To Peter
wishing you a Happy Xmas
from
Mr & Mrs Dungate.

THE BLACK ARROW
and
PRINCE OTTO

Robert Louis Stevenson
1850-1894

THE BLACK ARROW

and

PRINCE OTTO

R. L. STEVENSON

With Introductions by

ROSALINE MASSON

and

PATRICK BRAYBROOKE

COLLINS

LONDON AND GLASGOW

GENERAL EDITOR: G. F. MAINE

THE BLACK ARROW *first published, 1888*
PRINCE OTTO *first published, 1885*
This Edition. 1953
Reprint, 1957
Reprint, 1958

Printed in Great Britain by
COLLINS CLEAR-TYPE PRESS

ROBERT LOUIS STEVENSON

ROBERT LOUIS STEVENSON was born on November 12th 1850 in Edinburgh. He was the only child of Thomas Stevenson, a distinguished civil engineer and of his wife Margaret Isabella, daughter of the Reverend Lewis Balfour, minister of Colinton.

Stevenson's whole life was dominated by a pulmonary affliction, periods of comparative good health alternating with prolonged spells of acute illness and invalidism. As a young child, owing to a religious upbringing in which the main emphasis was laid on sin and its dire consequences in after-life, he lived in terror of death and damnation, indulged in disturbing guilt phantasies and suffered from constant nightmares. Of all games he liked hide-and-seek best for it lent itself to any kind of make-believe. For the same reason he liked the "Penny plain and Twopence Coloured" toy theatres to which he had been initiated at the age of six.

He went successively to a number of schools, mainly at Edinburgh, but his schooling was neither exacting nor very strenuous. In 1863 he accompanied his parents on a long tour through southern France and Italy; other holidays were spent at Scottish holiday resorts and later at Swanston, near Edinburgh. In 1867 he entered Edinburgh University to study for a science degree, but he was bent on becoming a writer, not a civil engineer.

Stevenson loved his native city—its architectural beauties, its history and associations—but he hated its climate which was bad for him and was deeply disturbed by an element of deceitfulness and duplicity which seemed to him characteristic of town and inhabitants alike. There was the polite, highly respectable façade, and behind it a life of squalor, vice and misery. His own life as a young man brought him into close contact with the less polite, less respectable side of Edinburgh, and his views on matters of religion, morals and sex led to many conflicts with his father. In 1871 he abandoned his engineering studies and started reading law, his intention, however, of taking up a literary career remaining unchanged. (In 1874 he was called to the Scottish Bar but never practised in earnest).

In 1873 he made the acquaintance of Mrs. Sitwell and Sidney Colvin, then Professor of Fine Art at Cambridge, and from this meeting sprang a lifelong friendship which was of the greatest importance to Stevenson's development and literary career. Sidney Colvin later became editor of his works and correspondence. During the winter of 1873-74 spent in the south of France, he began to write stories and essays, many of which appeared in the *Cornhill* magazine, and were collected later in the volume *Virginibus Puerisque* (1881). The next three years (1875-78) were spent in congenial company mostly in France, especially at Fontainebleau and Barbizon. There he met his future wife Mrs. Osbourne an American lady who, estranged from her husband, had come to spend some time in Europe, accompanied by her son Lloyd and her daughter Isobel.

By now his writings were beginning to attract the pubblic's attention. His first two books: *An Inland Voyage* and *Travels with a Donkey in the Cévennes* appeared in 1878 and 1879 respectively.

In the summer of 1878 he left England for San Francisco where two years later he married Mrs. Osbourne, by then divorced. Later in 1880 the couple returned to Europe. Their movements during the next seven years were dictated by the grim realities of Stevenson's health. Davos (1880-82), the French Riviera (1882-84), Bournemouth (1884-87) were their successive places of residence, with occasional visits to Scotland and London. During these years Stevenson wrote and published some of his most famous works: *Treasure Island*, first serialised in the periodical *Young Folks*, appeared in 1883; *Prince Otto* in 1885; *The Strange Case of Dr. Jekyll and Mr. Hyde* in 1886; *Kidnapped* in the same year; *The Black Arrow* in 1887. In between appeared books on travels, short stories and volumes of poetry. In 1885 in Bournemouth, Stevenson made the acquaintance of Henry James, with whom he established an intimate and lasting friendship.

In August 1887, accompanied by his wife, his stepson and his mother—his father having died that year—Stevenson left Europe for America, never to return. He remained in America just under a year, mostly at a health resort at Saranac Lake, during which time he contributed a series of articles for *Scribner's Magazine*, wrote the novel *The Wrong Box* (in collaboration with Lloyd Osbourne) and began *The Master of Ballantrae*.

In June 1888, he set out with his family on a cruise to the South Pacific, which took him to the Marquesas, Tahiti and Honolulu (where he spent six months and visited the leper settlement of Molokai) and then from Honolulu (in June 1889) to the Gilbert Islands, arriving in Samoa at Christmas 1889. After a short visit to Sidney, and further cruises, Stevenson decided to live permanently in Samoa. In November 1890 he settled at Vailima where he built a house and gradually established himself as a sort of Island Chieftain, surrounded by his family and faithful retainers. He took an active part in the island's internal political affairs, recording his experiences and observations in *A Footnote to History* (1892). Other works written during that time include: *The Wrecker* (in collaboration with Lloyd Osbourne), *The Ebb-Tide*, *Catriona*, and finally *Weir of Hermiston* left unfinished at his death.

Stevenson's last years at Samoa were happy, and his health much better than it had been during most of his life. He died suddenly on December 3rd 1894, and was buried with all the honours and ceremonial due to a chieftain, on top of Mount Vaea 1300 feet above the Pacific. He was mourned not only by his family and his islanders but by the whole civilized world.

H. d. R.

THE BLACK ARROW

CONTENTS

PROLOGUE

BOOK FIVE

CROOKBACK

INTRODUCTION

In March 1883 Stevenson and his wife settled at Hyères; and Stevenson, in very weak health after a miserable winter of constant hæmorrhages, fever and exhaustion, and continual flittings from one place to another, at last seemed to have found a congenial home, peace and comfort. His soul was satisfied by the beauty of the scenery, the view of mountains 'as graceful as Apollo, as severe as Zeus.' His racked body was soothed by a settled abiding-place,—a home, to which he could invite his friends to come; and a garden—he boasted of 'my roses, and my aloes, and my figmarigolds, and my olives.' It was at Hyères that the clever and faithful French maidservant, Valentine Roch, was engaged, and she greatly added to the comfort of the household arrangements. In May he was able to write to Mr. Gosse that he thought he should be able this year to live and keep 'my family.'

It was in these circumstances and in this mood that, on May 26th, 1883, Stevenson set to work on *The Black Arrow*.

Before they had been very long at Hyères, Mr. Henderson, the discerning editor of *Young Folks*, in spite of *Treasure Island* not having been popular when it had been published in *Young Folks*, and not having increased the circulation whilst it ran there, wrote and asked Stevenson for another serial—another story for boys. And Stevenson gladly consented. He wrote to Henley to tell him of the order. To Henley he calls it 'another Butcher's Boy.' This means that it was a story written to make money for the housekeeping bills. In time of money stress, Stevenson, after he had housekeeping bills, used the butcher as the synonym for that order of expenses; at Bournemouth it was 'Byles the Butcher,' and he complained sadly that when he 'wanted to live' he seemed to hear 'the butcher's cart resounding through the neighbourhood.'

Stevenson spoke disparagingly of his work at first. He called it 'tushery' in his account to Henley, because of the archaic diction in which it abounded—he and Henley often used the term in regard to fiction which employed archaic dialect. 'Tushery, by the mass! Ay, friend, a whole tale of tushery. And every tusher tushes me so free, that I may be tushed if the whole thing is worth a tush.'

The Black Arrow was avowedly written in rivalry to a one-time popular exponent of 'tushery,' Alfred R. Phillips, who contributed adventure stories to *Young Folks*. A serial by him, called *Don Salva, the Brave*, ran there concurrently with Stevenson's *Treasure Island* in the winter of 1881-2, was given precedence of position, and quite eclipsed *Treasure Island* in popularity with *Young Folks* readers. When *The Black Arrow* was published in book form in 1888, Stevenson, in his dedication (dated Saranac Lake, April 8th, 1888) refers to this bygone rivalry, and, whilst generously acknowledging his rival's 'well-won priority,' shows an almost ingenuous satisfaction in remembrance that whereas readers of *Young Folks* 'thought less than nothing of' *Treasure Island, The Black Arrow* 'was supposed to mark a clear advance.'

Stevenson placed his story in the time of the Wars of the Roses, and drew the material for it from his memory of bygone studies—those studies he had turned to in the July days of 1875, when, after 'steering through all sorts of breakers with my tongue in my cheek,' he had gone to the peace of little Swanston, and sought forgetfulness in the fascinations of fifteenth century poetry and history—the *Paston Letters, The Trial of Joan of Arc*, and kindred books.

And, tushery or not, the writing of *The Black Arrow* came easily to him. The first six chapters were written in a week. The reviewer in *The Academy* considered the opening chapters the only ones worthy of the author: if this were right it would seem as if Stevenson, like Browning's bird, 'never could recapture the first fine careless rapture'; but all readers will not agree with that reviewer, and will think that the note of careless rapture is well maintained to the end. Stevenson certainly wrote the book with little effort, and it was never, like so many of his books, cast aside and taken up again after an interval. All that summer at Hyères, and during little journeys to places near, he wrote steadily, and often it must have meant writing against time, for the story began to appear in *Young Folks* (it ran as a serial from June 30th to October 20th) before the author had completed it. It was in July, when he had been three months at work on the story, that Stevenson and his wife went to Royat, and were joined there by his parents. His father was, as with *Treasure Island* at Braemar, full of helpful and sympathetic interest in what his son was writing, and made useful suggestions.

Chapter after chapter was sent off as it was written, till, at the end of summer, Stevenson despatched the final instalment to Mr. Henderson at Red Lion Court, and, back at Hyères, awaited the final proofs.

They came in due course, and with them a letter from that important and anonymous functionary, the Reader. There is no longer any need to protect his anonymity, for, in 1922, he himself allowed his name to appear with his account of his connexion with Stevenson[1]; and in quoting his letter, Mr. James Dow's meeting with Stevenson may be given in his own words:—

'The "slips of the pen" to which I drew his attention—few and far between—were attributable to ill-health and human fallibility . . . the principal one in *The Black Arrow* caused me to write him the following note,—

'"To the Author.

'"DEAR SIR.—At the risk of incurring your displeasure, I venture to point out to you what may be an intentional omission, but which, I think, is probably an oversight.

'"There were four arrows, to be used with deadly intent. Three have been accounted for. In this concluding instalment the fourth is not mentioned; nor is there any indication of the fate of Sir Oliver, for whom the fourth arrow was evidently intended. This has occurred to me all the more forcibly because Sir Oliver's dreadful terror of a violent death has been on more than one occasion so vividly represented.

'"Believe me, Sir, to be, not your critic, but your servant

'"The Reader, Y.F."'

Quick and delighted came the response, dated from La Solitude, Hyères-les-Palmiers, Var.—'Thanks to you, Sir, he shall die the death. . . . I enclose slips 49-50-51; and to-morrow or next day, having butchered the priest, I shall dispatch the rest.'

The fourth arrow found its mark in the black heart of Sir Daniel Brackley:

'An arrow flew, and with a great choked cry of agony and anger, the Knight of Tunstall threw up his hands and fell forward in the snow.'

But the author evidently could not bring himself to 'butcher the priest', despite his declared intention, for in the final meeting between Ellis Duckworth, the avenger, and Richard Shelton, Ellis promises that 'the Black Arrow flieth nevermore—the fellowship is broken. They that still live shall come to their quiet and ripe end, in Heaven's good time, for me. . . .' Most readers will agree that to 'butcher the priest' would have been inappropriate, even distasteful, for Sir Oliver was merely Sir Daniel's creature, a pitiable rather than heroic figure.

[1] *I Can Remember Robert Louis Stevenson, ed.* Rosaline Masson, pp. 206-209.

Months afterwards, when Stevenson was on his way to Bournemouth, he stopped in London purposely in order to call at Red Lion House and meet his critic and Reader. In Mr. James Dow's letter describing the visit, he says that Stevenson, 'unheeding Mr. Henderson's entreaties not to attempt to mount the flights of stairs necessary (he was exceedingly ill), said, "I will ascend the stairs and see the Reader, though I die for it!" But he was so exhausted by the effort that when he entered the reading closet he was speechless.'

Yes, it was true what old Jules Simoneau of Monterey once said of Stevenson—'Louis Stevenson, 'e nevaire forget.'

In November, Stevenson wrote to tell Mr. Colvin of the success of *The Black Arrow*, and that another story was asked for. This, also written for the sake of the money it would bring in, was to be *Kidnapped*. Both *Treasure Island*, which had not been a success as a serial, and *Kidnapped*, written three years later than *The Black Arrow*, were published in book form before it; *Treasure Island* in 1883, and *Kidnapped* in 1886; but before Stevenson had been a month in America—that is, in the October of 1887, at Saranac,—Mr. McClure the publisher called on him and asked leave to publish *The Black Arrow* serially in his newspaper syndicate. It 'lay unknown to the world in the back files of *Henderson's Weekly*,' and Stevenson, having no copy, had to send to London and get the files. There being no copyright in America, 'any American paper might cut in, get a file of *Henderson's Weekly*, and come out ahead of me'; so Mr. McClure advertised and published the story under a different title, *The Outlaws of Tunstall Forest*. The well-known American artist, Mr. Will H. Low, Stevenson's intimate friend from Fontainebleau days, illustrated it; and the tale made more money than any other novel that Mr. McClure's syndicate ever published. Under its original title, *The Black Arrow: A Tale of Two Roses*, it was published in book form the following year, 1888, by Cassell in England and Charles Scribner's Sons in America.

It is always interesting to see what contemporary criticism made of a book that has become famous. *The Academy* was tepid and patronising; *The Athenæum* slated it; but *The Spectator* lauded it to the skies. Stevenson was, to *The Academy* reviewer, 'The most engaging among our young writers,' and he is warned that 'if he cares to maintain his place among the crowd of competitors whom he himself has taught, he must give us his best.' To *The Athenæum* reviewer, 'The perusal of *The Black Arrow* has been a hard task.' But *The Spectator* reviewer, with all the dignity of the editorial plural of the Victorian era, declares at the outset, 'We should ourselves prefer *The Black Arrow* to any story Mr. Stevenson has published except *Treasure Island*'; and farther on he states authoritatively, ' If *Ivanhoe* be the most brilliant tale for boys which genius ever penned, *The Black Arrow* certainly deserves to be placed next to it.'

Stevenson's own judgment rather leant to the side of his detractors. ' It is scarcely a work of genius,' was the best he ever said of it.

But, though many critics will concede as much, it remains undeniable that there are rich flashes of genius in it. Perhaps the most arresting of these is the character of the young Duke, Richard of Gloucester, ' Crookback.' It stands out like an opal caught by the firelight; it is as exquisite and meticulous a bit of character carving as any Stevenson has ever done; but it is merely a passing figure on the stage of his story, not a sustained character study.

What Stevenson wrote with relish, and finished perfectly, was generally something that had lain in his mind for long time, something which had attracted him and about which he had allowed his imagination to play. So it evidently was with Crookback: we have his own words for it: ' he is a fellow whose hellish energy has always fixed my attention.'

Genius also is stamped on many of the descriptions of scenery in *The Black Arrow*. Who but Stevenson, or perhaps Hardy, could give in so few and such exactly right words the character and atmosphere of a bit of country as in this passage?—

' . . . He saw behind him the whole fenny plain as far as Kettley, and the Till wandering among woody islets, and in front of him, the white line of highroad winding through the forest . . . the two lads, winged by what Dick had seen, hurried through the remainder of the outwood, crossed the road in safety, and began to mount into the high ground of Tunstall Forest. The trees grew more and more in groves, with heathy places in between, sandy, gorsy, and dotted with old yews. The ground became more and more uneven, full of pits and hillocks. And with every step of the ascent the wind still blew the shriller, and the trees bent before the gusts like fishing-rods.'

And this was written from memory, at Hyères, far from the fenny plains of England.

In any criticism of *The Black Arrow* it is necessary to remember that the book was written for boys. It is by the judgment of boys that its success in the fulfilment of its destiny must stand or fall. And what is the judgment of boys? *The Black Arrow* is a favourite prize: its sale is to this day kept up by its inclusion in every prize list. Stevenson himself recognised the test, and saw it applied. In a letter to Mr. Archer, who had told him that his little son, with whom Stevenson used to correspond, liked *The Black Arrow*, Stevenson says: 'I am sorry indeed to hear that my esteemed correspondent Tolmarcher has such poor taste in literature. . . . Well, after all, if Tolmarcher likes it, it has not been written in vain.'

How many thousand of boys, yesterday, to-day, and to-morrow, will endorse this? As long as the boyhood of this country is healthy and active and manly, and loves to read of the open air combined with battle, murder, and sudden death, so long will *The Black Arrow* be read.

ROSALINE MASSON

PROLOGUE

JOHN AMEND-ALL

On a certain afternoon, in the late spring time, the bell upon Tunstall Moat House was heard ringing at an unaccustomed hour. Far and near, in the forest and in the fields along the river, people began to desert their labours and hurry towards the sound; and in Tunstall hamlet a group of poor country-folk stood wondering at the summons.

Tunstall hamlet at that period, in the reign of old Henry VI., wore much the same appearance that it wears to-day. A score or so of houses, heavily framed with oak, stood scattered in a long green valley ascending from the river. At the foot, the road crossed a bridge, and mounting on the other side, disappeared into the fringes of the forest on its way to the Moat House, and farther forth to Holywood Abbey. Half-way up the village the church stood among yews. On every side the slopes were crowned and the view bounded by the green elms and greening oak-trees of the forest.

Hard by the bridge there was a stone cross upon a knoll, and here the group had collected—half a dozen women and one tall fellow in a russet smock—discussing what the bell betided. An express had gone through the hamlet half an hour before, and drunk a pot of ale in the saddle, not daring to dismount for the hurry of his errand; but he had been ignorant himself of what was forward, and only bore sealed letters from Sir Daniel Brackley to Sir Oliver Oates, the parson, who kept the Moat House in the master's absence.

But now there was the noise of a horse; and soon, out of the edge of the wood, and over the echoing bridge, there rode up young Master Richard Shelton, Sir Daniel's ward. He, at the least, would know, and they hailed him and begged him to explain. He drew bridle willingly enough—a young fellow not yet eighteen, sunbrowned and gray-eyed, in a jacket of deer's leather, with a black velvet collar, a green hood upon his head, and a steel crossbow at his back. The express, it appeared, had brought great news. A battle was impending. Sir Daniel had sent for every man who could draw a bow or carry a bill to go post-haste to Kettley, under pain of his severe displeasure; but for whom they were to fight, or of where the battle was expected, Dick knew nothing. Sir Oliver would come shortly himself, and

Bennet Hatch was arming at that moment, for he it was who should lead the party.

'It is the ruin of this kind land,' a woman said. 'If the barons live at war, ploughfolk must eat roots.'

'Nay,' said Dick, 'every man that follows shall have sixpence a day, and archers twelve.'

'If they live,' returned the woman, 'that may very well be; but how if they die, my master?'

'They cannot better die than for their natural lord,' said Dick.

'No natural lord of mine,' said the man in the smock. 'I followed the Walsinghams; so we all did down Brierly way, till two years ago come Candlemas. And now I must side with Brackley! It was the law that did it; call ye that natural? But now, what with Sir Daniel and what with Sir Oliver—that knows more of law than honesty—I have no natural lord but poor King Harry the Sixt, God bless him!—the poor innocent that cannot tell his right hand from his left.'

'Ye speak with an ill tongue, friend,' answered Dick, 'to miscall your good master and my lord the king in the same libel. But King Harry—praise he the saints!—has come again into his right mind, and will have all things peaceably ordained. And as for Sir Daniel, y' are very brave behind his back. But I will be no tale-bearer; and let that suffice.'

'I say no harm of you, Master Richard,' returned the peasant. 'Y' are a lad; but when ye come to a man's inches ye will find ye have an empty pocket. I say no more: the saints help Sir Daniel's neighbours, and the Blessed Maid protect his wards!'

'Clipsby,' said Richard, 'you speak what I cannot hear with honour. Sir Daniel is my good master and my guardian.'

'Come, now, will ye read me a riddle?' returned Clipsby. 'On whose side is Sir Daniel?'

'I know not,' said Dick, colouring a little; for his guardian had changed sides continually in the troubles of that period, and every change had brought him some increase of fortune.

'Ay,' returned Clipsby, 'you, nor no man. For, indeed, he is one that goes to bed Lancaster and gets up York.'

Just then the bridge rang under horse-shoe iron, and the party turned and saw Bennet Hatch come galloping—a brown-faced, grizzled fellow, heavy of hand and grim of mien, armed with sword and spear, a steel salet on his head, a leather jack upon his body. He was a great man in these parts; Sir Daniel's right hand in peace and war, and at that time, by his master's interest, bailiff of the hundred.

'Clipsby,' he shouted, 'off to the Moat House, and send all other laggards the same gate. Bowyer will give you jack and salet. We must ride before curfew. Look to it: he that is last at the lychgate Sir Daniel shall reward. Look to it right well! I know you for a man of naught. Nance,' he added, to one of the women, 'is old Appleyard up town?'

'I'll warrant you,' replied the woman. 'In his field, for sure.'

So the group dispersed, and, while Clipsby walked leisurely over the bridge, Bennet and young Shelton rode up the road together, through the village and past the church.

'Ye will see the old shrew,' said Bennet. 'He will waste more time grumbling and prating of Harry the Fift than would serve a man to shoe a horse. And all because he has been to the French wars!'

The house to which they were bound was the last in the village, standing alone among lilacs; and beyond it, on three sides, there was open meadow rising towards the borders of the wood.

Hatch dismounted, threw his rein over the fence, and walked down the field, Dick keeping close at his elbow, to where the old soldier was digging, knee-deep in his cabbages, and now and again, in a cracked voice, singing a snatch of song. He was all dressed in leather, only his hood and tippet were of black frieze, and tied with scarlet; his face was like a walnut-shell, both for colour and wrinkles; but his old gray eye was still clear enough, and his sight unabated. Perhaps he was deaf; perhaps he thought it unworthy of an old archer of Agincourt to pay any heed to such disturbances; but neither the surly notes of the alarm-bell, nor the near approach of Bennet and the lad, appeared at all to move him; and he continued obstinately digging, and piped up, very thin and shaky:—

'Now, dear lady, if thy will be,
I pray you that you will rue on me.'

'Nick Appleyard,' said Hatch, 'Sir Oliver commends him to you, and bids that ye shall come within this hour to the Moat House, there to take command.'

The old fellow looked up.

'Save you, my masters!' he said, grinning. 'And where goeth Master Hatch?'

'Master Hatch is off to Kettley, with every man that we can horse,' returned Bennet. 'There is a fight toward, it seems, and my lord stays a reinforcement.'

'Ay, verily,' returned Appleyard. 'And what will ye leave me to garrison withal?'

'I leave you six good men, and Sir Oliver to boot,' answered Hatch.

'It'll not hold the place,' said Appleyard; 'the number sufficeth not. It would take two score to make it good.'

'Why, it's for that we came to you, old shrew!' replied the other. 'Who else is there but you that could do aught in such a house with such a garrison?'

'Ay, when the pinch comes, ye remember the old shoe,' returned Nick. 'There is not a man of you can back a horse or hold a bill; and as for archery—St. Michael! if old Harry the Fift were back again, he would stand and let ye shoot at him for a farthing a shoot!'

'Nay, Nick, there's some can draw a good bow yet,' said Bennet.

'Draw a good bow!' cried Appleyard. 'Yes! But who'll shoot me a good shoot? It's there the eye comes in, and the head between your shoulders. Now, what might you call a long shoot, Bennet Hatch?'

'Well,' said Bennet, looking about him, 'it would be a long shoot from here into the forest.'

'Ay, it would be a longish shoot,' said the old fellow, turning to look over his shoulder; and then he put up his hand over his eyes, and stood staring.

'Why, what are you looking at?' asked Bennet, with a chuckle. 'Do you see Harry the Fift?'

The veteran continued looking up the hill in silence. The sun shone broadly over the shelving meadows; a few white sheep wandered browsing; all was still but the distant jangle of the bell.

'What is it, Appleyard?' asked Dick.

'Why, the birds,' said Appleyard.

And, sure enough, over the top of the forest, where it ran down in a tongue among the meadows, and ended in a pair of goodly green elms, about a bowshot from the field where they were standing, a flight of birds was skimming to and fro, in evident disorder.

'What of the birds?' said Bennet.

'Ay!' returned Appleyard, 'y' are a wise man to go to war, Master Bennet. Birds are a good sentry; in forest places they be the first line of battle. Look you, now, if we lay here in camp, there might be archers skulking down to get the wind of us; and here would you be, none the wiser!'

'Why, old shrew,' said Hatch, 'there be no men nearer us than Sir Daniel's, at Kettley; y' are as safe as in London Tower; and ye raise scares upon a man for a few chaffinches and sparrows!

'Hear him!' grinned Appleyard. 'How many a rogue would

give his two crop ears to have a shoot at either of us! Saint Michael, man! they hate us like two pole-cats!'

'Well, sooth it is, they hate Sir Daniel,' answered Hatch, a little sobered.

'Ay, they hate Sir Daniel, and they hate every man that serves with him,' said Appleyard; 'and in the first order of hating, they hate Bennet Hatch and old Nicholas the bowman. See ye here: if there was a stout fellow yonder in the wood-edge, and you and I stood fair for him—as, by Saint George, we stand!—which, think ye, would he choose?'

'You, for a good wager,' answered Hatch.

'My surcoat to a leather belt, it would be you!' cried the old archer. 'Ye burned Grimstone, Bennet—they'll ne'er forgive you that, my master. And as for me, I'll soon be in a good place, God grant, and out of bow-shoot—ay, and cannon-shoot—of all their malices. I am an old man, and draw fast to homeward, where the bed is ready. But for you, Bennet, y' are to remain behind here at your own peril, and if ye come to my years unhanged, the old true-blue English spirit will be dead.'

'Y' are the shrewishest old dolt in Tunstall Forest,' returned Hatch, visibly ruffled by these threats. 'Get ye to your arms before Sir Oliver come, and leave prating for one good while. An' ye had talked so much with Harry the Fift, his ears would ha' been richer than his pocket.'

An arrow sang in the air, like a huge hornet: it struck old Appleyard between the shoulderblades, and pierced him clean through, and he fell forward on his face among the cabbages. Hatch, with a broken cry, leapt into the air; then, stooping double, he ran for the cover of the house. And in the meanwhile Dick Shelton had dropped behind a lilac, and had his crossbow bent and shouldered, covering the point of the forest.

Not a leaf stirred. The sheep were patiently browsing; the birds had settled. But there lay the old man, with a clothyard arrow standing in his back; and there were Hatch holding to the gable, and Dick crouching and ready behind the lilac bush.

'D'ye see aught?' cried Hatch.

'Not a twig stirs,' cried Dick.

'I think shame to leave him lying,' said Bennet, coming forward once more with hesitating steps and a very pale countenance. 'Keep a good eye on the wood, Master Shelton—keep a clear eye on the wood. The saints assoil us! here was a good shoot!'

Bennet raised the old archer on his knee. He was not yet dead; his face worked, and his eyes shut and opened like machinery, and he had a most horrible, ugly look of one in pain.

'Can ye hear, old Nick?' asked Hatch. 'Have ye a last wish before ye wend, old brother?'

'Pluck out the shaft, and let me pass, a' Mary's name!' gasped Appleyard. 'I be done with old England. Pluck it out!'

'Master Dick,' said Bennet, 'come hither, and pull me a good pull upon the arrow. He would fain pass, the poor sinner.'

Dick laid down his crossbow, and pulling hard upon the arrow, drew it forth. A gush of blood followed; the old archer scrambled half upon his feet, called once more upon the name of God, and then fell dead. Hatch, upon his knees among the cabbages, prayed fervently for the welfare of the passing spirit. But even as he prayed, it was plain that his mind was still divided, and he kept ever an eye upon the corner of the wood from which the shot had come. When he had done, he got to his feet again, drew off one of his mailed gauntlets, and wiped his pale face, which was all wet with terror.

'Ay,' he said, 'it'll be my turn next.'

'Who hath done this, Bennet?' Richard asked, still holding the arrow in his hand.

'Nay, the saints know,' said Hatch. 'Here are a good two score Christian souls that we have hunted out of house and holding, he and I. He has paid his shot, poor shrew, nor will it be long, mayhap, ere I pay mine. Sir Daniel driveth over hard.'

'This is a strange shaft,' said the lad, looking at the arrow in his hand.

'Ay, by my faith!' cried Bennet. 'Black, end black-feathered. Here is an ill-favoured shaft, by my sooth! for black, they say, bodes burial. And here be words written. Wipe the blood away. What read ye?'

'"*Appulyaird fro Jon Amend-All,*"' read Shelton. 'What should this betoken?'

'Nay, I like it not,' returned the retainer, shaking his head. 'John Amend-All! Here is a rogue's name for those that be up in the world! But why stand here to make a mark? Take him by the knees, good Master Shelton, while I lift him by the shoulders, and let us lay him in his house. This will be a rare shog to poor Sir Oliver; he will turn paper-colour; he will pray like a windmill.'

They took up the old archer, and carried him between them into his house, where he had dwelt alone. And there they laid him on the floor, out of regard for the mattress, and sought, as best they might, to straighten and compose his limbs.

Appleyard's house was clean and bare. There was a bed, with a blue cover, a cupboard, a great chest, a pair of joint-stools, a hinged table in the chimney-corner, and hung upon the wall the old soldier's armoury of bows and defensive armour. Hatch began to look about him curiously.

'Nick had money,' he said. 'He may have had three score pounds put by. I would I could light upon 't! When ye lose an old friend, Master Richard, the best consolation is to heir him. See, now, this chest. I would go a mighty wager there is a bushel of gold therein. He had a strong hand to get, and a hard hand to keep withal, had Appleyard the archer. Now may God rest his spirit! Near eighty year he was afoot and about, and ever getting; but now he's on the broad of his back, poor shrew, and no more lacketh; and if his chattels came to a good friend, he would be merrier, methinks, in heaven.'

'Come, Hatch,' said Dick, 'respect his stone-blind eyes. Would ye rob the man before his body? Nay, he would walk!'

Hatch made several signs of the cross; but by this time his natural complexion had returned, and he was not easily to be dashed from any purpose. It would have gone hard with the chest had not the gate sounded, and presently after the door of the house opened and admitted a tall, portly, ruddy, black-eyed man of near fifty, in a surplice and black robe.

'Appleyard,' the newcomer was saying, as he entered, but he stopped dead. 'Ave Maria!' he cried. 'Saints be our shield! What cheer is this?'

'Cold cheer with Appleyard, sir parson,' answered Hatch, with perfect cheerfulness. 'Shot at his own door, and alighteth even now at purgatory gates. Ay! there, if tales be true, he shall lack neither coal nor candle.'

Sir Oliver groped his way to a joint-stool, and sat down upon it, sick and white.

'This is a judgment! Oh, a great stroke!' he sobbed, and rattled off a leash of prayers.

Hatch meanwhile reverently doffed his salet and knelt down.

'Ay, Bennet,' said the priest, somewhat recovering, 'and what may this be? What enemy hath done this?'

'Here, Sir Oliver, is the arrow. See, it is written upon with words,' said Dick.

'Nay,' cried the priest, 'this is a foul hearing! John Amend-All! A right Lollardy word. And black of hue, as for an omen! Sirs, this knave arrow likes me not. But it importeth rather to take counsel. Who should this be? Bethink you, Bennet. Of so many black ill-willers, which should he be that doth so hardily outface us? Simnel? I do much question it. The Walsinghams? Nay, they are not yet so broken; they still think to have the law over us, when times change. There was Simon Malmesbury, too. How think ye, Bennet?'

'What think ye, sir,' returned Hatch, 'of Ellis Duckworth?'

'Nay, Bennet, never. Nay, not he,' said the priest. 'There cometh never any rising, Bennet, from below—so all judicious chroniclers concord in their opinion; but rebellion travelleth ever downward from above; and when Dick, Tom, and Harry take them to their bills, look ever narrowly to see what lord is profited thereby. Now, Sir Daniel, having once more joined him to the Queen's party, is in ill odour with the Yorkist lords. Thence, Bennet, comes the blow—by what procuring, I yet seek; but therein lies the nerve of this discomfiture.'

'An't please you, Sir Oliver,' said Bennet, 'the axles are so hot in this country that I have long been smelling fire. So did this poor sinner, Appleyard. And, by your leave, men's spirits are so foully inclined to all of us, that it needs neither York nor Lancaster to spur them on. Hear my plain thoughts: You, that are a clerk, and Sir Daniel, that sails on any wind, ye have taken many men's goods, and beaten and hanged not a few. Y'are called to count for this; in the end, I wot not how, ye have ever the uppermost at law, and ye think all patched. But give me leave, Sir Oliver: the man that ye have dispossessed and beaten is but the angrier, and some day, when the black devil is by, he will up with his bow and clout me a yard of arrow through your inwards.'

'Nay, Bennet, y'are in the wrong. Bennet, ye should be glad to be corrected,' said Sir Oliver. 'Y'are a prater, Bennet, a talker, a babbler; your mouth is wider than your two ears. Mend it, Bennet, mend it.'

'Nay, I say no more. Have it as ye list,' said the retainer.

The priest now rose from the stool, and from the writing-case that hung about his neck took forth wax and a taper, and a flint and steel. With these he sealed up the chest and the cupboard with Sir Daniel's arms, Hatch looking on disconsolate; and then the whole party proceeded, somewhat timorously, to sally from the house and get to horse.

''Tis time we were on the road, Sir Oliver,' said Hatch, as he held the priest's stirrup while he mounted.

'Ay; but, Bennet, things are changed,' returned the parson. 'There is now no Appleyard—rest his soul!—to keep the garrison. I shall keep you, Bennet. I must have a good man to rest me on in this day of black arrows. "The arrow that flieth by day," said the evangel; I have no mind of the context; nay, I am a sluggard priest, I am too deep in men's affairs. Well, let us ride forth, Master Hatch. The jackmen should be at the church by now.'

So they rode forward down the road, with the wind after

them, blowing the tails of the parson's cloak; and behind them, as they went, clouds began to arise and blot out the sinking sun. They had passed three of the scattered houses that make up Tunstall hamlet, when, coming to a turn, they saw the church before them. Ten or a dozen houses clustered immediately round it; but to the back the churchyard was next the meadows. At the lych-gate, near a score of men were gathered, some in the saddle, some standing by their horses' heads. They were variously armed and mounted; some with spears, some with bills, some with bows, and some bestriding plough-horses, still splashed with the mire of the furrow; for these were the very dregs of the country, and all the better men and the fair equipments were already with Sir Daniel in the field.

'We have not done amiss, praised be the cross of Holywood! Sir Daniel will be right well content,' observed the priest, inwardly numbering the troop.

'Who goes? Stand! if ye be true!' shouted Bennet.

A man was seen slipping through the churchyard among the yews; and at the sound of this summons he discarded all concealment, and fairly took to his heels for the forest. The men at the gate, who had been hitherto unaware of the stranger's presence, woke and scattered. Those who had dismounted began scrambling into the saddle: the rest rode in pursuit; but they had to make the circuit of the consecrated ground, and it was plain their quarry would escape them. Hatch, roaring an oath, put his horse at the hedge, to head him off; but the beast refused, and sent his rider sprawling in the dust. And though he was up again in a moment, and had caught the bridle, the time had gone by, and the fugitive had gained too great a lead for any hope of capture.

The wisest of all had been Dick Shelton. Instead of starting in a vain pursuit, he had whipped his cross-bow from his back, bent it, and set a quarrel to the string; and now, when the others had desisted, he turned to Bennet, and asked if he should shoot.

'Shoot! shoot!' cried the priest, with sanguinary violence.

'Cover him, Master Dick,' said Bennet. 'Bring me him down like a ripe apple.'

The fugitive was now within but a few leaps of safety; but this last part of the meadow ran very steeply uphill, and the man ran slower in proportion. What with the grayness of the falling night, and the uneven movements of the runner, it was no easy aim; and as Dick levelled his bow, he felt a kind of pity, and a half desire that he might miss. The quarrel sped.

The man stumbled and fell, and a great cheer arose from Hatch and the pursuers. But they were counting their corn before the harvest. The man fell lightly; he was lightly afoot again, turned and waved his cap in a bravado, and was out of sight next moment in the margin of the wood.

'And the plague go with him!' cried Bennet. 'He has thieves' heels: he can run, by St. Banbury! But you touched him, Master Shelton; he has stolen your quarrel, may he never have good I grudge him less!'

'Nay, but what made he by the church!' asked Sir Oliver. 'I am shrewdly afeared there has been mischief here. Clipsby, good fellow, get ye down from your horse, and search thoroughly among the yews.'

Clipsby was gone but a little while ere he returned, carrying a paper.

'This writing was pinned to the church door,' he said, handing it to the parson. 'I found naught else, sir parson.'

'Now, by the power of Mother Church,' cried Sir Oliver, 'but this runs hard on sacrilege! For the king's good pleasure, or the lord of the manor—well! But that every run-the-hedge in a green jerkin should fasten papers to the chancel door—nay, it runs hard on sacrilege, hard; and men have burned for matters of less weight! But what have we here? The light falls apace. Good Master Richard, y' have young eyes. Read me, I pray, this libel.'

Dick Shelton took the paper in his hand and read it aloud. It contained some lines of a very rugged doggerel, hardly ever rhyming, written in a gross character, and most uncouthly spelt. With the spelling somewhat bettered, this is how they ran:—

'I had four blak arrows under my belt,
Four for the greefs that I have felt,
Four for the nomber of ill menne
That have oppressid me now and then.

One is gone; one is wele sped;
Old Apulyaird is ded.

One is for Maister Bennet Hatch,
That burned Grimstone, walls and thatch.

One for Sir Oliver Oates,
That cut Sir Harry Shelton's throat.

Sir Daniel, ye shull have the fourt;
We shull think it fair sport.

Ye shull each have your own part,
A blak arrow in each blak heart.
Get ye to your knees for to pray:
Ye are ded theeves, by yea and nay.

'JON AMEND-ALL
'of the Green Wood,
'And his jolly fellaweship.

'Item, we have mo arrowes and goode hempen cord for otheres of your following.'

'Now, well-a-day for charity and the Christian graces!' cried Sir Oliver lamentably. 'Sirs, this is an ill world, and groweth daily worse. I will swear upon the cross of Holywood I am as innocent of that good knight's hurt, whether in act or purpose, as the babe unchristened. Neither was his throat cut; for therein they are again in error, as there still live credible witnesses to show.'

'It boots not, sir parson,' said Bennet. 'Here is unseasonable talk.'

'Nay, Master Bennet, not so. Keep ye in your due place, good Bennet,' answered the priest. 'I shall make my innocence appear. I will upon no consideration lose my poor life in error. I take all men to witness that I am clear of this matter. I was not even in the Moat House. I was sent of an errand before nine upon the clock——'

'Sir Oliver,' said Hatch, interrupting, 'since it please you not to stop this sermon, I will take other means. Goffe, sound to horse.'

And while the tucket was sounding, Bennet moved close to the bewildered parson, and whispered violently in his ear.

Dick Shelton saw the priest's eye turned upon him for an instant in a startled glance. He had some cause for thought; for this Sir Harry Shelton was his own natural father. But he never said a word, and kept his countenance unmoved.

Hatch and Sir Oliver discussed together for awhile their altered situation; ten men, it was decided between them, should be reserved, not only to garrison the Moat House, but to escort the priest across the wood. In the meantime, as Bennet was to remain behind, the command of the reinforcement was given to Master Shelton. Indeed, there was no choice; the men were loutish fellows, dull and unskilled in war, while Dick was not only popular, but resolute and grave beyond his age. Although his youth had been spent in these rough country places, the lad had been well taught in letters by Sir Oliver, and Hatch himself had shown him the management of arms and the first principles of command. Bennet had always been kind and helpful; he was one of those who are cruel as the grave to those they call their enemies, but ruggedly faithful and well-willing to their friends; and now, while Sir Oliver entered the next house to write, in his swift, exquisite penmanship, a memorandum of the last occurrences to his master, Sir Daniel Brackley, Bennet came up to his pupil to wish him God-speed upon his enterprise.

'Ye must go the long way about, Master Shelton,' he said; 'round by the bridge, for your life! Keep a sure man fifty paces afore you, to draw shots; and go softly till y'are past the wood. If the rogues fall upon you, ride for 't; ye will do naught by standing. And keep ever forward, Master Shelton; turn me not back again, an ye love your life; there is no help in Tunstall, mind ye that. And now, since ye go to the great wars about the king, and I continue to dwell here in extreme jeopardy of my life, and the saints alone can certify if we shall meet again below, I give you my last counsels now at your riding. Keep an eye on Sir Daniel; he is unsure. Put not your trust in the jack-priest; he intendeth not amiss, but doth the will of others; it is a hand-gun for Sir Daniel! Get you good lordship where ye go; make you strong friends; look to it. And think ever a paternoster-while on Bennet Hatch. There are worse rogues afoot than Bennet. So, God-speed!'

'And Heaven be with you, Bennet!' returned Dick. 'Ye were a good friend to me-ward, and so I shall say ever.'

'And look ye, master,' added Hatch, with a certain embarrassment, 'if this Amend-All should get a shaft into me, ye might, mayhap, lay out a gold mark or mayhap a pound for my poor soul; for it is like to go stiff with me in purgatory.'

'Ye shall have your will of it, Bennet,' answered Dick. 'But, what cheer, man! We shall meet again, where ye shall have more need of ale than masses.'

'The saints so grant it, Master Dick!' returned the other. 'But here comes Sir Oliver. An' he were as quick with the long-bow as with the pen, he would be a brave man-at-arms.'

Sir Oliver gave Dick a sealed packet, with this superscription: 'To my ryght worchypful master, Sir Daniel Brackley, knyght, be thys delyvered in haste.'

And Dick, putting it in the bosom of his jacket, gave the word and set forth westward up the village.

Book One

THE TWO LADS

B.P.2

I

At the Sign of the Sun in Kettley

SIR DANIEL and his men lay in and about Kettley that night, warmly quartered and well patrolled. But the Knight of Tunstall was one who never rested from money-getting; and even now, when he was on the brink of an adventure which should make or mar him, he was up an hour after midnight to squeeze poor neighbours. He was one who trafficked greatly in disputed inheritances; it was his way to buy out the most unlikely claimant, and then, by the favour he curried with great lords about the king, procure unjust decisions in his favour; or, if that was too roundabout, to seize the disputed manor by force of arms, and rely on his influence and Sir Oliver's cunning in the law to hold what he had snatched. Kettley was one such place; it had come very lately into his clutches; he still met with opposition from the tenants; and it was to overawe discontent that he had led his troops that way.

By two in the morning, Sir Daniel sat in the inn room, close by the fireside, for it was cold at that hour among the fens of Kettley. By his elbow stood a pottle of spiced ale. He had taken off his visored headpiece, and sat with his bald head and thin, dark visage resting on one hand, wrapped warmly in a sanguine-coloured cloak. At the lower end of the room about a dozen of his men stood sentry over the door or lay asleep on benches; and, somewhat nearer hand, a young lad, apparently of twelve or thirteen, was stretched in a mantle on the floor. The host of the Sun stood before the great man.

'Now, mark me, mine host,' Sir Daniel said, 'follow but mine orders, and I shall be your good lord ever. I must have good men for head boroughs, and I will have Adam-a-More high constable; see to it narrowly. If other men be chosen, it shall avail you nothing; rather it shall be found to your sore cost. For those that have paid rent to Walsingham I shall take good measure—you among the rest, mine host.'

'Good knight,' said the host, 'I will swear upon the cross of Holywood I did but pay to Walsingham under compulsion. Nay, bully knight, I love not the rogue Walsingham; they were as poor as thieves, bully knight. Give me a great lord like you. Nay; ask me among the neighbours, I am stout for Brackley.'

'It may be,' said Sir Daniel drily. 'Ye shall then pay twice.' The innkeeper made a horrid grimace; but this was a piece of bad luck that might readily befall a tenant in these unruly times, and he was perhaps glad to make his peace so easily.

'Bring up yon fellow, Selden!' cried the knight.

And one of his retainers led up a poor, cringing old man, as pale as a candle, and all shaking with the fen fever.

'Sirrah,' said Sir Daniel, 'your name?'

'An't please your worship,' replied the man, 'my name is Condall—Condall of Shoreby, at your good worship's pleasure.'

'I have heard you ill reported on,' returned the knight. 'Ye deal in treason, rogue; ye trudge the country leasing; y' are heavily suspicioned of the death of severals. How, fellow, are ye so bold? But I will bring you down.'

'Right honourable and my reverend lord,' the man cried, 'here is some hodge-podge, saving your good presence. I am but a poor private man, and have hurt none.'

'The under-sheriff did report of you most vilely,' said the knight. '"Seize me," saith he, "that Tyndal of Shoreby."'

'Condall, my good lord; Condall is my poor name,' said the unfortunate.

'Condall or Tyndal, it is all one,' replied Sir Daniel coolly. 'For, by my sooth, y' are here, and I do mightily suspect your honesty. If you would save your neck, write me swiftly an obligation for twenty pound.'

'For twenty pound, my good lord!' cried Condall. 'Here is midsummer madness! My whole estate amounteth not to seventy shillings.'

'Condall or Tyndal,' returned Sir Daniel, grinning, 'I will run my peril of that loss. Write me down twenty, and when I have recovered all I may, I will be good lord to you, and pardon you the rest.'

'Alas! my good lord, it may not be; I have no skill to write,' said Condall.

'Well-a-day!' returned the knight. 'Here, then, is no remedy. Yet I would fain have spared you, Tyndal, had my conscience suffered. Selden, take me this old shrew softly to the nearest elm, and hang me him tenderly by the neck, where I may see him at my riding. Fare ye well, good Master Condall, dear Master Tyndal; y' are post-haste for Paradise; fare ye then well!'

'Nay, my right pleasant lord,' replied Condall, forcing an obsequious smile, 'an ye be so masterful, as doth right well become you, I will even, with all my poor skill, do your bidding.'

'Friend,' quoth Sir Daniel, 'ye will now write two score. Go to! y' are too cunning for a livelihood of seventy shillings. Selden, see him write me this in good form, and have it duly witnessed.'

And Sir Daniel, who was a very merry knight, none merrier in England, took a drink of his mulled ale, and lay back, smiling.

Meanwhile, the boy upon the floor began to stir, and presently sat up and looked about him with a scare.

'Hither,' said Sir Daniel; and as the other rose at his command and came slowly towards him, he leaned back and laughed outright. 'By the rood!' he cried, 'a sturdy boy!'

The lad flashed crimson with anger, and darted a look of hate out of his dark eyes. Now that he was on his legs, it was more difficult to make certain of his age. His face looked somewhat older in expression, but it was as smooth as a young child's; and in bone and body he was unusually slender, and somewhat awkward of gait.

'Ye have called me, Sir Daniel,' he said. 'Was it to laugh at my poor plight?'

'Nay, now, let laugh,' said the knight. 'Good shrew, let laugh, I pray you. An ye could see yourself, I warrant ye would laugh the first.'

'Well,' cried the lad, flushing, 'ye shall answer this when ye answer for the other. Laugh while yet ye may!'

'Nay, now, good cousin,' replied Sir Daniel, with some earnestness, 'think not that I mock at you, except in mirth, as between kinsfolk and singular friends. I will make you a marriage of a thousand pounds, go to! and cherish you exceedingly. I took you, indeed, roughly, as the time demanded; but from henceforth I shall ungrudgingly maintain and cheerfully serve you. Ye shall be Mrs. Shelton—Lady Shelton, by my troth! for the lad promiseth bravely. Tut! ye will not shy for honest laughter; it purgeth melancholy. They are no rogues who laugh, good cousin. Good mine host, lay me a meal now for my cousin, Master John. Sit ye down, sweetheart, and eat.'

'Nay,' said Master John, 'I will break no bread. Since ye force me to this sin, I will fast for my soul's interest. But, good mine host, I pray you of courtesy give me a cup of fair water; I shall be much beholden to your courtesy indeed.'

'Ye shall have a dispensation, go to!' cried the knight. 'Shalt be well shriven, by my faith! Content you, then, and eat.'

But the lad was obstinate, drank a cup of water, and, once more wrapping himself closely in his mantle, sat in a far corner, brooding.

In an hour or two there rose a stir in the village of sentries challenging and the clatter of arms and horses; and then a troop drew up by the inn door, and Richard Shelton, splashed with mud, presented himself upon the threshold.

'Save you, Sir Daniel,' he said.

'How! Dickie Shelton!' cried the knight; and at the mention of Dick's name the other lad looked curiously across. 'What maketh Bennet Hatch?'

'Please you, sir knight, to take cognisance of this packet from Sir Oliver, wherein are all things fully stated,' answered Richard, presenting the priest's letter. 'And please you farther, ye were best make all speed to Risingham; for on the way hither we encountered one riding furiously with letters, and by his report, my Lord of Risingham was sore bested, and lacked exceedingly your presence.'

'How say you? Sore bested?' returned the knight. 'Nay, then, we will make speed sitting down, good Richard. As the world goes in this poor realm of England, he that rides softliest rides surest. Delay, they say, begetteth peril; but it is rather this itch of doing that undoes men; mark it, Dick. But let me see, first, what cattle ye have brought. Selden, a link here at the door!'

And Sir Daniel strode forth into the village street, and, by the red glow of a torch, inspected his new troops. He was an unpopular neighbour and an unpopular master; but as a leader of war he was well beloved by those who rode behind his pennant. His dash, his proved courage, his forethought for the soldiers' comfort, even his rough gibes, were all to the taste of the bold blades in jack and salet.

'Nay, by the rood!' he cried, 'what poor dogs are these? Here be some as crooked as a bow, and some as lean as a spear. Friends, ye shall ride in the front of the battle; I can spare you, friends. Mark me this old villain on the piebald! A two-year mutton riding on a hog would look more soldierly! Ha! Clipsby, are ye there, old rat? Y' are a man I could lose with a good heart; ye shall go in front of all, with a bull's-eye painted on your jack, to be the better butt for archery; sirrah, ye shall show me the way.'

'I will show you any way, Sir Daniel, but the way to change sides,' returned Clipsby sturdily.

Sir Daniel laughed a guffaw.

'Why, well said!' he cried. 'Hast a shrewd tongue in thy mouth, go to! I will forgive you for that merry word. Selden, see them fed, both man and brute.'

The knight re-entered the inn.

'Now, friend Dick,' he said, 'fall to. Here is good ale and bacon. Eat, while that I read.'

Sir Daniel opened the packet, and as he read his brow darkened. When he had done he sat a little, musing. Then he looked sharply at his ward.

'Dick,' said he, 'y' have seen this penny rhyme?'

The lad replied in the affirmative.

'It bears your father's name,' continued the knight; 'and our poor shrew of a parson is, by some mad soul, accused of slaying him.'

'He did most eagerly deny it,' answered Dick.

'He did?' cried the knight, very sharply. 'Heed him not. He has a loose tongue; he babbles like a jack-sparrow. Some day, when I may find the leisure, Dick, I will myself more fully inform you of these matters. There was one Duckworth shrewdly blamed for it; but the times were troubled, and there was no justice to be got.'

'It befell at the Moat House?' Dick ventured, with a beating at his heart.

'It befell between the Moat House and Holywood,' replied Sir Daniel calmly: but he shot a covert glance, black with suspicion, at Dick's face. 'And now,' added the knight, 'speed you with your meal; ye shall return to Tunstall with a line from me.'

Dick's face fell sorely.

'Prithee, Sir Daniel,' he cried, 'send one of the villains! I beseech you let me to the battle. I can strike a stroke, I promise you.'

'I misdoubt it not,' replied Sir Daniel, sitting down to write. 'But here, Dick, is no honour to be won. I lie in Kettley till I have sure tidings of the war, and then ride to join me with the conqueror. Cry not on cowardice; it is but wisdom, Dick; for this poor realm so tosseth with rebellion, and the king's name and custody so changeth hands, that no man may be certain of the morrow. Toss-pot and Shuttle-wit run in, but my Lord Good-Counsel sits o' one side, waiting.'

With that, Sir Daniel, turning his back to Dick, and quite at the farther end of the long table, began to write his letter, with his mouth on one side, for this business of the Black Arrow stuck sorely in his throat.

Meanwhile, young Shelton was going on heartily enough with his breakfast, when he felt a touch upon his arm, and a very soft voice whispering in his ear.

'Make not a sign, I do beseech you,' said the voice, 'but of your charity teach me the straight way to Holywood. Beseech you, now, good boy, comfort a poor soul in peril and extreme distress, and set me so far forth upon the way to my repose.'

'Take the path by the windmill,' answered Dick, in the same tone; 'it will bring you to Till Ferry; there inquire again.'

And without turning his head, he fell again to eating. But with the tail of his eye he caught a glimpse of the young lad called Master John stealthily creeping from the room.

'Why,' thought Dick, 'he is as young as I. "Good boy" doth he call me! An I had known, I should have seen the varlet hanged ere I had told him. Well, if he goes through the fen, I may come up with him, and pull his ears.'

Half an hour later, Sir Daniel gave Dick the letter, and bade him speed to the Moat House. And again, some half an hour after Dick's departure, a messenger came, in hot haste, from my Lord of Risingham.

'Sir Daniel,' the messenger said, 'ye lose great honour, by my sooth! The fight began again this morning ere the dawn, and we have beaten their van and scattered their right wing. Only the main battle standeth fast. An we had your fresh men, we should tilt them all into the river. What, sir knight! Will ye be the last? It stands not with your good credit.'

'Nay,' cried the knight, 'I was but now upon the march. Selden, sound me the tucket. Sir, I am with you on the instant. It is not two hours since the more part of my command came in, sir messenger. What would ye have? Spurring is good meat, but yet it killed the charger. Bustle, boys!'

By this time the tucket was sounding cheerily in the morning, and from all sides Sir Daniel's men poured into the main street and formed before the inn. They had slept upon their arms, with chargers saddled, and in ten minutes five-score men-at-arms and archers, cleanly equipped and briskly disciplined, stood ranked and ready. The chief part were in Sir Daniel's livery, murrey and blue, which gave the greater show to their array. The best armed rode first; and away out of sight, at the tail of the column, came the sorry reinforcement of the night before. Sir Daniel looked with pride along the line.

'Here be the lads to serve you in a pinch,' he said.

'They are pretty men, indeed,' replied the messenger. 'It but augments my sorrow that ye had not marched the earlier.'

'Well,' said the knight, 'what would ye? The beginning of a feast and the end of a fray, sir messenger'; and he mounted into his saddle. 'Why! how now!' he cried. 'John! Joanna! Nay, by the sacred rood! where is she? Host, where is that girl?'

'Girl, Sir Daniel?' cried the landlord. 'Nay, sir, I saw no girl.'

'Boy, then, dotard!' cried the knight. 'Could ye not see it was a wench? She in the murrey-coloured mantle—she that broke her fast with water, rogue—where is she?'

'Nay, the saints bless us! Master John, ye called him,' said the host. 'Well, I thought none evil. He is gone. I saw him—her—I saw her in the stable a good hour agone; 'a was saddling a gray horse.'

'Now, by the rood!' cried Sir Daniel, 'the wench was worth five hundred pound to me and more.'

'Sir knight,' observed the messenger, with bitterness, 'while that ye are here, roaring for five hundred pounds, the realm of England is elsewhere being lost and won.'

'It is well said,' replied Sir Daniel. 'Selden, fall me out with six cross-bowmen; hunt me her down. I care not what it cost; but at my returning, let me find her at the Moat House. Be it upon your head. And now, sir messenger, we march.'

And the troop broke into a good trot, and Selden and his six men were left behind upon the street of Kettley, with the staring villagers.

2

In the Fen

It was near six in the May morning when Dick began to ride down into the fen upon his homeward way. The sky was all blue; the jolly wind blew loud and steady; the windmill-sails were spinning; and the willows over all the fen rippling and whitening like a field of corn. He had been all night in the saddle, but his heart was good and his body sound, and he rode right merrily.

The path went down into the marsh, till he lost sight of all the neighbouring landmarks but Kettley windmill on the knoll behind him, and the extreme top of Tunstall Forest far before. On either hand there were great fields of blowing reeds and willows, pools of water shaking in the wind, and treacherous bogs, as green as emerald, to tempt and to betray the traveller. The path lay almost straight through the morass. It was already very ancient; its foundation had been laid by Roman soldiery; in the lapse of ages much of it had sunk, and every here and there, for a few hundred yards, it lay submerged below the stagnant waters of the fen.

About a mile from Kettley, Dick came to one such break in the plain line of causeway, where the reeds and willows grew dispersedly like little islands and confused the eye. The gap, besides, was more than usually long; it was a place where any stranger might come readily to mischief; and Dick bethought him, with something like a pang, of the lad whom he had so imperfectly directed. As for himself, one look backward to where the windmill-sails were turning black against the blue of heaven—one look forward to the high ground of Tunstall Forest, and he was sufficiently directed and held straight on, the water washing to his horse's knees, as safe as on a highway.

Half-way across, and when he had already sighted the path rising high and dry upon the farther side, he was aware of a great splashing on his right, and saw a gray horse, sunk to its belly in the mud, and still spasmodically struggling. Instantly, as though it had divined the neighbourhood of help, the poor beast began to neigh most piercingly. It rolled, meanwhile, a blood-shot eye, insane with terror; and as it sprawled wallowing in the quag, clouds of stinging insects rose and buzzed about it in the air.

'Alack!' thought Dick, 'can the poor lad have perished? There is his horse, for certain—a brave gray! Nay, comrade, if thou criest to me so piteously, I will do all man can to help thee. Shalt not lie there to drown by inches!'

And he made ready his crossbow, and put a quarrel through the creature's head.

Dick rode on after this act of rugged mercy, somewhat sobered in spirit, and looking closely about him for any sign of his less happy predecessor in the way.

'I would I had dared to tell him further,' he thought; 'for I fear he has miscarried in the slough.'

And just as he was so thinking, a voice cried upon his name from the causeway side, and looking over his shoulder, he saw the lad's face peering from a clump of reeds.

'Are ye there?' he said, reining in. 'Ye lay so close among the reeds that I had passed you by. I saw your horse bemired, and put him from his agony; which, by my sooth! an ye had been a more merciful rider, ye had done yourself. But come forth out of your hiding. Here be none to trouble you.'

'Nay, good boy, I have no arms, nor skill to use them if I had,' replied the other, stepping forth upon the pathway.

'Why call me "boy"?' cried Dick. 'Y' are not, I trow, the elder of us twain.'

'Good Master Shelton,' said the other, 'prithee forgive me. I have none the least intention to offend. Rather I would in every way beseech your gentleness and favour, for I am now worse bested than ever, having lost my way, my cloak, and my poor horse. To have a riding-rod and spurs, and never a horse to sit upon! And before all,' he added, looking ruefully upon his clothes—' before all, to be so sorrily besmirched!'

'Tut!' cried Dick. 'Would ye mind a ducking? Blood of wound or dust of travel—that's a man's adornment.'

'Nay, then, I like him better plain,' observed the lad. 'But, prithee, how shall I do? Prithee, good Master Richard, help me with your good counsel. If I come not safe to Holywood, I am undone.'

'Nay,' said Dick, dismounting, 'I will give more than counsel. Take my horse, and I will run awhile, and when I am weary we shall change again, that so, riding and running, both may go the speedier.'

So the change was made, and they went forward as briskly as they durst on the uneven causeway, Dick with his hand upon the other's knee.

'How call ye your name?' asked Dick.

'Call me John Matcham,' replied the lad.

'And what make ye to Holywood?' Dick continued.

'I seek sanctuary from a man that would oppress me,' was the answer. 'The good Abbot of Holywood is a strong pillar to the weak.'

'And how came ye with Sir Daniel, Master Matcham?' pursued Dick.

'Nay,' cried the other, 'by the abuse of force! He hath taken me by violence from my own place; dressed me in these weeds; ridden with me till my heart was sick; gibed me till I could 'a' wept; and when certain of my friends pursued, thinking to have me back, claps me in the rear to stand their shot! I was even grazed in the right foot, and walk but lamely. Nay, there shall come a day between us; he shall smart for all!'

'Would ye shoot at the moon with a hand-gun?' said Dick. ''Tis a valiant knight, and hath a hand of iron. An he guessed I had made or meddled with your flight, it would go sore with me.'

'Ay, poor boy,' returned the other, 'y' are his ward, I know it. By the same token, so am I, or so he saith; or else he hath bought my marriage—I wot not rightly which; but it is some handle to oppress me by.'

'Boy again!' said Dick.

'Nay, then, shall I call you girl, good Richard?' asked Matcham.

'Never a girl for me,' returned Dick. 'I do abjure the crew of them!'

'Ye speak boyishly,' said the other. 'Ye think more of them than ye pretend.'

'Not I,' said Dick stoutly. 'They come not in my mind. A plague of them, say I! Give me to hunt and to fight and to feast, and to live with jolly foresters. I never heard of a maid yet that was for any service, save one only; and she, poor shrew, was burned for a witch and the wearing of men's clothes in spite of nature.'

Master Matcham crossed himself with fervour, and appeared to pray.

'What make ye?' Dick inquired.

'I pray for her spirit,' answered the other, with a somewhat troubled voice.

'For a witch's spirit?' Dick cried. 'But pray for her, an ye list; she was the best wench in Europe, was this Joan of Arc. Old Appleyard the archer ran from her, he said, as if she had been Mahoun. Nay, she was a brave wench.'

'Well, but, good Master Richard,' resumed Matcham, 'an ye like maids so little, y' are no true natural man; for God made them twain by intention, and brought true love into the world, to be man's hope and woman's comfort.'

'Faugh!' said Dick. 'Y' are a milk-sopping baby, so to harp on women. An ye think I be no true man, get down upon the path, and whether at fists, backsword, or bow and arrow, I will prove my manhood on your body.'

'Nay, I am no fighter,' said Matcham eagerly. 'I meant no tittle of offence. I meant but pleasantry. And if I talk of women, it is because I heard ye were to marry.'

'I to marry!' Dick exclaimed. 'Well, it is the first I hear of it. And with whom was I to marry?'

'One Joan Sedley,' replied Matcham, colouring. 'It was Sir Daniel's doing; he hath money to gain upon both sides; and, indeed, I have heard the poor wench bemoaning herself pitifully of the match. It seems she is of your mind, or else distasted to the bridegroom.

'Well! marriage is like death, it comes to all,' said Dick, with resignation. 'And she bemoaned herself? I pray ye now, see there how shuttle-witted are these girls: to bemoan herself before that she had seen me? Do I bemoan myself? Not I. An I be to marry, I will marry dry-eyed! But if ye know her, prithee, of what favour is she? fair or foul? And is she shrewish or pleasant?'

'Nay, what matters it?' said Matcham. 'An y' are to marry, ye can but marry. What matters foul or fair? These be but toys. Y' are no milksop, Master Richard; ye will wed with dry eyes, anyhow.'

'It is well said,' replied Shelton. 'Little I reck.'

'Your lady wife is like to have a pleasant lord,' said Matcham.

'She shall have the lord Heaven made her for,' returned Dick. 'I trow there be worse as well as better.'

'Ay, the poor wench!' cried the other.

'And why so poor?' asked Dick.

'To wed a man of wood,' replied his companion. 'O me, for a wooden husband!'

'I think I be a man of wood, indeed,' said Dick, 'to trudge afoot the while you ride my horse; but it is good wood, I trow.'

'Good Dick, forgive me,' cried the other. 'Nay, y' are the best heart in England; I but laughed. Forgive me now, sweet Dick.'

'Nay, no fool words,' returned Dick, a little embarrassed by his companion's warmth. 'No harm is done. I am not touchy, praise the saints.'

And at that moment the wind, which was blowing straight behind them as they went, brought them the rough flourish of Sir Daniel's trumpeter.

'Hark!' said Dick, 'the tucket soundeth.'

'Ay,' said Matcham, 'they have found my flight, and now I am unhorsed!' and he became pale as death.

'Nay, what cheer!' returned Dick. 'Y' have a long start, and we are near the ferry. And it is I, methinks, that am unhorsed.'

'Alack, I shall be taken!' cried the fugitive. 'Dick, kind Dick, beseech ye help me but a little!'

'Why, now, what aileth thee?' said Dick. 'Methinks I help you very patently. But my heart is sorry for so spiritless a fellow! And see ye here, John Matcham—sith John Matcham is your name—I, Richard Shelton, tide what betideth, come what may, will see you safe in Holywood. The saints so do to me again if I default you. Come, pick me up a good heart, Sir White-face. The way betters here; spur me the horse. Go faster! faster! Nay, mind not for me; I can run like a deer.'

So, with the horse trotting hard, and Dick running easily alongside, they crossed the remainder of the fen, and came out upon the banks of the river by the ferryman's hut.

3

The Fen Ferry

THE river Till was a wide, sluggish, clayey water, oozing out of fens, and in this part of its course it strained among some score of willow-covered, marshy islets.

It was a dingy stream: but upon this bright, spirited morning everything was become beautiful. The wind and the martens broke it up into innumerable dimples; and the reflection of the sky was scattered over all the surface in crumbs of smiling blue.

A creek ran up to meet the path, and close under the bank the ferryman's hut lay snugly. It was of wattle and clay, and the grass grew green upon the roof.

Dick went to the door and opened it. Within, upon a foul old russet cloak, the ferryman lay stretched and shivering; a great hulk of a man, but lean and shaken by the country fever.

'Hey, Master Shelton,' he said, 'be ye for the ferry? Ill times, ill times! Look to yourself. There is a fellowship abroad. Ye were better turn round on your two heels and try the bridge.'

'Nay; time's in the saddle,' answered Dick. 'Time will ride, Hugh Ferryman. I am hot in haste.'

'A wilful man!' returned the ferryman, rising. 'An ye win safe to the Moat House, y' have done lucky; but I say no more.' And then catching sight of Matcham, 'Who be this?' he asked, as he paused, blinking, on the threshold of his cabin.

'It is my kinsman, Master Matcham,' answered Dick.

'Give ye good day, good ferryman,' said Matcham, who had dismounted, and now came forward, leading the horse. 'Launch me your boat, I prithee; we are sore in haste.'

The gaunt ferryman continued staring.

'By the mass!' he cried at length, and laughed with open throat.

Matcham coloured to his neck and winced; and Dick, with an angry countenance, put his hand on the lout's shoulder.

'How now, churl!' he cried. 'Fall to thy business, and leave mocking thy betters.'

Hugh Ferryman grumblingly undid his boat, and shoved it a little forth into the deep water. Then Dick led in the horse, and Matcham followed.

'Ye be mortal small made, master,' said Hugh, with a wide grin; 'something o' the wrong model, belike. Nay, Master Shelton, I am for you,' he added, getting to his oars. 'A cat may look at a king. I did but take a shot of the eye at Master Matcham.'

'Sirrah, no more words,' said Dick. 'Bend me your back.'

They were by that time at the mouth of the creek, and the view opened up and down the river. Everywhere it was enclosed with islands. Clay banks were falling in, willows nodding, reeds waving, martens dipping and piping. There was no sign of man in the labyrinth of waters.

'My master,' said the ferryman, keeping the boat steady with one oar, 'I have a shrewd guess that John-a-Fenne is on the island. He bears me a black grudge to all Sir Daniel's. How if I turned me upstream and landed you an arrow-flight above the path? Ye were best not meddle with John Fenne.'

'How, then? is he of this company?' asked Dick.

'Nay, mum is the word,' said Hugh. 'But I would go up water, Dick. How if Master Matcham came by an arrow?' and he laughed again.

'Be it so, Hugh,' answered Dick.

'Look ye, then,' pursued Hugh. 'Sith it shall so be, unsling me your crossbow—so: now make it ready—good; place me a quarrel. Ay, keep it so, and look upon me grimly.'

'What meaneth this?' asked Dick.

'Why, my master, if I steal you across, it must be under force or fear,' replied the ferryman; 'for else, if John Fenne got wind of it, he were like to prove my most distressful neighbour.'

'Do these churls ride so roughly?' Dick inquired. 'Do they command Sir Daniel's own ferry?'

'Nay,' whispered the ferryman, winking. 'Mark me! Sir Daniel shall down. His time is out. He shall down. Mum!' And he bent over his oars.

They pulled a long way up the river, turned the tail of an island, and came softly down a narrow channel next the opposite bank. Then Hugh held water in mid-stream.

'I must land you here among the willows,' he said.

'Here is no path but willow swamps and quagmires,' answered Dick.

'Master Shelton,' replied Hugh, 'I dare not take ye nearer down, for your own sake now. He watcheth me the ferry, lying on his bow. All that go by and owe Sir Daniel goodwill, he shooteth down like rabbits. I heard him swear it by the rood. An I had not known you of old days—ay, and from so high upward—I would 'a' let you go on; but for old days' remembrance, and because ye had this toy with you that's not fit for wounds or warfare, I did risk my two poor ears to have you over whole. Content you; I can no more, on my salvation!'

Hugh was still speaking, lying on his oars, when there came a great shout from among the willows on the island, and sounds followed as of a strong man breasting roughly through the wood.

'A murrain!' cried Hugh. 'He was on the upper island all the while!' He pulled straight for the shore. 'Threat me with your bow, good Dick; threat me with it plain,' he added. 'I have tried to save your skins, save you mine!'

The boat ran into a tough thicket of willows with a crash.

Matcham, pale, but steady and alert, at a sign from Dick, ran along the thwarts and leaped ashore; Dick, taking the horse by the bridle, sought to follow, but what with the animal's bulk, and what with the closeness of the thicket, both stuck fast. The horse neighed and trampled; and the boat, which was swinging in an eddy, came on and off and pitched with violence.

'It may not be, Hugh; here is no landing,' cried Dick; but he still struggled valiantly with the obstinate thicket and the startled animal.

A tall man appeared upon the shore of the island, a long-bow in his hand. Dick saw him for an instant, with the corner of his eye, bending the bow with a great effort, his face crimson with hurry.

'Who goes?' he shouted. 'Hugh, who goes?'

''Tis Master Shelton, John,' replied the ferryman.

'Stand, Dick Shelton!' bawled the man upon the island. 'Ye shall have no hurt, upon the rood! Stand! Back out, Hugh Ferryman.'

Dick cried a taunting answer.

'Nay, then, ye shall go afoot,' returned the man; and he let drive an arrow.

The horse, struck by the shaft, lashed out in agony and terror; the boat capsized, and next moment all were struggling in the eddies of the river.

When Dick came up, he was within a yard of the bank; and before his eyes were clear his hand had closed on something firm and strong that instantly began to drag him forward. It was the riding-rod, that Matcham, crawling forth upon an overhanging willow, had opportunely thrust into his grasp.

'By the mass!' cried Dick, as he was helped ashore, 'that makes a life I owe you. I swim like a cannon-ball.' And he turned instantly towards the island.

Midway over, Hugh Ferryman was swimming with his up-turned boat, while John-a-Fenne, furious at the ill-fortune of his shot, bawled to him to hurry.

'Come, Jack,' said Shelton, 'run for it! Ere Hugh can hale his barge across, or the pair of 'em can get it righted, we may be out of cry.'

And adding example to his words, he began to run, dodging among the willows, and in marshy places leaping from tussock to tussock. He had no time to look for his direction; all he could do was to turn his back upon the river, and put all his heart to running.

Presently, however, the ground began to rise, which showed him he was still in the right way, and soon after they came forth upon a slope of solid turf, where elms began to mingle with the willows.

But here Matcham, who had been dragging far into the rear, threw himself fairly down.

'Leave me, Dick!' he cried pantingly; 'I can no more.'

Dick turned, and came back to where his companion lay.

'Nay, Jack, leave thee!' he cried. 'That were a knave's trick, to be sure, when ye risked a shot and a ducking, ay, and a drowning too, to save my life. Drowning, in sooth; for why I did not pull you in along with me, the saints alone can tell!'

'Nay,' said Matcham, 'I would 'a' saved us both, good Dick, for I can swim.'

'Can ye so?' cried Dick, with open eyes. It was the one manly accomplishment of which he was himself incapable. In the order of the things that he admired, next to having killed a man in single fight came swimming. 'Well,' he said, 'here is a lesson to despise no man. I promised to care for you as far as Holywood, and, by the rood, Jack, y' are more capable to care for me.'

'Well, Dick, we're friends now,' said Matcham.

'Nay, I never was unfriends,' answered Dick. 'Y'are a brave lad in your way, albeit something of a milksop, too. I never met your like before this day. But, prithee, fetch back your breath, and let us on. Here is no place for chatter.'

'My foot hurts shrewdly,' said Matcham.

'Nay, I had forgot your foot,' returned Dick. 'Well, we must go the gentlier. I would I knew rightly where we were. I have clean lost the path; yet that may be for the better, too. An they watch the ferry, they watch the path, belike, as well. I would Sir Daniel were back with two-score men; he would sweep me these rascals as the wind sweeps leaves. Come, Jack, lean ye on my shoulder, ye poor shrew. Nay, y' are not tall enough. What age are ye, for a wager?—twelve?'

'Nay, I am sixteen,' said Matcham.

'Y' are poorly grown to height, then,' answered Dick. 'But take my hand. We shall go softly, never fear. I owe you a life; I am a good repayer, Jack, of good or evil.'

They began to go forward up the slope.

'We must hit the road, early or late,' continued Dick; 'and then for a fresh start. By the mass! but y' 'ave a rickety hand Jack. If I had a hand like that, I would think shame. I tell you,' he went on, with a sudden chuckle, 'I swear by the mass I believe Hugh Ferryman took you for a maid.'

'Nay, never!' cried the other, colouring high.

''A did, though, for a wager!' Dick exclaimed. 'Small

blame to him. Ye look liker maid than man; and I tell ye more—y' are a strange-looking rogue for a boy; but for a hussy, Jack, ye would be right fair—ye would. Ye would be well-favoured for a wench.'

'Well,' said Matcham, 'ye know right well that I am none.'

'Nay, I know that; I do but jest,' said Dick. 'Ye'll be a man before your mother, Jack. What cheer, my bully! Ye shall strike shrewd strokes. Now, which, I marvel, of you or me, shall be first knighted, Jack? for knighted I shall be, or die for 't. "Sir Richard Shelton, Knight": it soundeth bravely. But "Sir John Matcham" soundeth not amiss.'

'Prithee, Dick, stop till I drink,' said the other, pausing where a little clear spring welled out of the slope into a gravelled basin no bigger than a pocket. 'And O, Dick, if I might come by anything to eat!—my very heart aches with hunger.'

'Why, fool, did ye not eat at Kettley?' said Dick.

'I made a vow—it was a sin I had been led into,' stammered Matcham; 'but now, if it were but dry bread, I would eat it greedily.'

'Sit ye, then, and eat,' said Dick, 'while that I scout a little forward for the road.' And he took a wallet from his girdle, wherein were bread and pieces of dry bacon, and, while Matcham fell heartily to, struck farther forth among the trees.

A little beyond there was a dip in the ground, where a streamlet soaked among dead leaves; and beyond that, again, the trees were better grown and stood wider, and oak and beech began to take the place of willow and elm. The continued tossing and pouring of the wind among the leaves sufficiently concealed the sounds of his footsteps on the mast; it was for the ear what a moonless night is to the eye; but for all that Dick went cautiously, slipping from one big trunk to another, and looking sharply about him as he went. Suddenly a doe passed like a shadow through the underwood in front of him, and he paused, disgusted at the chance. This part of the wood had been certainly deserted, but now that the poor deer had run, she was like a messenger he should have sent before him to announce his coming; and instead of pushing farther, he turned him to the nearest well-grown tree, and rapidly began to climb.

Luck had served him well. The oak on which he had mounted was one of the tallest in that quarter of the wood, and easily out-topped its neighbours by a fathom and a half; and when Dick had clambered into the topmost fork and clung there, swinging dizzily in the great wind, he saw behind him the whole fenny plain as far as Kettley, and the Till wandering among woody islets, and in front of him the white line of high-road winding through the forest. The boat had been righted—it was even now midway on the ferry. Beyond that there was no sign of man, nor aught moving but the wind. He was about to descend, when, taking a last view, his eye lit upon a string of moving points about the middle of the fen. Plainly a small troop was threading the causeway, and that at a good pace; and this gave him some concern as he shinned vigorously down the trunk and returned across the wood for his companion.

4

A greenwood company

MATCHAM was well rested and revived; and the two lads, winged by what Dick had seen, hurried through the remainder of the outwood, crossed the road in safety, and began to mount into the high ground of Tunstall Forest. The trees grew more and more in groves, with heathy places in between, sandy, gorsy, and dotted with old yews. The ground became more and more uneven, full of pits and hillocks. And with every step of the ascent the wind still blew the shriller, and the trees bent before the gusts like fishing-rods.

They had just entered one of the clearings, when Dick suddenly clapped down upon his face among the brambles, and began to crawl slowly backward towards the shelter of the grove. Matcham, in great bewilderment, for he could see no reason for this flight, still imitated his companion's course; and it was not until they had gained the harbour of a thicket that he turned and begged him to explain.

For all reply, Dick pointed with his finger.

At the far end of the clearing, a fir grew high above the neighbouring wood, and planted its black shock of foliage clear against the sky. For about fifty feet above the ground the trunk grew straight and solid like a column. At that level, it split into two massive boughs; and in the fork, like a mast-headed seaman, there stood a man in a green tabard, spying far and wide. The sun glistened upon his hair; with one hand he shaded his eyes to look abroad, and he kept slowly rolling his head from side to side with the regularity of a machine.

The lads exchanged glances.

'Let us try to the left,' said Dick. 'We had near fallen foully, Jack.'

Ten minutes afterwards they struck into a beaten path.

'Here is a piece of forest that I know not,' Dick remarked. 'Where goeth me this track?'

'Let us even try,' said Matcham.

A few yards farther the path came to the top of a ridge and began to go down abruptly into a cup-shaped hollow. At the foot, out of a thick wood of flowering hawthorn, two or three roofless gables, blackened as if by fire, and a single tall chimney marked the ruins of a house.

'What may this be?' whispered Matcham.

'Nay, by the mass, I know not,' answered Dick. 'I am all at sea. Let us go warily.'

With beating hearts, they descended through the hawthorns. Here and there they passed signs of recent cultivation; fruit-trees and pot-herbs ran wild among the thicket; a sun-dial had fallen in the grass; it seemed they were treading what once had been a garden. Yet a little farther and they came forth before the ruins of the house.

It had been a pleasant mansion and a strong. A dry ditch was dug deep about it; but it was now choked with masonry, and bridged by a fallen rafter. The two farther walls still stood, the sun shining through their empty windows; but the remainder of the building had collapsed, and now lay in a great cairn of ruin, grimed with fire. Already in the interior a few plants were springing green among the chinks.

'Now I bethink me,' whispered Dick, 'this must be Grimstone. It was a hold of one Simon Malmesbury; Sir Daniel was his bane! 'Twas Bennet Hatch that burned it, now five years agone. In sooth, 'twas pity, for it was a fair house.'

Down in the hollow, where no wind blew, it was both warm and still, and Matcham, laying one hand upon Dick's arm, held up a warning finger.'

'Hist!' he said.

Then came a strange sound, breaking on the quiet. It was twice repeated ere they recognised its nature. It was the sound of a big man clearing his throat; and just then a hoarse, untuneful voice broke into singing:—

'Then up and spake the master, the king of the outlaws:
"What make ye here, my merry men, among the greenwood shaws?
And Gamelyn made answer—he looked never adown:
"O, they must need to walk in wood that may not walk in town!"'

The singer paused, a faint click of iron followed, and then silence.

The two lads stood looking at each other. Whoever he might be, their invisible neighbour was just beyond the ruin. And suddenly the colour came into Matcham's face, and next moment he had crossed the fallen rafter, and was climbing cautiously on the huge pile of lumber that filled the interior of the roofless house. Dick would have withheld him, had he been in time; as it was, he was fain to follow.

Right in the corner of the ruin, two rafters had fallen crosswise, and protected a clear space no larger than a pew in church. Into this the lads silently lowered themselves. There they were perfectly concealed, and through an arrow loophole commanded a view upon the farther side.

Peering through this, they were struck stiff with terror at their predicament. To retreat was impossible; they scarce dared to breathe. Upon the very margin of the ditch, not thirty feet from where they crouched, an iron cauldron bubbled and steamed above a glowing fire; and close by, in an attitude of listening, as though he had caught some sound of their clambering among the ruins, a tall, red-faced, battered-looking man stood poised, an iron spoon in his right hand, a horn and a formidable dagger at his belt. Plainly this was the singer; plainly he had been stirring the cauldron, when some incautious step among the lumber had fallen upon his ear. A little farther off another man lay slumbering, rolled in a brown cloak, with a butterfly hovering above his face. All this was in a clearing white with daisies; and at the extreme verge a bow, a sheaf of arrows, and part of a deer's carcass hung upon a flowering hawthorn.

Presently the fellow relaxed from his attitude of attention, raised the spoon to his mouth, tasted its contents, nodded, and then fell again to stirring and singing.

'"O, they must need to walk in wood that may not walk
in town,"'

he croaked, taking up his song where he had left it.

'"O, sir, we walk not here at all an evil thing to do,
But if we meet with the good king's deer to shoot a shaft
into."'

Still as he sang, he took from time to time another spoonful of the broth, blew upon it, and tasted it, with all the airs of an experienced cook. At length, apparently, he judged the mess was ready, for, taking the horn from his girdle, he blew three modulated calls.

The other fellow awoke, rolled over, brushed away the butterfly, and looked about him.

'How now, brother?' he said. 'Dinner?'

'Ay, sot,' replied the cook, 'dinner it is, and a dry dinner, too, with neither ale nor bread. But there is little pleasure in the greenwood now; time was when a good fellow could live here like a mitred abbot, set aside the rain and white frosts; he had his heart's desire both of ale and wine. But now are men's spirits dead, and this John Amend-All, save us and guard us! but a stuffed booby to scare crows withal.'

'Nay,' returned the other, 'y' are too set on meat and drinking, Lawless. Bide ye a bit; the good time cometh.'

'Look ye,' returned the cook, 'I have even waited for this good time sith that I was so high. I have been a grey friar; I have been a king's archer; I have been a shipman, and sailed the salt seas; and I have been in greenwood before this, forsooth! and shot the king's deer. What cometh of it? Naught! I were better to have bided in the cloister. John Abbot availeth more than John Amend-All. By'r Lady! here they come.'

One after another, tall likely fellows began to stroll into the lawn. Each as he came produced a knife and a horn cup, helped himself from the cauldron, and sat down upon the grass to eat. They were very variously equipped and armed; some in rusty smocks, and with nothing but a knife and an old bow; others in the height of forest gallantry, all in Lincoln green, both hood and jerkin, with dainty peacock arrows in their belts, a horn upon a baldrick, and a sword and dagger at their sides. They came in the silence of hunger, and scarce growled a salutation, but fell instantly to meat.

There were, perhaps, a score of them already gathered, when a sound of suppressed cheering arose close by among the hawthorns, and immediately after five or six woodmen carrying a stretcher debouched upon the lawn. A tall, lusty fellow, somewhat grizzled, and as brown as a smoked ham, walked before them with an air of some authority, his bow at his back, a bright boar-spear in his hand.

'Lads!' he cried, 'good fellows all, and my right merry friends, y' have sung this while on a dry whistle and lived at little ease. But what said I ever? Abide Fortune constantly; she turneth, turneth swift. And lo! here is her firstling—even that good creature, ale!'

There was a murmur of applause as the bearers set down the stretcher and displayed a goodly cask.

'And now haste, ye boys,' the man continued. 'There is work toward. A handful of archers are but now come to the ferry; murrey and blue is their wear; they are our butts—they shall all taste arrows—no man of them shall struggle through this wood. For, lads, we are here some fifty strong, each man of us most foully wronged; for some they have lost lands, and some friends; and some have been outlawed—all oppressed! Who, then, hath done this evil? Sir Daniel, by the rood! Shall he then profit? shall he sit snug in our houses? shall he till our fields? shall he suck the bone he robbed us of? I trow not. He getteth him strength at law; he gaineth cases; nay, there is one case he shall not gain—I have a writ here at my belt that, please the saints, shall conquer him.'

Lawless the cook was by this time already at his second horn of ale. He raised it, as if to pledge the speaker.

'Master Ellis,' he said, 'y' are for vengeance—well it becometh you!—but your poor brother o' the greenwood that had never lands to lose nor friends to think upon, looketh rather, for his poor part, to the profit of the thing. We had liever a gold noble and a pottle of canary wine than all the vengeances in purgatory.'

'Lawless,' replied the other, 'to reach the Moat House, Sir Daniel must pass the forest. We shall make that passage dearer, pardy, than any battle. Then, when he has got to earth with such ragged handful as escapeth us—all his great friends fallen and fled away, and none to give him aid—we shall beleaguer that old fox about, and great shall be the fall of him. 'Tis a fat buck; he will make a dinner for us all.'

'Ay,' returned Lawless, 'I have eaten many of these dinners beforehand; but the cooking of them is hot work, good Master Ellis. And meanwhile what do we? We make black arrows, we write rhymes, and we drink fair cold water, that discomfortable drink.'

'Y' are untrue, Will Lawless. Ye still smell of the Grey Friars' buttery; greed is your undoing,' answered Ellis. 'We took twenty pounds from Appleyard. We took seven marks from the messenger last night. A day ago we had fifty from the merchant.'

'And to-day,' said one of the men, 'I stopped a fat pardoner riding apace for Holywood. Here is his purse.

Ellis counted the contents.

'Five-score shillings!' he grumbled. 'Fool, he had more in his sandal, or stitched into his tippet. Y' are but a child, Tom Cuckow; ye have lost the fish.'

But, for all that, Ellis pocketed the purse with nonchalance. He stood leaning on his boar-spear, and looked round upon the rest. They, in various attitudes, took greedily of the venison pottage, and liberally washed it down with ale. This was a good day; they were in luck; but business pressed, and they were speedy in their eating. The first comers had by this time even despatched their dinner. Some lay down upon the grass and fell instantly asleep, like boa-constrictors; others talked together, or overhauled their weapons; and one, whose humour was particularly gay, holding forth an ale-horn, began to sing:—

'Here is no law in good green shaw,
  Here is no lack of meat;
'Tis merry and quiet, with deer for our diet,
  In summer, when all is sweet.

'Come winter again, with wind and rain—
  Come winter, with snow and sleet,
Get home to your places, with hoods on your faces,
  And sit by the fire and eat.'

All this while the two lads had listened and lain close; only Richard had unslung his crossbow, and held ready in one hand the windac, or grappling-iron, that he used to bend it. Otherwise they had not dared to stir; and this scene of forest life had gone on before their eyes like a scene upon a theatre. But now there came a strange interruption. The tall chimney which overtopped the remainder of the ruins rose right above their hiding-place. There came a whistle in the air, and then a sounding smack, and the fragments of a broken arrow fell about their ears. Some one from the upper quarters of the wood, perhaps the very sentinel they saw posted in the fir, had shot an arrow at the chimney-top.

Matcham could not restrain a little cry, which he instantly stifled, and even Dick started with surprise, and dropped the windac from his fingers. But to the fellows on the lawn, this shaft was an expected signal. They were all afoot together, tightening their belts, testing their bow-strings, loosening sword and dagger in the sheath. Ellis held up his hand; his face had suddenly assumed a look of savage energy; the white of his eyes shone in his sun-brown face.

'Lads,' he said, 'ye know your places. Let not one man's soul escape you. Appleyard was a whet before a meal; but now we go to table. I have three men whom I will bitterly avenge—Harry Shelton, Simon Malmesbury, and '—striking his broad bosom—'and Ellis Duckworth, by the mass!'

Another man came, red with hurry, through the thorns.

'’Tis not Sir Daniel!' he panted. 'They are but seven. Is the arrow gone?'

'It struck but now,' replied Ellis.

'A murrain!' cried the messenger. 'Methought I heard it whistle. And I go dinnerless!'

In the space of a minute, some running, some walking sharply, according as their stations were nearer or farther away, the men of the Black Arrow had all disappeared from the neighbourhood of the ruined house; and the cauldron, and the fire, which was now burning low, and the dead deer's carcase on the hawthorn, remained alone to testify they had been there.

5

'*Bloody as the Hunter*'

THE lads lay quiet till the last footstep had melted on the wind. Then they arose, and with many an ache, for they were weary with constraint, clambered through the ruins, and recrossed the ditch upon the rafter. Matcham had picked up the windac and went first, Dick following stiffly, with his cross-bow on his arm.

'And now,' said Matcham, 'forth to Holywood.'

'To Holywood!' cried Dick, 'when good fellows stand shot? Not I! I would see you hanged first, Jack!'

'Ye would leave me, would ye?' Matcham asked.

'Ay, by my sooth!' returned Dick. 'An I be not in time to warn these lads, I will go die with them. What! would ye have me leave my own men that I have lived among? I trow not! Give me my windac.'

But there was nothing further from Matcham's mind.

'Dick,' he said, 'ye sware before the saints that ye would see me safe to Holywood. Would ye be forsworn? Would you desert me—a perjurer?'

'Nay, I sware for the best,' returned Dick. 'I meant it, too; but now! But look ye, Jack, turn again with me. Let me but warn these men, and, if needs must, stand shot with them; then shall all be clear, and I will on again to Holywood and purge mine oath.'

'Ye but deride me,' answered Matcham. 'These men ye go to succour are the same that hunt me to my ruin.'

Dick scratched his head.

'I cannot help it, Jack,' he said. 'Here is no remedy. What would ye? Ye run no great peril, man; and these are in the way of death. Death! he added. 'Think of it! What a murrain do ye keep me here for? Give me the windac. Saint George! shall they all die?'

'Richard Shelton,' said Matcham, looking him squarely in the face, 'would ye, then, join party with Sir Daniel? Have ye not ears? Heard ye not this Ellis, what he said? or have ye no heart for your own kindly blood and the father that men slew? "Harry Shelton," he said; and Sir Harry Shelton was your father, as the sun shines in heaven.'

'What would ye?' Dick cried again. 'Would ye have me credit thieves?'

'Nay, I have heard it before now,' returned Matcham. 'The fame goeth currently, it was Sir Daniel slew him. He slew him under oath; in his own house he shed the innocent blood. Heaven wearies for the avenging on't; and you —the man's son —ye go about to comfort and defend the murderer!'

'Jack,' cried the lad, 'I know not. It may be; what know I? But, see here: This man has bred me up and fostered me, and his men I have hunted with and played among; and to leave them in the hour of peril—O, man, if I did that, I were stark dead to honour! Nay, Jack, ye would not ask it; ye would not wish me to be base.'

'But your father, Dick?' said Matcham, somewhat wavering. 'Your father? and your oath to me? Ye took the saints to witness.'

'My father?' cried Shelton. 'Nay, he would have me go! If Sir Daniel slew him, when the hour comes this hand shall slay Sir Daniel; but neither him nor his will I desert in peril. And for mine oath, good Jack, ye shall absolve me of it here. For the lives' sake of many men that hurt you not, and for mine honour, ye shall set me free.'

'I, Dick? never!' returned Matcham. 'An ye leave me, y' are forsworn, and so I shall declare it.'

'My blood heats,' said Dick. 'Give me the windac! Give it me!'

'I'll not,' said Matcham. 'I'll save you in your teeth.'

'Not?' cried Dick. 'I'll make you!'

'Try it,' said the other.

They stood, looking in each other's eyes, each ready for a spring. Then Dick leaped; and though Matcham turned instantly and fled, in two bounds he was overtaken, the windac was twisted from his grasp, he was thrown roughly to the ground, and Dick stood across him, flushed and menacing, with doubled fist. Matcham lay where he had fallen, with his face in the grass, not thinking of resistance.

Dick bent his bow.

'I'll teach you!' he cried fiercely. 'Oath or no oath, you may go hang for me!'

And he turned and began to run. Matcham was on his feet at once, and began running after him.

'What d'ye want?' cried Dick, stopping. 'What make ye after me? Stand off!'

'I will follow an I please,' said Matcham. 'This wood is free to me.'

'Stand back, by'r Lady!' returned Dick, raising his bow.

'Ah, y'are a brave boy!' retorted Matcham. 'Shoot!'

Dick lowered his weapon in some confusion.

'See here,' he said. 'Y' have done me ill enough. Go, then. Go your way in fair wise; or, whether I will or not, I must even drive you to it.'

'Well,' said Matcham doggedly, 'y' are the stronger. Do your worst. I shall not leave to follow thee, Dick, unless thou makest me,' he added.

Dick was almost beside himself. It went against his heart to beat a creature so defenceless; and, for the life of him, he knew no other way to rid himself of this unwelcome, and, as he began to think, perhaps untrue companion.

'Y' are mad, I think,' he cried. 'Fool-fellow, I am hasting to your foes; as fast as foot can carry me, go I thither.'

'I care not, Dick,' replied the lad. 'If y' are bound to die, Dick, I'll die too. I would liever go with you to prison than to go free without you.'

'Well,' returned the other, 'I may stand no longer prating. Follow me, if ye must; but if ye play me false, it shall but little advance you, mark ye that. Shalt have a quarrel in thine inwards, boy.'

So saying, Dick took once more to his heels, keeping in the margin of the thicket, and looking briskly about him as he went. At a good pace he rattled out of the dell, and came again into the more open quarters of the wood. To the left a little eminence appeared, spotted with golden gorse, and crowned with a black tuft of firs.

'I shall see from there,' he thought, and struck for it across a heathy clearing.

He had gone but a few yards, when Matcham touched him on the arm, and pointed. To the eastward of the summit there was a dip, and, as it were, a valley passing to the other side; the heath was not yet out; all the ground was rusty, like an unscoured buckler and dotted sparingly with yews; and there, one following another, Dick saw half a score green jerkins mounting the ascent, and marching at their head, conspicuous by his boar-spear, Ellis Duckworth in person. One after another gained the top, showed for a moment against the sky, and then dipped upon the farther side, until the last was gone.

Dick looked at Matcham with a kindlier eye.

'So y' are to be true to me, Jack?' he asked. 'I thought ye were of the other party.'

Matcham began to sob.

'What cheer!' cried Dick. 'Now the saints behold us! would ye snivel for a word?'

'Ye hurt me,' sobbed Matcham. 'Ye hurt me when ye threw me down. Y' are a coward to abuse your strength.'

'Nay, that is fool's talk,' said Dick roughly. 'Y' had no title to my windac, Master John. I would 'a' done right to have well basted you. If ye go with me, ye must obey me; and so, come.'

Matcham had half a thought to stay behind; but, seeing that Dick continued to scour full-tilt towards the eminence, and not so much as looked across his shoulder, he soon thought better of that, and began to run in turn. But the ground was very difficult and steep; Dick had already a long start, and had, at any rate, the lighter heels, and he had long since come to the summit, crawled forward through the firs, and ensconced himself in a thick tuft of gorse, before Matcham, panting like a deer, rejoined him, and lay down in silence by his side.

Below, in the bottom of a considerable valley, the short cut from Tunstall hamlet wound downwards to the ferry. It was well beaten, and the eye followed it easily from point to point. Here it was bordered by open glades; there the forest closed upon it; every hundred yards it ran beside an ambush. Far down the path, the sun shone on seven steel salets, and from time to time, as the trees opened, Selden and his men could be seen riding briskly, still bent upon Sir Daniel's mission. The wind had somewhat fallen, but still tussled merrily with the trees, and, perhaps, had Appleyard been there, he would have drawn a warning from the troubled conduct of the birds.

'Now, mark,' Dick whispered. 'They be already well advanced into the wood; their safety lieth rather in continuing forward. But see ye where this wide glade runneth down before us, and in the midst of it, these two-score trees make like an island? There were their safety. An they but come sound as far as that, I will make shift to warn them. But my heart misgiveth me; they are but seven against so many, and they but carry crossbows. The long-bow, Jack, will have the uppermost ever.'

Meanwhile, Selden and his men still wound up the path,

ignorant of their danger, and momentarily drew nearer hand. Once, indeed, they paused, drew into a group, and seemed to point and listen. But it was something from far away across the plain that had arrested their attention—a hollow growl of cannon that came, from time to time, upon the wind, and told of the great battle. It was worth a thought, to be sure; for if the voice of the big guns were thus become audible in Tunstall Forest, the fight must have rolled ever eastward, and the day, by consequence, gone sore against Sir Daniel and the lords of the dark rose.

But presently the little troop began again to move forward, and came next to a very open, heathy portion of the way, where but a single tongue of forest ran down to join the road. They were but just abreast of this, when an arrow shone flying. One of the men threw up his arms, his horse reared, and both fell and struggled together in a mass. Even from where the boys lay they could hear the rumour of the men's voices crying out; they could see the startled horses prancing, and, presently, as the troop began to recover from their first surprise, one fellow beginning to dismount. A second arrow from somewhat farther off glanced in a wide arch; a second rider bit the dust. The man who was dismounting lost hold upon the rein, and his horse fled galloping, and dragged him by the foot along the road, bumping from stone to stone, and battered by the fleeing hoofs. The four who still kept the saddle instantly broke and scattered; one wheeled and rode, shrieking, towards the ferry; the other three, with loose rein and flying raiment, came galloping up the road from Tunstall. From every clump they passed an arrow sped. Soon a horse fell, but the rider found his feet and continued to pursue his comrades till a second shot despatched him. Another man fell; then another horse; out of the whole troop there was but one fellow left, and he on foot; only, in different directions, the noise of the galloping of three riderless horses was dying fast into the distance.

All this time not one of the assailants had for a moment showed himself. Here and there along the path, horse or man rolled, undespatched, in his agony; but no merciful enemy broke cover to put them from their pain.

The solitary survivor stood bewildered in the road beside his fallen charger. He had come the length of that broad glade, with the island of timber, pointed out by Dick. He was not, perhaps, five hundred yards from where the boys lay hidden; and they could see him plainly, looking to and fro in deadly expectation. But nothing came; and the man began to pluck up his courage, and suddenly unslung and bent his bow. At the same time, by something in his action, Dick recognised Selden.

At this offer of resistance, from all about him in the covert of the woods there went up the sound of laughter. A score of men, at least, for this was the very thickest of the ambush, joined in this cruel and untimely mirth. Then an arrow glanced over Selden's shoulder; and he leaped and ran a little back. Another dart struck quivering at his heel. He made for the cover. A third shaft leaped out right in his face, and fell short in front of him. And then the laughter was repeated loudly, rising and re-echoing from different thickets.

It was plain that his assailants were but baiting him, as men, in those days, baited the poor bull, or as the cat still trifles with the mouse. The skirmish was well over; farther down the road, a fellow in green was already calmly gathering the arrows; and now, in the evil pleasure of their hearts, they gave themselves the spectacle of their poor fellow-sinner in his torture.

Selden began to understand; he uttered a roar of anger, shouldered his crossbow, and sent a quarrel at a venture into the wood. Chance favoured him, for a slight cry responded. Then, throwing down his weapon, Selden began to run before him up the glade, and almost in a straight line for Dick and Matcham.

The companions of the Black Arrow now began to shoot in earnest. But they were properly served; their chance had passed; most of them had now to shoot against the sun; and Selden, as he ran, bounded from side to side to baffle and deceive their aim. Best of all, by turning up the glade he had defeated their preparations; there were no marksmen posted higher up than the one whom he had just killed or wounded; and the confusion of the foresters' counsels soon became apparent. A whistle sounded thrice, and then again twice. It was repeated from another quarter. The woods on either side became full of the sound of people bursting through the underwood; and a bewildered deer ran out into the open, stood for a second on three feet, with nose in air, and then plunged again into the thicket.

Selden still ran, bounding; ever and again an arrow followed him, but still would miss. It began to appear as if he might escape. Dick had his bow armed, ready to support him; even Matcham, forgetful of his interest, took sides at heart for the poor fugitive; and both lads glowed and trembled in the ardour of their hearts.

He was within fifty yards of them, when an arrow struck him, and he fell. He was up again, indeed, upon the instant; but now he ran staggering, and, like a blind man, turned aside from his direction.

Dick leaped to his feet and waved to him.

'Here!' he cried. 'This way! here is help! Nay, run, fellow—run!'

But just then a second arrow struck Selden in the shoulder, between the plates of his brigandine, and, piercing through his jack, brought him, like a stone, to earth.

'Oh, the poor heart!' cried Matcham, with clasped hands.

And Dick stood petrified upon the hill, a mark for archery.

Ten to one he had speedily been shot—for the foresters were furious with themselves, and taken unawares by Dick's appearance in the rear of their position—but instantly out of a quarter of the wood surprisingly near to the two lads, a stentorian voice arose, the voice of Ellis Duckworth.

'Hold!' it roared. 'Shoot not! Take him alive! It is young Shelton—Harry's son.'

And immediately after a shrill whistle sounded several times, and was again taken up and repeated farther off. The whistle, it appeared, was John Amend-All's battle trumpet, by which he published his directions.

'Ah, foul fortune!' cried Dick. 'We are undone. Swiftly, Jack, come swiftly.

And the pair turned and ran back through the open pine clump that covered the summit of the hill.

6

To the day's end

It was, indeed, high time for them to run. On every side the company of the Black Arrow was making for the hill. Some, being better runners, or having open ground to run upon, had far outstripped the others, and were already close upon the goal; some, following valleys, had spread out to right and left, and outflanked the lads on either side.

Dick plunged into the nearest cover. It was a tall grove of oaks, firm under foot and clear of underbrush, and as it lay downhill, they made good speed. There followed next a piece of open, which Dick avoided, holding to his left. Two minutes after, and the same obstacle arising, the lads followed the same course. Thus it followed that, while the lads, bending continually to the left, drew nearer and nearer to the high road and the river which they had crossed an hour or two before, the great bulk of their pursuers were leaning to the other hand, and running towards Tunstall.

The lads paused to breathe. There was no sound of pursuit. Dick put his ear to the ground, and still there was nothing; but the wind, to be sure, still made a turmoil in the trees, and it was hard to make certain.

'On again!' said Dick; and, tired as they were, Matcham limping with his injured foot, they pulled themselves together, and once more pelted down the hill.

Three minutes later, they were breasting through a low thicket of evergreen. High overhead, the tall trees made a continuous roof of foliage. It was a pillared grove, as high as a cathedral, and, except for the hollies among which the lads were struggling, open and smoothly swarded.

On the other side, pushing through the last fringe of evergreen, they blundered forth again into the open twilight of the grove.

'Stand!' cried a voice.

And there, between the huge stems, not fifty feet before them, they beheld a stout fellow in green, sore blown with running, who instantly drew an arrow to the head and covered them. Matcham stopped with a cry; but Dick, without a pause, ran straight upon the forester, drawing his dagger as he went. The other, whether he was startled by the daring of the onslaught, or whether he was hampered by his orders, did not shoot: he stood wavering; and before he had time to come to himself, Dick bounded at his throat, and sent him sprawling backward on the turf. The arrow went one way and the bow another with a sounding twang. The disarmed forester grappled his assailant; but the dagger shone and descended twice. Then came a couple of groans, and then Dick rose to his feet again, and the man lay motionless, stabbed to the heart.

'On!' said Dick; and he once more pelted forward, Matcham trailing in the rear. To say truth, they made but poor speed of it by now, labouring dismally as they ran, and catching for their breath like fish. Matcham had a cruel stitch, and his head swam; and as for Dick, his knees were like lead. But they kept up the form of running with undiminished courage.

Presently they came to the end of the grove. It stopped abruptly; and there, a few yards before them, was the high road from Risingham to Shoreby, lying, at this point, between two even walls of forest.

At the sight Dick paused; and as soon as he stopped running, he became aware of a confused noise, which rapidly grew louder. It was at first like the rush of a very high gust of wind, but it soon became more definite, and resolved itself into the galloping of horses; and then, in a flash, a whole company of men-at-arms came driving round the corner, swept before the lads, and were gone again upon the instant. They rode as for their lives, in complete disorder; some of them were wounded; riderless horses galloped at their side with bloody saddles. They were plainly fugitives from the great battle.

The noise of their passage had scarce begun to die away towards Shoreby, before fresh hoofs came echoing in their wake, and another deserter clattered down the road; this time a single rider, and, by his splendid armour, a man of high degree. Close after him there followed several baggage-wagons, fleeing at an ungainly canter, the drivers flailing at the horses as if for life. These must have run early in the day; but their cowardice was not to save them. For just before they came abreast of where the lads stood wondering, a man in hacked armour, and seemingly beside himself with fury, overtook the wagons, and with the truncheon of a sword began to cut the drivers down. Some leaped from their places and plunged into the wood; the others he sabred as they sat, cursing them the while for cowards in a voice that was scarce human.

All this time the noise in the distance had continued to increase; the rumble of carts, the clatter of horses, the cries of men, a great, confused rumour, came swelling on the wind; and it was plain that the rout of a whole army was pouring, like an inundation, down the road.

Dick stood sombre. He had meant to follow the highway till the turn for Holywood, and now he had to change his plan. But above all, he had recognised the colours of Earl Risingham, and he knew that the battle had gone finally against the rose of Lancaster. Had Sir Daniel joined, and was he now a fugitive and ruined? or had he deserted to the side of York, and was he forfeit to honour? It was an ugly choice.

'Come,' he said sternly; and, turning on his heel, he began to walk forward through the grove, with Matcham limping in his rear.

For some time they continued to thread the forest in silence. It was now growing late; the sun was setting in the plain beyond Kettley; the tree-tops overhead glowed golden; but the shadows had begun to grow darker and the chill of the night to fall.

'If there was anything to eat!' cried Dick suddenly, pausing as he spoke.

Matcham sat down and began to weep.

'Ye can weep for your own supper, but when it was to save men's lives, your heart was hard enough,' said Dick contemptuously. 'Y' 'ave seven deaths upon your conscience, Master John; I'll ne'er forgive you that.'

'Conscience!' cried Matcham, looking fiercely up. 'Mine!

And ye have the man's red blood upon your dagger! And wherefore did ye slay him, the poor soul? He drew his arrow, but he let not fly; he held you in his hand, and spared you! 'Tis as brave to kill a kitten as a man that not defends himself.'

Dick was struck dumb.

'I slew him fair. I ran me in upon his bow,' he cried.

'It was a coward blow,' returned Matcham. 'Y' are but a lout and bully, Master Dick; ye but abuse advantages; let there come a stronger, we will see you truckle at his boot! Ye care not for vengeance, neither—for your father's death that goes unpaid, and his poor ghost that clamoureth for justice. But if there come but a poor creature in your hands that lacketh skill and strength, and would befriend you, down she shall go!'

Dick was too furious to observe that 'she.'

'Marry!' he cried, 'and here is news! Of any two the one will still be stronger. The better man throweth the worse, and the worse is well served. Ye deserve a belting, Master Matcham, for your ill-guidance and unthankfulness to meward; and what ye deserve ye shall have.'

And Dick, who, even in his angriest temper, still preserved the appearance of composure, began to unbuckle his belt.

'Here shall be your supper,' he said grimly.

Matcham had stopped his tears; he was as white as a sheet, but he looked Dick steadily in the face and never moved. Dick took a step, swinging the belt. Then he paused, embarrassed by the large eyes and the thin, weary face of his companion. His courage began to subside.

'Say ye were in the wrong, then,' he said, lamely.

'Nay,' said Matcham, 'I was in the right. Come, cruel! I be lame; I be weary; I resist not; I ne'er did thee hurt; come beat me—coward!'

Dick raised the belt at this last provocation, but Matcham winced, and drew himself together with so cruel an apprehension, that his heart failed him yet again. The strap fell by his side, and he stood irresolute, feeling like a fool.

'A plague upon thee, shrew!' he said. 'An ye be so feeble of hand, ye should keep the closer guard upon your tongue. But I'll be hanged before I beat you!' and he put on his belt again. 'Beat you I will not,' he continued; 'but forgive you?—never. I know ye not; ye were my master's enemy; I lent you my horse; my dinner ye have eaten; y' 'ave called me a man o' wood, a coward, and a bully. Nay, by the mass! the measure is filled, and runneth over. 'Tis a great thing to be weak, I trow; ye can do your worst, yet shall none punish you; ye may steal a man's weapons in the hour of need, yet may the man not take his own again;—y' are weak forsooth! Nay, then, if one cometh charging at you with a lance, and crieth he is weak ye must let him pierce your body through! Tut! fool words!'

'And yet ye beat me not,' returned Matcham.

'Let be,' said Dick—'let be. I will instruct you. Y' 'ave been ill-nurtured, methinks, and yet ye have the makings of some good, and, beyond all questions, saved me from the river. Nay, I had forgotten it; I am as thankless as thyself. But, come, let us on. An we be for Holywood this night, ay, or to-morrow early, we had best set forward speedily.'

But though Dick had talked himself back into his usual good-humour, Matcham had forgiven him nothing. His violence, the recollection of the forester whom he had slain—above all, the vision of the upraised belt, were things not easily to be forgotten.

'I will thank you, for the form's sake,' said Matcham. 'But, in sooth, good Master Shelton, I had liever find my way alone. Here is a wide wood; prithee, let each choose his path; I owe you a dinner and a lesson. Fare ye well!'

'Nay,' cried Dick, 'if that be your tune, so be it, and a plague be with you!'

Each turned aside, and they began walking off severally, with no thought of the direction, intent solely on their quarrel. But Dick had not gone ten paces ere his name was called, and Matcham came running after.

'Dick,' he said, 'it were unmannerly to part so coldly. Here is my hand, and my heart with it. For all that wherein you have so excellently served and helped me—not for the form, but from the heart, I thank you. Fare ye right well.'

'Well, lad,' returned Dick, taking the hand which was offered him, 'good speed to you, if speed you may. But I misdoubt it shrewdly. Y' are too disputatious.'

So then they separated for the second time; and presently it was Dick who was running after Matcham.

'Here,' he said, 'take my crossbow; shalt not go unarmed.'

'A crossbow!' said Matcham. 'Nay, boy, I have neither the strength to bend nor yet the skill to aim with it. It were no help to me, good boy. But yet I thank you.'

The night had now fallen, and under the trees they could no longer read each other's face.

'I will go some little way with you,' said Dick. 'The night is dark. I would fain leave you on a path, at least. My mind misgiveth me, y' are likely to be lost.'

Without any more words, he began to walk forward, and the other once more followed him. The blackness grew thicker and thicker; only here and there, in open places, they saw the sky, dotted with small stars. In the distance, the noise of the rout of the Lancastrian army still continued to be faintly audible; but with every step they left it farther in the rear.

At the end of half an hour of silent progress they came forth upon a broad patch of heathy open. It glimmered in the light of the stars, shaggy with fern and islanded with clumps of yew. And here they paused and looked upon each other.

'Y' are weary?' Dick said.

'Nay, I am so weary,' answered Matcham, 'that methinks I could lie down and die.'

'I hear the chiding of a river,' returned Dick. 'Let us go so far forth, for I am sore athirst.'

The ground sloped down gently, and, sure enough, in the bottom, they found a little murmuring river, running among willows. Here they threw themselves down together by the brink; and putting their mouths to the level of a starry pool, they drank their fill.

'Dick,' said Matcham, 'it may not be. I can no more.'

'I saw a pit as we came down,' said Dick. 'Let us lie down therein and sleep.'

'Nay, but with all my heart!' cried Matcham.

The pit was sandy and dry; a shock of brambles hung upon one edge, and made a partial shelter; and there the two lads lay down, keeping close together for the sake of warmth, their quarrel all forgotten. And soon sleep fell upon them like a cloud, and under the dew and stars they rested peacefully.

7

The hooded face

THEY awoke in the gray of the morning; the birds were not yet in full song, but twittered here and there among the woods; the sun was not yet up, but the eastern sky was barred with solemn colours. Half-starved and over-weary as they were, they lay without moving, sunk in a delightful lassitude. And as they thus lay, the clang of a bell fell suddenly upon their ears.

'A bell!' said Dick, sitting up. 'Can we be, then, so near to Holywood?'

A little after, the bell clanged again, but this time somewhat nearer hand; and from that time forth, and still drawing nearer and nearer, it continued to sound brokenly abroad in the silence of the morning.

'Nay, what should this betoken?' said Dick, who was now broad awake.

'It is some one walking,' returned Matcham, 'and the bell tolleth ever as he moves.'

'I see that well,' said Dick. 'But wherefore? What maketh he in Tunstall Woods? Jack,' he added, 'laugh at me an ye will, but I like not the hollow sound of it.'

'Nay,' said Matcham, with a shiver, 'it hath a doleful note. An the day were not come——'

But just then the bell, quickening its pace, began to ring thick and hurried, and then it gave a single hammering jangle, and was silent for a space.

'It is as though the bearer had run for a paternoster-while, and then leaped the river,' Dick observed.

'And now beginneth he again to pace soberly forward,' added Matcham.

'Nay,' returned Dick—'nay, not so soberly, Jack. 'Tis a man that walketh you right speedily. 'Tis a man in some fear of his life, or about some hurried business. See ye not how swift the beating draweth near?'

'It is now close by,' said Matcham.

They were now on the edge of the pit; and as the pit itself was on a certain eminence, they commanded a view over the greater proportion of the clearing, up to the thick woods that closed it in.

The daylight, which was very clear and gray, showed them a riband of white footpath wandering among the gorse. It passed some hundred yards from the pit, and ran the whole length of the clearing, east and west. By the line of its course, Dick judged it should lead more or less directly to the Moat House.

Upon this path, stepping forth from the margin of the wood, a white figure now appeared. It paused a little, and seemed to look about; and then, at a slow pace, and bent almost double, it began to draw near across the heath. At every step the bell clanked. Face it had none; a white hood, not even pierced with eyeholes, veiled the head; and as the creature moved, it seemed to feel its way with the tapping of a stick. Fear fell upon the lads, as cold as death.

'A leper!' said Dick hoarsely.

'His touch is death,' said Matcham. 'Let us run.'

'Not so,' returned Dick. 'See ye not?—he is stone blind. He guideth him with a staff. Let us lie still; the wind bloweth towards the path, and he will go by and hurt us not. Alas, poor soul, and we should rather pity him!'

'I will pity him when he is by,' replied Matcham.

The blind leper was now about half-way towards them, and just then the sun rose and shone full on his veiled face. He had been a tall man before he was bowed by his disgusting sickness, and even now he walked with a vigorous step. The dismal beating of his bell, the pattering of the stick, the eyeglass screen before his countenance, and the knowledge that he was not only doomed to death and suffering, but shut out for ever from the touch of his fellow-men, filled the lads' bosoms with dismay; and at every step that brought him nearer, their courage and strength seemed to desert them.

As he came about level with the pit, he paused, and turned his face full upon the lads.

'Mary be my shield! He sees us!' said Matcham faintly.

'Hush!' whispered Dick. 'He doth but hearken. He is blind, fool!'

The leper looked or listened, whichever he was really doing, for some seconds. Then he began to move on again, but presently paused once more, and again turned and seemed to gaze upon the lads. Even Dick became dead-white and closed his eyes, as if by the mere sight he might become infected. But soon the bell sounded, and this time, without any further hesitation, the leper crossed the remainder of the little neath and disappeared into the covert of the woods.

'He saw us,' said Matcham. 'I could swear it!'

'Tut!' returned Dick, recovering some sparks of courage. 'He but heard us. He was in fear, poor soul! An ye were blind, and walked in a perpetual night, ye would start yourself, if ever a twig rustled or a bird cried "Peep."'

'Dick, good Dick, he saw us,' repeated Matcham. 'When a man hearkeneth, he doth not as this man; he doth otherwise, Dick. This was seeing; it was not hearing. He means foully. Hark, else, if his bell be not stopped!'

Such was the case. The bell rang no longer.

'Nay,' said Dick, 'I like not that. Nay,' he cried again, 'I like that little. What may this betoken? Let us go, by the mass!'

'He hath gone east,' added Matcham. 'Good Dick, let us go westward straight. I shall not breathe till I have my back turned upon that leper.'

'Jack, y' are too cowardly,' replied Dick. 'We shall go fair for Holywood, or as fair, at least, as I can guide you, and that will be due north.'

They were afoot at once, passed the stream upon some stepping-stones, and began to mount on the other side, which was steeper, towards the margin of the wood. The ground became very uneven, full of knolls and hollows; trees grew scattered or in clumps; it became difficult to choose a path, and the lads somewhat wandered. They were weary, besides, with yesterday's exertions and the lack of food, and they moved but heavily and dragged their feet among the sand.

Presently, coming to the top of a knoll, they were aware of the leper, some hundred feet in front of them, crossing the line of their march by a hollow. His bell was silent, his staff no longer tapped the ground, and he went before him with the swift and assured footsteps of a man who sees. Next moment he had disappeared into a little thicket.

The lads, at the first glimpse, had crouched behind a tuft of gorse; there they lay, horror-struck.

'Certain, he pursueth us,' said Dick—'certain. He held the clapper of his bell in one hand, saw ye? that it should not sound. Now may the saints aid and guide us, for I have no strength to combat pestilence!'

'What maketh he?' cried Matcham. 'What doth he want? Who ever heard the like, that a leper, out of mere malice, should pursue unfortunates? Hath he not his bell to that very end, that people may avoid him? Dick, there is below this something deeper.'

'Nay, I care not,' moaned Dick; 'the strength is gone out of me; my legs are like water. The saints be mine assistance!'

'Would ye lie there idle?' cried Matcham. 'Let us back into the open. We have the better chance; he cannot steal upon us unawares.'

'Not I,' said Dick. 'My time is come; and peradventure he may pass us by.'

'Bend me, then, your bow!' cried the other. 'What! will ye be a man?'

Dick crossed himself. 'Would ye have me shoot upon a leper?' he cried. 'The hand would fail me. Nay, now,' he added—'nay, now, let be! With sound men I will fight, but not with ghosts and lepers. Which this is, I wot not. One or other, Heaven be our protection!'

'Now,' said Matcham, 'if this be man's courage, what a poor thing is man! But sith ye will do naught, let us lie close.'

Then came a single, broken jangle on the bell.

'He hath missed his hold upon the clapper,' whispered Matcham. 'Saints! how near he is!'

But Dick answered never a word; his teeth were near chattering.

Soon they saw a piece of the white robe between some bushes; then the leper's head was thrust forth from behind a trunk, and he seemed narrowly to scan the neighbourhood before he once again withdrew. To their stretched senses the whole bush appeared alive with rustlings and the creak of twigs; and they heard the beating of each other's heart.

Suddenly, with a cry, the leper sprang into the open close by, and ran straight upon the lads. They, shrieking aloud, separated and began to run different ways. But their horrible enemy fastened upon Matcham, ran him swiftly down, and had him almost instantly a prisoner. The lad gave one scream that echoed high and far over the forest, he had one spasm of struggling, and then all his limbs relaxed, and he fell limp into his captor's arms.

Dick heard the cry and turned. He saw Matcham fall; and on the instant his spirit and his strength revived. With a cry of pity and anger, he unslung and bent his arblast. But ere he had time to shoot, the leper held up his hand.

'Hold your shot, Dickon!' cried a familiar voice. 'Hold your shot, mad wag! Know ye not a friend?'

And then laying down Matcham on the turf, he undid the hood from off his face, and disclosed the features of Sir Daniel Brackley.

'Sir Daniel!' cried Dick.

'Ay, by the mass, Sir Daniel!' returned the knight. 'Would ye shoot upon your guardian, rogue? But here is this——' And here he broke off, and pointing to Matcham, asked—'How call ye him, Dick?'

'Nay,' said Dick. 'I call him Master Matcham. Know ye him not? He said ye knew him!'

'Ay,' replied Sir Daniel, 'I know the lad'; and he chuckled. 'But he has fainted; and, by my sooth, he might have had less to faint for. Hey, Dick? Did I put the fear of death upon you?'

'Indeed, Sir Daniel, ye did that,' said Dick, and sighed again at the mere recollection. 'Nay, sir, saving your respect, I had as lief 'a' met the devil in person; and to speak truth, I am yet all a-quake. But what made ye, sir, in such a guise?'

Sir Daniel's brow grew suddenly black with anger.

'What made I?' he said. 'Ye do well to mind me of it! What? I skulked for my poor life in my own wood of Tunstall, Dick. We were ill sped at the battle; we but got there to be swept among the rout. Where be all my good men-at-arms? Dick, by the mass, I know not! We were swept down; the shot fell thick among us; I have not seen one man in my own colours since I saw three fall. For myself, I came sound to Shoreby, and being mindful of the Black Arrow, got me this gown and bell, and came softly by the path for the Moat House.

There is no disguise to be compared with it, the jingle of this bell would scare me the stoutest outlaw in the forest; they would all turn pale to hear it. At length I came by you and Matcham. I could see but evilly through this same hood, and was not sure of you, being chiefly, and for many a good cause, astonished at the finding you together. Moreover, in the open, where I had to go slowly and tap with my staff, I feared to disclose myself. But see,' he added, 'this poor shrew begins a little to revive. A little good canary will comfort the heart of it.'

The knight, from under his long dress, produced a stout bottle, and began to rub the temples and wet the lips of the patient, who returned gradually to consciousness, and began to roll dim eyes from one to another.

'What cheer, Jack!' said Dick. 'It was no leper, after all; it was Sir Daniel! See!'

'Swallow me a good draught of this,' said the knight. 'This will give you manhood. Thereafter, I will give you both a meal, and we shall all three on to Tunstall. For, Dick,' he continued, laying forth bread and meat upon the grass, 'I will avow to you, in all good conscience, it irks me sorely to be safe between four walls. Not since I backed a horse have I been pressed so hard; peril of life, jeopardy of land and livelihood, and to sum up, all these losels in the wood to hunt me down. But I be not yet shent. Some of my lads will pick me their way home. Hatch hath ten fellows; Selden, he had six. Nay, we shall soon be strong again; and if I can but buy my peace with my right fortunate and undeserving Lord of York, why, Dick, we'll be a man again and go a-horseback!'

And so saying, the knight filled himself a horn of canary, and pledged his ward in dumb show.

'Selden,' Dick faltered—'Selden——' And he paused again.

Sir Daniel put down the wine untasted.

'How!' he cried, in a changed voice. 'Selden? Speak! What of Selden?'

Dick stammered forth the tale of the ambush and the massacre.

The knight heard in silence; but as he listened, his countenance became convulsed with rage and grief.

'Now here,' he cried, 'on my right hand, I swear to avenge it! If that I fail, if that I spill not ten men's souls for each, may this hand wither from my body! I broke this Duckworth like a rush; I beggared him to his door; I burned the thatch above his head; I drove him from this country; and now, cometh he back to beard me? Nay, but, Duckworth, this time it shall go bitter hard!'

He was silent for some time, his face working.

'Eat!' he cried suddenly. 'And you here,' he added to Matcham, 'swear me an oath to follow straight to the Moat House.'

'I will pledge mine honour,' replied Matcham.

'What make I with your honour?' cried the knight. 'Swear me upon your mother's welfare!'

Matcham gave the required oath; and Sir Daniel readjusted the hood over his face, and prepared his bell and staff. To see him once more in that appalling travesty somewhat revived the horror of his two companions. But the knight was soon upon his feet.

'Eat with despatch,' he said, 'and follow me yarely to mine house.'

And with that he set forth again into the woods; and presently after the bell began to sound, numbering his steps, and the two lads sat by their untasted meal, and heard it die slowly away uphill into the distance.

'And so ye go to Tunstall!' Dick inquired.

'Yea, verily,' said Matcham, 'when needs must! I am braver behind Sir Daniel's back than to his face.'

They ate hastily, and set forth along the path through the airy upper levels of the forest, where great beeches stood apart among green lawns, and the birds and squirrels made merry on the boughs. Two hours later, they began to descend upon the other side, and already, among the tree-tops, saw before them the red walls and roofs of Tunstall House.

'Here,' said Matcham, pausing, 'ye shall take your leave of your friend Jack, whom y' are to see no more. Come, Dick, forgive him what he did amiss, as he, for his part, cheerfully and lovingly forgiveth you.'

'And wherefore so?' asked Dick. 'An we both go to Tunstall, I shall see you yet again, I trow, and that right often.'

'Ye'll never again see poor Jack Matcham,' replied the other 'that was so fearful and burthensome, and yet plucked you from the river; ye'll not see him more, Dick, by mine honour!' He held his arms open, and the lads embraced and kissed. 'And Dick,' continued Matcham, 'my spirit bodeth ill. Y' are now to see a new Sir Daniel; for heretofore hath all prospered in his hands exceedingly, and fortune followed him; but now, methinks, when his fate has come upon him, and he runs the adventure of his life, he will prove but a foul lord to both of us. He may be brave in battle, but he hath the liar's eye; there is fear in his eye, Dick, and fear is as cruel as the wolf! We go down into that house, Saint Mary guide us forth again!'

And so they continued their descent in silence, and came

out at last before Sir Daniel's forest stronghold, where it stood, low and shady, flanked with round towers and stained with moss and lichen, in the lilied waters of the moat. Even as they appeared, the doors were opened, the bridge lowered, and Sir Daniel himself, with Hatch and the parson at his side, stood ready to receive them.

Book Two

THE MOAT HOUSE

8

Dick asks questions

THE Moat House stood not far from the rough forest road. Externally it was a compact rectangle of red stone, flanked at each corner by a round tower, pierced for archery and battlemented at the top. Within, it enclosed a narrow court. The moat was perhaps twelve feet wide, crossed by a single drawbridge. It was supplied with water by a trench, leading to a forest pool, and commanded, through its whole length, from the battlements of the two southern towers. Except that one or two tall and thick trees had been suffered to remain within half a bowshot of the walls, the house was in a good posture for defence.

In the court, Dick found a part of the garrison, busy with preparations for defence, and gloomily discussing the chances of a siege. Some were making arrows, some sharpening swords that had long been disused; but even as they worked, they shook their heads.

Twelve of Sir Daniel's party had escaped the battle, run the gauntlet through the wood, and come alive to the Moat House. But out of this dozen, three had been gravely wounded: two at Risingham in the disorder of the rout, one by John Amend-All's marksmen as he crossed the forest. This raised the force of the garrison, counting Hatch, Sir Daniel, and young Shelton, to twenty-two effective men. And more might be continually expected to arrive. The danger lay not, therefore, in the lack of men.

It was the terror of the black arrow that oppressed the spirits of the garrison. For their open foes of the party of York, in these most changing times, they felt but a far-away concern. 'The world,' as people said in those days, 'might change again' before harm came. But for their neighbours in the wood they trembled. It was not Sir Daniel alone who was a mark for hatred. His men, conscious of impunity, had carried themselves cruelly through all the country. Harsh commands had been harshly executed; and of the little band that now sat talking in the court, there was not one but had been guilty of some act of oppression or barbarity. And now, by the fortune of war, Sir Daniel had become powerless to protect his instruments; now, by the issue of some hours of battle, at which many of them had not been present, they had all become punishable traitors to the State, outside the buckler of the law, a shrunken company in a poor fortress that was hardly tenable, and exposed upon all sides to the just resentment of their victims. Nor had there been lacking grisly advertisements of what they might expect.

At different periods of the evening and the night, no fewer than seven riderless horses had come neighing in terror to the gate. Two were from Selden's troop; five belonged to men who had ridden with Sir Daniel to the field. Lastly, a little before dawn, a spearman had come staggering to the moat-side, pierced by three arrows; even as they carried him in, his spirit had departed; but by the words that he uttered in his agony, he must have been the last survivor of a considerable company of men.

Hatch himself showed, under his sun-brown, the pallor of anxiety; and when he had taken Dick aside and learned the fate of Selden, he fell on a stone bench and fairly wept. The others, from where they sat on stools or door-steps in the sunny angle of the court, looked at him with wonder and alarm, but none ventured to inquire the cause of his emotion.

'Nay, Master Shelton,' said Hatch at last—'nay, but what said I? We shall all go. Selden was a man of his hands; he was like a brother to me. Well, he has gone second; well, we shall all follow! For what said their knave rhyme?—"A black arrow in each black heart." Was it not so it went? Appleyard, Selden, Smith, old Humphrey gone; and there lieth poor John Carter, crying, poor sinner, for the priest.'

Dick gave ear. Out of a low window, hard by where they were talking, groans and murmurs came to his ear.

'Lieth he there?' he asked.

'Ay, in the second porter's chamber,' answered Hatch. 'We could not bear him farther, soul and body were so bitterly at odds. At every step we lifted him, he thought to wend. But now, methinks, it is the soul that suffereth. Ever for the priest he crieth, and Sir Oliver, I wot not why, still cometh not. 'Twill be a long shrift; but poor Appleyard and poor Selden, they had none.'

Dick stooped to the window and looked in. The little cell was low and dark, but he could make out the wounded soldier lying moaning on his pallet.

'Carter, poor friend, how goeth it?' he asked.

'Master Shelton,' returned the man, in an excited whisper, 'for the dear light of heaven, bring the priest. Alack, I am sped: I am brought very low down; my hurt is to the death,

Ye may do me no more service; this shall be the last. Now, for my poor soul's interest, and as a loyal gentleman, bestir you; for I have that matter on my conscience that shall drag me deep.'

He groaned, and Dick heard the grating of his teeth, whether in pain or terror.

Just then Sir Daniel appeared upon the threshold of the hall. He had a letter in one hand.

'Lads,' he said, 'we have had a shog, we have had a tumble; wherefore, then, deny it? Rather it imputeth to get speedily again to saddle. This old Harry the Sixt has had the undermost. Wash we, then, our hands of him. I have a good friend that rideth next the duke, the Lord of Wensleydale. Well, I have writ a letter to my friend, praying his good lordship, and offering large satisfaction for the past and reasonable surety for the future. Doubt not but he will lend a favourable ear. A prayer without gifts is like a song without music; I surfeit him with promises, boys—I spare not to promise. What, then, is lacking? Nay, a great thing—wherefore should I deceive you?— a great thing and a difficult: a messenger to bear it. The woods—y' are not ignorant of that—lie thick with our ill-willers. Haste is most needful; but without sleight and caution all is nought. Which, then, of this company will take me this letter, bear it to my Lord of Wensleydale, and bring me the answer back?'

One man instantly arose.

'I will, an't like you,' said he. 'I will even risk my carcase.'

'Nay, Dicky Bower, not so,' returned the knight. 'It likes me not. Y' are sly, indeed, but not speedy. Ye were a laggard ever.'

'An't be so, Sir Daniel, here am I,' cried another.

'The saints forfend!' said the knight. 'Y' are speedy, but not sly. Ye would blunder me head-foremost into John Amend-All's camp. I thank you both for your good courage; but, in sooth, it may not be.'

Then Hatch offered himself, and he also was refused.

'I want you here, good Bennet; y' are my right hand, indeed,' returned the knight; and then several coming forward in a group, Sir Daniel at length selected one and gave him the letter.

'Now,' he said, 'upon your good speed and better discretion we do all depend. Bring me a good answer back, and before three weeks I will have purged my forest of these vagabonds that brave us to our faces. But mark it well, Throgmorton: the matter is not easy. Ye must steal forth under night, and go like a fox; and how ye are to cross the Till I know not, neither by the bridge nor ferry.'

'I can swim,' returned Throgmorton. 'I will come soundly, fear not.'

'Well, friend, get ye to the buttery,' replied Sir Daniel. 'Ye shall swim first of all in nut-brown ale.' And with that he turned back into the hall.

'Sir Daniel hath a wise tongue,' said Hatch, aside, to Dick. 'See, now, where many a lesser man had glossed the matter over, he speaketh it out plainly to his company. Here is a danger, 'a saith, and here difficulty; and jesteth in the very saying. Nay, by Saint Barbary, he is a born captain! Not a man but he is some deal heartened up! See how they fall again to work.'

This praise of Sir Daniel put a thought in the lad's head.

'Bennet,' he said, 'how came my father by his end?'

'Ask me not that,' replied Hatch. 'I had no hand nor knowledge in it; furthermore, I will even be silent, Master Dick. For look you, in a man's own business, there he may speak; but of hearsay matters and of common talk, not so. Ask me Sir Oliver—ay, or Carter, if ye will; not me.'

And Hatch set off to make the rounds, leaving Dick in a muse.

'Wherefore would he not tell me?' thought the lad. 'And wherefore named he Carter? Carter—nay, then Carter had a hand in it, perchance.'

He entered the house, and passing some little way along a flagged and vaulted passage, came to the door of the cell where the hurt man lay groaning. At his entrance Carter started eagerly.

'Have ye brought the priest?' he cried.

'Not yet awhile,' returned Dick. 'Y' 'ave a word to tell me first. How came my father, Harry Shelton, by his death?'

The man's face altered instantly.

'I know not,' he replied doggedly.

'Nay, ye know well,' returned Dick. 'Seek not to put me by.'

'I tell you I know not,' repeated Carter.

'Then,' said Dick, 'ye shall die unshriven. Here am I, and here shall stay. There shall no priest come near you, rest assured. For of what avail is penitence, an ye have no mind to right those wrongs ye had a hand in? and without penitence, confession is but mockery.'

'Ye say what ye mean not, Master Dick,' said Carter composedly. 'It is ill threatening the dying, and becometh you (to speak truth) little. And for as little as it commends you, it shall serve you less. Stay, an ye please. Ye will condemn my soul—ye shall learn nothing! There is my last word to you.' And the wounded man turned upon the other side.

Now, Dick, to say truth, had spoken hastily, and was ashamed of his threat. But he made one more effort.

'Carter,' he said, 'mistake me not. I know ye were but an instrument in the hands of others; a churl must obey his lord; I would not bear heavily on such an one. But I begin to learn upon many sides that this great duty lieth on my youth and ignorance, to avenge my father. Prithee, then, good Carter, set aside the memory of my threatenings, and in pure good-will and honest penitence, give me a word of help.'

The wounded man lay silent; nor, say what Dick pleased, could he extract another word from him.

'Well,' said Dick, 'I will go call the priest to you as ye desired; for howsoever ye be in fault to me or mine, I would not be willingly in fault to any, least of all to one upon the last change.'

Again the old soldier heard him without speech or motion; even his groans he had suppressed; and as Dick turned and left the room, he was filled with admiration for that rugged fortitude.

'And yet,' he thought, 'of what use is courage without wit? Had his hands been clean, he would have spoken; his silence did confess the secret louder than words. Nay, upon all sides, proof floweth on me. Sir Daniel, he or his men, hath done this thing.'

Dick paused in the stone passage with a heavy heart. At that hour, in the ebb of Sir Daniel's fortune, when he was beleaguered by the archers of the Black Arrow, and proscribed by the victorious Yorkists, was Dick, also, to turn upon the man who had nourished and taught him, who had severely punished indeed, but yet unwearyingly protected his youth? The necessity, if it should prove to be one, was cruel.

'Pray Heaven he be innocent!' he said.

And then steps sounded on the flagging, and Sir Oliver came gravely towards the lad.

'One seeketh you earnestly,' said Dick.

'I am upon the way, good Richard,' said the priest. 'It is this poor Carter. Alack, he is beyond cure.'

'And yet his soul is sicker than his body,' answered Dick.

'Have ye seen him?' asked Sir Oliver, with a manifest start.

'I do but come from him,' replied Dick.

'What said he—what said he?' snapped the priest, with extraordinary eagerness.

'He but cried for you the more piteously, Sir Oliver. It were well done to go the faster, for his hurt is grievous,' returned the lad.

'I am straight for him,' was the reply. 'Well, we have all our sins. We must all come to our latter day, good Richard.'

'Ay, sir; and it were well if we all came fairly,' answered Dick.

The priest dropped his eyes, and with an inaudible benediction hurried on.

'He, too!' thought Dick—'he, that taught me in piety! Nay, then, what a world is this, if all that care for me be blood-guilty of my father's death! Vengeance! Alas! what a sore fate is mine, if I must be avenged upon my friends!'

The thought put Matcham in his head. He smiled at the remembrance of his strange companion, and then wondered where he was. Ever since they had come together to the doors of the Moat House the younger lad had disappeared, and Dick began to weary for a word with him.

About an hour after, mass being somewhat hastily run through by Sir Oliver, the company gathered in the hall for dinner. It was a long, low apartment, strewn with green rushes, and the walls hung with arras in a design of savage men and questing bloodhounds; here and there hung spears and bows and bucklers; a fire blazed in the big chimney; there were arras-covered benches round the wall, and in the midst the table, fairly spread, awaited the arrival of the diners. Neither Sir Daniel nor his lady made their appearance. Sir Oliver himself was absent, and here again there was no word of Matcham. Dick began to grow alarmed, to recall his companion's melancholy forebodings, and to wonder to himself if any foul play had befallen him in that house.

After dinner he found Goody Hatch, who was hurrying to my lady Brackley.

'Goody,' he said, 'where is Master Matcham, I prithee? I saw ye go in with him when we arrived.'

The old woman laughed aloud.

'Ah, Master Dick,' she said, 'y' have a famous bright eye in your head, to be sure!' and laughed again.

'Nay, but where is he, indeed?' persisted Dick.

'Ye will never see him more,' she returned; 'never. It is sure.'

'An I do not,' returned the lad, 'I will know the reason why. He came not hither of his full free will; such as I am, I am his best protector, and I will see him justly used. There be too many mysteries; I do begin to weary of the game!'

But as Dick was speaking, a heavy hand fell on his shoulder. It was Bennet Hatch that had come unperceived behind him. With a jerk of his thumb the retainer dismissed his wife.

'Friend Dick,' he said, as soon as they were alone, 'are ye a moonstruck natural? An ye leave not certain things in peace, ye were better in the salt sea than here in Tunstall Moat House. Y' have questioned me; y' have baited Carter; y' have frighted the jack-priest with hints. Bear ye more wisely, fool; and even now when Sir Daniel calleth you, show me a smooth face, for the love of wisdom. Y' are to be sharply questioned. Look to your answers.'

'Hatch,' returned Dick, 'in all this I smell a guilty conscience.'

'An ye go not the wiser, ye will soon smell blood,' replied Bennet. 'I do but warn you. And here cometh one to call you.'

And indeed, at that very moment, a messenger came across the court to summon Dick into the presence of Sir Daniel.

9

The two oaths

Sir Daniel was in the hall; there he paced angrily before the fire, awaiting Dick's arrival. None was by except Sir Oliver, and he sat discreetly backward, thumbing and muttering over his breviary.

'Y' have sent for me, Sir Daniel?' said young Shelton.

'I have sent for you indeed,' replied the knight. 'For what cometh to mine ears? Have I been to you so heavy a guardian that ye make haste to credit ill of me? Or sith that ye see me, for the nonce, some worsted, do ye think to quit my party? By the mass, your father was not so! Those he was near, those he stood by, come wind or weather. But you, Dick, y' are a fair-day friend, it seemeth, and now seek to clear yourself of your allegiance.'

'An't please you, Sir Daniel, not so,' returned Dick firmly. 'I am grateful and faithful, where gratitude and faith are due. And before more is said, I thank you, and I thank Sir Oliver; y' have great claims upon me, both—none can have more; I were a hound if I forgot them.'

'It is well,' said Sir Daniel; and then, rising into anger: 'Gratitude and faith are words, Dick Shelton,' he continued; 'but I look to deeds. In this hour of my peril, when my name is attainted, when my lands are forfeit, when this wood is full of men that hunger and thirst for my destruction, what doth gratitude? what doth faith? I have but a little company remaining; is it grateful or faithful to poison me their hearts with your insidious whisperings? Save me from such gratitude! But, come, now, what is it ye wish? Speak; we are here to answer. If ye have aught against me, stand forth and say it.'

'Sir,' replied Dick, 'my father fell when I was yet a child. It hath come to mine ears that he was foully done by. It hath come to mine ears—for I will not dissemble—that ye had a hand in his undoing. And in all verity—I shall not be at peace in mine own mind, nor very clear to help you, till I have certain resolution of these doubts.'

Sir Daniel sat down in a deep settle. He took his chin in his hand and looked at Dick fixedly.

'And ye think I would be guardian to the man's son that I had murdered?' he asked.

'Nay,' said Dick, 'pardon me if I answer churlishly; but indeed ye know right well a wardship is most profitable. All these years have ye not enjoyed my revenues, and led my men? Have ye not still my marriage? I wot not what it may be worth—it is worth something. Pardon me again; but if ye were base enough to slay a man under trust, here were, perhaps, reasons enough to move you to the lesser baseness.'

'When I was a lad of your years,' returned Sir Daniel sternly, 'my mind had not so turned upon suspicions. And Sir Oliver here,' he added, 'why should he, a priest, be guilty of this act?'

'Nay, Sir Daniel,' said Dick, 'but where the master biddeth, there will the dog go. It is well known this priest is but your instrument. I speak very freely; the time is not for courtesies. Even as I speak, so would I be answered. And answer get I none! Ye but put more questions. I rede ye beware, Sir Daniel; for in this way ye will but nourish and not satisfy my doubts.'

'I will answer you fairly, Master Richard,' said the knight. 'Were I to pretend ye have not stirred my wrath, I were no honest man. But I will be just even in anger. Come to me with these words when y' are grown and come to man's estate, and I am no longer your guardian, and so helpless to resent them. Come to me then, and I will answer you as ye merit with a buffet in the mouth. Till then ye have two courses: either swallow me down these insults, keep a silent tongue, and fight in the meanwhile for the man that fed and fought for your infancy; or else—the door standeth open, the woods are full of mine enemies—go.'

The spirit with which these words were uttered, the looks with which they were accompanied, staggered Dick; and yet he could not but observe that he had got no answer.

'I desire nothing more earnestly, Sir Daniel, than to believe you,' he replied. 'Assure me ye are free from this.'

'Will ye take my word of honour, Dick?' inquired the knight.

'That would I,' answered the lad.

'I give it you,' returned Sir Daniel. 'Upon my word of honour, upon the eternal welfare of my spirit, and as I shall answer for my deeds hereafter, I had no hand nor portion in your father's death.'

He extended his hand, and Dick took it eagerly. Neither of them observed the priest, who, at the pronunciation of that solemn and false oath, had half arisen from his seat in an agony of horror and remorse.

'Ah,' cried Dick, 'ye must find it in your greatheartedness to pardon me! I was a churl indeed to doubt of you. But ye have my hand upon it; I will doubt no more.'

'Nay, Dick,' replied Sir Daniel, 'y' are forgiven. Ye know not the world and its calumnious nature.'

'I was the more to blame,' added Dick, 'in that the rogues pointed, not directly, at yourself, but at Sir Oliver.'

As he spoke, he turned towards the priest, and paused in the middle of the last word. This tall, ruddy, corpulent, high-stepping man had fallen, you might say, to pieces; his colour was gone, his limbs were relaxed, his lips stammered prayers; and now, when Dick's eyes were fixed upon him suddenly, he cried out aloud, like some wild animal, and buried his face in his hands.

Sir Daniel was by him in two strides, and shook him fiercely by the shoulder. At the same moment Dick's suspicions reawakened.

'Nay,' he said, 'Sir Oliver may swear also. 'Twas him they accused.'

'He shall swear,' said the knight.

Sir Oliver speechlessly waved his arms.

'Ay, by the mass! but ye shall swear,' cried Sir Daniel, beside himself with fury. 'Here, upon this book, ye shall swear,' he continued, picking up the breviary, which had fallen to the ground. 'What! Ye make me doubt you! Swear, I say; swear.'

But the priest was still incapable of speech. His terror of Sir Daniel, his terror of perjury, risen to about an equal height, strangled him.

And just then, through the high stained-glass window of the hall, a black arrow crashed, and struck, and stuck quivering in the midst of the long table.

Sir Oliver, with a loud scream, fell fainting on the rushes; while the knight, followed by Dick, dashed into the court and up the nearest cork-screw stair to the battlements. The sentries were all on the alert. The sun shone quietly on green lawns dotted with trees, and on the wooded hills of the forest which enclosed the view. There was no sign of a besieger.

'Whence came that shot?' asked the knight.

'From yonder clump, Sir Daniel,' returned a sentinel.

The knight stood a little, musing. Then he turned to Dick. 'Dick,' he said, 'keep me an eye upon these men; I leave you in charge here. As for the priest, he shall clear himself, or I will know the reason why. I do almost begin to share in your suspicions. He shall swear, trust me, or we shall prove him guilty.

Dick answered somewhat coldly, and the knight, giving him a piercing glance, hurriedly returned to the hall. His first glance was for the arrow. It was the first of these missiles he had seen, and as he turned it to and fro, the dark hue of it touched him with some fear. Again there was some writing: one word—'Earthed.'

'Ay,' he broke out, 'they know I am home, then. Earthed! Ay, but there is not a dog among them fit to dig me out.'

Sir Oliver had come to himself, and now scrambled to his feet.

'Alack, Sir Daniel!' he moaned, 'y' 'ave sworn a dread oath; y' are doomed to the end of time.'

'Ay,' returned the knight, 'I have sworn an oath, indeed, thou chuckle-head; but thyself shalt swear a greater. It shall be on the blessed cross of Holywood. Look to it; get the words ready. It shall be sworn to-night.'

'Now, may Heaven lighten you!' replied the priest; 'may Heaven incline your heart from this iniquity!'

'Look you, my good father,' said Sir Daniel, 'if y' are for piety, I say no more; ye begin late, that is all. But if y' are in any sense bent upon wisdom, hear me. This lad beginneth to irk me like a wasp. I have a need for him, for I would sell his marriage. But I tell you, in all plainness, if that he continue to weary me, he shall go join his father. I give orders now to change him to the chamber above the chapel. If that ye can swear your innocency with a good solid oath and an assured countenance, it is well; the lad will be at peace a little, and I will spare him. If that ye stammer or blench, or anyways boggle at the swearing, he will not believe you; and, by the mass, he shall die. There is for your thinking on.'

'The chamber above the chapel!' gasped the priest.

'That same,' replied the knight. 'So if ye desire to save him, save him; and if ye desire not, prithee, go to, and let me be at peace! For an I had been an hasty man, I would already have put my sword through you, for your intolerable cowardice and folly. Have ye chosen? Say!'

'I have chosen,' said the priest. 'Heaven pardon me, I will do evil for good. I will swear for the lad's sake.'

'So is it best!' said Sir Daniel. 'Send for him, then, speedily. Ye shall see him alone. Yet I shall have an eye on you. I shall be here in the panel room.'

The knight raised the arras and let it fall again behind him. There was the sound of a spring opening; then followed the creaking of trod stairs.

Sir Oliver, left alone, cast a timorous glance upward at the arras-covered wall, and crossed himself with every appearance of terror and contrition.

'Nay, if he is in the chapel room,' the priest murmured, 'were it at my soul's cost, I must save him.'

Three minutes later, Dick, who had been summoned by another messenger, found Sir Oliver standing by the hall table, resolute and pale.

'Richard Shelton,' he said, 'ye have required an oath from me. I might complain, I might deny you; but my heart is moved toward you for the past, and I will even content you as ye choose. By the true cross of Holywood, I did not slay your father.'

'Sir Oliver,' returned Dick, 'when first we read John Amend-All's paper, I was convinced of so much. But suffer me to put two questions. Ye did not slay him; granted. But had ye no hand in it?'

'None,' said Sir Oliver. And at the same time he began to contort his face, and signal with his mouth and eyebrows, like one who desired to convey a warning, yet dared not utter a sound.

Dick regarded him in wonder; then he turned, and looked all about him at the empty hall.

'What make ye?' he inquired.

'Why, naught,' returned the priest, hastily smoothing his countenance. 'I make naught; I do but suffer; I am sick. I—I—prithee, Dick, I must be gone. On the true cross of Holywood, I am clean innocent alike of violence or treachery. Content ye, good lad. Farewell!'

And he made his escape from the apartment with unusual alacrity.

Dick remained rooted to the spot, his eyes wandering about the room, his face a changing picture of various emotions—wonder, doubt, suspicion, and amusement. Gradually, as his mind grew clearer, suspicion took the upper hand, and was succeeded by certainty of the worst. He raised his head, and, as he did so, violently started. High upon the wall there was the figure of a savage hunter woven in the tapestry. With one hand he held a horn to his mouth; in the other he brandished a stout spear. His face was dark, for he was meant to represent an African.

Now here was what had startled Richard Shelton. The sun had moved away from the hall windows, and at the same time the fire had blazed up high on the wide hearth, and shed a changeful glow upon the roof and hangings. In this light the figure of the black hunter had winked at him with a white eyelid.

He continued staring at the eye. The light shone upon it like a gem; it was liquid, it was alive. Again the white eyelid closed upon it for a fraction of a second, and the next moment it was gone.

There could be no mistake. The live eye that had been watching him through an hole in the tapestry was gone. The firelight no longer shone on a reflecting surface.

And instantly Dick awoke to the terrors of his position. Hatch's warning, the mute signals of the priest, this eye that had observed him from the wall, ran together in his mind. He saw he had been put upon his trial, that he had once more betrayed his suspicions, and that, short of some miracle, he was lost.

'If I cannot get me forth out of this house,' he thought, 'I am a dead man! And this poor Matcham, too—to what a cockatrice's nest have I not led him!'

He was still so thinking, when there came one in haste, to bid him help in changing his arms, his clothing, and his two or three books, to a new chamber.

'A new chamber?' he repeated. 'Wherefore so? What chamber?'

''Tis one above the chapel,' answered the messenger.

'It hath stood long empty,' said Dick, musing. 'What manner of room is it?'

'Nay, a brave room,' returned the man. 'But yet'—lowering his voice—'they call it haunted.'

'Haunted?' repeated Dick, with a chill. 'I have not heard of it. Nay, then, and by whom?'

The messenger looked about him; and then, in a low whisper, 'By the sacrist of St. John's,' he said. 'They had him there to sleep one night, and in the morning—whew!—he was gone. The devil had taken him, they said; the more betoken, he had drunk late the night before.'

Dick followed the man with black forebodings.

10

The room over the Chapel

FROM the battlements nothing further was observed. The sun journeyed westward and at last went down; but to the eyes of all these eager sentinels, no living thing appeared in the neighbourhood of Tunstall House.

When the night was at length fairly come Throgmorton was led to a room overlooking an angle of the moat. Thence he was lowered with every precaution; the ripple of his swimming was audible for a brief period; then a black figure was observed to land by the branches of a willow and crawl away among the grass. For some half-hour Sir Daniel and Hatch stood eagerly giving ear; but all remained quiet. The messenger had got away in safety.

Sir Daniel's brow grew clearer. He turned to Hatch.

'Bennet,' said he, 'this John Amend-All is no more than a man, ye see. He sleepeth. We will make a good end of him. Go to!'

All the afternoon and evening Dick had been ordered hither and thither, one command following another, till he was bewildered with the number and the hurry of commissions. All that time he had seen no more of Sir Oliver, and nothing of Matcham; and yet both the priest and the young lad ran continually in his mind. It was now his chief purpose to escape from Tunstall Moat House as speedily as might be; and yet, before he went, he desired a word with both of these.

At length, with a lamp in one hand, he mounted to his new apartment. It was large, low, and somewhat dark. The window looked upon the moat, and although it was so high up, it was heavily barred. The bed was luxurious, with one pillow of down, and one of lavender, and a red coverlet worked in a pattern of roses. All about the walls were cupboards, locked and padlocked, and concealed from view by hangings of dark-coloured arras. Dick made the round, lifting the arras, sounding the panels, seeking vainly to open the cupboards. He assured himself that the door was strong, and the bolt solid; then he set down his lamp upon a bracket, and once more looked all around.

For what reason had he been given this chamber? It was larger and finer than his own. Could it conceal a snare? Was there a secret entrance? Was it indeed haunted? His blood ran a little chilly in his veins.

Immediately over him the heavy foot of a sentry trod the leads.

Below him, he knew, was the arched roof of the chapel; and next to the chapel was the hall. Certainly there was a secret passage in the hall; the eye that had watched him from the arras gave him proof of that. Was it not more than probable that the passage extended to the chapel, and if so, that it had an opening in his room?

To sleep in such a place, he felt, would be foolhardy. He made his weapons ready, and took his position in a corner of the room behind the door. If ill was intended he would sell his life dear.

The sound of many feet, the challenge, and the password sounded overhead along the battlements; the watch was being changed.

And just then there came a scratching at the door of the chamber, it grew a little louder; then a whisper:—

'Dick, Dick, it is I!'

Dick ran to the door, drew the bolt, and admitted Matcham. He was very pale, and carried a lamp in one hand and a drawn dagger in the other.

'Shut me the door,' he whispered. 'Swift, Dick! This house is full of spies; I hear their feet follow me in the corridors; I hear them breathe behind the arras.'

'Well, content you,' returned Dick, 'it is closed. We are safe for this while, if there be safety anywhere within these walls. But my heart is glad to see you. By the mass, lad, I thought ye were sped. Where hid ye?'

'It matters not,' returned Matcham. 'Since we be met, it matters not. But, Dick, are your eyes open? Have they told ye of to-morrow's doings?'

'Not they,' replied Dick. 'What make they to-morrow?'

'To-morrow, or to-night, I know not,' said the other; 'but one time or other, Dick, they do intend upon your life. I had the proof of it: I have heard them whisper; nay, they as good as told me.'

'Ay,' returned Dick, 'is it so? I had thought as much.'

And he told him the day's occurrences at length.

When it was done, Matcham arose and began, in turn, to examine the apartment.

'No,' he said, 'there is no entrance visible. Yet 'tis a pure certainty there is one. Dick, I will stay by you. An' y' are to die, I will die with you. And I can help—look! I have stolen a dagger—I will do my best! And meanwhile, an ye know of any issue, any sally-port we could get opened, or any window that we might descend by, I will most joyfully face any jeopardy to flee with you.'

'Jack,' said Dick, 'by the mass, Jack, y' are the best soul, and the truest, and the bravest in all England! Give me your hand, Jack.'

And he grasped the other's hand in silence.

'I will tell you,' he resumed. 'There is a window out of which the messenger descended; the rope should still be in the chamber. 'Tis a hope.'

'Hist!' said Matcham.

Both gave ear. There was a sound below the floor; then it paused, and then began again.

'Some one walketh in the room below,' whispered Matcham.

'Nay,' returned Dick, 'there is no room below; we are above the chapel. It is my murderer in the secret passage. Well, let him come: it shall go hard with him!' And he ground his teeth.

'Blow me the lights out,' said the other. 'Perchance he will betray himself.'

They blew out both the lamps and lay still as death. The footfalls underneath were very soft, but they were clearly audible. Several times they came and went; and then there was a loud jar of a key turning in a lock, followed by a considerable silence.

Presently the steps began again, and then, all of a sudden, a chink of light appeared in the planking of the room in a far corner. It widened; a trap-door was being opened, letting in a gush of light. They could see the strong hand pushing it up; and Dick raised his crossbow, waiting for the head to follow.

But now there came an interruption. From a distant corner of the Moat House shouts began to be heard, and first one voice, and then several, crying aloud upon a name. This noise had plainly disconcerted the murderer, for the trap-door was silently lowered to its place, and the steps hurriedly returned, passed once more close below the lads, and died away in the distance.

Here was a moment's respite. Dick breathed deep, and then, and not till then, he gave ear to the disturbance which had interrupted the attack, and which was now rather increasing than diminishing. All about the Moat House feet were running, doors were opening and slamming, and still the voice of Sir Daniel towered above all this bustle, shouting for 'Joanna.'

'Joanna!' repeated Dick. 'Why, who the murrain should this be? Here is no Joanna, nor ever hath been. What meaneth it?'

Matcham was silent. He seemed to have drawn farther away. But only a little faint starlight entered by the window, and at the far end of the apartment, where the pair were, the darkness was complete.

'Jack,' said Dick, 'I wot not where ye were all day. Saw ye this Joanna?'

'Nay,' returned Matcham, 'I saw her not.'

'Nor heard tell of her?' he pursued.

The steps drew nearer. Sir Daniel was still roaring the name of Joanna from the courtyard.

'Did ye hear of her?' repeated Dick.

'I heard of her,' said Matcham.

'How your voice twitters! What aileth you?' said Dick. ''Tis a most excellent good fortune, this Joanna; it will take their minds from us.'

'Dick,' cried Matcham, 'I am lost; we are both lost! Let us flee if there be yet time. They will not rest till they have found me. Or, see! let me go forth; when they have found me, ye may flee. Let me forth, Dick—good Dick, let me away!'

She was groping for the bolt, when Dick at last comprehended.

'By the mass!' he cried, 'y' are no Jack; y' are Joanna Sedley; y' are the maid that would not marry me!'

The girl paused, and stood silent and motionless. Dick, too, was silent for a little; then he spoke again.

'Joanna,' he said, 'y' 'ave saved my life, and I have saved yours; and we have seen blood flow, and been friends and enemies—ay, and I took my belt to thrash you; and all that time I thought ye were a boy. But now death has me, and my time's out, and before I die I must say this: Y' are the best maid and the bravest under heaven, and, if only I could live, I would marry you blindly: and, live or die, I love you!'

She answered nothing.

'Come,' he said, 'speak up, Jack. Come, be a good maid, and say ye love me!'

'Why, Dick,' she cried, 'would I be here?'

'Well, see ye here,' continued Dick, 'an we but escape whole, we'll marry; and an we're to die, we die, and there's an end on't. But now that I think, how found ye my chamber?'

'I asked it of Dame Hatch,' she answered.

'Well, the dame's staunch,' he answered; 'she'll not tell upon you. We have time before us.'

And just then, as if to contradict his words, feet came down the corridor, and a fist beat roughly on the door.

'Here!' cried a voice. 'Open, Master Dick; open!'

Dick neither moved nor answered.

'It is all over,' said the girl; and she put her arms about Dick's neck.

One after another, men came trooping to the door. Then Sir Daniel arrived himself, and there was a sudden cessation of the noise.

'Dick,' cried the knight, 'be not an ass. The Seven Sleepers had been awake ere now. We know she is within there. Open, then, the door, man.'

Dick was silent again.

'Down with it,' said Sir Daniel. And immediately his followers fell savagely upon the door with foot and fist. Solid as it was, and strongly bolted, it would soon have given way, but once more fortune interfered. Over the thunderstorm of blows the cry of a sentinel was heard; it was followed by another; shouts ran along the battlements, shouts answered out of the wood. In the first moment of alarm it sounded as if the foresters were carrying the Moat House by assault. And Sir Daniel and his men, desisting instantly from their attack upon Dick's chamber, hurried to defend the walls.

'Now,' cried Dick, 'we are saved.'

He seized the great old bedstead with both hands, and bent himself in vain to move it.

'Help me, Jack. For your life's sake, help me stoutly!' he cried.

Between them, with a huge effort, they dragged the big frame of oak across the room, and thrust it endwise to the chamber door.

'Ye do but make things worse,' said Joanna, sadly. 'He will then enter by the trap.'

'Not so,' replied Dick. 'He durst not tell his secret to so many. It is by the trap that we shall flee. Hark! The attack is over. Nay, it was none!'

It had, indeed, been no attack; it was the arrival of another party of stragglers from the defeat of Risingham that had disturbed Sir Daniel. They had run the gauntlet under cover of the darkness; they had been admitted by the great gate; and now with a great stamping of hoofs and jingle of accoutrements and arms, they were dismounting in the court.

'He will return anon,' said Dick. 'To the trap!'

He lighted a lamp, and they went together into the corner of the room. The open chink through which some light still glittered was easily discovered, and, taking a stout sword from his small armoury, Dick thrust it deep into the seam, and weighed strenuously on the hilt. The trap moved, gaped a little, and at length came widely open. Seizing it with their hands, the two young folk threw it back. It disclosed a few steps descending, and at the foot of them, where the would-be murderer had left it, a burning lamp.

'Now,' said Dick, 'go first and take the lamp. I will follow to close the trap.'

So they descended one after the other, and as Dick lowered the trap, the blows began once again to thunder on the panels of the door.

II

The passage

THE passage in which Dick and Joanna now found themselves was narrow, dirty, and short. At the other end of it a door stood partly open; the same door, without doubt, that they had heard the man unlocking. Heavy cobwebs hung from the roof, and the paved flooring echoed hollow under the lightest tread.

Beyond the door there were two branches, at right angles. Dick chose one of them at random, and the pair hurried, with echoing footsteps, along the hollow of the chapel roof. The top of the arched ceiling rose like a whale's back in the dim glimmer of the lamp. Here and there were spy-holes, concealed, on the other side, by the carving of the cornice; and looking down through one of these, Dick saw the paved floor of the chapel—the altar, with its burning tapers—and stretched before it on the steps, the figure of Sir Oliver praying with uplifted hands.

At the other end, they descended a few steps. The passage grew narrower; the wall upon one hand was now of wood; the noise of people talking, and a faint flickering of lights, came through the interstices; and presently they came to a round hole about the size of a man's eye, and Dick, looking down through it, beheld the interior of the hall, and some half a dozen men sitting, in their jacks, about the table, drinking deep and demolishing a venison pie. These were certainly some of the late arrivals.

'Here is no help,' said Dick. 'Let us try back.'

'Nay,' said Joanna; 'maybe the passage goeth farther.'

And she pushed on. But a few yards farther the passage ended at the top of a short flight of steps; and it became plain that, as long as the soldiers occupied the hall, escape was impossible upon that side.

They retraced their steps with all imaginable speed, and set forward to explore the other branch. It was exceedingly narrow, scarce wide enough for a large man; and it led them continually up and down by little breakneck stairs, until even Dick had lost all notion of his whereabouts.

At length it grew both narrower and lower; the stairs continued to descend; the walls on either hand became damp and slimy to the touch; and far in front of them they heard the squeaking and scuttling of the rats.

'We must be in the dungeons,' Dick remarked.

'And still there is no outlet,' added Joanna.

'Nay, but an outlet there must be!' Dick answered.

Presently, sure enough, they came to a sharp angle, and then the passage ended in a flight of steps. On the top of that there was a solid flag of stone by way of trap, and to this they both set their backs. It was immovable.

'Some one holdeth it,' suggested Joanna.

'Not so,' said Dick; 'for were a man as strong as ten he must still yield a little. But this resisteth like dead rock. There is a weight upon the trap. Here is no issue; and, by my sooth, good Jack, we are here as fairly prisoners as though the gyves were on our ankle-bones. Sit ye then down, and let us talk. After a while we shall return, when perchance they shall be less carefully upon their guard; and, who knoweth? we may break out and stand a chance. But, in my poor opinion, we are as good as shent.'

'Dick!' she cried, 'alas the day that ever ye should have seen me! For like a most unhappy and unthankful maid, it is I have led you hither.'

'What cheer!' returned Dick. 'It was all written, and that which is written, willy nilly, cometh still to pass. But tell me a little what manner of maid ye are, and how ye came into Sir Daniel's hands; that will do better than to bemoan yourself, whether for your sake or mine.'

'I am an orphan, like yourself, of father and mother,' said Joanna; 'and for my great misfortune, Dick, and hitherto for yours, I am a rich marriage. My Lord Foxham had me to ward; yet it appears Sir Daniel bought the marriage of me from the king, and a right dear price he paid for it. So here was I, poor babe, with two great and rich men fighting which should marry me, and I still at nurse! Well, then the world changed, and there was a new Chancellor, and Sir Daniel bought the warding of me over the Lord Foxham's head. And then the world changed again, and Lord Foxham bought my marriage over Sir Daniel's, and from then to now it went on ill betwixt the two of them. But still Lord Foxham kept me in his hands, and was a good lord to me. And at last I was to be married—or sold, if ye like it better. Five hundred pounds Lord Foxham was to get for me. Hamley was the groom's name, and to-morrow, Dick, of all days in the year, was I to be betrothed. Had it not come to Sir Daniel, I had been wedded, sure—and never seen thee, Dick—dear Dick!'

And here she took his hand, and kissed it with the prettiest grace; and Dick drew her hand to him and did the like.

'Well,' she went on, 'Sir Daniel took me unawares in the garden, and made me dress in these men's clothes, which is a deadly sin for a woman; and, besides, they fit me not. He rode with me to Kettley, as ye saw, telling me I was to marry you; but I, in my heart, made sure I would marry Hamley in his teeth.'

'Ay!' cried Dick, 'and so ye loved this Hamley?'

'Nay,' replied Joanna, 'not I. I did but hate Sir Daniel. And then, Dick, ye helped me, and ye were right kind, and very bold, and my heart turned towards you in mine own despite; and now, if we can in any way compass it, I would marry you with right goodwill. And if, by cruel destiny, it may not be, still ye'll be dear to me. While my heart beats, it'll be true to you.'

'And I,' said Dick, 'that never cared a straw for any manner of woman until now, I took to you when I thought ye were a boy. I had a pity to you, and knew not why. When I would have belted you, the hand failed me. But when ye owned ye were a maid, Jack—for still I will call you Jack—I made sure ye were the maid for me. Hark!' he said, breaking off—'one cometh.'

And indeed a heavy tread was now audible in the echoing passage, and the rats again fled in armies.

Dick reconnoitred his position. The sudden turn gave him a post of vantage. He could thus shoot in safety from the cover of the wall. But it was plain the light was too near him, and, running some way forward, he set down the lamp in the middle of the passage, and then returned to watch.

Presently, at the far end of the passage, Bennet hove in sight. He seemed to be alone, and he carried in his hand a burning torch, which made him the better mark.

'Stand, Bennet!' cried Dick. 'Another step and y' are dead.'

'So here ye are,' returned Hatch, peering forward into the darkness. 'I see you not. Aha! y' 'ave done wisely, Dick; y' 'ave put your lamp before you. By my sooth, but, though it was done to shoot my own knave body, I do rejoice to see ye profit of my lessons! And now, what make ye? what seek ye here? Why would ye shoot upon an old, kind friend? And have ye the young gentlewoman there?'

'Nay, Bennet, it is I should question and you answer,' replied Dick. 'Why am I in this jeopardy of my life? Why do men come privily to slay me in my bed? Why am I now fleeing in mine own guardian's strong house, and from the friends that I have lived among and never injured?'

'Master Dick, Master Dick,' said Bennet, 'what told I you? Y' are brave, but the most uncrafty lad that I can think upon!'

'Well,' returned Dick, 'I see ye know all, and that I am doomed indeed. It is well. Here where I am, I stay. Let Sir Daniel get me out if he be able!'

Hatch was silent for a space.

'Hark ye,' he began. 'I return to Sir Daniel, to tell him where ye are, and how posted; for, in truth, it was to that end he sent me. But you, if ye are no fool, had best begone ere I return.'

'Begone!' repeated Dick. 'I would begone already, an I wist how. I cannot move the trap.'

'Put me your hand into the corner, and see what ye find there, replied Bennet. 'Throgmorton's rope is still in the brown chamber. Fare ye well.'

And Hatch, turning upon his heel, disappeared again into the windings of the passage.

Dick instantly returned for his lamp, and proceeded to act upon the hint. At one corner of the trap there was a deep cavity in the wall. Pushing his arm into the aperture, Dick found an iron bar, which he thrust vigorously upwards. There followed a snapping noise, and the slab of stone instantly started in its bed.

They were free of the passage. A little exercise of strength easily raised the trap; and they came forth into a vaulted chamber, opening on one hand upon the court, where one or two fellows, with bare arms, were rubbing down the horses of the last arrivals. A torch or two, each stuck in an iron ring against the wall, changefully lit up the scene.

12

How Dick changed sides

DICK, blowing out his lamp lest it should attract attention, led the way upstairs and along the corridor. In the brown chamber the rope had been made fast to the frame of an exceedingly heavy and ancient bed. It had not been detached, and Dick, taking the coil to the window, began to lower it slowly and cautiously into the darkness of the night. Joan stood by; but as the rope lengthened, and still Dick continued to pay it out, extreme fear began to conquer her resolution.

'Dick,' she said, 'is it so deep? I may not essay it. I should infallibly fall, good Dick.'

It was just at the delicate moment of the operations that she spoke. Dick started; the remainder of the coil slipped from his grasp, and the end fell with a splash into the moat. Instantly, from the battlement above, the voice of a sentinel cried, 'Who goes?'

'A murrain!' cried Dick. 'We are paid now! Down with you—take the rope.'

'I cannot,' she cried, recoiling.

'An ye cannot, no more can I,' said Shelton. 'How can I swim the moat without you? Do ye desert me, then?'

'Dick,' she gasped, 'I cannot. The strength is gone from me.'

'By the mass, then, we are all shent!' he shouted, stamping his foot; and then, hearing steps, he ran to the room door and sought to close it.

Before he could shoot the bolt, strong arms were thrusting it back upon him from the other side. He struggled for a second; then, feeling himself overpowered, ran back to the window. The girl had fallen against the wall in the embrasure of the window; she was more than half insensible; and when he tried to raise her in his arms, her body was limp and unresponsive.

At the same moment the men who had forced the door against him laid hold upon him. The first he poniarded at a blow, and the others falling back for a second in some disorder, he profited by the chance, bestrode the window-sill, seized the cord in both hands, and let his body slip.

The cord was knotted, which made it the easier to descend; but so furious was Dick's hurry, and so small his experience of such gymnastics, that he span round and round in mid-air like a criminal upon a gibbet, and now beat his head, and now bruised his hands, against the rugged stonework of the wall. The air roared in his ears; he saw the stars overhead, and the reflected stars below him in the moat, whirling like dead leaves before the tempest. And then he lost hold and fell, and soused head over ears into the icy water.

When he came to the surface his hand encountered the rope, which, newly lightened of his weight, was swinging wildly to and fro. There was a red glow overhead, and looking up, he saw, by the light of several torches and a cresset full of burning coals, the battlements lined with faces. He saw the men's eyes turning hither and thither in quest of him; but he was too far below, the light reached him not, and they looked in vain.

And now he perceived that the rope was considerably too long, and he began to struggle as well as he could towards the other side of the moat, still keeping his head above water. In this way he got much more than half-way over; indeed, the bank was almost within reach before the rope began to draw him back by its own weight. Taking his courage in both hands, he left go and made a leap for the trailing sprays of willow that had already, that same evening, helped Sir Daniel's messenger to land. He went down, rose again, sank a second time, and then his hand caught a branch, and with the speed of thought he had dragged himself into the thick of the tree and clung there, dripping and panting, and still half uncertain of his escape.

But all this had not been done without a considerable splashing, which had so far indicated his position to the men along the battlements. Arrows and quarrels fell thick around him in the darkness, thick like driving hail; and suddenly a torch was thrown down—flared through the air in its swift passage—stuck for a moment on the edge of the bank, where it burned high and lit up its whole surroundings like a bonfire—and then, in a good hour for Dick, slipped off, plumped into the moat, and was instantly extinguished.

It had served its purpose. The marksmen had had time to see the willow, and Dick ensconced among its boughs; and though the lad instantly sprang higher up the bank and ran for his life, he was yet not quick enough to escape a shot. An arrow struck him in the shoulder, another grazed his head.

The pain of his wounds lent him wings; and he had no sooner got upon the level than he took to his heels and ran straight before him in the dark, without a thought for the direction of his flight.

For a few steps missiles followed him, but these soon ceased; and when at length he came to a halt and looked behind, he was already a good way from the Moat House, though he could still see the torches moving to and fro along its battlements.

He leaned against a tree, streaming with blood and water, bruised, wounded, and alone. For all that, he had saved his life for that bout; and though Joanna remained behind in the power of Sir Daniel, he neither blamed himself for an accident that it had been beyond his power to prevent, nor did he augur any fatal consequences to the girl herself. Sir Daniel was cruel, but he was not likely to be cruel to a young gentlewoman who had other protectors, willing and able to bring him to account. It was more probable he would make haste to marry her to some friend of his own.

'Well,' thought Dick, 'between then and now I will find the means to bring that traitor under; for I think, by the mass, that I be now absolved from any gratitude or obligation; and when war is open, there is a fair chance for all.'

In the meanwhile, here he was in a sore plight.

For some little way farther he struggled forward through the forest; but what with the pain of his wounds, the darkness of the night, and the extreme uneasiness and confusion of his mind, he soon became equally unable to guide himself or to continue to push through the close undergrowth, and he was fain at length to sit down and lean his back against a tree.

When he awoke from something betwixt sleep and swooning, the gray of the morning had begun to take the place of night. A little chilly breeze was bustling among the trees, and as he still sat staring before him, only half awake, he became aware of something dark that swung to and fro among the branches, some hundred yards in front of him. The progressive brightening of the day and the return of his own senses at last enabled him to recognise the object. It was a man hanging from the bough of a tall oak. His head had fallen forward on his breast; but at every stronger puff of wind his body spun round and round, and his legs and arms tossed, like some ridiculous plaything.

Dick clambered to his feet, and, staggering and leaning on the tree-trunks as he went, drew near to this grim object.

The bough was perhaps twenty feet above the ground, and the poor fellow had been drawn up so high by his executioners, that his boots swung clear above Dick's reach; and as his hood had been drawn over his face, it was impossible to recognise the man.

Dick looked about him right and left; and at last he perceived that the other end of the cord had been made fast to the trunk of a little hawthorn which grew, thick with blossom, under the lofty arcade of the oak. With his dagger, which alone remained to him of all his arms, young Shelton severed the rope, and instantly, with a dead thump, the corpse fell in a heap upon the ground.

Dick raised the hood; it was Throgmorton, Sir Daniel's messenger. He had not gone far upon his errand. A paper, which had apparently escaped the notice of the men of the Black Arrow, stuck from the bosom of his doublet, and Dick, pulling it forth, found it was Sir Daniel's letter to Lord Wensleydale.

'Come,' thought he, 'if the world changes yet again, I may have the wherewithal to shame Sir Daniel—nay, and perchance to bring him to the block.'

And he put the paper in his own bosom, said a prayer over the dead man, and set forth again through the woods.

His fatigue and weakness increased; his ears sang, his steps faltered, his mind at intervals failed him, so low had he been brought by loss of blood. Doubtless he made many deviations from his true path, but at last he came out upon the high-road, not very far from Tunstall hamlet.

A rough voice bid him stand.

'Stand?' repeated Dick. 'By the mass, but I am nearer falling.'

And he suited the action to the word, and fell all his length upon the road.

Two men came forth out of the thicket, each in green forest jerkin, each with long-bow and quiver and short sword.

'Why, Lawless,' said the younger of the two, 'it is young Shelton.'

'Ay, this will be as good as bread to John Amend-All,' returned the other. 'Though, faith, he hath been to the wars. Here is a tear in his scalp that must 'a' cost him many a good ounce of blood.'

'And here,' added Greensheve, 'is a hole in his shoulder that must have pricked him well. Who hath done this, think ye? If it be one of ours, he may all to prayer; Ellis will give him a short shrift and a long rope.'

'Up with the cub,' said Lawless. 'Clap him on my back.'

And then, when Dick had been hoisted to his shoulders, and he had taken the lad's arms about his neck, and got a firm hold of him, the ex-Grey Friar added,—

'Keep ye the post, brother Greensheve. I will on with him by myself.'

So Greensheve returned to his ambush on the wayside, and Lawless trudged down the hill, whistling as he went, with Dick, still in a dead faint, comfortably settled on his shoulders.

The sun rose as he came out of the skirts of the wood and saw Tunstall hamlet straggling up the opposite hill. All seemed quiet, but a strong post of some half a score of archers lay close by the bridge on either side of the road, and, as soon as they perceived Lawless with his burden, began to bestir themselves and set arrow to string like vigilant sentries.

'Who goes?' cried the man in command.

'Will Lawless, by the rood—ye know me as well as your own hand,' returned the outlaw, contemptuously.

'Give the word, Lawless,' returned the other.

'Now, Heaven lighten thee, thou great fool,' replied Lawless. 'Did I not tell it thee myself? But ye are all mad for this playing at soldiers. When I am in the greenwood, give me greenwood ways; and my word for this tide is, "A fig for all mock soldiery!"'

'Lawless, ye but show an ill example; give us the word, fool jester,' said the commander of the post.

'And if I had forgotten it?' asked the other.

'An ye had forgotten it—as I know y' 'ave not—by the mass, I would clap an arrow into your big body,' returned the first.

'Nay, an y' are so ill a jester,' said Lawless, 'ye shall have your word for me. "Duckworth and Shelton" is the word;

and here, to the illustration, is Shelton on my shoulders, and to Duckworth do I carry him.'

'Pass, Lawless,' said the sentry.

'And where is John?' asked the Grey Friar.

'He holdeth a court, by the mass, and taketh rents as to the manner born!' cried another of the company.

So it proved. When Lawless got as far up the village as the little inn, he found Ellis Duckworth surrounded by Sir Daniel's tenants, and, by the right of his good company of archers, coolly taking rents, and giving written receipts in return for them. By the faces of the tenants, it was plain how little this proceeding pleased them; for they argued very rightly that they would simply have to pay them twice.

As soon as he knew what had brought Lawless, Ellis dismissed the remainder of the tenants, and, with every mark of interest and apprehension, conducted Dick into an inner chamber of the inn. There the lad's hurts were looked to; and he was recalled, by simple remedies, to consciousness.

'Dear lad,' said Ellis, pressing his hand, 'y' are in a friend's hand that loved your father, and loves you for his sake. Rest ye a little quietly, for ye are somewhat out of case. Then shall ye tell me your story, and betwixt the two of us we shall find a remedy for all.'

A little later in the day, and after Dick had awakened from a comfortable slumber to find himself still very weak, but clearer in mind and easier in body, Ellis returned, and sitting down by the bedside, begged him, in the name of his father, to relate the circumstances of his escape from Tunstall Moat House. There was something in the strength of Duckworth's frame, in the honesty of his brown face, in the clearness and shrewdness of his eyes, that moved Dick to obey him; and from first to last the lad told him the story of his two days' adventures.

'Well,' said Ellis, when he had done, 'see what the kind saints have done for you, Dick Shelton, not alone to save your body in so numerous and deadly perils, but to bring you into my hands that have no dearer wish than to assist your father's son. Be but true to me—and I see y' are true—and betwixt you and me, we shall bring that false-heart traitor to the death.'

'Will ye assault the house?' asked Dick.

'I were mad, indeed, to think of it,' returned Ellis. 'He hath too much power; his men gather to him; those that gave me the slip last night, and by the mass came in so handily for you—those have made him safe. Nay, Dick, to the contrary, thou and I and our brave bowmen, we must all slip from this forest speedily, and leave Sir Daniel free.'

'My mind misgiveth me for Jack,' said the lad.

'For Jack!' repeated Duckworth. 'Oh, I see, for the wench! Nay, Dick, I promise you if there come talk of any marriage we shall act at once; till then, or till the time is ripe, we shall all disappear, even like shadows at morning; Sir Daniel shall look east and west, and see none enemies; he shall think, by the mass, that he hath dreamed awhile, and hath now awakened in his bed. But our four eyes, Dick, shall follow him right close, and our four hands—so help us all the army of the saints!—shall bring that traitor low!'

Two days later Sir Daniel's garrison had grown to such a strength that he ventured on a sally, and at the head of some two score horsemen pushed without opposition as far as Tunstall hamlet. Not an arrow flew, not a man stirred in the thicket; the bridge was no longer guarded, but stood open to all comers; and as Sir Daniel crossed it, he saw the villagers looking timidly from their doors.

Presently one of them, taking heart of grace, came forward, and, with the lowliest salutations, presented a letter to the knight.

His face darkened as he read the contents. It ran thus:—

'*To the most untrue and cruel gentylman, Sir Daniel Brackley, Knyght, These:*—

'I fynde ye were untrue and unkynd fro the first. Ye have my father's blood upon your hands; let be, it will not wasshe. Some day ye shall perish by my procurement, so much I let you to wytte; and I let you to wytte farther, that if ye seek to wed to any other the gentylwoman, Mistress Joan Sedley, whom that I am bound upon a great oath to wed myself, the blow will be very swift. The first step thereinne will be thy first step to the grave.

'RIC. SHELTON.'

Book Three

MY LORD FOXHAM

13

The House by the shore

MONTHS had passed away since Richard Shelton made his escape from the hands of his guardian. These months had been eventful for England. The party of Lancaster, which was then in the very article of death, had once more raised its head. The Yorkists defeated and dispersed, their leader butchered on the field, it seemed, for a very brief season in the winter following upon the events already recorded, as if the House of Lancaster had finally triumphed over its foes.

The small town of Shoreby-on-the-Till was full of the Lancastrian nobles of the neighbourhood. Earl Risingham was there, with three hundred men-at-arms; Lord Shoreby, with two hundred; Sir Daniel himself, high in favour and once more growing rich on confiscations, lay in a house of his own, on the main street, with three score men. The world had changed indeed.

It was a black, bitter cold evening in the first week of January, with a hard frost, a high wind, and every likelihood of snow before the morning.

In an obscure alehouse in a by-street near the harbour three or four men sat drinking ale and eating a hasty mess of eggs. They were all likely, lusty, weather-beaten fellows, hard of hand, bold of eye; and though they wore plain tabards, like country ploughmen, even a drunken soldier might have looked twice before he sought a quarrel in such company.

A little apart before the huge fire sat a younger man, almost a boy, dressed in much the same fashion, though it was easy to see by his looks that he was better born, and might have worn a sword, had the time suited.

'Nay,' said one of the men at the table, 'I like it not. Ill will come of it. This is no place for jolly fellows. A jolly fellow loveth open country, good cover, and scarce foes; but here we are shut in a town, girt about with enemies; and, for the bullseye of misfortune, see if it snow not ere the morning.'

''Tis for Master Shelton there,' said another, nodding his head towards the lad before the fire.

'I will do much for Master Shelton,' returned the first; 'but to come to the gallows for any man—nay, brothers, not that!'

The door of the inn opened, and another man entered hastily and approached the youth before the fire.

'Master Shelton,' he said, 'Sir Daniel goeth forth with a pair of links and four archers.'

Dick (for this was our young friend) rose instantly to his feet.

'Lawless,' he said, 'ye will take John Capper's watch. Greensheve, follow with me. Capper, lead forward. We will follow him this time, an he go to York.'

The next moment they were outside in the dark street, and Capper, the man who had just come, pointed to where two torches flared in the wind at a little distance.

The town was already sound asleep; no one moved upon the streets, and there was nothing easier than to follow the party without observation. The two link-bearers went first; next followed a single man, whose long cloak blew about him in the wind; and the rear was brought up by the four archers, each with his bow upon his arm. They moved at a brisk walk, threading the intricate lanes and drawing nearer to the shore.

'He hath gone each night in this direction?' added Dick, in a whisper.

'This is the third night running, Master Shelton,' returned Capper, 'and still at the same hour and with the same small following, as though his end were secret.'

Sir Daniel and his six men were now come to the outskirts of the country. Shoreby was an open town, and though the Lancastrian lords who lay there kept a strong guard on the main roads, it was still possible to enter or depart unseen by any of the lesser streets or across the open country.

The lane which Sir Daniel had been following came to an abrupt end. Before him there was a stretch of rough down, and the noise of the sea-surf was audible upon one hand. There were no guards in the neighbourhood, nor any light in that quarter of the town.

Dick and his two outlaws drew a little closer to the object of their chase, and presently, as they came forth from between the houses and could see a little farther upon either hand, they were aware of another torch drawing near from another direction.

'Hey,' said Dick, 'I smell treason.'

Meanwhile Sir Daniel had come to a full halt. The torches were stuck into the sand, and the men lay down, as if to await the arrival of the other party.

This drew near at a good rate. It consisted of four men only—a pair of archers, a varlet with a link, and a cloaked gentleman walking in their midst.

'Is it you, my lord?' cried Sir Daniel.

'It is I, indeed; and if ever true knight gave proof I am that man,' replied the leader of the second troop; 'for who would not rather face giants, sorcerers, or pagans, than this pinching cold?'

'My lord,' returned Sir Daniel, 'beauty will be the more beholden, misdoubt it not. But shall we forth? for the sooner ye have seen my merchandise, the sooner shall we both get home.'

'But why keep ye her here, good knight?' inquired the other. 'An she be so young, and so fair, and so wealthy, why do ye not bring her forth among her mates? Ye would soon make her a good marriage, and no need to freeze your fingers and risk arrow-shots by going abroad at such untimely seasons in the dark.'

'I have told you, my lord,' replied Sir Daniel, 'the reason thereof concerneth me only. Neither do I purpose to explain it further. Suffice it that if ye be weary of your old gossip, Daniel Brackley, publish it abroad that y' are to wed Joanna Sedley, and I give you my word ye will be quit of him right soon. Ye will find him with an arrow in his back.'

Meantime the two gentlemen were walking briskly forward over the down; the three torches going before them, stooping against the wind and scattering clouds of smoke and tufts of flame, and the rear brought up by the six archers.

Close upon the heels of these, Dick followed. He had, of course, heard no word of this conversation; but he had recognised in the second of the speakers old Lord Shoreby himself, a man of an infamous reputation, whom even Sir Daniel affected, in public, to condemn.

Presently they came close down upon the beach. The air smelt salt, the noise of the surf increased; and here, in a large walled garden, there stood a small house of two storeys, with stables and other offices.

The foremost torch-bearer unlocked a door in the wall, and after the whole party had passed into the garden, again closed and locked it on the other side.

Dick and his men were thus excluded from any further following, unless they should scale the wall and thus put their necks in a trap.

They sat down in a tuft of furze and waited. The red glow of the torches moved up and down to and fro within the enclosure, as if the linkbearers steadily patrolled the garden.

Twenty minutes passed, and then the whole party issued forth again upon the down; and Sir Daniel and the baron, after an elaborate salutation, separated and turned severally homeward, each with his own following of men and lights.

As soon as the sound of the steps had been swallowed by the wind, Dick got to his feet as briskly as he was able, for he was stiff and aching with the cold.

'Capper, ye will give me a back up,' he said.

They advanced, all three, to the wall; Capper stooped, and Dick, getting upon his shoulders, clambered on to the cope-stone.

'Now, Greensheve,' whispered Dick, 'follow me up here; lie flat upon your face, that ye may be the less seen; and be ever ready to give me a hand if I fall foully on the other side.'

And so saying he dropped into the garden.

It was all pitch dark; there was no light in the house. The wind whistled shrill among the poor shrubs, and the surf beat upon the beach; there was no other sound. Cautiously Dick footed it forth, stumbling among bushes, and groping with his hands; and presently the crisp noise of gravel under foot told him that he had struck upon an alley.

Here he paused, and taking his crossbow from where he kept it concealed under his long tabard, he prepared it for instant action, and went forward once more with greater resolution and assurance. The path led him straight to the group of buildings.

All seemed to be sorely dilapidated: the windows of the house were secured by crazy shutters; the stables were open and empty; there was no hay in the hay-loft, no corn in the corn-box. Any one would have supposed the place to be deserted; but Dick had good reason to think otherwise. He continued his inspection, visiting the offices, trying all the windows. At length he came round to the sea side of the house, and there, sure enough, there burned a pale light in one of the upper windows.

He stepped back a little way, till he thought he could see the movement of a shadow on the wall of the apartment. Then he remembered that in the stable his groping hand had rested for a moment on a ladder, and he returned with all despatch to bring it. The ladder was very short, but yet, by standing on the topmost round, he could bring his hands as high as the iron bars of the window; and seizing these, he raised his body by main force until his eyes commanded the interior of the room.

Two persons were within: the first he readily knew to be Dame Hatch; the second, a tall and beautiful and grave young lady, in a long, embroidered dress—could that be Joanna Sedley? his old wood-companion, Jack, whom he had thought to punish with a belt?

He dropped back again to the top round of the ladder in a kind of amazement. He had never thought of his sweetheart as of so superior a being, and he was instantly taken with a feeling of diffidence. But he had little opportunity for thought. A low 'Hist!' sounded from close by, and he hastened to descend the ladder.

'Who goes?' he whispered.

'Greensheve,' came the reply, in tones similarly guarded.

'What want ye?' asked Dick.

'The house is watched, Master Shelton,' returned the outlaw. 'We are not alone to watch it; for even as I lay on my belly on the wall I saw men prowling in the dark, and heard them whistle softly one to the other.'

'By my sooth,' said Dick, 'but this is passing strange! Were they not men of Sir Daniel's?'

'Nay, sir, that they were not,' returned Greensheve, 'for if I have eyes in my head, every man-Jack of them weareth me a white badge in his bonnet, something chequered with dark.'

'White, chequered with dark?' repeated Dick. 'Faith, 'tis a badge I know not. It is none of this country's badges. Well, an that be so, let us slip as quietly forth from this garden as we may; for here we are in an evil posture for defence. Beyond all question there are men of Sir Daniel's in that house, and to be taken between two shots is a beggarman's position. Take me this ladder; I must leave it where I found it.'

They returned the ladder to the stable, and groped their way to the place where they had entered.

Capper had taken Greensheve's position on the cope, and now he leaned down his hand, and, first one and then the other, pulled them up.

Cautiously and silently they dropped again upon the other side; nor did they dare to speak until they had returned to their old ambush in the gorse.

'Now, John Capper,' said Dick, 'back with you to Shoreby, even as for your life. Bring me instantly what men ye can collect. Here shall be the rendezvous; or if the men be scattered and the day be near at hand before they muster, let the place be something farther back, and by the entering in of the town. Greensheve and I lie here to watch. Speed ye, John Capper, and the saints aid you to despatch! And now, Greensheve,' he continued, as soon as Capper had departed, 'let thou and I go round about the garden in a wide circuit. I would fain see whether thine eyes betrayed thee.'

Keeping well outwards from the wall, and profiting by every height and hollow, they passed about two sides, beholding nothing. On the third side the garden wall was built close upon the beach, and to preserve the distance necessary to their purpose, they had to go some way down upon the sands. Although the tide was still pretty far out, the surf was so high, and the sands so flat, that at each breaker a great sheet of froth and water came careering over the expanse, and Dick and Greensheve made this part of their inspection' wading, now to the ankles, and now as deep as to the knees, in the salt and icy waters of the German Ocean.

Suddenly, against the comparative whiteness of the garden wall, the figure of a man was seen, like a faint Chinese shadow, violently signalling with both arms. As he dropped again to the earth, another arose a little farther on and repeated the same performance. And so, like a silent watchword, these gesticulations made the round of the beleaguered garden.

'They keep good watch,' Dick whispered.

'Let us back to land, good master,' answered Greensheve. 'We stand here too open; for, look ye, when the seas break heavy and white out there behind us, they shall see us plainly against the foam.'

'Ye speak sooth,' returned Dick. 'Ashore with us, right speedily.'

14

A skirmish in the dark

THOROUGHLY drenched and chilled, the two adventurers returned to their position in the gorse.

'I pray Heaven that Capper make good speed!' said Dick. 'I vow a candle to St. Mary of Shoreby if he come before the hour!'

'Y' are in a hurry, Master Dick?' asked Greensheve.

'Ay, good fellow,' answered Dick; 'for in that house lieth my lady, whom I love, and who should these be that lie about her secretly by night? Unfriends for sure!'

'Well,' returned Greensheve, 'an John come speedily, we shall give a good account of them. They are not two score at the outside—I judge so by the spacing of their sentries—and, taken where they are, lying so widely, one score would scatter them like sparrows. And yet, Master Dick, an she be in Sir Daniel's power already, it will little hurt that she should change into another's. Who should these be?'

'I do suspect the Lord of Shoreby,' Dick replied. 'When came they?'

'They began to come, Master Dick,' said Greensheve, 'about the time ye crossed the wall. I had not lain there the space of a minute ere I marked the first of the knaves crawling round the corner.'

The last light had been already extinguished in the little house when they were wading in the wash of the breakers, and it was impossible to predict at what moment the lurking men about the garden wall might make their onslaught. Of two evils, Dick preferred the least. He preferred that Joanna should remain under the guardianship of Sir Daniel rather than pass into the clutches of Lord Shoreby; and his mind was made up, if the house should be assaulted, to come at once to the relief of the besieged.

But the time passed, and still there was no movement. From quarter of an hour to quarter of an hour the same signal passed about the garden wall, as if the leader desired to assure himself of the vigilance of his scattered followers; but in every other particular the neighbourhood of the little house lay undisturbed.

Presently Dick's reinforcements began to arrive. The night was not yet old before nearly a score of men crouched beside him in the gorse.

Separating these into two bodies, he took the command of the smaller himself, and entrusted the larger to the leadership of Greensheve.

'Now, Kit,' said he to this last, 'take me your men to the near angle of the garden wall upon the beach. Post them strongly, and wait till that ye hear me falling on upon the other side. It is those upon the sea-front that I would fain make certain of, for there will be the leader. The rest will run; even let them. And now lads, let no man draw an arrow; ye will but hurt friends. Take to the steel, and keep to the steel; and if we have the uppermost, I promise every man of you a gold noble when I come to mine estate.'

Out of the odd collection of broken men, thieves, murderers, and ruined peasantry whom Duckworth had gathered together to serve the purposes of his revenge, some of the boldest and most experienced in war had volunteered to follow Richard Shelton. The service of watching Sir Daniel's movements in the town of Shoreby had from the first been irksome to their temper, and they had of late began to grumble loudly and threaten to disperse. The prospect of a sharp encounter and possible spoils restored them to good humour, and they joyfully prepared for battle.

Their long tabards thrown aside, they appeared, some in plain green jerkins, and some in stout leathern jacks; under their hoods many wore bonnets strengthened by iron plates; and for offensive armour, swords, daggers, a few stout boar-spears, and a dozen of bright bills, put them in a posture to engage even regular feudal troops. The bows, quivers, and tabards were concealed among the gorse, and the two bands set resolutely forward.

Dick, when he had reached the other side of the house, posted his six men in a line, about twenty yards from the garden wall, and took position himself a few paces in front. Then they all shouted with one voice, and closed upon the enemy.

These, lying widely scattered, stiff with cold, and taken unawares, sprang stupidly to their feet, and stood undecided. Before they had time to get their courage about them, or even to form an idea of the number and mettle of their assailants, a similar shout of onslaught sounded in their ears from the far side of the enclosure. Thereupon they gave themselves up for lost and ran.

In this way the two small troops of the men of the Black Arrow closed upon the sea-front of the garden wall, and took a part of the strangers, as it were, between two fires; while the whole of the remainder ran for their lives in different directions, and were soon scattered in the darkness.

For all that the fight was but beginning. Dick's outlaws, although they had the advantage of the surprise, were still considerably outnumbered by the men they had surrounded. The tide had flowed in the meanwhile; the beach was narrowed to a strip; and on this wet field, between the surf and the garden wall, there began, in the darkness, a doubtful, furious, and deadly contest.

The strangers were well armed; they fell in silence upon their assailants; and the affray became a series of single combats. Dick, who had come first into the mellay, was engaged by three; the first he cut down at the first blow, but the other two coming upon him hotly he was fain to give ground before their onset. One of these two was a huge fellow, almost a giant for stature, and armed with a two-handed sword, which he brandished like a switch. Against this opponent, with his reach of arm and the length and weight of his weapon, Dick and his bill were quite defenceless; and had the other continued to join vigorously in the attack, the lad must have indubitably fallen. This second man, however, less in stature and slower in his movements, paused for a moment to peer about him in the darkness, and to give ear to the sounds of the battle.

The giant still pursued his advantage, and still Dick fled before him, spying for his chance. Then the huge blade flashed and descended, and the lad, leaping on one side and running in, slashed sideways and upwards with his bill. A roar of agony responded, and before the wounded man could raise his formidable weapon, Dick, twice repeating his blow, had brought him to the ground.

The next moment he was engaged upon more equal terms with his second pursuer. Here there was no great difference in size, and though the man, fighting with sword and dagger against a bill, and being wary and quick of fence, had a certain superiority of arms, Dick more than made it up by his greater agility on foot. Neither at first gained any obvious advantage; but the older man was still insensibly profiting by the ardour of the younger to lead him where he would; and presently Dick found that they had crossed the whole width of the beach, and were now fighting above the knees in the spume and bubble of the breakers. Here his own superior activity was rendered useless; he found himself more or less at the discretion of his foe; yet a little, and he had his back turned upon his own men, and saw that this adroit and skilful adversary was bent upon drawing him farther and farther away.

Dick ground his teeth. He determined to decide the combat instantly; and when the wash of the next wave had ebbed and left them dry, he rushed in, caught a blow upon his bill, and leaped right at the throat of his opponent. The man went down backwards, with Dick still upon the top of him; and the next wave, speedily succeeding the last, buried him below a rush of water.

While he was still submerged, Dick forced his dagger from his grasp, and rose to his feet victorious.

'Yield ye!' he said. 'I give you life.'

'I yield me,' said the other, getting to his knees. 'Ye fight, like a young man, ignorantly and foolhardily; but, by the array of the saints, ye fight bravely!'

Dick turned to the beach. The combat was still raging doubtfully in the night; over the hoarse roar of the breakers steel clanged upon steel, and cries of pain and the shout of battle resounded.

'Lead me to your captain, youth,' said the conquered knight. 'It is fit this butchery should cease.'

'Sir,' replied Dick, 'so far as these brave fellows have a captain, the poor gentleman who addresses you is he.'

'Call off your dogs, then, and I will bid my villains hold,' returned the other.

There was something noble both in the voice and manner of his late opponent, and Dick instantly dismissed all fears of treachery.

'Lay down your arms, men!' cried the stranger knight. 'I have yielded me, upon promise of life.'

The tone of the stranger was one of absolute command, and almost instantly the din and confusion of the mellay ceased.

'Lawless,' cried Dick, 'are ye safe?'

'Ay,' cried Lawless, 'safe and hearty.'

'Light me the lantern,' said Dick.

'Is not Sir Daniel here?' inquired the knight.

'Sir Daniel?' echoed Dick. 'Now, by the rood, I pray not. It would go ill with me if he were.'

'Ill with *you*, fair sir?' inquired the other. 'Nay, then, if ye be not of Sir Daniel's party, I profess I comprehend no longer. Wherefore, then, fell ye upon mine ambush? in what quarrel, my young and very fiery friend? to what earthly purpose? and, to make a clear end of questioning, to what good gentleman have I surrendered?'

But before Dick could answer, a voice spoke in the darkness from close by. Dick could see the speaker's black and white badge, and the respectful salute which he addressed to his superior.

'My lord,' said he, 'if these gentlemen be unfriends to Sir Daniel, it is a pity, indeed, we should have been at blows with them; but it were tenfold greater that either they or we should linger here. The watchers in the house—unless they be all dead or deaf—have heard our hammering this quarter-hour agone; instantly they have signalled to the town; and unless we be the livelier in our departure, we are like to be taken, both of us, by a fresh foe.'

'Hawksley is in the right,' added the lord. 'How please ye, sir? Whither shall we march?'

'Nay, my lord,' said Dick, 'go where you will for me. I do begin to suspect we have some ground of friendship, and if, indeed, I began our acquaintance somewhat ruggedly, I would not churlishly continue. Let us, then, separate, my lord, you laying your right hand in mine; and at the hour and place that ye shall name, let us encounter and agree.'

'Y' are too trustful, boy,' said the other; 'but this time your trust is not misplaced. I will meet you at the point of day at St. Bride's Cross. Come, lads, follow!'

The strangers disappeared from the scene with a rapidity that seemed suspicious; and, while the outlaws fell to the congenial task of rifling the dead bodies, Dick made once more the circuit of the garden wall to examine the front of the house. In a little upper loophole of the roof he beheld a light set; and as it would certainly be visible in town from the back windows of Sir Daniel's mansion, he doubted not that this was the signal feared by Hawksley, and that ere long the lances of the Knight of Tunstall would arrive upon the scene.

He put his ear to the ground, and it seemed to him as if he heard a jarring and hollow noise from townward. Back to the beach he went hurrying. But the work was already done; the last body was disarmed and stripped to the skin, and four fellows were already wading seaward to commit it to the mercies of the deep.

A few minutes later, when there debouched out of the nearest lanes of Shoreby some two score horsemen, hastily arrayed and moving at the gallop of their steeds, the neighbourhood of the house beside the sea was entirely silent and deserted.

Meanwhile, Dick and his men had returned to the alehouse of the Goat and Bagpipes to snatch some hours of sleep before the morning tryst.

15

St. Bride's Cross

St. Bride's Cross stood a little way back from Shoreby, on the skirts of Tunstall Forest. Two roads met: one, from Holywood across the forest; one, that road from Risingham down which we saw the wrecks of a Lancastrian army fleeing in disorder. Here the two joined issue, and went on together down the hill to Shoreby; and a little back from the point of junction, the summit of a little knoll was crowned by the ancient and weather-beaten cross.

Here, then, about seven in the morning, Dick arrived. It was as cold as ever; the earth was all gray and silver with the hoar-frost, and the day began to break in the east with many colours of purple and orange.

Dick set him down upon the lowest step of the cross, wrapped himself well in his tabard, and looked vigilantly upon all sides. He had not long to wait. Down the road from Holywood a gentleman in very rich and bright armour, and wearing over that a surcoat of the rarest furs, came pacing on a splendid charger. Twenty yards behind him followed a clump of lancers: but these halted as soon as they came in view of the trysting-place, while the gentleman in the fur surcoat continued to advance alone.

His visor was raised, and showed a countenance of great command and dignity, answerable to the richness of his attire and arms. And it was with some confusion of manner that Dick arose from the cross and stepped down the bank to meet his prisoner.

'I thank you, my lord, for your exactitude,' he said, louting very low. 'Will it please your lordship to set foot to earth?'

'Are ye here alone, young man?' inquired the other.

'I was not so simple,' answered Dick; 'and, to be plain with your lordship, the woods upon either hand of this cross lie full of mine honest fellows lying on their weapons.'

'Y' 'ave done wisely,' said the lord. 'It pleaseth me the rather, since last night ye fought foolhardily, and more like a savage Saracen lunatic than any Christian warrior. But it becomes not to me to complain that had the undermost.'

'Ye had the undermost indeed, my lord, since ye so fell,' returned Dick; 'but had the waves not holpen me, it was I that should have had the worst. Ye were pleased to make me yours with several dagger marks, which I still carry. And in fine, my lord, methinks I had all the danger, as well as all the profit, of that little blind-man's medley on the beach.'

'Y' are shrewd enough to make light of it, I see,' returned the stranger.

'Nay, my lord, not shrewd,' replied Dick, 'in that I shoot at no advantage to myself. But when, by the light of this new day, I see how stout a knight hath yielded, not to my arms alone, but to fortune, and the darkness, and the surf—and how easily the battle had gone otherwise, with a soldier so untried and rustic as myself—think it not strange, my lord, if I feel confounded with my victory.'

'Ye speak well,' said the stranger. 'Your name?'

'My name, an't like you, is Shelton,' answered Dick.

'Men call me the Lord Foxham,' added the other.

'Then, my lord, and under your good favour, ye are guardian to the sweetest maid in England,' replied Dick; 'and for your ransom, and the ransom of such as were taken with you on the beach, there will be no uncertainty of terms. I pray you, my lord, of your goodwill and charity, yield me the hand of my mistress, Joan Sedley; and take ye, upon the other part, your liberty, the liberty of these your followers, and (if ye will have it) my gratitude and service till I die.'

'But are ye not ward to Sir Daniel? Methought, if y' are Harry Shelton's son, that I had heard it so reported,' said Lord Foxham.

'Will it please you, my lord, to alight? I would fain tell you fully who I am, how situate, and why so bold in my demands. Beseech you, my lord, take place upon these steps, hear me to a full end, and judge me with allowance.'

And so saying, Dick lent a hand to Lord Foxham to dismount; led him up the knoll to the cross; installed him in the place where he had himself been sitting; and standing respectfully before his noble prisoner, related the story of his fortunes up to the events of the evening before.

Lord Foxham listened gravely, and, when Dick had done, 'Master Shelton,' he said, 'ye are a most fortunate-unfortunate young gentleman; but what fortune y' 'ave had, that ye have amply merited; and what unfortune, ye have noways deserved. Be of good cheer; for ye have made a friend who is devoid neither of power nor favour. For yourself, although it fits not for a person of your birth to herd with outlaws, I must own ye are both brave and honourable; very dangerous in battle, right courteous in peace; a youth of excellent disposition and brave bearing. For your estates, ye will never see them till the world shall change again; so long as Lancaster hath the strong hand, so long shall Sir Daniel enjoy them for his own. For my ward, it is another matter; I had promised her before to a gentleman, a kinsman of my house, one Hamley; the promise is old——'

'Ay, my lord, and now Sir Daniel hath promised her to my Lord Shoreby,' interrupted Dick. 'And his promise, for all it is but young, is still the likelier to be made good.'

''Tis the plain truth,' returned his lordship. 'And considering, moreover, that I am your prisoner, upon no better composition than my bare life, and over and above that, that the maiden is unhappily in other hands, I will so far consent. Aid me with your good fellows——'

'My lord,' cried Dick, 'they are these same outlaws that ye blame me for consorting with.'

'Let them be what they will, they can fight,' returned Lord Foxham. 'Help me, then; and if between us we regain the maid, upon my knightly honour, she shall marry you!'

Dick bent his knee before his prisoner; but he, leaping up lightly from the cross, caught the lad up and embraced him like a son.

'Come,' he said, 'an y' are to marry Joan, we must be early friends.'

16

The 'Good Hope'

An hour thereafter, Dick was back at the Goat and Bagpipes, breaking his fast, and receiving the report of his messengers and sentries. Duckworth was still absent from

Shoreby; and this was frequently the case, for he played many parts in the world, shared many different interests, and conducted many various affairs. He had founded that fellowship of the Black Arrow, as a ruined man longing for vengeance and money; and yet among those who knew him best, he was thought to be the agent and emissary of the great King-maker of England, Richard, Earl of Warwick.

In his absence, at any rate, it fell upon Richard Shelton to command affairs in Shoreby; and, as he sat at meat, his mind was full of care, and his face heavy with consideration. It had been determined, between him and the Lord Foxham, to make one bold stroke that evening, and, by brute force, to set Joanna free. The obstacles, however, were many; and as one after another of his scouts arrived, each brought him more discomfortable news.

Sir Daniel was alarmed by the skirmish of the night before. He had increased the garrison of the house in the garden; but not content with that, he had stationed horsemen in all the neighbouring lanes, so that he might have instant word of any movement. Meanwhile, in the court of his mansion, steeds stood saddled, and the riders, armed at every point, awaited but the signal to ride.

The adventure of the night appeared more and more difficult of execution, till suddenly Dick's countenance lightened.

'Lawless!' he cried, 'you that were a shipman, can ye steal me a ship?'

'Master Dick,' replied Lawless, 'if ye would back me, I would agree to steal York Minster.'

Presently after, these two set forth and descended to the harbour. It was a considerable basin, lying among sand-hills, and surrounded with patches of down, ancient ruinous lumber, and tumble-down slums of the town. Many decked ships and many open boats either lay there at anchor, or had been drawn up on the beach. A long duration of bad weather had driven them from the high seas into the shelter of the port; and the great trooping of black clouds, and the cold squalls that followed one another, now with a sprinkling of dry snow, now in a mere swoop of wind, promised no improvement, but rather threatened a more serious storm in the immediate future.

The seamen, in view of the cold and the wind, had, for the most part, slunk ashore, and were now roaring and singing in the shoreside taverns. Many of the ships already rode unguarded at their anchors; and as the day wore on, and the weather offered no appearance of improvement, the number was continually being augmented. It was to these deserted ships, and, above all, to those of them that lay far out, that Lawless directed his attention; while Dick, seated upon an anchor that was half embedded in the sand, and giving ear, now to the rude, potent, and boding voices of the gale, and now to the hoarse singing of the shipmen in a neighbouring tavern, soon forgot his immediate surroundings and concerns in the agreeable recollection of Lord Foxham's promise.

He was disturbed by a touch upon his shoulder. It was Lawless, pointing to a small ship that lay somewhat by itself, and within but a little of the harbour mouth, where it heaved regularly and smoothly on the entering swell. A pale gleam of winter sunshine fell at that moment on the vessel's deck, relieving her against a bank of scowling cloud; and in this momentary glitter Dick could see a couple of men hauling the skiff alongside.

'There, sir,' said Lawless, 'mark ye it well! There is the ship for to-night.'

Presently the skiff put out from the vessel's side, and the two men, keeping her head well to the wind, pulled lustily for shore. Lawless turned to a loiterer.

'How call ye her?' he asked, pointing to the little vessel.

'They call her the *Good Hope*, of Dartmouth,' replied the loiterer. 'Her captain, Arblaster by name. He pulleth the bow oar in yon skiff.'

This was all that Lawless wanted. Hurriedly thanking the man, he moved round the shore to a certain sandy creek, for which the skiff was heading. There he took up his position, and as soon as they were within earshot, opened fire on the sailors of the *Good Hope*.

'What! Gossip Arblaster!' he cried. 'Why, ye be well met; nay, gossip, ye be right well met, upon the rood! And is that the *Good Hope*? Ay, I would know her among ten thousand!—a sweet shear, a sweet boat! But marry come up, my gossip, will ye drink? I have come into mine estate, which doubtless ye remember to have heard on. I am now rich; I have left to sail upon the sea; I do sail now, for the most part, upon spiced ale. Come, fellow, thy hand upon't! Come, drink with an old shipfellow!'

Skipper Arblaster, a long-faced, elderly, weather-beaten man, with a knife hanging about his neck by a plaited cord, and for all the world like any modern seaman in his gait and bearing, had hung back in obvious amazement and distrust. But the name of an estate, and a certain air of tipsified simplicity and good-fellowship which Lawless very well affected, combined to conquer his suspicious jealousy; his countenance relaxed, and he at once extended his open hand and squeezed that of the outlaw in a formidable grasp.

'Nay,' he said, 'I cannot mind you. But what o' that? I would drink with any man gossip, and so would my man Tom. Man Tom,' he added, addressing his follower, 'here is my gossip, whose name I cannot mind, but no doubt a very good seaman. Let's go drink with him and his shore friend.'

Lawless led the way, and they were soon seated in an alehouse, which, as it was very new, and stood in an exposed and solitary station, was less crowded than those nearer to the centre of the port. It was but a shed of timber, much like a block-house in the backwoods of to-day, and was coarsely furnished with a press or two, a number of naked benches, and boards set upon barrels to play the part of tables. In the middle, and besieged by half a hundred violent draughts, a fire of wreck-wood blazed and vomited thick smoke.

'Ay, now,' said Lawless, 'here is a shipman's joy—a good fire and a good stiff cup ashore, with foul weather without and an off-sea gale a-snoring in the roof! Here's to the *Good Hope*! May she ride easy!'

'Ay,' said Skipper Arblaster, ''tis good weather to be ashore in, that is sooth. Man Tom, how say ye to that? Gossip, ye speak well, though I can never think upon your name; but ye speak very well. May the *Good Hope* ride easy! Amen.'

'Friend Dickon,' resumed Lawless, addressing his commander, 'ye have certain matters on hand, unless I err? Well, prithee be about them incontinently. For here I be with the choice of all good company, two tough old shipmen; and till that ye return I will go warrant these brave fellows will bide here and drink me cup for cup. We are not like shoremen, we old, tough tarry-Johns!'

'It is well meant,' returned the skipper. 'Ye can go, boy; for I will keep your good friend and my good gossip company till curfew—ay, and by St. Mary, till the sun get up again! For look ye, when a man hath been long enough at sea, the salt getteth me into the clay upon his bones; and let him drink a draw-well, he will never be quenched.'

Thus encouraged upon all hands, Dick rose, saluted his company, and going forth again into the gusty afternoon, got him as speedily as he might to the Goat and Bagpipes. Thence he sent word to my Lord Foxham that, so soon as ever the evening closed, they would have a stout boat to keep the sea in. And then leading along with him a couple of outlaws who had some experience of the sea, he returned himself to the harbour and the little sandy creek.

The skiff of the *Good Hope* lay among many others, from which it was easily distinguished by its extreme smallness and fragility. Indeed, when Dick and his two men had taken their places, and begun to put forth out of the creek into the open harbour, the little cockle dipped into the swell and staggered under every gust of wind, like a thing upon the point of sinking.

The *Good Hope*, as we have said, was anchored far out, where the swell was heaviest. No other vessel lay nearer than several cables' length; those that were the nearest were themselves entirely deserted; and as the skiff approached, a thick flurry of snow and a sudden darkening of the weather further concealed the movements of the outlaws from all possible espial. In a trice they had leaped upon the heaving deck, and the skiff was dancing at the stern. The *Good Hope* was captured.

She was a good stout boat, decked in the bows and amidships, but open in the stern. She carried one mast, and was rigged between a felucca and a lugger. It would seem that Skipper Arblaster had made an excellent venture, for the hold was full of pieces of French wine; and in the little cabin, besides the Virgin Mary in the bulkhead which proved the captain's piety, there were many lockfast chests and cupboards, which showed him to be rich and careful.

A dog, who was the sole occupant of the vessel, furiously barked and bit the heels of the boarders; but he was soon kicked into the cabin, and the door shut upon his just resentment. A lamp was lit and fixed in the shrouds to mark the vessel clearly from the shore; one of the wine-pieces in the hold was broached, and a cup of excellent Gascony emptied to the adventure of the evening; and then, while one of the outlaws began to get ready his bow and arrows and prepare to hold the ship against all comers, the other hauled in the skiff and got overboard, where he held on, waiting for Dick.

'Well, Jack, keep a good watch,' said the young commander, preparing to follow his subordinate. 'Ye will do right well.'

'Why,' returned Jack, 'I shall do excellent well indeed, so long as we lie here; but once we put the nose of this poor ship outside the harbour——See, there she trembles! Nay, the poor shrew heard the words, and the heart misgave her in her oak-tree ribs. But look, Master Dick! how black the weather gathers!'

The darkness ahead was, indeed, astonishing. Great billows heaved up out of the blackness, one after another; and one after another the *Good Hope* buoyantly climbed, and giddily plunged upon the farther side. A thin sprinkle of snow and thin flakes of foam came flying and powdered the deck; and the wind harped dismally among the rigging.

'In sooth, it looketh evilly,' said Dick. 'But what cheer! 'Tis but a squall, and presently it will blow over.' But, in spite of his words, he was depressingly affected by the bleak disorder of the sky and the wailing and fluting of the wind; and as he got over the side of the *Good Hope* and made once more for the landing-creek with the best speed of oars, he crossed himself devoutly, and recommended to Heaven the lives of all who should adventure on the sea.

At the landing-creek there had already gathered about a dozen of the outlaws. To these the skiff was left, and they were bidden embark without delay.

A little farther up the beach Dick found Lord Foxham hurrying in quest of him, his face concealed with a dark hood, and his bright armour covered by a long russet mantle of a poor appearance.

'Young Shelton,' he said, 'are ye for sea, then, truly?'

'My lord,' replied Richard, 'they lie about the house with horsemen; it may not be reached from the land side without alarum; and, Sir Daniel once advertised of our adventure, we can no more carry it to a good end than, saving your presence, we could ride upon the wind. Now, in going round by sea, we do run some peril by the elements; but, what much outweighteth all, we have a chance to make good our purpose and bear off the maid.'

'Well,' returned Lord Foxham, 'lead on. I will, in some sort, follow you for shame's sake; but I own I would I were in bed.'

'Here, then,' said Dick. 'Hither we go to fetch our pilot.'

And he led the way to the rude alehouse where he had given rendezvous to a portion of his men. Some of these he found lingering round the door outside; others had pushed more boldly in, and, choosing place as near as possible to where they saw their comrade, gathered close about Lawless and the two shipmen. These, to judge by the distempered countenance and cloudy eye, had long since gone beyond the boundaries of moderation; and as Richard entered, closely followed by Lord Foxham, they were all three tuning up an old, pitiful sea-ditty, to the chorus of the wailing of the gale.

The young leader cast a rapid glance about the shed. The fire had just been replenished, and gave forth volumes of black smoke, so that it was difficult to see clearly in the farther corners. It was plain, however, that the outlaws very largely outnumbered the remainder of the guests. Satisfied upon this point, in case of any failure in the operation of his plan, Dick strode up to the table and resumed his place upon the bench.

'Hey?' cried the skipper tipsily, 'who are ye, hey?'

'I want a word with you without, Master Arblaster,' returned Dick; 'and here is what we shall talk of.' And he showed him a gold noble in the glimmer of the firelight.

The shipman's eyes burned, although he still failed to recognise our hero.

'Ay, boy,' he said, 'I am with you. Gossip, I will be back anon. Drink fair, gossip'; and, taking Dick's arm to steady his uneven steps, he walked to the door of the alehouse.

As soon as he was over the threshold, ten strong arms had seized and bound him; and in two minutes more, with his limbs trussed one to another, and a good gag in his mouth, he had been tumbled neck and crop into a neighbouring hay-barn. Presently, his man Tom, similarly secured, was tossed beside him, and the pair were left to their uncouth reflections for the night.

And now, as the time for concealment had gone by, Lord Foxham's followers were summoned by a preconcerted signal, and the party, boldly taking possession of as many boats as their numbers required, pulled in a flotilla for the light in the rigging of the ship. Long before the last man had climbed to the deck of the *Good Hope*, the sound of furious shouting from the shore showed that a part, at least, of the seamen had discovered the loss of their skiffs.

But it was now too late, whether for recovery or revenge. Out of some forty fighting men now mustered in the stolen ship, eight had been to sea, and could play the part of mariners. With the aid of these, a slice of sail was got upon her. The cable was cut. Lawless, vacillating on his feet, and still shouting the chorus of sea-ballads, took the long tiller in his hands; and the *Good Hope* began to flit forward into the darkness of the night, and to face the great waves beyond the harbour-bar.

Richard took his place beside the weather rigging. Except for the ship's own lantern, and for some lights in Shoreby town, that were already fading to leeward, the whole world of air was as black as in a pit. Only from time to time, as the *Good Hope* swooped dizzily down into the valley of the rollers, a crest would break—a great cataract of snowy foam would leap in one instant into being—and, in an instant more, would stream into the wake and vanish.

Many of the men lay holding on and praying aloud; many more were sick, and had crept into the bottom, where they sprawled among the cargo. And what with the extreme violence of the motion, and the continued drunken bravado of Lawless, still shouting and singing at the helm, the stoutest heart on board may have nourished a shrewd misgiving as to the result.

But Lawless, as if guided by an instinct, steered the ship across the breakers, struck the lee of a great sandbank, where they sailed for a while in smooth water, and presently after laid her alongside a rude, stone pier, where she was hastily made fast, and lay ducking and grinding in the dark.

17

The 'Good Hope' (continued)

THE pier was not far distant from the house in which Joanna lay; it now only remained to get the men on shore, to surround the house with a strong party, burst in the door, and carry off the captive. They might then regard themselves as done with the *Good Hope*; it had placed them on the rear of their enemies; and the retreat, whether they should succeed or fail in the main enterprise, would be directed with a greater measure of hope in the direction of the forest and my Lord Foxham's reserve.

To get the men on shore, however, was no easy task; many had been sick, all were pierced with cold; the promiscuity and disorder on board had shaken their discipline; the movement of the ship and the darkness of the night had cowed their spirits. They made a rush upon the pier; my lord, with his sword drawn on his own retainers, must throw himself in front; and this impulse of rabblement was not restrained without a certain clamour of voices, highly to be regretted in the case.

When some degree of order had been restored, Dick, with a few chosen men, set forth in advance. The darkness on shore, by contrast with the flashing of the surf, appeared before him like a solid body; and the howling and whistling of the gale drowned any lesser noise.

He had scarce reached the end of the pier, however, when there fell a lull of the wind; and in this he seemed to hear on shore the hollow footing of horses and the clash of arms. Checking his immediate followers, he passed forward a step or two alone, even setting foot upon the down; and here he made sure he could detect the shape of men and horses moving. A strong discouragement assailed him. If their enemies were really on the watch, if they had beleaguered the shoreward end of the pier, he and Lord Foxham were taken in a posture of very poor defence—the sea behind, the men jostled in the dark upon a narrow causeway. He gave a cautious whistle, the signal previously agreed upon.

It proved to be a signal for more than he desired. Instantly there fell, through the black night, a shower of arrows sent at a venture; and so close were the men huddled on the pier that more than one was hit, and the arrows were answered with cries of both fear and pain. In this first discharge, Lord Foxham was struck down; Hawksley had him carried on board again at once; and his men, during the brief remainder of the skirmish, fought (when they fought at all) without guidance. That was, perhaps, the chief cause of the disaster which made haste to follow.

At the shore end of the pier, for perhaps a minute, Dick held his own with a handful; one or two were wounded upon either side; steel crossed steel; nor had there been the least signal of advantage, when, in the twinkling of an eye, the tide turned against the party from the ship. Some one cried out that all was lost; the men were in the very humour to lend an ear to a discomfortable counsel; the cry was taken up. 'On board, lads, for your lives!' cried another. A third, with the true instinct of the coward, raised that inevitable report on all retreats: 'We are betrayed!' And in a moment the whole mass of men went surging and jostling backward down the pier, turning their defenceless backs on their pursuers and piercing the night with craven outcry.

One coward thrust off the ship's stern, while another still held her by the bows. The fugitives leaped, screaming, and were hauled on board, or fell back and perished in the sea. Some were cut down upon the pier by the pursuers. Many were injured on the ship's deck in the blind haste and terror of the moment, one man leaping upon another, and a third on both. At last, and whether by design or accident, the bows of the *Good Hope* were liberated; and ever-ready Lawless, who had maintained his place at the helm through all the hurly-burly by sheer strength of body and a liberal use of the cold steel, instantly clapped her on the proper tack. The ship began to move once more forward on the stormy sea, its scuppers running blood, its deck heaped with fallen men, sprawling and struggling in the dark.

Thereupon, Lawless sheathed his dagger, and turning to his next neighbour, 'I have left my mark on them, gossip,' said he, 'the yelping, coward hounds.'

Now, while they were all leaping and struggling for their lives, the men had not appeared to observe the rough shoves and cutting stabs with which Lawless had held his post in the confusion. But perhaps they had already begun to understand somewhat more clearly, or perhaps another ear had overheard the helmsman's speech.

Panic-stricken troops recover slowly, and men who have just disgraced themselves by cowardice, as if to wipe out the memory of their fault, will sometimes run straight into the opposite extreme of insubordination. So it was now; and the same men who had thrown away their weapons and been hauled, feet foremost, into the *Good Hope*, began to cry out upon their leaders, and demand that some one should be punished.

This growing ill-feeling turned upon Lawless.

In order to get a proper offing, the old outlaw had put the head of the *Good Hope* to seaward.

'What!' bawled one of the grumblers, 'he carrieth us to seaward!'

''Tis sooth,' cried another. 'Nay, we are betrayed for sure.'

And they all began to cry out in chorus that they were betrayed, and in shrill tones and with abominable oaths bade Lawless go about-ship and bring them speedily ashore. Lawless, grinding his teeth, continued in silence to steer the true course, guiding the *Good Hope* among the formidable billows. To their empty terrors, as to their dishonourable threats, between drink and dignity he scorned to make reply. The malcontents drew together a little abaft the mast, and it was plain they were like barnyard cocks, 'crowing for courage.' Presently they would be fit for any extremity of injustice or ingratitude. Dick began to mount by the ladder, eager to interpose; but one of the outlaws, who was also something of a seaman, got beforehand.

'Lads,' he began, 'y' are right wooden heads, I think. For to get back, by the mass, we must have an offing, must we not? And this old Lawless——'

Some one struck the speaker on the mouth, and the next moment, as a fire springs among dry straw, he was felled upon the deck, trampled under the feet, and despatched by the daggers of his cowardly companions. At this the wrath of Lawless rose and broke.

'Steer yourselves,' he bellowed, with a curse; and, careless of the result, he left the helm.

The *Good Hope* was, at that moment, trembling on the summit of a swell. She subsided, with sickening velocity, upon the farther side. A wave, like a great black bulwark, hove immediately in front of her; and, with a staggering blow, she plunged head-foremost through that liquid hill. The green water passed right over her from stem to stern, as high as a man's knees: the sprays ran higher than the mast; and she rose again upon the other side, with an appalling, tremulous indecision, like a beast that has been deadly wounded.

Six or seven of the malcontents had been carried bodily

overboard; and as for the remainder, when they found their tongues again, it was to bellow to the saints and wail upon Lawless to come back and take the tiller.

Nor did Lawless wait to be twice bidden. The terrible result of his fling of just resentment sobered him completely. He knew, better than any one on board, how nearly the *Good Hope* had gone bodily down below their feet; and he could tell, by the laziness with which she met the sea, that the peril was by no means over.

Dick, who had been thrown down by the concussion and half drowned, rose wading to his knees in the swamped well of the stern, and crept to the old helmsman's side.

'Lawless,' he said, 'we do all depend on you; y' are a brave, steady man, indeed, and crafty in the management of ships; I shall put three sure men to watch upon your safety.'

'Bootless, my master, bootless,' said the steersman, peering forward through the dark. 'We come every moment somewhat clearer of these sandbanks; with every moment, then, the sea packeth upon us heavier, and for all these whimperers, they will presently be on their backs. For, my master, 'tis a right mystery, but true, there never yet was a bad man that was a good shipman. None but the honest and the bold can endure me this tossing of a ship.'

'Nay, Lawless,' said Dick, laughing, 'that is a right shipman's byword, and hath no more of sense than the whistle of the wind. But, prithee, how go we? Do we lie well? Are we in good case?'

'Master Shelton,' replied Lawless, 'I have been a Grey Friar—I praise fortune—an archer, a thief, and a shipman. Of all these coats, I had the best fancy to die in the Grey Friar's, as ye may readily conceive, and the least fancy to die in John Shipman's tarry jacket; and that for two excellent good reasons: first, that the death might take a man suddenly; and second, for the horror of that great salt smother and welter under my foot here'—and Lawless stamped with his foot. 'Howbeit,' he went on, 'an I die not a sailor's death, and that this night, I shall owe a tall candle to our Lady.'

'Is it so?' asked Dick.

'It is right so,' replied the outlaw. 'Do ye not feel how heavy and dull she moves upon the waves? Do ye not hear the water washing in her hold? She will scarce mind the rudder even now. Bide till she has settled a bit lower; and she will either go down below your boots like a stone image, or drive ashore here, under our lee, and come all to pieces like a twist of string.'

'Ye speak with a good courage,' returned Dick. 'Ye are not then appalled?'

'Why, master,' answered Lawless, 'if ever a man had an ill crew to come to port with, it is I—a renegade friar, a thief, and all the rest on't. Well, ye may wonder, but I keep a good hope in my wallet; and if that I be to drown, I will drown with a bright eye, Master Shelton, and a steady hand.'

Dick returned no answer, but he was surprised to find the old vagabond of so resolute a temper, and fearing some fresh violence or treachery, set forth upon his quest for three sure men. The great bulk of the men had now deserted the deck, which was continually wetted with the flying sprays, and where they lay exposed to the shrewdness of the winter wind. They had gathered, instead, into the hold of the merchandise, among the butts of wine, and lighted by two swinging lanterns.

Here a few kept up the form of revelry, and toasted each other deep in Arblaster's Gascony wine. But as the *Good Hope* continued to tear through the smoking waves, and toss her stem and stern alternately high in air and deep into white foam, the number of these jolly companions diminished with every moment and with every lurch. Many sat apart, tending their hurts, but the majority were already prostrated with sickness and lay moaning in the bilge.

Greensheve, Cuckow, and a young fellow of Lord Foxham's whom Dick had already remarked for his intelligence and spirit, were still, however, both fit to understand and willing to obey. These Dick set as a bodyguard about the person of the steersman, and then, with a last look at the black sky and sea, he turned and went below into the cabin, whither Lord Foxham had been carried by his servants.

18

The 'Good Hope' (concluded)

THE moans of the wounded baron blended with the wailing of the ship's dog. The poor animal, whether he was merely sick at heart to be separated from his friends, or whether he indeed recognised some peril in the labouring of the ship, raised his cries, like minute-guns, above the roar of wave and weather; and the more superstitious of the men heard, in these sounds, the knell of the *Good Hope*.

Lord Foxham had been laid in a berth, upon a fur cloak. A little lamp burned dim before the Virgin in the bulk-head and by its glimmer Dick could see the pale countenance and hollow eyes of the hurt man.

'I am sore hurt,' said he. 'Come near to my side, young Shelton; let there be one by me who, at least, is gentle born; for after having lived nobly and richly all the days of my life, this is a sad pass that I should get my hurt in a little ferreting skirmish, and die here, in a foul, cold ship upon the sea, among broken men and churls.'

'Nay, my lord,' said Dick, 'I rather pray to the saints that ye will recover you of your hurt, and come soon and sound ashore.'

'How?' demanded his lordship. 'Come sound ashore? There is, then, a question of it?'

'The ship laboureth—the sea is grievous and contrary,' replied the lad; 'and by what I can learn of my fellow that steereth us, we shall do well, indeed, if we come dryshod to land.'

'Ha!' said the baron gloomily, 'thus shall every terror attend upon the passage of my soul! Sir, pray rather to live hard, that ye may die easy, than to be fooled and fluted all through life, as to the pipe and tabor, and, in the last hour, be plunged among misfortunes! Howbeit. I have that upon my mind that must not be delayed. We have no priest aboard?'

'None,' replied Dick.

'Here, then, to my secular interests,' resumed Lord Foxham; 'ye must be as good a friend to me dead, as I found you a gallant enemy when I was living. I fall in an evil hour for me, for England, and for them that trusted me. My men are being brought by Hamley—he that was your rival: they will rendezvous in the long room at Holywood; this ring from off my finger will accredit you to represent mine orders; and I shall write, besides, two words upon this paper, bidding Hamley yield to you the damsel. Will ye obey? I know not.'

'But, my lord, what orders?' inquired Dick.

'Ay,' quoth the baron, 'ay—the orders;' and he looked upon Dick with hesitation. 'Are ye Lancaster or York?' he asked, at length.

'I shame to say it,' answered Dick, 'I can scarce clearly answer. But so much I think is certain: since I serve with Ellis Duckworth, I serve the House of York. Well, if that be so, I declare for York.'

'It is well,' returned the other; 'it is exceeding well. For, truly, had ye said Lancaster, I wot not for the world what I had done. But sith ye are for York, follow me. I came hither but to watch these lords at Shoreby, while mine excellent young lord, Richard of Gloucester,[1] prepareth a sufficient force to fall upon and scatter them. I have made me notes of their strength, what watch they keep, and how they lie; and these I was to deliver to my young lord on Sunday, an hour before noon, at St. Bride's Cross beside the forest. This tryst I am not like to keep, but I pray you, of courtesy, to keep it in my stead; and see that not pleasure, nor pain, tempest, wound, nor pestilence withhold you from the hour and place, for the welfare of England lieth upon this cast.'

'I do soberly take this upon me,' said Dick. 'In so far as in me lieth, your purpose shall be done.'

'It is good,' said the wounded man. 'My lord Duke shall order you farther, and if ye obey him with spirit and good will, then is your fortune made. Give me the lamp a little nearer to mine eyes, till that I write these words for you.'

He wrote a note 'to his worshipful kinsman, Sir John Hamley'; and then a second, which he left without external superscription.

'This is for the Duke,' he said. 'The word is "England and Edward," and the counter, "England and York."'

'And Joanna, my lord?' asked Dick.

'Nay, ye must get Joanna how ye can,' replied the baron. 'I have named you for my choice in both these letters; but ye must get her for yourself, boy. I have tried, as ye see here before you, and have lost my life. More could no man do.'

By this time the wounded man began to be very weary; and Dick, putting the precious papers in his bosom, bade him be of good cheer, and left him to repose.

The day was beginning to break, cold and blue, with flying squalls of snow. Close under the lee of the *Good Hope*, the coast lay in alternate rocky headlands and sandy bays; and farther inland the wooded hill-tops of Tunstall showed along the sky. Both the wind and the sea had gone down; but the vessel wallowed deep, and scarce rose upon the waves.

Lawless was still fixed at the rudder; and by this time nearly all the men had crawled on deck, and were now gazing, with blank faces, upon the inhospitable coast.

'Are we going ashore?' asked Dick.

'Ay,' said Lawless, 'unless we get first to the bottom.'

And just then the ship rose so languidly to meet a sea, and the water weltered so loudly in her hold, that Dick involuntarily seized the steersman by the arm.

'By the mass!' cried Dick, as the bows of the *Good Hope*

1 At the date of this story, Richard Crookback could not have been created Duke of Gloucester; but for clearness, with the reader's leave, he shall so be called.

reappeared above the foam, 'I thought we had foundered, indeed; my heart was at my throat.'

In the waist, Greensheve, Hawksley, and the better men of both companies were busy breaking up the deck to build a raft; and to these Dick joined himself, working the harder to drown the memory of his predicament. But, even as he worked, every sea that struck the poor ship, and every one of her dull lurches, as she tumbled wallowing among the waves, recalled him with a horrid pang to the immediate proximity of death.

Presently, looking up from his work, he saw that they were close in below a promontory; a piece of ruinous cliff, against the base of which the sea broke white and heavy, almost over-plumbed the deck; and, above that again, a house appeared, crowning a down.

Inside the bay, the seas ran gaily, raised the *Good Hope* upon her foam-flecked shoulders, carried her beyond the control of the steersman, and in a moment dropped her with a great concussion on the sand, and began to break over her, half-mast high, and roll her to and fro. Another great wave followed, raised her again, and carried her yet farther in; and then a third succeeded, and left her far inshore of the more dangerous breakers, wedged upon a bank.

'Now, boys,' cried Lawless, 'the saints have had a care of us, indeed. The tide ebbs; let us but sit down and drink a cup of wine, and before half an hour ye may all march me ashore as safe as on a bridge.'

A barrel was broached, and, sitting in what shelter they could find from the flying snow and spray, the shipwrecked company handed the cup around, and sought to warm their bodies and restore their spirits.

Dick, meanwhile, returned to Lord Foxham, who lay in great perplexity and fear, the floor of his cabin washing knee-deep in water, and the lamp, which had been his only light, broken and extinguished by the violence of the blow.

'My lord,' said young Shelton, 'fear not at all; the saints are plainly for us; the seas have cast us high upon a shoal, and as soon as the tide hath somewhat ebbed, we may walk ashore upon our feet.'

It was nearly an hour before the vessel was sufficiently deserted by the ebbing sea, and they could set forth for the land, which appeared dimly before them through a veil of driving snow.

Upon a hillock on one side of their way a party of men lay huddled together, suspiciously observing the movements of the new arrivals.

'They might draw near and offer us some comfort,' Dick remarked.

'Well, an they come not to us, let us even turn aside to them,' said Hawksley. 'The sooner we come to a good fire and a dry bed, the better for my poor lord.'

But they had not moved far in the direction of the hillock before the men, with one consent, rose suddenly to their feet, and poured a flight of well-directed arrows on the shipwrecked company.

'Back! back!' cried his lordship. 'Beware, in Heaven's name, that ye reply not!'

'Nay,' cried Greensheve, pulling an arrow from his leather jack. 'We are in no posture to fight, it is certain, being drenching wet, dogweary, and three parts frozen; but, for the love of old England, what aileth them to shoot thus cruelly on their poor country people in distress?'

'They take us to be French pirates,' answered Lord Foxham. 'In these most troublesome and degenerate days we cannot keep our own shores of England; but our old enemies, whom we once chased on sea and land, do now range at pleasure, robbing and slaughtering and burning. It is the pity and reproach of this poor land.'

The men upon the hillock lay, closely observing them, while they trailed upward from the beach, and wound inland among desolate sand-hills; for a mile or so they even hung upon the rear of the march, ready, at a sign, to pour another volley on the weary and dispirited fugitives; and it was only when, striking at length upon a firm, high road, Dick began to call his men to some more martial order, that these jealous guardians of the coast of England silently disappeared among the snow. They had done what they desired; they had protected their own homes and farms, their own families and cattle; and their private interest being thus secured, it mattered not the weight of a straw to any of them, although the Frenchman should carry blood and fire to every other parish in the realm of England.

Book Four

THE DISGUISE

19

The Den

The place where Dick had struck the line of a high road was not far from Holywood, and within nine or ten miles of Shoreby-on-the-Till; and here, after making sure that they were pursued no longer, the two bodies separated. Lord Foxham's followers departed, carrying their wounded master towards the comfort and security of the great abbey; and Dick, as he saw them wind away and disappear in the thick curtain of the falling snow, was left alone with near upon a dozen outlaws, the last remainder of his troop of volunteers.

Some were wounded; one and all were furious at their ill-success and long exposure; and though they were now too cold and hungry to do more, they grumbled and cast sullen looks upon their leaders. Dick emptied his purse among them, leaving himself nothing; thanked them for the courage they had displayed, though he could have found it more readily in his heart to rate them for poltroonery; and having thus somewhat softened the effect of his prolonged misfortune, despatched them to find their way, either severally or in pairs, to Shoreby and the Goat and Bagpipes.

For his own part, influenced by what he had seen on board of the *Good Hope*, he chose Lawless to be his companion on the walk. The snow was falling, without pause or variation, in one even, blinding cloud; the wind had been strangled, and now blew no longer; and the whole world was blotted out and sheeted down below that silent inundation. There was great danger of wandering by the way and perishing in drifts; and Lawless, keeping half a step in front of his companion, and holding his head forward like a hunting dog upon the scent, inquired his way of every tree, and studied out their path as though he were conning a ship among dangers.

About a mile into the forest they came to a place where several ways met, under a grove of lofty and contorted oaks. Even in the narrow horizon of the falling snow, it was a spot that could not fail to be recognised; and Lawless evidently recognised it with particular delight.

'Now, Master Richard,' said he, 'an y' are not too proud to be the guest of a man who is neither a gentleman by birth nor so much as a good Christian, I can offer you a cup of wine and a good fire to melt the marrow in your frozen bones.'

'Lead on, Will,' answered Dick. 'A cup of wine and a good fire! Nay, I would go a far way round to see them.'

Lawless turned aside under the bare branches of the grove, and, walking resolutely forward for some time, came to a steepish hollow or den, that had now drifted a quarter full of snow. On the verge a great beech tree hung, precariously rooted; and here the old outlaw, pulling aside some bushy underwood, bodily disappeared into the earth.

The beech had, in some violent gale, been half uprooted, and had torn up a considerable stretch of turf; and it was under this that old Lawless had dug out his forest hiding-place. The roots served him for rafters, the turf was his thatch, for walls and floor he had his mother the earth. Rude as it was, the hearth in one corner, blackened by fire, and the presence in another of a large oaken chest well fortified with iron, showed it at one glance to be the den of a man, and not the burrow of a digging beast.

Though the snow had drifted at the mouth and sifted in upon the floor of this earth cavern, yet was the air much warmer than without; and when Lawless had struck a spark, and the dry furze bushes had begun to blaze and crackle on the hearth, the place assumed, even to the eye, an air of comfort and of home.

With a sigh of great contentment Lawless spread his broad hands before the fire, and seemed to breathe the smoke.

'Here, then,' he said, 'is this old Lawless's rabbit hole; pray Heaven there come no terrier! Far have I rolled hither and thither, and here and about, since that I was fourteen years of mine age and first ran away from mine abbey, with the sacrist's gold chain and a mass book that I sold for four marks. I have been in England and France and Burgundy, and in Spain too, on a pilgrimage for my poor soul; and upon the sea, which is no man's country. But here is my place, Master Shelton. This is my native land, this burrow in the earth. Come rain or wind—and whether it's April, and the birds all sing, and the blossoms fall about my bed, or whether it's winter, and I sit alone with my good gossip the fire, and robin redbreast twitters in the woods—here is my church and market, my wife and child. It's here I come back to, and it's here, so please the saints, that I would like to die.'

''Tis a warm corner, to be sure,' replied Dick, 'and a pleasant, and a well hid.'

'It had need to be,' returned Lawless, 'for an they found it,

Master Shelton, it would break my heart. But here,' he added, burrowing with his stout fingers in the sandy floor, 'here is my wine cellar, and ye shall have a flask of excellent strong stingo.'

Sure enough, after but a little digging, he produced a big leathern bottle of about a gallon, nearly three parts full of a very heady and sweet wine; and when they had drunk to each other comradely, and the fire had been replenished and blazed up again, the pair lay at full length, thawing and steaming, and divinely warm.

'Master Shelton,' observed the outlaw, 'y' 'ave had two mischances this last while, and y' are like to lose the maid—do I take it aright?'

'Aright,' returned Dick, nodding his head.

'Well, now,' continued Lawless, 'hear an old fool that hath been nigh-hand everything, and seen nigh-hand all. Ye go too much on other people's errands, Master Dick. Ye go on Ellis's; but he desireth rather the death of Sir Daniel. Ye go on Lord Foxham's; well—the saints preserve him!—doubtless he meaneth well. But go ye upon your own, good Dick. Come right to the maid's side. Court her, lest that she forget you. Be ready; and when the chance shall come, off with her at the saddlebow.'

'Ay, but, Lawless, beyond doubt she is now in Sir Daniel's own mansion,' answered Dick.

'Thither, then, go we,' replied the outlaw. Dick stared at him.

'Nay, I mean it,' nodded Lawless. 'And if y' are of so little faith, and stumble at a word, see here!'

And the outlaw, taking a key from about his neck, opened the oak chest, and dipping and groping deep among its contents, produced first a friar's robe, and next a girdle of rope; and then a huge rosary of wood, heavy enough to be counted as a weapon.

'Here,' he said, 'is for you. On with them!'

And then, when Dick had clothed himself in this clerical disguise, Lawless produced some colours and a pencil, and proceeded, with the greatest cunning, to disguise his face. The eyebrows he thickened and produced; to the moustache, which was yet hardly visible, he rendered a like service; while, by a few lines around his eye, he changed the expression and increased the apparent age of this young monk.

'Now,' he resumed, 'when I have done the like, we shall make as bonny a pair of friars as the eye could wish. Boldly to Sir Daniel's we shall go, and there be hospitably welcome for the love of Mother Church.'

'And how, dear Lawless,' cried the lad, 'shall I repay you?'

'Tut, brother,' replied the outlaw, 'I do naught but for my pleasure. Mind not for me. I am one, by the mass, that mindeth for himself. When that I lack, I have a long tongue and a voice like the monastery bell—I do ask, my son; and where asking faileth, I do most usually take.'

The old rogue made a humorous grimace; and although Dick was displeased to lie under so great favours to so equivocal a personage, he was yet unable to restrain his mirth.

With that, Lawless returned to the big chest, and was soon similarly disguised; but below his gown, Dick wondered to observe him conceal a sheaf of black arrows.

'Wherefore do ye that?' asked the lad. 'Wherefore arrows, when ye take no bow?'

'Nay,' replied Lawless lightly, ''tis like there will be heads broke—not to say backs—ere you and I win sound from where we're going to; and if any fall, I would our fellowship should come by the credit on't. A black arrow, Master Dick, is the seal of our abbey; it showeth you who writ the bill.'

'An ye prepare so carefully,' said Dick. 'I have here some papers that, for mine own sake, and the interest of those that trusted me, were better left behind than found upon my body. Where shall I conceal them, Will?'

'Nay,' replied Lawless, 'I will go forth into the wood and whistle me three verses of a song; meanwhile, do you bury them where ye please, and smooth the sand upon the place.'

'Never!' cried Richard. 'I trust you, man. I were base indeed if I not trusted you.'

'Brother, y' are but a child,' replied the old outlaw, pausing and turning his face upon Dick from the threshold of the den. 'I am a kind old Christian, and no traitor to men's blood, and no sparer of mine own in a friend's jeopardy. But fool, child, I am a thief by trade and birth and habit. If my bottle were empty and my mouth dry, I would rob you, dear child, as sure as I love, honour, and admire your parts and person! Can it be clearer spoken? No.'

And he stumped forth through the bushes with a snap of his big fingers.

Dick, thus left alone, after a wondering thought upon the inconsistencies of his companion's character, hastily produced, reviewed, and buried his papers. One only he reserved to carry along with him, since it in nowise compromised his friends, and yet might serve him, in a pinch, against Sir Daniel. That was the knight's own letter to Lord Wensleydale, sent by Throgmorton, on the morrow of the defeat at Risingham, and found next day by Dick upon the body of the messenger.

Then, treading down the embers of the fire, Dick left the den, and rejoined the old outlaw, who stood awaiting him under the leafless oaks, and was already beginning to be powdered by the falling snow. Each looked upon the other, and each laughed, so thorough and so droll was the disguise.

'Yet I would it were but summer and a clear day,' grumbled the outlaw, 'that I might see myself in the mirror of a pool. There be many of Sir Daniel's men that know me; and if we fell to be recognised, there might be two words for you, my brother, but as for me, in a paternoster while, I should be kicking in a rope's-end.'

Thus they set forth together along the road to Shoreby, which, in this part of its course, kept near the margin of a forest, coming forth from time to time in the open country, and passing beside poor folks' houses and small farms.

Presently, at sight of one of these, Lawless pulled up.

'Brother Martin,' he said in a voice capitally disguised, and suited to his monkish robe, 'let us enter and seek alms from these poor sinners. *Pax vobiscum!* Ay,' he added, in his own voice, ''tis as I feared; I have somewhat lost the whine of it; and by your leave, good Master Shelton, ye must suffer me to practise in these country places, before that I risk my fat neck by entering Sir Daniel's. But look ye a little, what an excellent thing it is to be a Jack-of-all-trades! An I had not been a shipman, ye had infallibly gone down in the *Good Hope*; an I had not been a thief, I could not have painted me your face! and but that I had been a Grey Friar, and sung loud in the choir, and ate hearty at the board, I could not have carried this disguise, but the very dogs would have spied us out and barked at us for shams.'

He was by this time close to the window of the farm, and he rose on his tiptoes and peeped in.

'Nay,' he cried, 'better and better. We shall here try our false faces with a vengeance, and have a merry jest on Brother Capper to boot.'

And so saying he opened the door and led the way into the house.

Three of their own company sat at the table, greedily eating. Their daggers, stuck beside them in the board, and the black and menacing looks which they continued to shower upon the people of the house, proved that they owed their entertainment rather to force than favour. On the two monks, who now, with a sort of humble dignity, entered the kitchen of the farm, they seemed to turn with a particular resentment; and one—it was John Capper in person—who seemed to play the leading part, instantly and rudely ordered them away.

'We want no beggars here!' he cried.

But another—although he was far from recognising Dick and Lawless—inclined to more moderate counsels.

'Not so,' he cried. 'We be strong men, and take: these be weak, and crave; but in the latter end these shall be uppermost and we below. Mind him not, my father; but come, drink of my cup, and give me a benediction.'

'Y' are men of a light mind, carnal and accursed,' said the monk. 'Now, may the saints forbid that ever I should drink with such companions! But here, for the pity I bear to sinners, here I do leave you a blessed relic, the which, for your soul's interest, I bid you kiss and cherish.'

So far Lawless thundered upon them like a preaching friar; but with these words he drew from under his robe a black arrow, tossed it on the board in front of the three startled outlaws, turned in the same instant, and, taking Dick along with him, was out of the room and out of sight among the falling snow before they had time to utter a word or move a finger.

'So,' he said, 'we have proved our false faces, Master Shelton. I will now adventure my poor carcase where ye please.'

'Good!' returned Richard. 'It irks me to be doing. Set we on for Shoreby!'

20

'*In mine enemies' house*'

Sir Daniel's residence in Shoreby was a tall, commodious, plastered mansion, framed in carven oak, and covered by a low-pitched roof of thatch. To the back there stretched a garden, full of fruit-trees, alleys, and thick arbours, and overlooked from the far end by the tower of the abbey church.

The house might contain, upon a pinch, the retinue of a greater person than Sir Daniel; but even now it was filled with hubbub. The court rang with arms and horse-shoe-iron; the kitchen roared with cookery like a bees'-hive; minstrels, and the players of instruments, and the cries of tumblers, sounded from the hall. Sir Daniel, in his profusion, in the gaiety and gallantry of his establishment, rivalled with Lord Shoreby, and eclipsed Lord Risingham.

All guests were made welcome. Minstrels, tumblers, players of chess, sellers of relics, medicines, perfumes and enchantments, and along with these every sort of priest, friar, or pilgrim, were made welcome to the lower table, and slept together in the ample lofts, or on the bare boards of the long dining-hall.

On the afternoon following the wreck of the *Good Hope*, the buttery, the kitchens, the stables, the covered cart-shed that surrounded two sides of the court, were all crowded by idle people, partly belonging to Sir Daniel's establishment, and attired in his livery of murrey and blue, partly nondescript strangers attracted to the town by greed, and received by the knight through policy, and because it was the fashion of the time.

The snow, which still fell without interruption, the extreme chill of the air, and the approach of night, combined to keep them under shelter. Wine, ale, and money were all plentiful; many sprawled gambling in the straw of the barn, many were still drunken from the noontide meal. To the eye of a modern it would have looked like the sack of a city; to the eye of a contemporary it was like any other rich and noble household at a festive season.

Two monks—a young and an old—had arrived late, and were now warming themselves at a bonfire in a corner of the shed. A mixed crowd surrounded them—jugglers, mountebanks, and soldiers; and with these the elder of the two had soon engaged so brisk a conversation, and exchanged so many loud guffaws and country witticisms, that the group momentarily increased in number.

The younger companion, in whom the reader has already recognised Dick Shelton, sat from the first somewhat backward, and gradually drew himself away. He listened, indeed, closely, but he opened not his mouth; and by the grave expression of his countenance, he made but little account of his companion's pleasantries.

At last his eye, which travelled continually to and fro, and kept a guard upon all the entrances of the house, lit upon a little procession entering by the main gate and crossing the court in an oblique direction. Two ladies, muffled in thick furs, led the way, and were followed by a pair of waiting-women and four stout men-at-arms. The next moment they had disappeared within the house; and Dick, slipping through the crowd of loiterers in the shed, was already giving hot pursuit.

'The taller of these twain was Lady Brackley,' he thought; 'and where Lady Brackley is, Joan will not be far.'

At the door of the house the four men-at-arms had ceased to follow, and the ladies were now mounting the stairway of polished oak, under no better escort than that of the two waiting women. Dick followed close behind. It was already the dusk of the day; and in the house the darkness of the night had almost come. On the stair-landings torches flared in iron holders; down the long tapestried corridors a lamp burned by every door. And where the door stood open, Dick could look in upon arras-covered walls, and rush-bescattered floors, glowing in the light of the wood-fires.

Two floors were passed, and at every landing the younger and shorter of the two ladies had looked back keenly at the monk. He, keeping his eyes lowered, and affecting the demure manners that suited his disguise, had but seen her once, and was unaware that he had attracted her attention. And now, on the third floor, the party separated, the younger lady continuing to ascend alone, the other, followed by the waiting-maids, descended the corridor to the right.

Dick mounted with a swift foot, and holding to the corner, thrust forth his head and followed the three women with his eyes. Without turning or looking behind them, they continued to descend the corridor.

'It is right well,' thought Dick. 'Let me but know my Lady Brackley's chamber, and it will go hard and I find not Dame Hatch upon an errand.'

And just then a hand was laid upon his shoulder, and, with a bound and a choked cry, he turned to grapple his assailant.

He was somewhat abashed to find, in the person whom he had so roughly seized, the short young lady in the furs. She, on her part, was shocked and terrified beyond expression, and hung trembling in his grasp.

'Madam,' said Dick, releasing her, 'I cry you a thousand pardons; but I have no eyes behind, and, by the mass, I could not tell ye were a maid.'

The girl continued to look at him, but, by this time, terror began to be succeeded by surprise, and surprise by suspicion. Dick, who could read these changes on her face, became, alarmed for his own safety in that hostile house.

'Fair maid,' he said, affecting easiness, 'suffer me to kiss your hand, in token ye forgive my roughness, and I will even go.'

'Y' are a strange monk, young sir,' returned the young lady, looking him both boldly and shrewdly in the face; 'and now that my first astonishment hath somewhat passed away, I can spy the layman in each word you utter. What do ye here? Why are ye thus sacrilegiously tricked out? Come ye in peace or war? And why spy ye after Lady Brackley like a thief?'

'Madam,' quoth Dick, 'of one thing I pray you to be very sure: I am no thief. And even if I come here in war, as in some degree I do, I make no war upon fair maids, and I hereby entreat them to copy me so far, and leave me be. For, indeed, fair mistress, cry out—if such be your pleasure—cry but once, and say what ye have seen, and the poor gentleman before you is merely a dead man. I cannot think ye would be cruel,' added Dick; and taking the girl's hand gently in both of his, he looked at her with courteous admiration.

'Are ye then a spy—a Yorkist?' asked the maid.

'Madam,' he replied, 'I am indeed a Yorkist, and in some sort, a spy. But that which bringeth me into this house, the same which will win for me the pity and interest of your kind heart, is neither of York nor Lancaster. I will wholly put my life in your discretion. I am a lover, and my name——'

But here the young lady clapped her hand suddenly upon Dick's mouth, looked hastily up and down and east and west, and, seeing the coast clear, began to drag the young man, with great strength and vehemence, upstairs.

'Hush!' she said, 'and come. 'Shalt talk hereafter.'

Somewhat bewildered, Dick suffered himself to be pulled upstairs, bustled along a corridor, and thrust suddenly into a chamber, lit, like so many of the others, by a blazing log upon the hearth.

'Now,' said the young lady, forcing him down upon a stool, 'sit ye there and attend my sovereign good pleasure. I have life and death over you, and I will not scruple to abuse my power. Look to yourself; y' 'ave cruelly mauled my arm. He knew not I was a maid, quoth he! Had he known I was a maid, he had ta'en his belt to me, forsooth!'

And with these words she whipped out of the room, and left Dick gaping with wonder, and not very sure if he were dreaming or awake.

'Ta'en my belt to her!' he repeated. 'Ta'en my belt to her!' And the recollection of that evening in the forest flowed back upon his mind, and he once more saw Matcham's wincing body and beseeching eyes.

And then he was recalled to the dangers of the present. In the next room he heard a stir, as of a person moving; then followed a sigh, which sounded strangely near; and then the rustle of skirts and tap of feet once more began. As he stood hearkening, he saw the arras wave along the hall; there was the sound of a door being opened, the hangings divided, and, lamp in hand, Joanna Sedley entered the apartment.

She was attired in costly stuffs of deep and warm colours, such as befit the winter and the snow. Upon her head, her hair had been gathered together and became her as a crown. And she, who had seemed so little and so awkward in the attire of

Matcham, was now tall like a young willow, and swam across the floor as though she scorned the drudgery of walking.

Without a start, without a tremor, she raised her lamp and looked at the young monk.

'What make ye here, good brother?' she inquired. 'Ye are doubtless ill-directed. Whom do ye require?' And she set her lamp upon the bracket.

'Joanna,' said Dick; and then his voice failed him. 'Joanna,' he began again, 'ye said ye loved me; and the more fool I, but I believed it!'

'Dick!' she cried. 'Dick!'

And then, to the wonder of the lad, this beautiful and tall young lady made but one step of it, and threw her arms about his neck, and gave him a hundred kisses all in one.

'Oh, the fool fellow!' she cried. 'Oh, dear Dick! Oh, if ye could see yourself! Alack!' she added, pausing, 'I have spoilt you, Dick! I have knocked some of the paint off. But that can be mended. What cannot be mended, Dick— or I much fear it cannot!—is my marriage with Lord Shoreby.'

'Is it decided, then?' asked the lad.

'To-morrow, before noon, Dick, in the abbey church,' she answered, 'John Matcham and Joanna Sedley both shall come to a right miserable end. There is no help in tears, or I could weep mine eyes out. I have not spared myself to pray, but Heaven frowns on my petition. And, dear Dick—good Dick—but that ye can get me forth of this house before the morning, we must even kiss and say good-bye.'

'Nay,' said Dick, 'not I; I will never say that word. 'Tis like despair; but while there's life, Joanna, there is hope. Yet will I hope. Ay, by the mass, and triumph! Look ye, now, when ye were but a name to me, did I not follow—did I not rouse good men—did I not stake my life upon the quarrel? And now that I have seen you for what you are—the fairest maid and stateliest of England—think ye I would turn?—if the deep sea were there, I would straight through it; if the way were full of lions, I would scatter them like mice.'

'Ay,' she said drily, 'ye make a great ado about a sky-blue robe!'

'Nay, Joan,' protested Dick, ''tis not alone the robe. But lass, ye were disguised. Here am I disguised; and, to the proof, do I not cut a figure of fun—a right fool's figure?'

'Ay, Dick, an' that ye do!' she answered, smiling.

'Well, then!' he returned, triumphant. 'So was it with you, poor Matcham, in the forest. In sooth, ye were a wench to laugh at. But now!'

So they ran on, holding each other by both hands, exchanging smiles and lovely looks, and melting minutes into seconds; and so they might have continued all night long. But presently there was a noise behind them; and they were aware of the short young lady, with her finger on her lips.

'Saints!' she cried, 'but what a noise ye keep! Can ye not speak in compass? And now, Joanna, my fair maid of the woods, what will ye give your gossip for bringing you your sweetheart?'

Joanna ran to her, by way of answer, and embraced her fierily.

'And you, sir,' added the young lady, 'what do ye give me?'

'Madam,' said Dick, 'I would fain offer to pay you in the same money.'

'Come, then,' said the lady, 'it is permitted you.'

But Dick, blushing like a peony, only kissed her hand.

'What ails ye at my face, fair sir?' she inquired, curtseying to the very ground; and then, when Dick had at length and most tepidly embraced her, 'Joanna,' she added, 'your sweetheart is very backward under your eyes; but I warrant you, when first we met, he was more ready. I am all black and blue, wench; trust me never, if I be not black and blue! And now,' she continued, 'have ye said your sayings? for I must speedily dismiss the paladin.'

But at this they both cried out that they had said nothing, that the night was still very young, and that they would not be separated so early.

'And supper?' asked the young lady. 'Must we not go down to supper?'

'Nay, to be sure!' cried Joan. 'I had forgotten.'

'Hide me, then,' said Dick, 'put me behind the arras, shut me in a chest, or what ye will, so that I may be here on your return. Indeed, fair lady,' he added, 'bear this in mind, that we are sore bested, and may never look upon each other's face from this night forward till we die.'

At this the young lady melted; and when, a little after, the bell summoned Sir Daniel's household to the board, Dick was planted very stiffly against the wall, at a place where a division in the tapestry permitted him to breathe the more freely, and even to see into the room.

He had not been long in this position when he was somewhat strangely disturbed. The silence in that upper storey of the house was only broken by the flickering of the flames and the hissing of a green log in the chimney; but presently, to Dick's strained hearing, there came the sound of some one walking with extreme precaution; and soon after the door opened, and a little black-faced, dwarfish fellow, in Lord Shoreby's colours, pushed first his head and then his crooked body into the chamber. His mouth was open, as though to hear the better; and his eyes, which were very bright, flitted restlessly and swiftly to and fro. He went round and round the room, striking here and there upon the hangings: but Dick, by a miracle, escaped his notice. Then he looked below the furniture, and examined the lamp; and at last, with an air of cruel disappointment, was preparing to go away as silently as he had come, when down he dropped upon his knees, picked up something from among the rushes on the floor, examined it, and with every signal of delight, concealed it in the wallet at his belt.

Dick's heart sank, for the object in question was a tassel from his own girdle; and it was plain to him that this dwarfish spy, who took a malign delight in his employment, would lose no time in bearing it to his master, the baron. He was half-tempted to throw aside the arras, fall upon the scoundrel, and, at the risk of his life, remove the tell-tale token. And while he was still hesitating, a new cause of concern was added. A voice, hoarse and broken by drink, began to be audible from the stair; and presently after, uneven, wandering, and heavy footsteps sounded without along the passage.

'What make ye here, my merry men, among the greenwood shaws?' sang the voice. 'What make ye here? Hey! sots, what make ye here!' it added, with a rattle of drunken laughter; and then once more breaking into song:—

> 'If ye should drink the clary wine,
> Fat Friar John, ye friend o' mine—
> If I should eat, and ye should drink,
> Who shall sing the mass, d'ye think?'

Lawless, alas! rolling drunk, was wandering the house, seeking for a corner wherein to slumber off the effect of his potations. Dick inwardly raged. The spy, at first terrified, had grown reassured as he found he had to deal with an intoxicated man, and now, with a movement of cat-like rapidity, slipped from the chamber, and was gone from Richard's eyes.

What was to be done? If he lost touch of Lawless for the night he was left impotent, whether to plan or carry forth Joanna's rescue. If, on the other hand, he dared to address the drunken outlaw, the spy might still be lingering within sight, and the most fatal consequences ensue.

It was, nevertheless, upon this last hazard that Dick decided. Slipping from behind the tapestry, he stood ready in the doorway of the chamber, with a warning hand upraised. Lawless flushed crimson, with his eyes injected, vacillating on his feet, drew still unsteadily nearer. At last he hazily caught sight of his commander, and, in despite of Dick's imperious signals, hailed him instantly and loudly by his name.

Dick leaped upon and shook the drunkard furiously.

'Beast!' he hissed—'beast, and no man! It is worse than treachery to be so witless. We may all be shent for thy sotting.'

But Lawless only laughed and staggered, and tried to clap young Shelton on the back.

And just then Dick's quick ear caught a rapid brushing in the arras. He leaped towards the sound, and the next moment a piece of the wall-hanging had been torn down, and Dick and the spy were sprawling together in its folds. Over and over they rolled, grappling for each other's throat, and still baffled by the arras, and still silent in their deadly fury. But Dick was by much the stronger, and soon the spy lay prostrate under his knee, and, with a single stroke of the long poniard, ceased to breathe.

21

The dead spy

THROUGHOUT this furious and rapid passage, Lawless had looked on helplessly, and even when all was over, and Dick, already re-arisen to his feet, was listening with the most passionate attention to the distant bustle in the lower storeys of the house, the old outlaw was still wavering on his legs like a shrub in a breeze of wind, and still stupidly staring on the face of the dead man.

'It is well,' said Dick at length; 'they have not heard us, praise the saints! But, now, what shall I do with this poor spy? At least, I will take my tassel from his wallet.'

So saying, Dick opened the wallet; within he found a few pieces of money, the tassel, and a letter addressed to Lord Wensleydale, and sealed with my Lord Shoreby's seal. The name awoke Dick's recollections; and he instantly broke the wax and read the contents of the letter. It was short, but to Dick's delight, it gave evident proof that Lord Shoreby was treacherously corresponding with the House of York.

The young fellow usually carried his ink-horn and implements about him, and so now, bending a knee beside the body of the dead spy, he was able to write these words upon a corner of the paper:—

'My Lord of Shoreby, ye that writt the letter, wot ye why your man is ded! But let me rede you, marry not.

'Jon Amend-All.'

He laid this paper on the breast of the corpse; and then Lawless, who had been looking on upon these last manœuvres with some flickering returns of intelligence, suddenly drew a black arrow from below his robe, and therewith pinned the paper in its place. The sight of this disrespect, or, as it almost seemed, cruelty to the dead, drew a cry of horror from young Shelton; but the old outlaw only laughed.

'Nay, I will have the credit for mine order,' he hiccupped. 'My jolly boys must have the credit on't—the credit, brother'; and then, shutting his eyes tight and opening his mouth like a precentor, he began to thunder, in a formidable voice:—

'If ye should drink the clary wine——'

'Peace, sot!' cried Dick, and thrust him hard against the wall. 'In two words—if so be that such a man can understand me who hath more wine than wit in him— in two words, and, a-Mary's name, begone out of this house, where, if ye continue to abide, ye will not only hang yourself, but me also! Faith, then, up foot! beware, or, by the mass, I may forget that I am in some sort your captain, and in some your debtor! Go!'

The sham monk was now, in some degree, recovering the use of his intelligence; and the ring in Dick's voice, and the glitter in Dick's eye, stamped home the meaning of his words.

'By the mass,' cried Lawless, 'an I be not wanted, I can go'; and he turned tipsily along the corridor and proceeded to flounder downstairs, lurching against the wall.

So soon as he was out of sight, Dick returned to his hiding-place, resolutely fixed to see the matter out. Wisdom, indeed, moved him to be gone; but love and curiosity were stronger.

Time passed slowly for the young man, bolt upright behind the arras. The fire in the room began to die down, and the lamp to burn low and to smoke. And still there was no word of the return of any one to these upper quarters of the house; still the faint hum and chatter of the supper party sounded from far below; and still, under the thick fall of the snow, Shoreby town lay silent upon every side.

At length, however, feet and voices began to draw near upon the stair; and presently after several of Sir Daniel's guests arrived upon the landing, and, turning down the corridor, beheld the torn arras and the body of the spy.

Some ran forward and some back, and all together began to cry aloud.

At the sound of their cries, guests, men-at-arms, ladies, servants and, in a word, all the inhabitants of that great house, came flying from every direction, and began to join their voices to the tumult.

Soon a way was cleared, and Sir Daniel came forth in person, followed by the bridegroom of the morrow, my Lord Shoreby.

'My lord,' said Sir Daniel, 'have I not told you of this knave Black Arrow? To the proof, behold it! There it stands, and, by the rood, my gossip, in a man of yours, or one that stole your colours?'

'In good sooth, it was a man of mine,' replied Lord Shoreby, hanging back. 'I would I had more such. He was keen as a beagle and secret as a mole.'

'Ay, gossip, truly?' asked Sir Daniel keenly. 'And what came he smelling up so many stairs in my poor mansion? But he will smell no more.'

'An't please you, Sir Daniel,' said one, 'here is a paper written upon with some matter, pinned upon his breast.'

'Give it me, arrow and all,' said the knight. And when he had taken into his hand the shaft, he continued for some time to gaze upon it in a sullen musing. 'Ay,' he said, addressing Lord Shoreby, 'here is a hate that followeth hard and close upon my heels. This black stick, or its just likeness, shall yet bring me down. And, gossip, suffer a plain knight to counsel you; and if these hounds begin to wind you, flee! 'Tis like a sickness—it still hangeth, hangeth upon the limbs. But let us see what they have written. It is as I thought, my lord; y' are marked, like an old oak, by the woodman; to-morrow or next day, by will come the axe. But what wrote ye in a letter?'

Lord Shoreby snatched the paper from the arrow, read it, crumpled it between his hands, and, overcoming the reluctance which had hitherto withheld him from approaching, threw himself on his knees beside the body and eagerly groped in the wallet.

He rose to his feet with a somewhat unsettled countenance.

'Gossip,' he said, 'I have indeed lost a letter here that much imported; and could I lay my hand upon the knave that took it, he should incontinently grace a halter. But let us, first of all, secure the issues of the house. Here is enough harm already, by St. George!'

Sentinels were posted close around the house and garden; a sentinel on every landing of the stair, a whole troop in the main entrance-hall, and yet another about the bonfire in the shed. Sir Daniel's followers were supplemented by Lord Shoreby's;

there was thus no lack of men or weapons to make the house secure, or to entrap a lurking enemy, should one be there.

Meanwhile the body of the spy was carried out through the falling snow and deposited in the abbey church.

It was not until these dispositions had been taken, and all had returned to a decorous silence, that the two girls drew Richard Shelton from his place of concealment, and made a full report to him of what had passed. He, upon his side, recounted the visit of the spy, his dangerous discovery, and speedy end.

Joanna leaned back very faint against the curtained wall.

'It will avail but little,' she said. 'I shall be wed to-morrow, in the morning, after all?'

'What!' cried her friend. 'And here is our paladin that driveth lions like mice! Ye have little faith, of a surety. But come, friend lion-driver, give us some comfort; speak and let us hear bold counsels.'

Dick was confounded to be thus outfaced with his own exaggerated words; but though he coloured, he still spoke stoutly.

'Truly,' said he, 'we are in straits. Yet, could I but win out of this house for half an hour, I do honestly tell myself that all might still go well; and for the marriage, it should be prevented.'

'And for the lions,' mimicked the girl, 'they shall be driven.'

'I crave your excuse,' said Dick. 'I speak not now in any boasting humour, but rather as one inquiring after help or counsel; for if I get not forth of this house through these sentinels, I can do less than naught. Take me, I pray you, rightly.'

'Why said ye he was rustic, Joan?' the girl inquired. 'I warrant he hath a tongue in his head; ready, soft, and bold is his speech at pleasure. What would ye more?'

'Nay,' sighed Joanna, with a smile, 'they have changed me my friend Dick, 'tis sure enough. When I beheld him, he was rough indeed. But it matters little; there is no help for my hard case, and I must still be Lady Shoreby!'

'Nay, then,' said Dick, 'I will even make the adventure. A friar is not much regarded; and if I found a good fairy to lead me up, I may find another belike to carry me down. How call they the name of this spy?'

'Rutter,' said the young lady; 'and an excellent good name to call him by. But how mean ye, lion-driver? What is in your mind to do?'

'To offer boldly to go forth,' returned Dick; 'and, if any stop me, to keep an unchanged countenance, and say I go to pray for Rutter. They will be praying over his poor clay even now.'

'The device is somewhat simple,' replied the girl, 'yet it may hold.'

'Nay,' said young Shelton, 'it is no device, but mere boldness, which serveth often better in great straits.'

'Ye say true,' she said. 'Well, go, a-Mary's name. And may Heaven speed you! Ye leave here a poor maid that loves you entirely, and another that is most heartily your friend. Be wary, for their sakes, and make not shipwreck of your safety.'

'Ay,' added Joanna, 'go, Dick. Ye run no more peril, whether ye go or stay. Go; ye take my heart with you; the saints defend you!'

Dick passed the first sentry with so assured a countenance that the fellow merely fidgeted and stared; but at the second landing the man carried his spear across and bade him name his business.

'*Pax vobiscum*,' answered Dick. 'I go to pray over the body of this poor Rutter.'

'Like enough,' returned the sentry; 'but to go alone is not permitted you.' He leaned over the oaken balusters and whistled shrill. 'One cometh,' he cried; and then motioned Dick to pass.

At the foot of the stairs he found the guard afoot and awaiting his arrival; and when he had once more repeated his story, the commander of the post ordered four men out to accompany him to the church.

'Let him not slip, my lads,' he said. 'Bring him to Sir Oliver, on your lives!'

The door was then opened; one of the men took Dick by either arm, another marched ahead with a link, and the fourth, with bent bow and the arrow on the string, brought up the rear. In this order they proceeded through the garden, under the thick darkness of the night and the scattering snow, and drew near to the dimly-illuminated windows of the abbey church.

At the western portal a picket of archers stood, taking what shelter they could find in the hollow of the arched doorways, and all powdered with the snow; and it was not until Dick's conductors had exchanged a word with these, that they were suffered to pass forth and enter the nave of the sacred edifice.

The church was doubtfully lighted by the tapers upon the great altar, and by a lamp or two that swung from the arched roof before the private chapels of illustrious families. In the midst of the choir the dead spy lay, his limbs piously composed, upon a bier.

A hurried mutter of prayer sounded along the arches; cowled figures knelt in the stalls of the choir, and on the steps of the high altar a priest in pontifical vestments celebrated mass.

Upon this fresh entrance, one of the cowled figures arose, and, coming down the steps which elevated the level of the choir above that of the nave, demanded from the leader of the four men what business brought him to the church. Out of respect for the service and the dead, they spoke in guarded tones; but the echoes of that huge, empty building caught up their words, and hollowly repeated and repeated them along the aisles.

'A monk!' returned Sir Oliver (for he it was), when he had heard the report of the archer. 'My brother, I looked not for your coming,' he added, turning to young Shelton. 'In all civility, who are ye? and at whose instance do ye join your supplication to ours?'

Dick, keeping his cowl about his face, signed to Sir Oliver to move a pace or two aside from the archers; and, so soon as the priest had done so, 'I cannot hope to deceive you, sir,' he said. 'My life is in your hands.'

Sir Oliver violently started; his stout cheeks grew pale, and for a space he was silent.

'Richard,' he said, 'what brings you here, I know not; but I much misdoubt it to be evil. Nevertheless, for the kindness that was, I would not willingly deliver you to harm. Ye shall sit all night beside me in the stalls: ye shall sit there till my Lord of Shoreby be married, and the party gone safe home; and if all goeth well, and ye have planned no evil, in the end ye shall go whither ye will. But if your purpose be bloody, it shall return upon your head. Amen!'

And the priest devoutly crossed himself, and turned and louted to the altar.

With that, he spoke a few words more to the soldiers, and taking Dick by the hand, led him up to the choir, and placed him in the stall beside his own, where, for mere decency, the lad had instantly to kneel and appear to be busy with his devotions.

His mind and his eyes, however, were continually wandering. Three of the soldiers, he observed, instead of returning to the house, had got them quietly into a point of vantage in the aisle; and he could not doubt that they had done so by Sir Oliver's command. Here, then, he was trapped. Here he must spend the night in the ghostly glimmer and shadow of the church, and looking on the pale face of him he slew; and here, in the morning, he must see his sweetheart married to another man before his eyes.

But, for all that, he obtained a command upon his mind, and built himself up in patience to await the issue.

22

In the Abbey Church

In Shoreby Abbey Church the prayers were kept up all night without cessation, now with the singing of psalms, now with a note or two upon the bell.

Rutter, the spy, was nobly waked. There he lay, meanwhile, as they had arranged him, his dead hands crossed upon his bosom, his dead eyes staring on the roof; and hard by, in the stall, the lad who had slain him waited, in sore disquietude, the coming of the morning.

Once only, in the course of the hours, Sir Oliver leaned across to his captive.

'Richard,' he whispered, 'my son, if ye mean me evil, I will certify, on my soul's welfare, ye design upon an innocent man. Sinful in the eye of Heaven I do declare myself; but sinful against you I am not, neither have been ever.'

'My father,' returned Dick, in the same tone of voice, 'trust me, I design nothing; but as for your innocence, I may not forget that ye cleared yourself but lamely.'

'A man may be innocently guilty,' replied the priest. 'He may be set blindfolded upon a mission, ignorant of its true scope. So it was with me. I did decoy your father to his death; but as Heaven sees us in this sacred place, I knew not what I did.'

'It may be,' returned Dick, 'but see what a strange web ye have woven, that I should be, at this hour, at once your prisoner and your judge; that ye should both threaten my days and deprecate my anger. Methinks, if ye had been all your life a true man and good priest, ye would neither thus fear nor thus detest me. And now to your prayers. I do obey you, since needs must; but I will not be burthened with your company.'

The priest uttered a sigh so heavy that it had almost touched the lad into some sentiment of pity, and he bowed his head upon his hands like a man borne down below a weight of care. He joined no longer in the psalms; but Dick could hear the beads rattle through his fingers and the prayers a-pattering between his teeth.

Yet a little, and the gray of the morning began to struggle through the painted casements of the church, and to put to shame the glimmer of the tapers. The light slowly broadened and brightened, and presently through the south-eastern clerestories a flush of rosy sunlight flickered on the walls. The storm was over; the great clouds had disburdened their snow and fled farther on, and the new day was breaking on a merry winter landscape sheathed in white.

A bustle of church officers followed; the bier was carried forth to the dead-house, and the stains of blood were cleansed from off the tiles, that no such ill-omened spectacle should disgrace the marriage of Lord Shoreby. At the same time, the very ecclesiastics who had been so dismally engaged all night began to put on morning faces, to do honour to the merrier ceremony which was about to follow. And further to announce the coming of the day, the pious of the town began to assemble and fall to prayer before their favourite shrines, or wait their turn at the confessionals.

Favoured by this stir, it was, of course, easily possible for any man to avoid the vigilance of Sir Daniel's sentries at the door; and presently Dick, looking about him warily, caught the eye of no less a person than Will Lawless, still in his monk's habit.

The outlaw, at the same moment, recognised his leader, and privily signed to him with hand and eye.

Now, Dick was far from having forgiven the old rogue his most untimely drunkenness, but he had no desire to involve him in his own predicament; and he signalled back to him, as plain as he was able, to begone.

Lawless, as though he had understood, disappeared at once behind a pillar, and Dick breathed again.

What, then, was his dismay to feel himself plucked by the sleeve and to find the old robber installed beside him, upon the next seat, and, to all appearance, plunged in his devotions!

Instantly Sir Oliver arose from his place, and, gliding behind the stalls, made for the soldiers in the aisle. If the priest's suspicions had been so lightly wakened, the harm was already done, and Lawless a prisoner in the church.

'Move not,' whispered Dick. 'We are in the plaguiest pass, thanks, before all things, to thy swinishness of yestereven. When ye saw me here, so strangely seated, where I have neither right nor interest, what a murrain! could ye not smell harm and get ye gone from evil?'

'Nay,' returned Lawless, 'I thought ye had heard from Ellis, and were here on duty.'

'Ellis!' echoed Dick. 'Is Ellis then returned?'

'For sure,' replied the outlaw. 'He came last night, and belted me sore for being in wine—so there ye are avenged, my master. A furious man is Ellis Duckworth! He hath ridden me hot-spur from Craven to prevent this marriage; and, Master Dick, ye know the way of him—do so he will!'

'Nay, then,' returned Dick, with composure, 'you and I, my poor brother, are dead men; for I sit here a prisoner upon suspicion, and my neck was to answer for this very marriage that he purposeth to mar. I had a fair choice, by the rood! to lose my sweetheart or else lose my life! Well, the cast is thrown—it is to be my life.'

'By the mass,' cried Lawless, half arising, 'I am gone!'

But Dick had his hand at once upon his shoulder.

'Friend Lawless, sit ye still,' he said. 'An ye have eyes, look yonder at the corner by the chancel arch; see ye not that, even upon the motion of your rising, yon armed men are up and ready to intercept you? Yield ye, friend. Ye were bold aboard ship, when ye thought to die a sea-death; be bold again, now that y' are to die presently upon the gallows.'

'Master Dick,' gasped Lawless, 'the thing hath come upon me somewhat of the suddenest. But give me a moment till I fetch my breath again; and, by the mass, I will be as stout-hearted as yourself.'

'Here is my bold fellow!' returned Dick. 'And yet, Lawless, it goes hard against the grain with me to die; but where whining mendeth nothing, wherefore whine?'

'Nay, that indeed!' chimed Lawless. 'And a fig for death at worst! It has to be done, my master, soon or late. And hanging in a good quarrel is an easy death, they say, though I could never hear of any that came back to say so.'

And so saying the stout old rascal leaned back in his stall, folded his arms, and began to look about him with the greatest air of insolence and unconcern.

'And for the matter of that,' Dick added, 'it is yet our best chance to keep quiet. We wot not yet what Duckworth purposes; and when all is said, and if the worst befall, we may yet clear our feet of it.'

Now that they ceased talking, they were aware of a very distant and thin strain of mirthful music which steadily drew nearer, louder, and merrier. The bells in the tower began to break forth into a doubling peal, and a greater and greater concourse of people to crowd into the church, shuffling the snow from off their feet, and clapping and blowing in their hands. The western door was flung wide open, showing a glimpse of sunlit, snowy street, and admitting in a great gust the shrewd air of the morning; and in short, it became plain by every sign that Lord Shoreby desired to be married very early in the day, and that the wedding-train was drawing near.

Some of Lord Shoreby's men now cleared a passage down the middle aisle, forcing the people back with lance-stocks; and just then, outside the portal, the secular musicians could be descried drawing near over the frozen snow, the fifers and trumpeters scarlet in the face with lusty blowing, the drummers and the cymbalists beating as for a wager.

These, as they drew near the door of the sacred building, filed off on either side, and marking time to their own vigorous music, stood stamping in the snow. As they thus opened their ranks, the leaders of this noble bridal train appeared behind and between them; and such was the variety and gaiety of their attire, such a display of silks and velvet, fur and satin, embroidery and lace, that the procession showed forth upon the snow like a flower-bed in a path or a painted window in a wall.

First came the bride, a sorry sight, as pale as winter, clinging to Sir Daniel's arm, and attended, as bridesmaid, by the short young lady who had befriended Dick the night before. Close behind, in the most radiant toilet, followed the bridegroom, halting on a gouty foot, and as he passed the threshold of the sacred building, and doffed his hat, his bald head was seen to be rosy with emotion.

And now came the hour of Ellis Duckworth.

Dick, who sat stunned among contrary emotions, grasping the desk in front of him, beheld a movement in the crowd, people jostling backward, and eyes and arms uplifted. Following these signs, he beheld three or four men with bent bows, leaning from the clerestory gallery. At the same instant they delivered their discharge, and before the clamour and cries of the astounded populace had time to swell fully upon the ear, they had flitted from their perch and disappeared.

The nave was full of swaying heads and voices screaming; the ecclesiastics thronged in terror from their places; the music ceased, and though the bells overhead continued for some seconds to clang upon the air, some wind of the disaster seemed to find its way at last even to the chamber where the ringers were leaping on their ropes, and they also desisted from their merry labours.

Right in the midst of the nave the bridegroom lay stone-dead, pierced by two black arrows. The bride had fainted. Sir Daniel stood, towering above the crowd in his surprise and anger, a clothyard shaft quivering in his left forearm, and his face streaming blood from another which had grazed his brow.

Long before any search could be made for them, the authors of this tragic interruption had clattered down a turnpike stair and decamped by a postern door.

But Dick and Lawless still remained in pawn; they had indeed arisen on the first alarm and pushed manfully to gain the door;

but what with the narrowness of the stalls, and the crowding of terrified priests and choristers, the attempt had been in vain, and they had stoically resumed their places.

And now, pale with horror, Sir Oliver rose to his feet and called upon Sir Daniel, pointing with one hand to Dick.

'Here,' he cried, 'is Richard Shelton—alas the hour!—blood guilty! Seize him!—bid him be seized! For all our lives' sakes, take him and bind him surely! He hath sworn our fall.'

Sir Daniel was blinded by anger—blinded by the hot blood that still streamed across his face.

'Where?' he bellowed. 'Hale him forth! By the cross of Holywood but he shall rue this hour.'

The crowd fell back, and a party of archers invaded the choir, laid rough hands on Dick, dragged him head foremost from the stall, and thrust him by the shoulders down the chancel steps. Lawless, on his part, sat as still as a mouse.

Sir Daniel, brushing the blood out of his eyes, stared blinkingly upon his captive.

'Ay,' he said, 'treacherous and insolent, I have thee fast; and by all potent oaths, for every drop of blood that now trickles in mine eyes, I will wring a groan out of thy carcase. Away with him!' he added. 'Here is no place. Off with him to my house. I will number every joint of thy body with a torture.'

But Dick, putting off his captors, uplifted his voice.

'Sanctuary!' he shouted. 'Sanctuary! Ho, there, my fathers! They would drag me from the church!'

'From the church thou hast defiled with murder, boy,' added a tall man, magnificently dressed.

'On what probation?' cried Dick. 'They do accuse me, indeed, of some complicity, but have not proved one tittle. I was, in truth, a suitor for this damsel's hand; and she, I will be bold to say, repaid my suit with favour. But what then? To love a maid is no offence, I trow—nay, nor to gain her love. In all else, I stand here free from guiltiness.'

There was a murmur of approval among the bystanders, so boldly Dick declared his innocence; but at the same time a throng of accusers arose upon the other side, crying how he had been found last night in Sir Daniel's house, how he wore a sacrilegious disguise; and in the midst of the babel, Sir Oliver indicated Lawless, both by voice and gesture, as accomplice to the fact. He, in his turn, was dragged from his seat and set beside his leader. The feelings of the crowd rose high on either side, and while some dragged the prisoners to and fro to favour their escape, others cursed and struck them with their fists.

Dick's ears rang and his brain swam dizzily, like a man struggling in the eddies of a furious river.

But the tall man who had already answered Dick, by a prodigious exercise of voice restored silence and order in the mob.

'Search them,' he said, 'for arms. We may so judge of their intentions.'

Upon Dick they found no weapon but his poniard, and this told in his favour, until one man officiously drew it from its sheath, and found it still uncleansed of the blood of Rutter. At this there was a great shout among Sir Daniel's followers, which the tall man suppressed by a gesture and an imperious glance. But when it came to the turn of Lawless, there was found under his gown a sheaf of arrows identical with those that had been shot.

'How say ye now?' asked the tall man frowningly of Dick.

'Sir,' replied Dick, 'I am here in sanctuary, is it not so? Well, sir, I see by your bearing that ye are high in station, and I read in your countenance the marks of piety and justice. To you, then, I will yield me prisoner, and that blithely, forgoing the advantage of this holy place. But rather than to be yielded into the discretion of that man—whom I do here accuse with a loud voice to be the murderer of my natural father and the unjust detainer of my lands and revenues—rather than that, I would beseech you, under favour, with your own gentle hand, to despatch me on the spot. Your own ears have heard him, how before that I was proven guilty he did threaten me with torments. It standeth not with your own honour to deliver me to my sworn enemy and old oppressor, but to try me fairly by the way of law, and, if that I be guilty indeed, to slay me mercifully.'

'My lord,' cried Sir Daniel, 'ye will not hearken to this wolf? His bloody dagger reeks him the lie into his face.'

'Nay, but suffer me, good knight,' returned the tall stranger; 'your own vehemence doth somewhat tell against yourself.'

And here the bride, who had come to herself some minutes past and looked wildly on upon this scene, broke loose from those that held her, and fell upon her knees before the last speaker.

'My Lord of Risingham,' she cried, 'hear me, in justice. I am here in this man's custody by mere force, reft from mine own people. Since that day I had never pity, countenance, nor comfort from the face of man—but from him only—Richard Shelton—whom they now accuse and labour to undo. My lord, if he was yesternight in Sir Daniel's mansion, it was I that brought him there; he came but at my prayer, and thought to do no hurt. While yet Sir Daniel was a good lord to him, he fought with them of the Black Arrow loyally; but when his foul guardian sought his life by practices, and he fled by night, for his soul's sake, out of that bloody house, whither was he to turn—he, helpless and penniless? Or if he be fallen among ill company, whom should ye blame—the lad that was unjustly handled, or the guardian that did abuse his trust?'

And then the short young lady fell on her knees by Joanna's side.

'And I, my good lord and natural uncle,' she added, 'I can bear testimony, on my conscience and before the face of all, that what this maiden saith is true. It was I, unworthy, that did lead the young man in.'

Earl Risingham had heard in silence, and when the voices ceased, he still stood silent for a space. Then he gave Joanna his hand to arise, though it was to be observed that he did not offer the like courtesy to her who had called herself his niece.

'Sir Daniel,' he said, 'here is a right intricate affair, the which, with your good leave, it shall be mine to examine and adjust. Content ye, then; your business is in careful hands; justice shall be done you; and in the meanwhile, get ye incontinently home, and have your hurts attended. The air is shrewd, and I would not ye took cold upon these scratches.'

He made a sign with his hand; it was passed down the nave by obsequious servants, who waited upon his smallest gesture. Instantly, without the church, a tucket sounded shrill, and through the open portal archers and men-at-arms, uniformly arrayed in the colours and wearing the badge of Lord Risingham, began to file into the church, took Dick and Lawless from those who still detained them, and, closing their files about the prisoners, marched forth again and disappeared.

As they were passing, Joanna held both her hands to Dick and cried him her farewell; and the bridesmaid, nothing downcast by her uncle's evident displeasure, blew him a kiss, with a 'Keep your heart up, lion-driver!' that for the first time since the accident called up a smile to the faces of the crowd.

23

Earl Risingham

EARL RISINGHAM, although by far the most important person then in Shoreby, was poorly lodged in the house of a private gentleman upon the extreme outskirts of the town. Nothing but the armed men at the doors, and the mounted messengers that kept arriving and departing, announced the temporary residence of a great lord.

Thus it was that, from lack of space, Dick and Lawless were clapped into the same apartment.

'Well spoken, Master Richard,' said the outlaw; 'it was excellently well spoken, and, for my part, I thank you cordially. Here we are in good hands; we shall be justly tried, and some time this evening decently hanged on the same tree.'

'Indeed, my poor friend, I do believe it,' answered Dick.

'Yet we have a string to our bow,' returned Lawless. 'Ellis Duckworth is a man out of ten thousand; he holdeth you right near his heart, both for your own and for your father's sake; and knowing you guiltless of this fact, he will stir earth and heaven to bear you clear.'

'It may not be,' said Dick. 'What can he do? He hath but a handful. Alack, if it were but to-morrow—could I but keep a certain tryst an hour before noon to-morrow—all were, I think, otherwise. But now there is no help.'

'Well,' concluded Lawless, 'an ye will stand to it for my innocence, I will stand to it for yours, and that stoutly. It shall naught avail us; but an I be to hang, it shall not be for lack of swearing.'

And then, while Dick gave himself over to his reflections, the old rogue curled himself down into a corner, pulled his monkish hood about his face, and composed himself to sleep. Soon he was loudly snoring, so utterly had his long life of hardship and adventure blunted the sense of apprehension.

It was long after noon, and the day was already failing, before the door was opened and Dick taken forth and led upstairs to where, in a warm cabinet, Earl Risingham sat musing over the fire.

On his captive's entrance he looked up.

'Sir,' he said, 'I knew your father, who was a man of honour, and this inclineth me to be the more lenient; but I may not hide from you that heavy charges lie against your character. Ye do consort with murderers and robbers; upon a clear probation ye have carried war against the king's peace; ye are suspected to have piratically seized upon a ship; ye are found skulking with a counterfeit presentment in your enemy's house; a man is slain that very evening——'

'An it like you, my lord,' Dick interposed, 'I will at once avow my guilt, such as it is. I slew this fellow Rutter; and to the proof'—searching in his bosom—'here is a letter from his wallet.'

Lord Risingham took the letter, and opened and read it twice.

'Ye have read this?' he inquired.

'I have read it,' answered Dick.

'Are ye for York or Lancaster?' the earl demanded.

'My lord, it was but a little while back that I was asked that question, and knew not how to answer it,' said Dick; 'but having answered once, I will not vary. My lord, I am for York.'

The earl nodded approvingly.

'Honestly replied,' he said. 'But wherefore, then, deliver me this letter?'

'Nay, but against traitors, my lord, are not all sides arrayed?' cried Dick.

'I would they were, young gentleman,' returned the earl; 'and I do at least approve your saying. There is more youth than guile in you, I do perceive; and were not Sir Daniel a mighty man upon our side, I were half tempted to espouse your quarrel. For I have inquired, and it appears you have been hardly dealt with, and have much excuse. But look ye, sir, I am, before all else, a leader in the Queen's interest; and though by nature a just man, as I believe, and leaning even to the excess of mercy, yet must I order my goings for my party's interest, and, to keep Sir Daniel, I would go far about.'

'My lord,' returned Dick, 'ye will think me very bold to counsel you; but do ye count upon Sir Daniel's faith? Methought he had changed sides intolerably often.'

'Nay, it is the way of England. What would ye have?' the earl demanded. 'But ye are unjust to the knight of Tunstall; and as faith goes, in this unfaithful generation, he hath of late been honourably true to us of Lancaster. Even in our last reverses he stood firm.'

'An it please you, then,' said Dick, 'to cast your eye upon this letter, ye might somewhat change your thought of him,' and he handed to the earl Sir Daniel's letter to Lord Wensleydale.

The effect upon the earl's countenance was instant; he lowered like an angry lion, and his hand, with a sudden movement, clutched at his dagger.

'Ye have read this also?' he asked.

'Even so,' said Dick. 'It is your lordship's own estate he offers to Lord Wensleydale.'

'It is my own estate, even as ye say!' returned the earl. 'I am your bedesman for this letter. It hath shown me a fox's hole. Command me, Master Shelton; I will not be backward in gratitude, and to begin with, York or Lancaster, true man or thief, I do now set you at freedom. Go, a-Mary's name! But judge it right that I retain and hang your fellow Lawless. The crime hath been most open, and it were fitting that some open punishment should follow.'

'My lord, I make it my first suit to you to spare him also,' pleaded Dick.

'It is an old condemned rogue, thief, and vagabond, Master Shelton,' said the earl. 'He hath been gallows-ripe this score of years. And, whether for one thing or another, whether to-morrow or the day after, where is the great choice?'

'Yet, my lord, it was through love to me that he came hither,' answered Dick, 'and I were churlish and thankless to desert him.'

'Master Shelton, ye are troublesome,' replied the earl severely. 'It is an evil way to prosper in this world. Howbeit, and to be quit of your importunity, I will once more humour you. Go, then, together; but go warily, and get swiftly out of Shoreby town. For this Sir Daniel (whom may the saints confound!) thirsteth most greedily to have your blood.'

'My lord, I do now offer you in words my gratitude, trusting at some brief date to pay you some of it in service,' replied Dick, as he turned from the apartment.

24

Arblaster again

When Dick and Lawless were suffered to steal, by a back way, out of the house where Lord Risingham held his garrison, the evening had already come.

They paused in shelter of the garden wall to consult on their best course. The danger was extreme. If one of Sir Daniel's men caught sight of them and raised the view-hallo, they would be run down and butchered instantly. And not only was the town of Shoreby a mere net of peril for their lives, but to make for the open country was to run the risk of the patrols.

A little way off, upon some open ground, they spied a windmill standing; and hard by that, a very large granary with open doors.

'How if we lay there until the night fall?' Dick proposed.

And Lawless, having no better suggestion to offer, they made a straight push for the granary at a run, and concealed themselves behind the door among some straw. The daylight rapidly departed; and presently the moon was silvering the frozen snow. Now or never was their opportunity to gain the Goat and Bagpipes unobserved and change their tell-tale garments. Yet even then it was advisable to go round by the outskirts, and not run the gauntlet of the market-place, where, in the concourse of people, they stood the more imminent peril to be recognised and slain.

This course was a long one. It took them not far from the house by the beach, now lying dark and silent, and brought them forth at last by the margin of the harbour. Many of the ships, as they could see by the clear moonshine, had weighed anchor, and, profiting by the calm sky, proceeded to far more distant parts; answerable to this, the rude alehouses along the beach (although, in defiance of the curfew law, they still shone with fire and candle) were no longer thronged with customers, and no longer echoed to the chorus of sea songs.

Hastily, half running, with their monkish raiment kilted to the knee, they plunged through the deep snow, and threaded the labyrinth of marine lumber; and they were already more than half-way round the harbour when, as they were passing close before an alehouse, the door suddenly opened and let out a gush of light upon their fleeting figures.

Instantly they stopped, and made believe to be engaged in earnest conversation.

Three men, one after another, came out of the alehouse, and the last closed the door behind him. All three were unsteady upon their feet, as if they had passed the day in deep potations, and they now stood wavering in the moonlight, like men who knew not what they would be after. The tallest of the three was talking in a loud, lamentable voice.

'Seven pieces of as good Gascony as ever a tapster broached,' he was saying, 'the best ship out o' the port o' Dartmouth, a Virgin Mary, parcel-gilt, thirteen pounds of good gold money——'

'I have had losses, too,' interrupted one of the others. 'I have had losses of mine own, gossip Arblaster. I was robbed at Martinmas of five shillings and a leather wallet well worth ninepence farthing.'

Dick's heart smote him at what he heard. Until that moment he had not perhaps thought twice of the poor skipper who had been ruined by the loss of the *Good Hope*; so careless, in those days, were men who wore arms of the goods and interests of their inferiors. But this sudden encounter reminded him sharply of the high-handed manner and ill ending of his enterprise; and both he and Lawless turned their heads the other way, to avoid the chance of recognition.

The ship's dog had, however, made his escape from the wreck and found his way back again to Shoreby. He was now at Arblaster's heels, and suddenly sniffing and pricking his ears, he darted forward and began to bark furiously at the two sham friars.

His master unsteadily followed him.

'Hey, shipmates!' he cried. 'Have ye ever a penny piece for a poor old shipman, clean destroyed by pirates? I am a man that would have paid for you both o' Thursday morning; and now here I be o' Saturday night, begging for a flagon of ale! Ask my man Tom, if ye misdoubt me. Seven pieces of good Gascon wine, a ship that was mine own, and was my father's before me, a Blessed Mary of plane-tree wood and parcel-gilt, and thirteen pounds in gold and silver. Hey! what say ye? A man that fought the French, too; for I have fought the French; I have cut more French throats upon the high seas than ever a man that sails out of Dartmouth. Come, a penny piece.'

Neither Dick nor Lawless durst answer him a word, lest he should recognise their voices; and they stood as helpless as a ship ashore, not knowing where to turn nor what to hope.

'Are ye dumb, boy?' inquired the skipper. 'Mates,' he added, with a hiccup, 'they be dumb. I like not this manner of discourtesy; for an a man be dumb, so be as he's courteous, he will still speak when he was spoken to, methinks.'

By this time the sailor Tom, who was a man of great personal strength, seemed to have conceived some suspicion of these two speechless figures; and being soberer than his captain, stepped suddenly before him, took Lawless roughly by the shoulder, and asked him, with an oath, what ailed him that he held his tongue. To this the outlaw, thinking all was over, made answer by a wrestling feint that stretched the sailor on the sand, and, calling upon Dick to follow him, took to his heels among the lumber.

The affair passed in a second. Before Dick could run at all, Arblaster had him in his arms; Tom, crawling on his face, had caught him by one foot, and the third man had a drawn cutlass brandishing above his head.

It was not so much the danger, it was not so much the annoyance, that now bowed down the spirits of young Shelton; it was the profound humiliation to have escaped Sir Daniel, convinced Lord Risingham, and now fall helpless in the hands of this old drunken sailor; and not merely helpless, but, as his conscience loudly told him when it was too late, actually guilty—actually the bankrupt debtor of the man whose ship he had stolen and lost.

'Bring me him back into the alehouse, till I see his face,' said Arblaster.

'Nay, nay,' returned Tom; 'but let us first unload his wallet, lest the other lads cry share.'

But though he was searched from head to foot, not a penny was found upon him; nothing but Lord Foxham's signet, which they plucked savagely from his finger.

'Turn me him to the moon,' said the skipper; and taking Dick by the chin, he cruelly jerked his head into the air. 'Blessed Virgin!' he cried, 'it is the pirate.'

'Hey!' cried Tom.

'By the Virgin of Bordeaux, it is the man himself!' repeated Arblaster. 'What, sea-thief, do I hold you?' he cried. 'Where is my ship? Where is my wine? Hey! have I you in my hands? Tom, give me one end of a cord here; I will so truss me this sea-thief, hand and foot together, like a basting turkey—marry, I will so bind him up—and thereafter I will so beat—so beat him!'

And so he ran on, winding the cord meanwhile about Dick's limbs with the dexterity peculiar to seamen, and at every turn and cross securing it with a knot, and tightening the whole fabric with a savage pull.

When he had done, the lad was a mere package in his hands—as helpless as the dead. The skipper held him at arm's length, and laughed aloud. Then he fetched him a stunning buffet on the ear; and then turned him about, and furiously kicked and kicked him. Anger rose up in Dick's bosom like a storm; anger strangled him, and he thought to have died; but when the sailor, tired of this cruel play, dropped him all his length upon the sand and turned to consult with his companions, he instantly regained command of his temper. Here was a momentary respite; ere they began again to torture him, he might have found some method to escape from this degrading and fatal misadventure.

Presently, sure enough, and while his captors were still discussing what to do with him, he took heart of grace, and, with a pretty steady voice, addressed them.

'My masters,' he began, 'are ye gone clean foolish? Here hath Heaven put into your hands as pretty an occasion to grow rich as ever shipman had—such as ye might make thirty oversea adventures and not find again—and, by the mass! what do ye? Beat me?—nay; so would an angry child. But for long-headed tarry-Johns, that fear not fire nor water, and that love gold as they love beef, methinks ye are not wise.'

'Ay,' said Tom, 'now y' are trussed ye would cozen us.'

'Cozen you!' repeated Dick. 'Nay, if ye be fools, it would be easy. But if ye be shrewd fellows, as I trow ye are, ye can see plainly where your interest lies. When I took your ship from you we were many, we were well clad and armed; but now, bethink you a little, who mustered that array? One incontestably that hath made much gold. And if he, being already rich, continueth to hunt after more even in the face of storms—bethink you once more—shall there not be a treasure somewhere hidden?'

'What meaneth he?' asked one of the men.

'Why, if ye have lost an old skiff and a few jugs of vinegary wine,' continued Dick, 'forget them, for the trash they are; and do ye rather buckle to an adventure worth the name, that shall, in twelve hours, make or mar you for ever. But take me up from where I lie, and let us go somewhere near at hand and talk across a flagon, for I am sore and frozen, and my mouth is half among the snow.'

'He seeks to cozen us,' said Tom contemptuously.

'Cozen! cozen!' cried the third man. 'I would I could see the man that could cozen me! He were a cozener indeed! Nay, I was not born yesterday. I can see a church when it hath a steeple on it; and for my part, gossip Arblaster, methinks there is some sense in this young man. Shall we go hear him, indeed? Say, shall we go hear him?'

'I would look gladly on a pottle of strong ale, good Master Pirret,' returned Arblaster. 'How say ye, Tom? But then the wallet is empty.'

'I will pay,' said the other, 'I will pay. I would fain see this matter out; I do believe, upon my conscience, there is gold in it.'

'Nay, if ye get again to drinking, all is lost!' cried Tom.

'Gossip Arblaster, ye suffer your fellow to have too much liberty,' returned Master Pirret. 'Would ye be led by a hired man? Fy, fy!'

'Peace, fellow!' said Arblaster, addressing Tom. 'Will ye put your oar in! Truly a fine pass, when the crew is to correct the skipper!'

'Well, then, go your way,' said Tom; 'I wash my hands of you.'

'Set him, then, upon his feet,' said Master Pirret. 'I know a privy place where we may drink and discourse.'

'If I am to walk, my friends, ye must set my feet at liberty,' said Dick, when he had been once more planted upright like a post.

'He saith true,' laughed Pirret. 'Truly, he could not walk accoutred as he is. Give it a slit—out with your knife and slit it, gossip.'

Even Arblaster paused at this proposal; but as his companion continued to insist, and Dick had the sense to keep the merest wooden indifference of expression, and only shrugged his shoulders over the delay, the skipper consented at last, and cut the cords which tied his prisoner's feet and legs. Not only did this enable Dick to walk, but the whole network of his bonds being proportionately loosened, he felt the arm behind his back begin to move more freely, and could hope, with time and trouble, to entirely disengage it. So much he owed already to the owlish silliness and greed of Master Pirret.

That worthy now assumed the lead, and conducted them to the very same rude alehouse where Lawless had taken Arblaster on the day of the gale. It was now quite deserted; the fire was a pile of red embers, radiating the most ardent heat; and when they had chosen their places, and the landlord had set before them a measure of mulled ale, both Pirret and Arblaster stretched forth their legs and squared their elbows like men bent upon a pleasant hour.

The table at which they sat, like all the others in the alehouse, consisted of a heavy, square board, set on a pair of barrels; and each of the four curiously assorted cronies sat at one side of the square, Pirret facing Arblaster, and Dick opposite to the common sailor.

'And now, young man,' said Pirret, 'to your tale. It doth appear, indeed, that ye have somewhat abused our gossip Arblaster; but what then? Make it up to him—show him but this chance to become wealthy—and I will go pledge he will forgive you.'

So far Dick had spoken pretty much at random; but it was now necessary, under the supervision of six eyes, to invent and tell some marvellous story, and, if it were possible, get back into his hands the all-important signet. To squander time was the first necessity. The longer his stay lasted, the more would his captors drink, and the surer should he be when he attempted his escape.

Well, Dick was not much of an inventor, and what he told was pretty much the tale of Ali Baba, with Shoreby and Tunstall Forest substituted for the East, and the treasures of the cavern rather exaggerated than diminished. As the reader is aware, it is an excellent story, and has but one drawback—that it is not true; and so as these three simple shipmen now heard it for the first time, their eyes stood out of their faces, and their mouths gaped like codfish at a fishmonger's.

Pretty soon a second measure of mulled ale was called for; and while Dick was artfully spinning out the incidents a third followed the second.

Here was the position of the parties towards the end:—

Arblaster, three-parts drunk and one-half asleep, hung helpless on his stool. Even Tom had been much delighted with the tale, and his vigilance had abated in proportion. Meanwhile, Dick had gradually wormed his right arm clear of its bonds, and was ready to risk all.

'And so,' said Pirret, 'y' are one of these?'

'I was made so,' replied Dick, 'against my will; but an I could but get a sack or two of gold coin to my share, I should be a fool indeed to continue dwelling in a filthy cave, and standing shot and buffet like a soldier. Here be we four; good! Let us, then, go forth into the forest to-morrow ere the sun be up. Could we come honestly by a donkey, it were better; but an we cannot, we have our four strong backs and I warrant me we shall come home staggering.'

Pirret licked his lips.

'And this magic,' he said—'this password, whereby the cave is opened—how call ye it, friend?'

'Nay, none know the word but the three chiefs,' returned Dick; 'but here is your great good fortune, that, on this very evening, I should be the bearer of a spell to open it. It is a thing not trusted twice a year beyond the captain's wallet.'

'A spell!' said Arblaster, half awakening, and squinting upon Dick with one eye. 'Aroint thee! no spells! I be a good Christian. Ask my man Tom, else.'

'Nay, but this is white magic,' said Dick. 'It doth naught with the devil; only the powers of numbers, herbs, and planets.'

'Ay, ay,' said Pirret; ''tis but white magic, gossip. There is no sin therein, I do assure you. But proceed, good youth. This spell—in what should it consist?'

'Nay, that I will incontinently show you,' answered Dick. 'Have ye there the ring ye took from my finger? Good! Now hold it forth before you by the extreme finger-ends, at the arm's length, and over against the shining of these embers. 'Tis so, exactly. Thus, then, is the spell.'

With a haggard glance, Dick saw the coast was clear between him and the door. He put up an internal prayer. Then whipping forth his arm, he made but one snatch of the ring, and at the same instant, levering up the table, he sent it bodily over upon the seaman Tom. He, poor soul, went down bawling under the ruins; and before Arblaster understood that anything was wrong, or Pirret could collect his dazzled wits, Dick had run to the door and escaped into the moonlit night.

The moon, which now rode in the mid-heavens, and the extreme whiteness of the snow, made the open ground about the harbour bright as day; and young Shelton leaping, with kilted robe, among the lumber, was a conspicuous figure from afar.

Tom and Pirret followed him with shouts; from every drinking-shop they were joined by others whom their cries aroused; and presently a whole fleet of sailors was in full pursuit. But Jack ashore was a bad runner, even in the fifteenth century, and Dick, besides, had a start, which he rapidly improved, until, as he drew near the entrance of a narrow lane, he even paused and looked laughingly behind him.

Upon the white floor of snow, all the shipmen of Shoreby came clustering in an inky mass, and tailing out rearward in isolated clumps. Every man was shouting or screaming; every man was gesticulating with both arms in air; some one was continually falling; and to complete the picture, when one fell, a dozen would fall upon the top of him.

The confused mass of sound which they rolled up as high as to the moon was partly comical and partly terrifying to the fugitive whom they were hunting. In itself, it was impotent, for he made sure no seaman in the port could run him down. But the mere volume of noise, in so far as it must awake all the sleepers in Shoreby, and bring all the skulking sentries to the street, did really threaten him with danger in the front. So, spying a dark doorway at a corner, he whipped briskly into it, and let the uncouth hunt go by him, still shouting and gesticulating, and all red with hurry, and white with tumbles in the snow.

It was a long while, indeed, before this great invasion of the town by the harbour came to an end, and it was long before silence was restored. For long, lost sailors were still to be heard pounding and shouting through the streets in all directions and in every quarter of the town. Quarrels followed, sometimes among themselves, sometimes with the men of the patrols; knives were drawn, blows given and received, and more than one dead body remained behind upon the snow.

When, a full hour later, the last seaman returned grumblingly to the harbour side and his particular tavern, it may fairly be questioned if he had ever known what manner of man he was pursuing, but it was absolutely sure that he had now forgotten. By next morning there were many strange stories flying; and a little while after, the legend of the devil's nocturnal visit was an article of faith with all the lads of Shoreby.

But the return of the last seaman did not, even yet, set free young Shelton from his cold imprisonment in the doorway.

For some time after there was a great activity of patrols; and special parties came forth to make the round of the place and report to one or other of the great lords, whose slumbers had been thus unusually broken.

The night was already well spent before Dick ventured from

his hiding-place and came, safe and sound, but aching with cold and bruises, to the door of the Goat and Bagpipes. As the law required, there was neither fire nor candle in the house; but he groped his way into a corner of the icy guest-room, found an end of the blanket, which he hitched around his shoulders, and creeping close to the nearest sleeper, was soon lost in slumber.

Book Five

CROOKBACK

25

The shrill trumpet

VERY early the next morning, before the first peep of the day, Dick arose, changed his garments, armed himself once more like a gentleman, and set forth for Lawless's den in the forest. There, it will be remembered, he had left Lord Foxham's papers; and to get these and be back in time for the tryst with the young Duke of Gloucester could only be managed by an early start, and the most vigorous walking.

The frost was more rigorous than ever; the air windless and dry, and stinging to the nostril. The moon had gone down, but the stars were still bright and numerous, and the reflection from the snow was clear and cheerful. There was no need for a lamp to walk by; nor, in that still but ringing air, the least temptation to delay.

Dick had crossed the greater part of the open ground between Shoreby and the forest, and had reached the bottom of the little hill, some hundred yards below the Cross of St. Bride, when, through the stillness of the black morn, there rang forth the note of a trumpet, so shrill, clear, and piercing, that he thought he had never heard the match of it for audibility. It was blown once, and then hurriedly a second time, and then the clash of steel succeeded.

At this young Shelton pricked his ears, and drawing his sword, ran forward up the hill.

Presently he came in sight of the cross, and was aware of a most fierce encounter raging on the road before it. There were seven or eight assailants, and but one to keep head against them; but so active and dexterous was this one, so desperately did he charge and scatter his opponents, so deftly keep his footing on the ice, that already, before Dick could intervene, he had slain one, wounded another, and kept the whole in check.

Still, it was by a miracle that he continued his defence, and at any moment, any accident, the least slip of foot or error of hand, his life would be a forfeit.

'Hold ye well, sir! Here is help!' cried Richard; and forgetting that he was alone, and that the cry was somewhat irregular, 'To the Arrow! to the Arrow!' he shouted, as he fell upon the rear of the assailants.

These were stout fellows also, for they gave not an inch at

this surprise, but faced about, and fell with astonishing fury upon Dick. Four against one, the steel flashed about him in the starlight: the sparks flew fiercely; one of the men opposed to him fell—in the stir of the fight he hardly knew why; then he himself was struck across the head, and though the steel cap below his hood protected him, the blow beat him down upon one knee, with a brain whirling like a windmill sail.

Meanwhile the man whom he had come to rescue, instead of joining in the conflict had, on the first sign of intervention, leaped aback and blown again, and yet more urgently and loudly, on that same shrill-voiced trumpet that began the alarm. Next moment, indeed, his foes were on him, and he was once more charging and fleeing, leaping, stabbing, dropping to his knee, and using indifferently sword and dagger, foot and hand, with the same unshaken courage and feverish energy and speed.

But that ear-piercing summons had been heard at last. There was a muffled rushing in the snow; and, in a good hour for Dick, who saw the sword-points glitter already at his throat, there poured forth out of the wood upon both sides a disorderly torrent of mounted men-at-arms, each cased in iron, and with visor lowered, each bearing his lance in rest, or his sword bared and raised, and each carrying, so to speak, a passenger, in the shape of an archer or page, who leaped one after another from their perches, and had presently doubled the array.

The original assailants, seeing themselves outnumbered and surrounded, threw down their arms without a word.

'Seize me these fellows!' said the hero of the trumpet; and when his order had been obeyed, he drew near to Dick and looked him in the face.

Dick, returning this scrutiny, was surprised to find in one who had displayed such strength, skill, and energy, a lad no older than himself—slightly deformed, with one shoulder higher than the other, and of a pale, painful, and distorted countenance.[1] The eyes, however, were very clear and bold.

'Sir,' said this lad, 'ye came in good time for me, and none too early.'

'My lord,' returned Dick, with a faint sense that he was in the presence of a great personage, 'ye are yourself so marvellous a good swordsman that I believe ye had managed them single-handed. Howbeit, it was certainly well for me that your men delayed no longer than they did.'

'How knew ye who I was?' demanded the stranger.

1 Richard Crookback would have been really far younger at this date.

'Even now, my lord,' Dick answered, 'I am ignorant of whom I speak with.'

'Is it so?' asked the other. 'And yet ye threw yourself head first into this unequal battle.'

'I saw one man valiantly contending against many,' replied Dick, 'and I had thought myself dishonoured not to bear him aid.'

A singular sneer played about the young nobleman's mouth as he made answer:—

'These are very brave words. But to the more essential—are ye Lancaster or York?'

'My lord, I make no secret; I am clear for York,' Dick answered.

'By the mass!' replied the other, 'it is well for you.'

And so saying, he turned towards one of his followers.

'Let me see,' he continued, in the same sneering and cruel tones—'let me see a clean end of these brave gentlemen. Truss me them up.'

There were but five survivors of the attacking party. Archers seized them by the arms; they were hurried to the borders of the wood, and each placed below a tree of suitable dimensions; the rope was adjusted; an archer, carrying the end of it, hastily clambered overhead, and before a minute was over, and without a word passing upon either hand, the five men were swinging by the neck.

'And now,' cried the deformed leader, 'back to your posts, and when I summon you next, be readier to attend.'

'My lord duke,' said one man 'beseech you, tarry not here alone. Keep but a handful of lances at your hand.'

'Fellow,' said the duke, 'I have forborne to chide you for your slowness. Cross me not, therefore. I trust my hand and arm, for all that I be crooked. Ye were backward when the trumpet sounded: and ye are now too forward with your counsels. But it is ever so; last with the lance and first with tongue. Let it be reversed.'

And with a gesture that was not without a sort of dangerous nobility, he waved them off.

The footmen climbed again to their seats behind the men-at-arms, and the whole party moved slowly away and disappeared in twenty different directions, under the cover of the forest.

The day was by this time beginning to break, and the stars to fade. The first gray glimmer of dawn shone upon the countenances of the two young men, who now turned once more to face each other.

'Here,' said the duke, 'ye have seen my vengeance, which is, like my blade, both sharp and ready. But I would not have you, for all Christendom, suppose me thankless. You that came to my aid with a good sword and a better courage—unless that ye recoil from my misshapenness—come to my heart.'

And so saying the young leader held out his arms for an embrace.

In the bottom of his heart Dick already entertained a great terror and some hatred for the man whom he had rescued; but the invitation was so worded that it would not have been merely discourteous, but cruel, to refuse or hesitate, and he hastened to comply.

'And now, my lord duke,' he said, when he had regained his freedom, 'do I suppose aright? Are ye my Lord Duke of Gloucester?'

'I am Richard of Gloucester,' returned the other. 'And you—how call they you?'

Dick told him his name, and presented Lord Foxham's signet, which the duke immediately recognised.

'Ye come too soon,' he said; 'but why should I complain? Ye are like me, that was here at watch two hours before the day. But this is the first sally of mine arms; upon this adventure, Master Shelton, shall I make or mar the quality of my renown. There lie mine enemies, under two old, skilled captains, Risingham and Brackley, well posted for strength, I do believe, but yet upon two sides without retreat, enclosed betwixt the sea, the harbour, and the river. Methinks, Shelton, here were a great blow to be stricken, an we could strike it silently and suddenly.'

'I do think so, indeed,' cried Dick, warming.

'Have ye my Lord Foxham's notes?' inquired the duke.

And then Dick, having explained how he was without them for the moment, made himself bold to offer information every jot as good, of his own knowledge.

'And for mine own part, my lord duke,' he added, 'an ye had men enough, I would fall on even at this present. For, look ye, at the peep of day the watches of the night are over; but by day they keep neither watch nor ward—only scour the outskirts with horsemen. Now, then, when the night-watch is already unarmed, and the rest are at their morning cup—now were the time to break them.'

'How many do ye count?' asked Gloucester.

'They number not two thousand,' Dick replied.

'I have seven hundred in the woods behind us,' said the duke; 'seven hundred follow from Kettley, and will be here anon;

behind these, and farther, are four hundred more; and my Lord Foxham hath five hundred half a day from here, at Holywood. Shall we attend their coming, or fall on?'

'My lord,' said Dick, 'when ye hanged these five poor rogues ye did decide the question. Churls although they were, in these uneasy times they will be lacked and looked for, and the alarm be given. Therefore, my lord, if ye do count upon the advantage of a surprise, ye have not, in my poor opinion, one whole hour in front of you.'

'I do think so, indeed,' returned Crookback. 'Well, before an hour, ye shall be in the thick on't, winning spurs. A swift man to Holywood, carrying Lord Foxham's signet; another along the road to speed my laggards! Nay, Shelton, by the rood, it may be done!'

Therewith he once more set his trumpet to his lips and blew.

This time he was not long kept waiting. In a moment the open space about the cross was filled with horse and foot. Richard of Gloucester took his place upon the steps, and despatched messenger after messenger to hasten the concentration of the seven hundred men that lay hidden in the immediate neighbourhood among the woods; and before a quarter of an hour had passed, all his dispositions being taken, he put himself at their head, and began to move down the hill towards Shoreby.

His plan was simple. He was to seize a quarter of the town of Shoreby lying on the right hand of the high road, and make his position good there in the narrow lanes until his reinforcements followed.

If Lord Risingham chose to retreat, Richard would follow upon his rear, and take him between two fires; or, if he preferred to hold the town he would be shut in a trap, there to be gradually overwhelmed by force of numbers.

There was but one danger, but that was imminent and great —Gloucester's seven hundred might be rolled up and cut to pieces in the first encounter, and, to avoid this, it was needful to make the surprise of their arrival as complete as possible.

The footmen, therefore, were all once more taken up behind the riders, and Dick had the signal honour meted out to him of mounting behind Gloucester himself. For as far as there was any cover the troops moved slowly, and when they came near the end of the trees that lined the highway, stopped to breathe and reconnoitre.

The sun was now well up, shining with a frosty brightness out of a yellow halo, and right over against the luminary, Shoreby, a field of snowy roofs, and ruddy gables, was rolling up its columns of morning smoke.

Gloucester turned round to Dick.

'In that poor place,' he said, 'where people are cooking breakfast, either you shall gain your spurs and I begin a life of mighty honour and glory in the world's eye, or both of us, as I conceive it, shall fall dead and be unheard of. Two Richards are we. Well then, Richard Shelton, they shall be heard about, these two! Their swords shall not ring more loudly on men's helmets than their names shall ring in people's ears.'

Dick was astonished at so great a hunger after fame, expressed with so great vehemence of voice and language; and he answered very sensibly and quietly that, for his part, he promised he would do his duty, and doubted not of victory if every one did the like.

By this time the horses were well breathed, and the leader holding up his sword and giving rein, the whole troop of chargers broke into the gallop and thundered, with their double load of fighting men, down the remainder of the hill and across the snow-covered plain that still divided them from Shoreby.

26

The battle of Shoreby

THE whole distance to be crossed was not above a quarter of a mile. But they had no sooner debouched beyond the cover of the trees than they were aware of people fleeing and screaming in the snowy meadows upon either hand. Almost at the same moment a great rumour began to arise, and spread and grow continually louder in the town; and they were not yet half-way to the nearest house before the bells began to ring backward from the steeple.

The young duke ground his teeth together. By these so early signals of alarm he feared to find his enemies prepared; and if he failed to gain a footing in the town, he knew that his small party would soon be broken and exterminated in the open.

In the town, however, the Lancastrians were far from being in so good a posture. It was as Dick had said. The night-guard had already doffed their harness; the rest were still hanging —unlatched, unbraced, all unprepared for battle—about their quarters; and in the whole of Shoreby there were not, perhaps, fifty men fully armed, or fifty chargers ready to be mounted.

The beating of the bells, the terrifying summons of men who ran about the streets crying and beating upon the doors, aroused in an incredibly short space at least two score out of that half hundred. These got speedily to horse, and, the alarm still flying wild and contrary, galloped in different directions.

Thus it befell that, when Richard of Gloucester reached the first house of Shoreby, he was met in the mouth of the street by a mere handful of lances, whom he swept before his onset as the storm chases the bark.

A hundred paces into the town, Dick Shelton touched the duke's arm; the duke, in answer, gathered his reins, put the shrill trumpet to his mouth, and blowing a concerted point, turned to the right hand out of the direct advance. Swerving like a single rider, his whole command turned after him, and, still at the full gallop of the chargers, swept up the narrow by-street. Only the last score of riders drew rein and faced about in the entrance; the footmen, whom they carried behind them, leapt at the same instant to the earth, and began, some to bend their bows, and others to break into and secure the houses upon either hand.

Surprised at this sudden change of direction, and daunted by the firm front of the rear-guard, the few Lancastrians, after a momentary consultation, turned and rode farther into town to seek for reinforcements.

The quarter of the town upon which, by the advice of Dick, Richard of Gloucester had now seized, consisted of five small streets of poor and ill-inhabited houses, occupying a very gentle eminence, and lying open towards the back.

The five streets being each secured by a good guard, the reserve would thus occupy the centre, out of shot, and yet ready to carry aid wherever it was needed.

Such was the poorness of the neighbourhood that none of the Lancastrian lords, and but few of their retainers, had been lodged therein; and the inhabitants, with one accord, deserted their houses and fled, squalling, along the streets or over garden walls.

In the centre, where the five ways all met, a somewhat ill-favoured alehouse displayed the sign of the Chequers; and here the Duke of Gloucester chose his headquarters for the day.

To Dick he assigned the guard of one of the five streets.

'Go,' he said, 'win your spurs. Win glory for me; one Richard for another. I tell you, if I rise, ye shall rise by the same ladder. Go,' he added, shaking him by the hand.

But, as soon as Dick was gone, he turned to a little shabby archer at his elbow.

'Go, Dutton, and that right speedily,' he added. 'Follow that lad. If ye find him faithful, ye answer for his safety, a head for a head. Woe unto you, if ye return without him! But if he be faithless—or, for one instant, ye misdoubt him—stab him from behind.'

In the meanwhile Dick hastened to secure his post. The street he had to guard was very narrow, and closely lined with houses, which projected and overhung the roadway; but narrow and dark as it was, since it opened upon the market-place of the town, the main issue of the battle would probably fall to be decided on that spot.

The market-place was full of townspeople fleeing in disorder; but there was as yet no sign of any foeman ready to attack, and Dick judged he had some time before him to make ready his defence.

The two houses at the end stood deserted, with open doors, as the inhabitants had left them in their flight, and from these he had the furniture hastily tossed forth and piled into a barrier in the entry of the lane. A hundred men were placed at his disposal, and of these he threw the more part into the houses, where they might lie in shelter and deliver their arrows from the windows. With the rest, under his own immediate eye, he lined the barricade.

Meanwhile the utmost uproar and confusion had continued to prevail throughout the town; and what with the hurried clashing of bells, the sounding of trumpets, the swift movement of bodies of horse, the cries of the commanders, and the shrieks of women, the noise was almost deafening to the ear. Presently, little by little, the tumult began to subside; and soon after, files of men in armour and bodies of archers began to assemble and form in line of battle in the market-place.

A large portion of this body were in murrey and blue, and in the mounted knight who ordered their array Dick recognised Sir Daniel Brackley.

Then there befell a long pause, which was followed by the almost simultaneous sounding of four trumpets from four different quarters of the town. A fifth rang in answer from the market-place, and at the same moment the files began to move, and a shower of arrows rattled about the barricade, and sounded like blows upon the walls of the two flanking houses.

The attack had begun, by a common signal, on all the five issues of the quarter. Gloucester was beleaguered upon every side; and Dick judged, if he would make good his post, he must rely entirely on the hundred men of his command.

Seven volleys of arrows followed one upon the other, and in the very thick of the discharges Dick was touched from behind upon the arm, and found a page holding out to him a leathern jack, strengthened with bright plates of mail.

'It is from my Lord of Gloucester,' said the page. 'He hath observed, Sir Richard, that ye went unarmed.'

Dick, with a glow at his heart at being so addressed, got to his feet and, with the assistance of the page, donned the defensive coat. Even as he did so, two arrows rattled harmlessly upon the plates, and a third struck down the page, mortally wounded at his feet.

Meanwhile the whole body of the enemy had been steadily drawing nearer across the market-place; and by this time were so close at hand that Dick gave the order to return their shot. Immediately, from behind the barrier and from the windows of the houses, a counterblast of arrows sped, carrying death. But the Lancastrians, as if they had but waited for a signal, shouted loudly in answer; and began to close at a run upon the barrier, the horsemen still hanging back, with visors lowered.

Then followed an obstinate and deadly struggle, hand to hand. The assailants wielding their falchions with one hand, strove with the other to drag down the structure of the barricade. On the other side, the parts were reversed; and the defenders exposed themselves like madmen to protect their rampart. So for some minutes the contest raged almost in silence, friend and foe falling one upon another. But it is always the easier to destroy; and when a single note upon the tucket recalled the attacking party from this desperate service, much of the barricade had been removed piecemeal, and the whole fabric had sunk to half its height, and tottered to a general fall.

And now the footmen in the market-place fell back, at a run, on every side. The horsemen, who had been standing in a line two deep, wheeled suddenly, and made their flank into their front; and as swift as a striking adder, the long, steel-clad column was launched upon the ruinous barricade.

Of the first two horsemen, one fell, rider and steed, and was ridden down by his companions. The second leaped clean upon the summit of the rampart, transpiercing an archer with his lance. Almost in the same instant he was dragged from the saddle and his horse despatched.

And then the full weight and impetus of the charge burst upon and scattered the defenders. The men-at-arms, surmounting their fallen comrades, and carried onward by the fury of their onslaught, dashed through Dick's broken line and poured thundering up the lane beyond, as a stream bestrides and pours across a broken dam.

Yet was the fight not over. Still, in the narrow jaws of the entrance, Dick and a few survivors plied their bills like woodmen; and already, across the width of the passage, there had been formed a second, a higher, and a more effectual rampart of fallen men and disembowelled horses, lashing in the agonies of death.

Baffled by this fresh obstacle, the remainder of the cavalry fell back; and as, at the sight of this movement, the flight of arrows redoubled from the casements of the houses, their retreat had, for a moment, almost degenerated into flight.

Almost at the same time, those who had crossed the barricade and charged farther up the street, being met before the door of the Chequers by the formidable hunchback and the whole reserve of the Yorkists, began to come scattering backward, in the excess of disarray and terror.

Dick and his fellows faced about, fresh men poured out of the houses; a cruel blast of arrows met the fugitives full in the face, while Gloucester was already riding down their rear; in the inside of a minute and a half there was no living Lancastrian in the street.

Then, and not till then, did Dick hold up his reeking blade and give the word to cheer.

Meanwhile Gloucester dismounted from his horse and came forward to inspect the post. His face was as pale as linen; but his eyes shone in his head like some strange jewel, and his voice, when he spoke, was hoarse and broken with the exultation of battle and success. He looked at the rampart, which neither friend nor foe could now approach without precaution, so fiercely did the horses struggle in the throes of death, and at the sight of that great carnage he smiled upon one side.

'Despatch these horses,' he said; 'they keep you from your vantage. Richard Shelton,' he added, 'ye have pleased me. Kneel.'

The Lancastrians had already resumed their archery, and the shafts fell thick in the mouth of the street; but the duke, minding them not at all, deliberately drew his sword and dubbed Richard a knight upon the spot.

'And now, Sir Richard,' he continued, 'if that ye see Lord Risingham, send me an express upon the instant. Were it your last man, let me hear of it incontinently. I had rather venture the post than lose my stroke at him. For mark me, all of ye,' he added, raising his voice, 'if Earl Risingham fall by another hand than mine, I shall count this victory a defeat.'

'My lord duke,' said one of his attendants, 'is your grace not weary of exposing his dear life unneedfully? Why tarry we here?'

'Catesby,' returned the duke, 'here is the battle, not elsewhere. The rest are but feigned onslaughts. Here must we vanquish. And for the exposure—if ye were an ugly hunchback and the children gecked at you upon the street, ye would count your body cheaper, and an hour of glory worth a life. Howbeit, if ye will, let us ride on and visit the other posts. Sir Richard here, my namesake, he shall still hold this entry, where he wadeth to the ankles in hot blood. Him can we trust. But mark it, Sir Richard, ye are not yet done. The worst is yet to ward. Sleep not.'

He came right up to young Shelton, looking him hard in the eyes, and taking his hand in both of his, gave it so extreme a squeeze that the blood had nearly spurted. Dick quailed before his eyes. The insane excitement, the courage, and the cruelty that he read therein, filled him with dismay about the future. This young duke's was indeed a gallant spirit, to ride foremost in the ranks of war; but after the battle, in the days of peace and in the circle of his trusted friends, that mind, it was to be dreaded, would continue to bring forth the fruits of death.

27

The battle of Shoreby (concluded)

DICK, once more left to his own counsels, began to look about him. The arrow-shot had somewhat slackened. On all sides the enemy were falling back, and the greater part of the market-place was now left empty, the snow here trampled into orange mud, there splashed with gore, scattered all over with dead men and horses, and bristling thick with feathered arrows.

On his own side the loss had been cruel. The jaws of the little street and the ruins of the barricade were heaped with the dead and dying; and out of the hundred men with whom he had begun the battle, there were not seventy left who could still stand to arms.

At the same time the day was passing. The first reinforcements might be looked for to arrive at any moment; and the Lancastrians, already shaken by the result of their desperate but unsuccessful onslaught, were in an ill temper to support a fresh invader.

There was a dial in the wall of one of the two flanking houses; and this, in the frosty, wintry sunshine, indicated ten of the forenoon.

Dick turned to the man who was at his elbow, a little insignificant archer, binding a cut in his arm.

'It was well fought,' he said, 'and, by my sooth, they will not charge us twice.'

'Sir,' said the little archer, 'ye have fought right well for York, and better for yourself. Never hath man in so brief space prevailed so greatly on the duke's affections. That he should have entrusted such a post to one he knew not is a marvel. But look to your head, Sir Richard! If ye be vanquished—ay, if ye give away one foot's breadth—axe or cord shall punish it; and I am set if ye do aught doubtful, I will tell you honestly, here to stab you from behind!'

Dick looked at the little man in amaze.

'You!' he cried. 'And from behind!'

'It is right so,' returned the archer; 'and because I like not the affair I tell it you. Ye must make the post good, Sir Richard, at your peril. O, our Crookback is a bold blade and a good warrior; but whether in cold blood or in hot, he will have all things done exact to his commandment. If any fail or hinder, they shall die the death.'

'Now, by the saints!' cried Richard, 'is this so? And will men follow such a leader?'

'Nay, they follow him gleefully,' replied the other; 'for if he be exact to punish, he is most open-handed to reward. And if he spare not the blood and sweat of others, he is ever liberal of his own, still in the first front of battle, still the last to sleep. He will go far, will Crookback Dick o' Gloucester!'

The young knight, if he had before been brave and vigilant, was now all the more inclined to watchfulness and courage. His sudden favour, he began to perceive, had brought perils in its train. And he turned from the archer, and once more scanned anxiously the market-place. It lay empty as before.

'I like not this quietude,' he said. 'Doubtless they prepare us some surprise.'

And, as if in answer to his remark, the archers began once more to advance against the barricade, and the arrows to fall thick. But there was something hesitating in the attack. They came not on roundly, but seemed rather to await a further signal.

Dick looked uneasily about him, spying for a hidden danger. And sure enough, about half-way up the little street a door was suddenly opened from within, and the house continued, for some seconds, and both by door and window, to disgorge a torrent of Lancastrian archers. These, as they leaped down, hurriedly stood to their ranks, bent their bows, and proceeded to pour upon Dick's rear a flight of arrows.

At the same time, the assailants in the market-place redoubled their shot, and began to close in stoutly upon the barricade.

Dick called down his whole command out of the houses, and facing them both ways, and encouraging their valour both by word and gesture, returned as best he could the double shower of shafts that fell about his post.

Meanwhile house after house was opened in the street, and the Lancastrians continued to pour out of the doors and leap down from the windows, shouting victory, until the number of enemies upon Dick's rear was almost equal to the number in his face. It was plain that he could hold the post no longer; what was worse, even if he could have held it, it had now become useless; and the whole Yorkist army lay in a posture of helplessness upon the brink of a complete disaster.

The men behind him formed the vital flaw in the general defence; and it was upon these that Dick turned, charging at the head of his men. So vigorous was the attack, that the Lancastrian archers gave ground and staggered, and, at last, breaking their ranks, began to crowd back into the houses from which they had so recently and so vaingloriously sallied.

Meanwhile the men from the market-place had swarmed across the undefended barricade and fell on hotly upon the other side; and Dick must once again face about, and proceed to drive them back. Once again the spirit of his men prevailed; they cleared the street in a triumphant style, but even as they did so the others issued again out of the houses, and took them, a third time, upon the rear.

The Yorkists began to be scattered; several times Dick found himself alone among his foes and plying his bright sword for life; several times he was conscious of a hurt. And meanwhile the fight swayed to and fro in the street without determinate result.

Suddenly Dick was aware of a great trumpeting about the outskirts of the town. The way-cry of York began to be rolled up to heaven, as by many and triumphant voices. And at the same time the men in front of him began to give ground rapidly, streaming out of the street and back upon the market-place. Some one gave the word to fly. Trumpets were blown distractedly, some for a rally, some to charge. It was plain that a great blow had been struck, and the Lancastrians were thrown, at least for the moment, into full disorder, and some degree of panic.

And then, like a theatre trick, there followed the last act of Shoreby battle. The men in front of Richard turned tail, like a dog that has been whistled home, and fled like the wind. At the same moment there came through the market-place a storm of horsemen, fleeing and pursuing, the Lancastrians turning back to strike with the sword, the Yorkists riding them down at the point of the lance.

Conspicuous in the mellay, Dick beheld the Crookback. He was already giving a foretaste of that furious valour and skill to cut his way across the ranks of war, which, years afterwards upon the field of Bosworth, and when he was stained with crimes, almost sufficed to change the fortunes of the day and the destiny of the English throne. Evading, striking, riding down, he so forced and so manœuvred his strong horse, so aptly defended himself, and so liberally scattered death to his opponents, that he was now far ahead of the foremost of his knights, hewing his way, with the truncheon of a bloody sword, to where Lord Risingham was rallying the bravest. A moment more and they had met; the tall, splendid, and famous warrior against the deformed and sickly boy.

Yet Shelton had never a doubt as to the result; and when the fight next opened for a moment, the figure of the earl had disappeared; but still, in the first of the danger, Crookback Dick was launching his big horse and plying the truncheon of his sword.

Thus, by Shelton's courage in holding the mouth of the street against the first attack, and by the opportune arrival of his seven hundred reinforcements, the lad, who was afterwards to be handed down to the execration of posterity under the name of Richard III., had won his first considerable fight.

28

The sack of Shoreby

THERE was not a foe left within striking distance; and Dick, as he looked ruefully about him on the remainder of his gallant force, began to count the cost of victory. He was himself, now that the danger was ended, so stiff and sore, so bruised and cut and broken, and, above all, so utterly exhausted by his desperate and unremitting labours in the fight, that he seemed incapable of any fresh exertion.

But this was not yet the hour for repose. Shoreby had been taken by assault; and though an open town, and not in any manner to be charged with the resistance, it was plain that these rough fighters would be not less rough now that the fight was over, and that the more horrid part of war would fall to be enacted. Richard of Gloucester was not the captain to protect the citizens from his infuriated soldiery; and even if he had the will, it might be questioned if he had the power.

It was therefore Dick's business to find and to protect Joanna; and with that end he looked about him at the faces of his men. The three or four who seemed likeliest to be obedient and to keep sober he drew aside; and promising them a rich reward and a special recommendation to the duke, led them across the market-place, now empty of horsemen, and into the streets upon the farther side.

Every here and there small combats of from two to a dozen still raged upon the open street; here and there a house was being besieged, the defenders throwing out stools and tables on the heads of the assailants. The snow was strewn with arms and corpses; but except for these partial combats the streets were deserted, and the houses, some standing open, and some shuttered and barricaded, had for the most part ceased to give out smoke.

Dick, threading the skirts of these skirmishers, led his followers briskly in the direction of the abbey church; but when he came the length of the main street, a cry of horror broke from his lips. Sir Daniel's great house had been carried by assault. The gates hung in splinters from the hinges, and a double throng kept pouring in and out through the entrance, seeking and carrying booty. Meanwhile, in the upper storeys, some resistance was still being offered to the pillagers; for just as Dick came within eyeshot of the building a casement was burst open from within, and a poor wretch in murrey and blue, screaming and resisting, was forced through the embrasure and tossed into the street below.

The most sickening apprehension fell upon Dick. He ran forward like one possessed, forced his way into the house among the foremost, and mounted without pause to the chamber on the third floor where he had last parted from Joanna. It was a mere wreck; the furniture had been overthrown, the cupboards broken open, and in one place a trailing corner of the arras lay smouldering on the embers of the fire.

Dick, almost without thinking, trod out the incipient conflagration, and then stood bewildered. Sir Daniel, Sir Oliver, Joanna, all were gone; but whether butchered in the rout or safe escaped from Shoreby, who should say?

He caught a passing archer by the tabard.

'Fellow,' he asked, 'were ye here when this house was taken?'

'Let be,' said the archer. 'A murrain! let be, or I strike.'

'Hark ye,' returned Richard, 'two can play at that. Stand and be plain.'

But the man, flushed with drink and battle, struck Dick upon the shoulder with one hand, while with the other he twitched away his garment. Thereupon the full wrath of the young leader burst from his control. He seized the fellow in his strong embrace, and crushed him on the plates of his mailed bosom like a child; then, holding him at arm's length, he bid him speak as he valued life.

'I pray you mercy!' gasped the archer. 'An I thought ye were so angry I would 'a' been charier of crossing you. I was here indeed.'

'Know ye Sir Daniel?' pursued Dick.

'Well do I know him,' returned the man.

'Was he in the mansion?'

'Ay, sir,' he was,' answered the archer; 'but even as we entered by the yard gate he rode forth by the garden.'

'Alone? cried Dick.

'He may 'a' had a score of lances with him,' said the man.

'Lances! No women, then?' asked Shelton.

'Troth, I saw not,' said the archer. 'But there were none in the house, if that be your quest.'

'I thank you,' said Dick. 'Here is a piece for your pains.' But groping in his wallet, Dick found nothing. 'Inquire for me to-morrow,' he added—'Richard Shel—Sir Richard Shelton,' he corrected, 'and I will see you handsomely rewarded.'

And then an idea struck Dick. He hastily descended to the courtyard, ran with all his might across the garden, and came to the great door of the church. It stood wide open; within, every corner of the pavement was crowded with fugitive burghers, surrounded by their families and laden with the most precious of their possessions, while, at the high altar, priests in full canonicals were imploring the mercy of God. Even as Dick entered, the loud chorus began to thunder in the vaulted roofs.

He hurried through the groups of refugees, and came to the door of the stair that led into the steeple. And here a tall churchman stepped before him and arrested his advance.

'Whither, my son?' he asked severely.

'My father,' answered Dick, 'I am here upon an errand of expedition. Stay me not. I command here for my Lord of Gloucester.'

'For my Lord of Gloucester?' repeated the priest. 'Hath, then, the battle gone so sore?'

'The battle, father, is at an end, Lancaster clean sped, my Lord of Risingham—Heaven rest him!—left upon the field. And now, with your good leave, I follow mine affairs.' And thrusting on one side the priest, who seemed stupefied at the news, Dick pushed open the door and rattled up the stairs four at a bound, and without pause or stumble, till he stepped upon the open platform at the top.

Shoreby Church tower not only commanded the town, as in a map, but looked far, on both sides, over sea and land. It was now near upon noon, the day exceeding bright, the snow dazzling. And as Dick looked around him, he could measure the consequences of the battle.

A confused, growling uproar reached him from the streets, and now and then, but very rarely, the clash of steel. Not a ship, not so much as a skiff remained in harbour; but the sea was dotted with sails and row-boats laden with fugitives. On shore, too, the surface of the snowy meadows was broken up with bands of horsemen, some cutting their way towards the borders of the forest, others, who were doubtless of the Yorkist side, stoutly interposing and beating them back upon the town. Over all the open ground there lay a prodigious quantity of fallen men and horses, clearly defined upon the snow.

To complete the picture, those of the foot soldiers as had not found place upon a ship still kept up an archery combat on the borders of the port, and from the cover of the shoreside taverns. In that quarter, also, one or two houses had been fired, and the smoke towered high in the frosty sunlight, and blew off to sea in voluminous folds.

Already close upon the margin of the woods, and somewhat in the line of Holywood, one particular clump of fleeing horsemen riveted the attention of the young watcher on the tower. It was fairly numerous; in no other quarter of the field did so many Lancastrians still hold together; thus they had left a wide, discoloured wake upon the snow, and Dick was able to trace them step by step from where they had left the town.

While Dick stood watching them, they had gained unopposed the first fringe of the leafless forest, and turning a little from their direction, the sun fell for a moment full on their array, as it was relieved against the dusky wood.

'Murrey and blue!' cried Dick. 'I swear it—murrey and blue!'

The next moment he was descending the stairway.

It was now his business to seek out the Duke of Gloucester, who, alone, in the disorder of the forces, might be able to supply him with a sufficiency of men. The fighting in the main town was now practically at an end; and as Dick ran hither and thither, seeking the commander, the streets were thick with wandering soldiers, some laden with more booty than they could well stagger under, others shouting drunk. None of them, when questioned, had the least notion of the duke's whereabouts; and, at last, it was by sheer good fortune that Dick found him, where he sat in the saddle, directing operations to dislodge the archers from the harbour side.

'Sir Richard Shelton, ye are well found,' he said. 'I owe you one thing that I value little, my life; and one that I can never pay you for, this victory. Catesby, if I had ten such captains as Sir Richard, I would march forthright on London. But now, sir, claim your reward.'

'Freely, my lord,' said Dick, 'freely and loudly. One hath escaped to whom I owe some grudges, and takes with him one whom I owe love and service. Give me, then, fifty lances, that I may pursue; and for any obligation that your graciousness is pleased to allow, it shall be clean discharged.'

'How call ye him?' inquired the duke.

'Sir Daniel Brackley,' answered Richard.

'Out upon him, double-face,' cried Gloucester. 'Here is no reward, Sir Richard; here is fresh service offered, and, if that ye bring his head to me, a fresh debt upon my conscience. Catesby, get him these lances; and you, sir, bethink ye, in the meanwhile, what pleasure, honour, or profit it shall be mine to give you.'

Just then the Yorkist skirmishers carried one of the shoreside taverns, swarming in upon it on three sides, and driving out or taking its defenders. Crookback Dick was pleased to cheer the exploit, and pushing his horse a little nearer, called to see the prisoners.

There were four or five of them—two men of my Lord Shoreby's and one of Lord Risingham's among the number, and last, but in Dick's eyes, not least, a tall, shambling, grizzled old shipman, between drunk and sober, and with a dog whimpering and jumping at his heels.

The young duke passed them for a moment under a severe review.

'Good,' he said. 'Hang them.'

And he turned the other way to watch the progress of the fight.

'My lord,' said Dick, 'so please you, I have found my reward. Grant me the life and liberty of yon old shipman.'

Gloucester turned and looked the speaker in the face.

'Sir Richard,' he said, 'I make not war with peacock's feathers, but steel shafts. Those that are mine enemies I slay, and that without excuse or favour. For, bethink ye, in this realm of England, that is so torn in pieces, there is not a man of mine but hath a brother or a friend upon the other party. If, then, I did begin to grant these pardons, I might sheathe my sword.'

'It may be so, my lord; and yet I will be over bold, and, at the risk of your disfavour, recall your lordship's promise,' replied Dick.

Richard of Gloucester flushed.

'Mark it right well,' he said harshly. 'I love not mercy, nor yet mercy-mongers. Ye have this day laid the foundations of high fortune. If ye oppose to me my word, which I have plighted, I will yield. But by the glory of heaven, there your favour dies!'

'Mine is the loss,' said Dick.

'Give him his sailor,' said the duke; and wheeling his horse, he turned his back upon young Shelton.

Dick was nor glad nor sorry. He had seen too much of the young duke to set great store on his affection; and the origin and growth of his own favour had been too flimsy and too rapid to inspire much confidence. One thing alone he feared—that the vindictive leader might revoke the offer of the lances. But here he did justice neither to Gloucester's honour (such as it was), nor, above all, to his decision. If he had once judged Dick to be the right man to pursue Sir Daniel, he was not one to change; and he soon proved it by shouting after Catesby to be speedy, for the paladin was waiting.

In the meanwhile, Dick turned to the old shipman, who had seemed equally indifferent to his condemnation and to his subsequent release.

'Arblaster,' said Dick, 'I have done you ill; but now, by the rood, I think I have cleared the score.'

But the old skipper only looked upon him dully and held his peace.

'Come,' continued Dick, 'a life is a life, old shrew, and it is more than ships or liquor. Say ye forgive me; for if your life is worth nothing to you, it hath cost me the beginnings of my fortune. Come, I have paid for it dearly; be not so churlish.'

'And I had had my ship,' said Arblaster, 'I would 'a' been forth and safe on the high seas—I and my man Tom. But ye took my ship, gossip, and I'm a beggar; and for my man Tom, a knave fellow in russet shot him down. "Murrain!" quoth he, and spake never again. "Murrain" was the last of his words, and the poor spirit of him passed. 'A will never sail no more, will my Tom.'

Dick was seized with unavailing penitence and pity; he sought to take the skipper's hand, but Arblaster avoided his touch.

'Nay,' said he, 'let be. Y' have played the devil with me, and let that content you.'

The words died in Richard's throat. He saw, through tears,

the poor old man, bemused with liquor and sorrow, go shambling away, with bowed head, across the snow, and the unnoticed dog whimpering at his heels; and for the first time began to understand the desperate game that we play in life, and how a thing once done is not to be changed or remedied by any penitence.

But there was no time left to him for vain regret. Catesby had now collected the horsemen, and riding up to Dick he dismounted and offered him his own horse.

'This morning,' he said, 'I was somewhat jealous of your favour; it hath not been of a long growth; and now, Sir Richard, it is with a very good heart that I offer you this horse—to ride away with.'

'Suffer me yet a moment,' replied Dick. 'This favour of mine—whereupon was it founded?'

'Upon your name,' answered Catesby. 'It is my lord's chief superstition. Were my name Richard, I should be an earl tomorrow.'

'Well, sir, I thank you,' returned Dick; 'and since I am little likely to follow these great fortunes, I will even say farewell. I will not pretend I was displeased to think myself upon the road to fortune; but I will not pretend, neither, that I am over sorry to be done with it. Command and riches, they are brave things, to be sure; but a word in your ear—yon duke of yours, he is a fearsome lad.'

Catesby laughed.

'Nay,' said he, 'of a verity he that rides with Crooked Dick will ride deep. Well, God keep us all from evil! Speed ye well.'

Thereupon Dick put himself at the head of his men, and giving the word of command, rode off.

He made straight across the town, following what he supposed to be the route of Sir Daniel, and spying around for any signs that might decide if he were right.

The streets were strewn with the dead and the wounded, whose fate, in the bitter frost, was far the more pitiable. Gangs of the victors went from house to house, pillaging and stabbing, and sometimes singing together as they went.

From different quarters, as he rode on, the sounds of violence and outrage came to young Shelton's ears; now the blows of the sledge-hammer on some barricaded door, and now the miserable shrieks of women.

Dick's heart had just been awakened. He had just seen the cruel consequences of his own behaviour; and the thought of the sum of misery that was now acting in the whole of Shoreby filled him with despair.

At length he reached the outskirts, and there, sure enough, he saw straight before him the same broad, beaten track across the snow that he had marked from the summit of the church. Here, then, he went the faster on; but still, as he rode, he kept a bright eye upon the fallen men and horses that lay beside the track. Many of these, he was relieved to see, wore Sir Daniel's colours, and the faces of some, who lay upon their backs, he even recognised.

About half-way between the town and the forest, those whom he was following had plainly been assailed by archers; for the corpses lay pretty closely scattered, each pierced by an arrow. And here Dick spied among the rest the body of a very young lad, whose face was somehow hauntingly familiar to him.

He halted his troop, dismounted, and raised the lad's head. As he did so, the hood fell back, and a profusion of long brown hair unrolled itself. At the same time the eyes opened.

'Ah! lion-driver!' said a feeble voice. 'She is farther on. Ride—ride fast!'

And then the poor young lady fainted once again.

One of Dick's men carried a flask of some strong cordial, and with this Dick succeeded in reviving consciousness. Then he took Joanna's friend upon his saddle-bow, and once more pushed toward the forest.

'Why do ye take me?' said the girl. 'Ye but delay your speed.'

'Nay, Mistress Risingham,' replied Dick. 'Shoreby is full of blood and drunkenness and riot. Here ye are safe; content ye.'

'I will not be beholden to any of your faction,' she cried; 'set me down.'

'Madam, ye know not what ye say,' returned Dick. 'Y' are hurt——'

'I am not, she said.' 'It was my horse was slain.'

'It matters not one jot,' replied Richard. 'Ye are here in the midst of open snow, and compassed about with enemies. Whether ye will or not, I carry you with me. Glad am I to have the occasion; for thus shall I repay some portion of our debt.'

For a little while she was silent. Then, very suddenly, she asked:—

'My uncle?'

'My Lord Risingham?' returned Dick. 'I would I had good news to give you, madam; but I have none. I saw him once in the battle, and once only. Let us hope the best.'

29

Night in the woods: Alicia Risingham

It was almost certain that Sir Daniel had made for the Moat House; but, considering the heavy snow, the lateness of the hour, and the necessity under which he would lie of avoiding the few roads and striking across the wood, it was equally certain that he could not hope to reach it ere the morrow.

There were two courses open to Dick; either to continue to follow in the knight's trail, and, if he were able, to fall upon him that very night in camp, or to strike out a path of his own, and seek to place himself between Sir Daniel and his destination.

Either scheme was open to serious objection, and Dick, who feared to expose Joanna to the hazards of a fight, had not yet decided between them when he reached the borders of the wood.

At this point Sir Daniel had turned a little to his left, and then plunged straight under a grove of very lofty timber. His party had then formed to a narrower front, in order to pass between the trees, and the track was trod proportionately deeper in the snow. The eye followed it, under the leafless tracery of the oaks, running direct and narrow; the trees stood over it, with knotty joints and the great, uplifted forest of their boughs; there was no sound, whether of man or beast; not so much as the stirring of a robin; and over the field of snow the winter sun lay golden among netted shadows.

'How say ye,' asked Dick of one of the men, 'to follow straight on, or strike across for Tunstall?'

'Sir Richard,' replied the man-at-arms, 'I would follow the line until they scatter.'

'Ye are, doubtless, right,' returned Dick; 'but we came right hastily upon the errand, even as the time commanded. Here are no houses, neither for food nor shelter, and by the morrow's dawn we shall know both cold fingers and an empty belly. How say ye, lads? Will ye stand a pinch for expedition's sake, or shall we turn by Holywood and sup with Mother Church? The case being somewhat doubtful, I will drive no man; yet if ye would suffer me to lead you, ye would choose the first.'

The men answered, almost with one voice, that they would follow Sir Richard where he would.

And Dick, setting spur to his horse, began once more to go forward.

The snow in the trail had been trodden very hard, and the pursuers had thus a great advantage over the pursued. They pushed on, indeed, at a round trot, two hundred hoofs beating alternately on the dull pavement of the snow, and the jingle of weapons and the snorting of horses raising a warlike noise along the arches of the silent wood.

Presently, the wide slot of the pursued came out upon the high road from Holywood; it was there, for a moment, indistinguishable; and, where it once more plunged into the unbeaten snow upon the farther side, Dick was surprised to see it narrower and lighter trod. Plainly, profiting by the road, Sir Daniel had begun already to scatter his command.

At all hazards, one chance being equal to another, Dick continued to pursue the straight trail; and that, after an hour's riding, in which it led into the very depth of the forest, suddenly split, like a bursting shell, into two dozen others, leading to every point of the compass.

Dick drew bridle in despair. The short winter's day was near an end; the sun, a dull red orange, shorn of rays, swam low among the leafless thickets; the shadows were a mile long upon the snow; the frost bit cruelly at the finger-nails; and the breath and steam of the horses mounted in a cloud.

'Well, we are outwitted,' Dick confessed. 'Strike we for Holywood, after all. It is still nearer us than Tunstall—or should be by the station of the sun.'

So they wheeled to their left, turning their backs on the red shield of sun, and made across country for the abbey. But now times were changed with them; they could no longer spank forth briskly on a path beaten firm by the passage of their foes, and for a goal to which that path itself conducted them. Now they must plough at a dull pace through the encumbering snow, continually pausing to decide their course, continually floundering in drifts. The sun soon left them; the glow of the west decayed; and presently they were wandering in a shadow of blackness under frosty stars.

Presently, indeed, the moon would clear the hilltops, and they might resume their march. But till then, every random step might carry them wider of their march. There was nothing for it but to camp and wait.

Sentries were posted; a spot of ground was cleared of snow, and after some failures, a good fire blazed in the midst. The men-at-arms sat close about this forest hearth, sharing such provisions as they had, and passing about the flask; and Dick, having collected the most delicate of this rough and scanty fare, brought it to Lord Risingham's niece, where she sat apart from the soldiery against a tree.

She sat upon one horse-cloth, wrapped in another, and stared straight before her at the firelit scene. At the offer of food she started, like one wakened from a dream, and then silently refused.

'Madam,' said Dick, 'let me beseech you, punish me not so cruelly. Wherein I have offended you, I know not; I have, indeed, carried you away, but with a friendly violence; I have, indeed, exposed you to the inclemency of night, but the hurry that lies upon me hath for its end the preservation of another, who is no less frail and no less unfriended than yourself. At least, madam, punish not yourself; and eat, if not for hunger, then for strength.'

'I will eat nothing at the hands that slew my kinsman,' she replied.

'Dear madam,' Dick cried, 'I swear to you upon the rood I touched him not.'

'Swear to me that he still lives,' she returned.

'I will not palter with you,' answered Dick. 'Pity bids me to wound you. In my heart I do believe him dead.'

'And ye ask me to eat!' she cried. 'Ay, and they call you "sir"! Y' have won your spurs by my good kinsman's murder. And had I not been fool and traitor both, and saved you in your enemy's house, ye should have died the death, and he—he that was worth twelve of you—were living.'

'I did but my man's best, even as your kinsman did upon the other party,' answered Dick. 'Were he still living—as I vow to Heaven I wish it!—he would praise, not blame me.'

'Sir Daniel hath told me,' she replied. 'He marked you at the barricade. Upon you, he saith, their party foundered; it was you that won the battle. Well, then, it was you that killed my good Lord Risingham, as sure as though ye had strangled him. And ye would have me eat with you—and your hands not washed from killing? But Sir Daniel hath sworn your downfall. He 'tis that will avenge me!'

The unfortunate Dick was plunged in gloom. Old Arblaster returned upon his mind, and he groaned aloud.

'Do ye hold me so guilty?' he said; 'you that defended me—you that are Joanna's friend?'

'What made ye in the battle?' she retorted. 'Y' are of no party; y' are but a lad—but legs and body, without government of wit or counsel! Wherefore did ye fight? For the love of hurt, pardy!'

'Nay,' cried Dick, 'I know not. But as the realm of England goes, if that a poor gentleman fight not upon the one side, perforce he must fight upon the other. He may not stand alone, 'tis not in nature.'

'They that have no judgment should not draw the sword,'

replied the young lady. 'Ye that fight but for a hazard, what are ye but a butcher? War is but noble by the cause, and y' have disgraced it.'

'Madam,' said the miserable Dick, 'I do partly see mine error. I have made too much haste; I have been busy before my time. Already I stole a ship—thinking, I do swear it, to do well—and thereby brought about the death of many innocent, and the grief and ruin of a poor old man whose face this very day hath stabbed me like a dagger. And for this morning, I did but design to do myself credit, and get fame to marry with, and, behold! I have brought about the death of your dear kinsman that was good to me. And what besides, I know not. For, alas! I may have set York upon the throne, and that may be the worser cause, and may do hurt to England. O! madam, I do see my sin. I am unfit for life. I will, for penance sake and to avoid worse evil, once I have finished this adventure, get me to a cloister. I will forswear Joanna and the trade of arms. I will be a friar, and pray for your good kinsman's spirit all my days.'

It appeared to Dick, in this extremity of his humiliation and repentance, that the young lady had laughed.

Raising his countenance, he found her looking down upon him in the firelight, with a somewhat peculiar but not unkind expression.

'Madam,' he cried, thinking the laughter to have been an illusion of his hearing, but still, from her changed looks, hoping to have touched her heart—'madam, will not this content you? I give up all to undo what I have done amiss; I make heaven certain for Lord Risingham. And all this upon the very day that I have won my spurs, and thought myself the happiest young gentleman on ground.'

'O, boy,' she said—'good boy!'

And then, to the extreme surprise of Dick, she first very tenderly wiped the tears away from his cheeks, and then, as if yielding to a sudden impulse, threw both her arms about his neck, drew up his face, and kissed him. A pitiful bewilderment came over simple-minded Dick.

'But come,' she said, with great cheerfulness, 'you that are a captain, ye must eat. Why sup ye not?'

'Dear Mistress Risingham,' replied Dick, 'I did but wait first upon my prisoner; but, to say truth, penitence will no longer suffer me to endure the sight of food. I were better to fast, dear lady, and to pray.'

'Call me Alicia,' she said; 'are we not old friends? And now, come, I will eat with you, bit for bit and sup for sup;

so if ye eat not, neither will I; but if ye eat hearty, I will dine like a ploughman.'

So there and then she fell to; and Dick, who had an excellent stomach, proceeded to bear her company, at first with great reluctance but gradually, as he entered into the spirit, with more and more vigour and devotion; until, at last, he forgot even to watch his model, and most heartily repaired the expenses of his day of labour and excitement.

'Lion-driver,' she said at length, 'ye do not admire a maid in a man's jerkin?'

The moon was now up; and they were only waiting to repose the wearied horses. By the moon's light, the still penitent but now well-fed Richard beheld her looking somewhat coquettishly down upon him.

'Madam——' he stammered, surprised at this new turn in her manners.

'Nay,' she interrupted, 'it skills not to deny; Joanna hath told me, but come, Sir Lion-driver, look at me—am I so homely?—come!'

And she made bright eyes at him.

'Ye are something smallish indeed——' began Dick.

And here again she interrupted him, this time with a ringing peal of laughter that completed his confusion and surprise.

'Smallish!' she cried. 'Nay, now, be honest as ye are bold; I am a dwarf, or little better; but for all that—come, tell me!—for all that, passably fair to look upon; is't not so?'

'Nay, madam, exceedingly fair,' said the distressed knight, pitifully trying to seem easy.

'And a man would be right glad to wed me?' she pursued.

'O, madam, right glad!' agreed Dick.

'Call me Alicia,' said she.

'Alicia,' quoth Sir Richard.

'Well, then, lion-driver,' she continued, 'sith that ye slew my kinsman, and left me without stay, ye owe me, in honour, every reparation; do ye not?'

'I do, madam,' said Dick. 'Although, upon my heart, I do hold me but partially guilty of that brave knight's blood.'

'Would ye evade me?' she cried.

'Madam, not so. I have told you; at your bidding, I will even turn me a monk,' said Richard.

'Then, in honour, ye belong to me?' she concluded.

'In honour, madam, I suppose——' began the young man.

'Go to!' she interrupted; 'ye are too full of catches. In honour do ye belong to me, till ye have paid the evil?'

'In honour I do,' said Dick.

'Hear, then,' she continued. 'Ye would make but a sad friar, methinks; and since I am to dispose of you at pleasure, I will even take you for my husband. Nay, now no words!' cried she. 'They will avail you nothing. For see how just it is, that ye who deprived me of one home, should supply me with another. And as for Joanna, she will be the first, believe me, to commend the change; for, after all, as we be dear friends, what matters it with which of us ye wed? Not one whit!'

'Madam,' said Dick, 'I will go into a cloister, an ye please to bid me; but to wed with any one in this big world besides Joanna Sedley, is what I will consent to neither for man's force nor yet for lady's pleasure. Pardon me if I speak my plain thoughts plainly; but where a maid is very bold, a poor man must even be the bolder.'

'Dick,' she said, 'ye sweet boy, ye must come and kiss me for that word. Nay, fear not, ye shall kiss me for Joanna, and when we meet I shall give it back to her, and say I stole it. And as for what ye owe me, why, dear simpleton, methinks ye were not alone in that great battle; and even if York be on the throne, it was not you that set him there. But for a good sweet, honest heart, Dick, y' are all that; and if I could find it in my soul to envy your Joanna anything, I would envy her your love.'

30

Night in the woods (concluded): Dick and Joan

THE horses had by this time finished the small store of provender, and fully breathed from their fatigues. At Dick's command the fire was smothered in snow; and while his men got once more wearily to saddle, he himself, remembering, somewhat late, true woodland caution, chose a tall oak, and nimbly clambered to the topmost fork. Hence he could look far abroad on the moonlit and snow-paved forest. On the south-west, dark against the horizon, stood those upland heathy quarters where he and Joanna had met with the terrifying misadventure of the leper. And there his eye was caught by a spot of ruddy brightness no bigger than a needle's eye.

He blamed himself sharply for his previous neglect. Were that, as it appeared to be, the shining of Sir Daniel's campfire he should long ago have seen and marched for it; above all, he should, for no consideration, have announced his neighbourhood by lighting a fire of his own. But now he must no longer squander valuable hours. The direct way to the uplands was about two miles in length; but it crossed by a very deep, precipitous dingle, impassable to mounted men; and for the sake of speed, it seemed to Dick advisable to desert the horses and attempt the adventure on foot.

Ten men were left to guard the horses; signals were agreed upon by which they could communicate in case of need; and Dick set forth at the head of the remainder, Alicia Risingham walking stoutly by his side.

The men had freed themselves of heavy armour, and left behind their lances; and they now marched with a very good spirit in the frozen snow, and under the exhilarating lustre of the moon. The descent into the dingle, where a stream strained sobbing through the snow and ice, was effected with silence and order; and on the farther side, being then within a short half-mile of where Dick had seen the glimmer of the fire, the party halted to breathe before the attack.

In the vast silence of the wood, the lightest sounds were audible from afar; and Alicia, who was keen of hearing, held up her finger warningly, and stooped to listen. All followed her example; but besides the groans of the choked brook in the dingle close behind, and the barking of a fox at a distance of many miles among the forest, to Dick's acutest hearkening not a breath was audible.

'But yet, for sure, I heard the clash of harness,' whispered Alicia.

'Madam,' returned Dick, who was more afraid of that young lady than of ten stout warriors, 'I would not hint ye were mistaken; but it might well have come from either of the camps.'

'It came not thence. It came from westward,' she declared.

'It may be what it will,' returned Dick; 'and it must be as heaven please. Reck we not a jot, but push on the livelier, and put it to the touch. Up, friends—enough breathed.'

As they advanced, the snow became more and more trampled with hoof-marks, and it was plain that they were drawing near to the encampment of a considerable force of mounted men. Presently they could see the smoke pouring from among the trees, ruddily coloured on its lower edge and scattering bright sparks.

And here, pursuant to Dick's orders, his men began to open out, creeping stealthily in the covert, to surround on every side the camp of their opponents. He himself, placing Alicia in the shelter of a bulky oak, stole straight forth in the direction of the fire.

At last, through an opening of the wood, his eye embraced the scene of the encampment. The fire had been built upon a heathy hummock of the ground, surrounded on three sides by thicket, and it now burned very strong, roaring aloud and brandishing flames. Around it there sat not quite a dozen people, warmly cloaked; but though the neighbouring snow was trampled down as by a regiment, Dick looked in vain for any horse. He began to have a terrible misgiving that he was out-manœuvred. At the same time, in a tall man with a steel salet, who was spreading his hands before the blaze, he recognised his old friend and still kindly enemy, Bennet Hatch; and in two others, sitting a little back, he made out, even in their male disguise, Joanna Sedley and Sir Daniel's wife.

'Well,' thought he to himself, 'even if I lose my horses, let me get my Joanna, and why should I complain?'

And then, from the farther side of the encampment, there came a little whistle, announcing that his men had joined, and the investment was complete.

Bennet, at the sound, started to his feet; but ere he had time to spring upon his arms, Dick hailed him.

'Bennet,' he said—'Bennet, old friend, yield ye. Ye will but spill men's lives in vain if ye resist.'

''Tis Master Shelton, by St. Barbary!' cried Hatch. 'Yield me? Ye ask much. What force have ye?'

'I tell you, Bennet, ye are both outnumbered and begirt,' said Dick. 'Cæsar and Charlemagne would cry for quarter. I have two score men at my whistle, and with one shoot of arrows I could answer for you all.'

'Master Dick,' said Bennet, 'it goes against my heart; but I must do my duty. The saints help you!' And therewith he raised a little tucket to his mouth and wound a rousing call.

Then followed a moment of confusion; for while Dick, fearing for the ladies, still hesitated to give the word to shoot, Hatch's little band sprang to their weapons and formed back to back as for a fierce resistance. In the hurry of their change of place, Joanna sprang from her seat and ran like an arrow to her lover's side.

'Here, Dick!' she cried, as she clasped his hand in hers.

But Dick still stood irresolute; he was yet young to the more deplorable necessities of war, and the thought of old Lady Brackley checked the command upon his tongue. His own men became restive. Some of them cried on him by name; others, of their own accord, began to shoot; and at the first discharge poor Bennet bit the dust. Then Dick awoke.

'On!' he cried. 'Shoot, boys, and keep to cover. England and York!'

But just then the dull beat of many horses on the snow suddenly arose in the hollow ear of the night, and, with incredible swiftness, drew nearer and swelled louder. At the same time, answering tuckets repeated and repeated Hatch's call.

'Rally, rally!' cried Dick. 'Rally upon me! Rally for your lives!'

But his men—afoot, scattered, taken in the hour when they counted on an easy triumph—began, instead, to give ground severally, and either stood wavering or dispersed into the thickets. And when the first of the horsemen came charging through the open avenues and fiercely riding their steeds into the underwood, a few stragglers were overthrown or speared among the brush, but the bulk of Dick's command had simply melted at the rumour of their coming.

Dick stood for a moment, bitterly recognising the fruits of his precipitate and unwise valour. Sir Daniel had seen the fire; he had moved out with his main force, whether to attack his pursuers or to take them in the rear if they should venture the assault. His had been throughout the part of a sagacious captain; Dick's the conduct of an eager boy. And here was the young knight, his sweetheart, indeed, holding him tightly by the hand, but otherwise alone, his whole command of men and horses dispersed in the night and the wide forest, like a paper of pins in a hay barn.

'The saints enlighten me!' he thought. 'It is well I was knighted for this morning's matter; this doth me little honour.'

And thereupon, still holding Joanna, he began to run.

The silence of the night was now shattered by the shouts of the men of Tunstall, as they galloped hither and thither, hunting fugitives; and Dick broke boldly through the underwood and ran straight before him like a deer. The silver clearness of the moon upon the open snow increased, by contrast, the obscurity of the thickets; and the extreme dispersion of the vanquished led the pursuers into widely divergent paths. Hence, in but a little while, Dick and Joanna paused, in a close covert, and heard the sounds of the pursuit, scattering abroad, indeed, in all directions, but yet fainting already in the distance.

'An I had but kept a reserve of them together,' Dick cried bitterly, 'I could have turned the tables yet! Well, we live and learn; next time it shall go better, by the rood.'

'Nay, Dick,' said Joanna, 'what matters it? Here we are together once again.'

He looked at her, and there she was—John Matcham, as of yore, in hose and doublet. But now he knew her; now, even in that ungainly dress, she smiled upon him, bright with love; and his heart was transported with joy.

'Sweetheart,' he said, 'if ye forgive this blunderer, what care I? Make we direct for Holywood; there lieth your good guardian and my better friend, Lord Foxham. There shall we be wed; and whether poor or wealthy, famous or unknown, what matters it? This day, dear love, I won my spurs; I was commended by great men for my valour; I thought myself the goodliest man of war in all broad England. Then, first, I fell out of my favour with the great; and now have I been well thrashed, and clean lost my soldiers. There was a downfall for conceit! But, dear, I care not—dear, if ye still love me and will wed, I would have my knighthood done away, and mind it not a jot.'

'My Dick!' she cried. 'And did they knight you?'

'Ay, dear, ye are my lady now,' he answered fondly; 'or ye shall, ere noon to-morrow—will ye not?'

'That will I, Dick, with a glad heart,' she answered.

'Ay, sir? Methought ye were to be a monk!' said a voice in their ears.

'Alicia!' cried Joanna.

'Even so,' replied the young lady, coming forward. 'Alicia, whom ye left for dead, and whom your lion-driver found, and brought to life again, and, by my sooth, made love to, if ye want to know.'

'I'll not believe it,' cried Joanna. 'Dick!'

'Dick!' mimicked Alicia. 'Dick, indeed! Ay, fair sir, and ye desert poor damsels in distress,' she continued, turning to the young knight. 'Ye leave them planted behind oaks. But they say true, the age of chivalry is dead.'

'Madam,' cried Dick, in despair, 'upon my soul I had forgotten you outright. Madam, ye must try to pardon me. Ye see, I had new found Joanna!'

'I did not suppose that ye had done it on purpose,' she retorted. 'But I will be cruelly avenged. I will tell a secret to my Lady Shelton—she that is to be,' she added, curtseying. 'Joanna,' she continued, 'I believe, upon my soul, your sweetheart is a bold fellow in a fight, but he is, let me tell you plainly, the softest-hearted simpleton in England. Go to—ye may do your pleasure with him! And now, fool children, first kiss me, either one of you, for luck and kindness; and then kiss each other just one minute by the glass, and not one second longer; and then let us all three set forth for Holywood as fast as we can stir; for these woods, methinks, are full of peril and exceeding cold.'

'But did my Dick make love to you?' asked Joanna, clinging to her sweetheart's side.

'Nay, fool girl,' returned Alicia, 'it was I made love to him. I offered to marry him, indeed; but he bade me go marry with my likes. These were his words. Nay, that I will say: he is more plain than pleasant. But now, children, for the sake of sense set forward. Shall we go once more over the dingle, or push straight for Holywood?'

'Why,' said Dick, 'I would like dearly to get upon a horse; for I have been sore mauled and beaten, one way and another, these last days, and my poor body is one bruise. But how think ye? If the men, upon the alarm of the fighting, had fled away, we should have gone about for nothing. 'Tis but some three short miles to Holywood direct; the bell hath not beat nine; the snow is pretty firm to walk upon, the moon clear; how if we went even as we are?'

'Agreed,' cried Alicia; but Joanna only pressed upon Dick's arm.

Forth, then, they went, through open leafless groves and down snow-clad alleys, under the white face of the winter moon; Dick and Joanna walking hand in hand and in a heaven of pleasure; and their light-minded companion, her own bereavements heartily forgotten, followed a pace or two behind, now rallying them upon their silence, and now drawing happy pictures of their future and united lives.

Still, indeed, in the distance of the wood, the riders of Tunstall might be heard urging their pursuit; and from time to time cries or the clash of steel announced the shock of enemies. But in these young folk, bred among the alarms of war, and fresh from such a multiplicity of dangers, neither fear nor pity could be lightly wakened. Content to find the sounds still drawing farther and farther away, they gave up their hearts to the enjoyment of the hour, walking already, as Alicia put it, in a wedding procession; and neither the rude solitude of the forest, nor the cold of the freezing night, had any force to shadow or distract their happiness.

At length, from a rising hill, they looked below them on the dell of Holywood. The great windows of the forest abbey shone with torch and candle; its high pinnacles and spires arose very clear and silent, and the gold rood upon the topmost summit glittered brightly in the moon. All about it, in the open glade, camp-fires were burning, and the ground was thick with huts; and across the midst of the picture the frozen river curved.

'By the mass,' said Richard, 'there are Lord Foxham's fellows still encamped. The messenger hath certainly miscarried. Well, then, so better. We have power at hand to face Sir Daniel.'

But if Lord Foxham's men still lay encamped in the long holm at Holywood, it was from a different reason from the one supposed by Dick. They had marched, indeed, for Shoreby;

but ere they were half-way thither, a second messenger met them, and bade them return to their morning's camp, to bar the road against Lancastrian fugitives, and to be so much nearer to the main army of York. For Richard of Gloucester, having finished the battle and stamped out his foes in that district, was already on the march to rejoin his brother; and not long after the return of my Lord Foxham's retainers, Crookback himself drew rein before the abbey door. It was in honour of this august visitor that the windows shone with lights; and at the hour of Dick's arrival with his sweetheart and her friend, the whole ducal party was being entertained in the refectory with the splendour of that powerful and luxurious monastery.

Dick, not quite with his good will, was brought before them. Gloucester, sick with fatigue, sat leaning upon one hand his white and terrifying countenance; Lord Foxham, half recovered from his wound, was in a place of honour on his left.

'How, sir?' asked Richard. 'Have ye brought me Sir Daniel's head?'

'My lord duke,' replied Dick, stoutly enough, but with a qualm at heart, 'I have not even the good fortune to return with my command. I have been, so please your grace, well beaten.'

Gloucester looked upon him with a formidable frown.

'I gave you fifty lances,[1] sir,' he said.

'My lord duke, I had but fifty men-at-arms,' replied the young knight.

'How is this?' said Gloucester. 'He did ask me fifty lances.'

'May it please your grace,' replied Catesby, smoothly, 'for a pursuit we gave him but the horsemen.'

'It is well,' replied Richard, adding, 'Shelton, ye may go.'

'Stay!' said Lord Foxham. 'This young man likewise had a charge from me. It may be he hath better sped. Say, Master Shelton, have ye found the maid?'

'I praise the saints, my lord,' said Dick, 'she is in this house.'

'Is it even so? Well, then, my lord the duke,' resumed Lord Foxham, 'with your good will, to-morrow, before the army march, I do propose a marriage. This young squire——'

'Young knight,' interrupted Catesby.

'Say ye so, Sir William?' cried Lord Foxham.

'I did myself, and for good service, dub him knight,' said Gloucester. 'He hath twice manfully served me. It is not valour of hands, it is a man's mind of iron, that he lacks. He will not rise, Lord Foxham. 'Tis a fellow that will fight indeed bravely

1 Technically, the term "lance" included a not quite certain number of foot soldiers attached to the man-at-arms.

in a mellay, but hath a capon's heart. Howbeit, if he is to marry, marry him in the name of Mary, and be done!'

'Nay, he is a brave lad—I know it,' said Lord Foxham. 'Content ye, then, Sir Richard. I have compounded this affair with Master Hamley, and to-morrow ye shall wed.'

Whereupon Dick judged it prudent to withdraw; but he was not yet clear of the refectory, when a man, but newly alighted at the gate, came running four stairs at a bound, and brushing through the abbey servants, threw himself on one knee before the duke.

'Victory, my lord,' he cried.

And before Dick had got to the chamber set apart for him as Lord Foxham's guest, the troops in the holm were cheering around their fires; for upon that same day, not twenty miles away, a second crushing blow had been dealt to the power of Lancaster.

31

Dick's revenge

THE next morning Dick was afoot before the sun, and having dressed himself to the best advantage with the aid of the Lord Foxham's baggage, and got good reports of Joan, he set forth on foot to walk away his impatience.

For some while he made rounds among the soldiery, who were getting to arms in the wintry twilight of the dawn and by the red glow of torches; but gradually he strolled farther afield, and at length passed clean beyond the outpost, and walked alone in the frozen forest, waiting for the sun.

His thoughts were both quiet and happy. His brief favour with the duke he could not find it in his heart to mourn; with Joan to wife, and my Lord Foxham for a faithful patron, he looked most happily upon the future; and in the past he found but little to regret.

As he thus strolled and pondered, the solemn light of the morning grew more clear, the east was already coloured by the sun, and a little scathing wind blew up the frozen snow. He turned to go home; but even as he turned, his eyes lit upon a figure behind a tree.

'Stand!' he cried. 'Who goes?'

The figure stepped forth and waved its hand like a dumb person. It was arrayed like a pilgrim, the hood lowered over the face, but Dick, in an instant, recognised Sir Daniel.

He strode up to him, drawing his sword; and the knight,

putting his hand in his bosom, as if to seize a hidden weapon, steadfastly awaited his approach.

'Well, Dickon,' said Sir Daniel, 'how is it to be? Do ye make war upon the fallen?'

'I made no war upon your life,' replied the lad; 'I was your true friend until ye sought for mine; but ye have sought for it greedily.'

'Nay—self-defence,' replied the knight. 'And now, boy, the news of this battle, and the presence of yon crooked devil here in mine own wood, have broken me beyond all help. I go to Holywood for sanctuary; thence over seas, with what I can carry, and to begin life again in Burgundy or France.'

'Ye may not go to Holywood,' said Dick.

'How! May not!' asked the knight.

'Look ye, Sir Daniel, this is my marriage morn,' said Dick; 'and yon sun that is to rise will make the brightest day that ever shone for me. Your life is forfeit—doubly forfeit, for my father's death and your own practices to me-ward. But I myself have done amiss; I have brought about men's deaths; and upon this glad day I will be neither judge nor hangman. An ye were the devil, I would not lay a hand on you. An ye were the devil, ye might go where ye will for me. Seek God's forgiveness; mine ye have freely. But to go on to Holywood is different. I carry arms for York, and I will suffer no spy within their lines. Hold it, then, for certain, if ye set one foot before another, I will uplift my voice and call the nearest post to seize you.'

'Ye mock me,' said Sir Daniel. 'I have no safety out of Holywood.'

'I care no more,' returned Richard. 'I let you go east, west, or south; north I will not. Holywood is shut against you. Go, and seek not to return. For, once ye are gone, I will warn every post about this army, and there will be so shrewd a watch upon all pilgrims that, once again, were ye the very devil, ye would find it ruin to make the essay.'

'Ye doom me,' said Sir Daniel gloomily.

'I doom you not,' returned Richard. 'If it so please you to set your valour against mine, come on; and though I fear it be disloyal to my party, I will take the challenge openly and fully, fight you with mine own single strength, and call for none to help me. So shall I avenge my father, with a perfect conscience.'

'Ay,' said Sir Daniel, 'y' have a long sword against my dagger.'

'I rely upon Heaven only,' answered Dick, casting his sword some way behind him on the snow. 'Now, if your ill fate bids you, come; and, under the pleasure of the Almighty, I make myself bold to feed your bones to foxes.'

'I did but try you, Dickon,' returned the knight, with an uneasy semblance of a laugh. 'I would not spill your blood.'

'Go then, ere it be too late,' replied Shelton. 'In five minutes I will call the post. I do perceive that I am too long-suffering. Had but our places been reversed, I should have been bound hand and foot some minutes past.'

'Well, Dickon, I will go,' replied Sir Daniel. 'When we next meet, it shall repent you that ye were so harsh.'

And with these words, the knight turned and began to move off under the trees. Dick watched him with strangely mingled feelings, as he went swiftly and warily, and ever and again turning a wicked eye upon the lad who had spared him, and whom he still suspected.

There was upon one side of where he went a thicket, strongly matted with green ivy, and, even in its winter state, impervious to the eye. Herein, all of a sudden, a bow sounded like a note of music. An arrow flew, and with a great choked cry of agony and anger, the Knight of Tunstall threw up his hands and fell forward in the snow.

Dick bounded to his side and raised him. His face desperately worked; his whole body was shaken by contorting spasms.

'Is the arrow black?' he gasped.

'It is black,' replied Dick gravely.

And then, before he could add one word, a desperate seizure of pain shook the wounded man from head to foot, so that his body leaped in Dick's supporting arms, and with the extremity of that pang his spirit fled in silence.

The young man laid him back gently on the snow and prayed for that unprepared and guilty spirit, and as he prayed the sun came up at a bound, and the robins began chirping in the ivy.

When he rose to his feet, he found another man upon his knees but a few steps behind him, and, still with uncovered head, he waited until that prayer also should be over. It took long; the man with his head bowed and his face covered with his hands, prayed like one in a great disorder or distress of mind; and by the bow that lay beside him, Dick judged that he was no other than the archer who had laid Sir Daniel low.

At length he also rose, and showed the countenance of Ellis Duckworth.

'Richard,' he said, very gravely, 'I heard you. Ye took the better part and pardoned; I took the worse, and there lies the clay of mine enemy. Pray for me.'

And he wrung him by the hand.

'Sir,' said Richard, 'I will pray for you indeed; though how I may prevail I wot not. But if ye have so long pursued revenge, and find it now of such a sorry flavour, bethink ye, were it not well to pardon others? Hatch—he is dead, poor shrew! I would have spared a better; and for Sir Daniel, here lies his body. But for the priest, if I might anywise prevail, I would have you let him go.'

A flash came into the eyes of Ellis Duckworth.

'Nay,' he said, 'the devil is still strong within me. But be at rest; the Black Arrow flieth nevermore—the fellowship is broken. They that still live shall come to their quiet and ripe end, in Heaven's good time, for me; and for yourself, go where your better fortune calls you, and think no more of Ellis.'

32

Conclusion

About nine in the morning, Lord Foxham was leading his ward, once more dressed as befitted her sex, and followed by Alicia Risingham, to the church of Holywood, when Richard Crookback, his brow already heavy with cares, crossed their path and paused.

'Is this the maid?' he asked; and when Lord Foxham had replied in the affirmative, 'Minion,' he added, 'hold up your face until I see its favour.'

He looked upon her sourly for a little.

'Ye are fair,' he said at last, 'and, as they tell me, dowered. How if I offered you a brave marriage, as became your face and parentage?'

'My lord duke,' replied Joanna, 'may it please your grace, I had rather wed with Sir Richard.'

'How so?' he asked harshly. 'Marry but the man I name to you, and he shall be my lord, and you my lady, before night. For Sir Richard, let me tell you plainly, he will die Sir Richard.'

'I ask no more of Heaven, my lord, than but to die Sir Richard's wife,' returned Joanna.

'Look ye at that, my lord,' said Gloucester, turning to Lord Foxham. 'Here be a pair for you. The lad, when for good services I gave him his choice of my favour, chose but the grace of an old, drunken shipman. I did warn him freely, but he was stout in his besottedness. "Here dieth your favour," said I; and he, my lord, with a most assured impertinence, "Mine be the loss," quoth he. It shall be so, by the rood!'

'Said he so?' cried Alicia. 'Then well said, lion-driver!'

'Who is this?' asked the duke.

'A prisoner of Sir Richard's,' answered Lord Foxham; 'Mistress Alicia Risingham.'

'See that she be married to a sure man,' said the duke.

'I had thought of my kinsman, Hamley, an it like your grace,' returned Lord Foxham. 'He hath well served the cause.'

'It likes me well,' said Richard. 'Let them be wedded speedily. Say, fair maid, will you wed?'

'My lord duke,' said Alicia, 'so as the man is straight——' And there, in a perfect consternation, the voice died on her tongue.

'He is straight, my mistress,' replied Richard calmly. 'I am the only crookback of my party; we are else passably well shapen. Ladies, and you, my lord,' he added, with a sudden change to grave courtesy, 'judge me not too churlish if I leave you. A captain, in the time of war, hath not the ordering of his hours.'

And with a very handsome salutation he passed on, followed by his officers.

'Alack,' cried Alicia, 'I am shent!'

'Ye know him not,' replied Lord Foxham. 'It is but a trifle; he hath already clean forgot your words.'

'He is, then, the very flower of knighthood,' said Alicia.

'Nay, he but mindeth other things,' returned Lord Foxham. 'Tarry we no more.'

In the chancel they found Dick waiting, attended by a few young men; and there were he and Joan united. When they came forth again, happy and yet serious, into the frosty air and sunlight, the long files of the army were already winding forward up the road; already the Duke of Gloucester's banner was unfolded and began to move from before the abbey in a clump of spears; and behind it, girt by steel-clad knights, the bold, black-hearted, and ambitious hunchback moved on towards his brief kingdom and his lasting infamy. But the wedding party turned upon the other side, and sat down, with sober merriment, to breakfast. The father cellarer attended on their wants, and sat with them at table. Hamley, all jealousy forgotten, began to ply the nowise loth Alicia with courtship. And there, amid the sounding of tuckets and the clash of armoured soldiery and horses continually moving forth, Dick and Joan sat side by side, tenderly held hands, and looked, with ever-growing affection, in each other's eyes.

Thenceforth the dust and blood of that unruly epoch passed them by. They dwelt apart from alarms in the green forest where their love began.

Two old men in the meanwhile enjoyed pensions in great prosperity and peace, and with perhaps a superfluity of ale and wine, in Tunstall hamlet. One had been all his life a shipman and continued to the last to lament his man Tom. The other, who had been a bit of everything, turned in the end towards piety, and made a most religious death under the name of Brother Honestus in the neighbouring abbey. So Lawless had his will, and died a friar.

PRINCE OTTO

TO

NELLY VAN DE GRIFT

(*MRS. ADULFO SANCHEZ, OF MONTEREY*)

At last, after so many years, I have the pleasure of re-introducing you to Prince Otto, *whom you will remember a very little fellow, no bigger in fact than a few sheets of memoranda written for me by your kind hand. The sight of his name will carry you back to an old wooden house embowered in creepers; a house that was far gone in the respectable stages of antiquity and seemed indissoluble from the green garden in which it stood, and that yet was a sea-traveller in its younger days, and had come round the Horn piecemeal in the belly of a ship, and might have heard the seamen stamping and shouting and the note of the boatswain's whistle. It will recall to you the nondescript inhabitants now so widely scattered:—the two horses, the dog, and the four cats, some of them still looking in your face as you read these lines;—the poor lady, so unfortunately married to an author;—the China boy, by this time, perhaps, baiting his line by the banks of a river in the Flowery Land;—and in particular the Scot who was then sick apparently unto death, and whom you did so much to cheer and keep in good behaviour.*

You may remember that he was full of ambitions and designs: so soon as he had his health again completely, you may remember the fortune he was to earn, the journeys he was to go upon, the delights he was to enjoy and confer, and (among other matters) the masterpiece he was to make of Prince Otto*!*

Well, we will not give in that we are finally beaten. We read together in those days the story of Braddock, and how, as he was carried dying from the scene of his defeat, he promised himself to do better another time; a story that will always touch a brave heart, and a dying speech worthy of a more fortunate commander. I try to be of Braddock's mind. I still mean to get my health again; I still purpose, by hook or crook, this book or the next, to launch a masterpiece; and I still intend—somehow, some time or other—to see your face and to hold your hand.

Meanwhile, this little paper traveller goes forth instead, crosses the great seas and the long plains and the dark mountains, and comes at last to your door in Monterey, charged with tender greetings. Pray you, take him in. He comes from a house where (even as in your own) there are gathered together some of the waifs of our company at Oakland; a house —for all its outlandish Gaelic name and distant station—where you are well-beloved. *R. L. S.*

Skerryvore,
Bournemouth.

CONTENTS

INTRODUCTION

It was during the three months that Stevenson spent at Monterey that his *Prince Otto* was planned. Stevenson was not quite thirty, much work was yet to be done, and this work was to be accomplished during those years in which he hardly ever knew what it was to be really well. His worldly position at this period was precarious. With almost a pathetic insistency, he demands that he must have money—journalism at two dollars a week was to him then, something that seemed a Divine clemency.

Prince Otto was planned when Stevenson was in the throes of a great literary activity. At Monterey he wrote an essay on the famous natural philosopher Thoreau, he created *The Pavilion on the Links*, a ' blood and thunder ' story, as he tells us, and he found time to write another story which remained unpublished.

In spite of all this activity, in spite of the commonplace journalism for the *Monterey Californian*, in spite of his desperate need of ' dibbs,' as he tells us; in spite of constant ill-health, Stevenson was able to spend many hours of crude enjoyment at Monterey. *Prince Otto* was born to the vision of the curious but picturesque friendship with Jules Simoneau, the delightful keeper of the little restaurant at Monterey, ' With Simoneau, Louis discussed the Universe.'

. . . . . .

From what we know of Stevenson it is quite obvious that he was very fond of his *Prince Otto*. It was to be a masterpiece, something really great, something that was to be worthy of a man who had left youth behind by several years. It is surely not merely ungracious, but also untrue, to suggest that Stevenson did not create a masterpiece with his *Prince Otto*. For on what ground could we say that this book was not a masterpiece? On the most unstable ground of literary criticism possible—the method of comparison. It is simply superficial to say that *Prince Otto* is inferior to *Dr. Jekyll and Mr. Hyde*, or that it is superior to *Treasure Island*. It would be just as unsatisfactory to state the converse. *Prince Otto* is one of those books which must be judged alone, any attempt to ' compare ' it can but lead to a disastrous miscarriage of justice.

Here Stevenson is in a mood of pleasant satire. He is dealing with that most delightful theme—a serious joke. Stevenson is often serious, but he can always joke. This is perhaps one of the supreme differences between Stevenson and so many satirists, this ability, that they seem to be serious and yet joke. For *Prince*

Otto is a serious book; it discusses something that we are thinking about more and more—rule by a Royal House. In a very few words Stevenson puts quite plainly one of the most formidable objections to the fact that the king's eldest son is, *ipso facto*, the next king. He makes Prince Otto himself admit the difficulty. It has to do with that problem of unworthy princes, being supplied with all the attributes of potential kingship. Prince Otto has been told by Dr. Gotthold—perhaps one of the sanest characters Stevenson has ever created—that he would make a deplorable sovereign.

' " Nay, Gotthold, I am not to be put by,' said Otto. " If I am constitutionally unfit to be a sovereign, what am I doing with this money, with this palace, with these guards? " '

It is almost as if Stevenson had put a very long telescope to his eye and had seen something of the mind of Mr. Wells and something of what so much of the political world is now thinking. And yet for all this we feel that at heart Otto would not have made such a bad king, and we feel that Stevenson really grasped the fact that kingship demands one inexorable condition. It is one of those numerous 'opinions' of Otto which makes him such a curious and complicated figure. The Prince is arguing with a convinced revolutionary, one of those persons who always speaks before he thinks.

' " Well, sir, the great thing for the good of one's country is, first of all, to be a good man." '

It may be that this direct statement is a little platitudinous; Stevenson cannot escape the charge, if it is a charge. There is a good deal of Stevenson the teacher in this book, it is inevitable that he should use platitudes.

In his sub-title Stevenson has called his *Prince Otto* a romance. It is something much more than this, for it is a romance carried to its logical conclusion, it is a dualism, a mixture of imagination and realism. It is this mixture perhaps of the unreal and the real which makes it possible to call Stevenson a philosopher in this book. Prince Otto is highly imaginative; he might be expected to appear out of the wings in a theatre, yet he might quite easily be sitting opposite us in a third-class smoking carriage. He is a symbol yet he is intensely human. Stevenson in almost a Shavian way has 'used' him, yet the using is not so obvious, that we say, almost angrily, that Prince Otto is simply Stevenson! Stevenson never forgets that if he is a philosopher he is also an artist. He does not fall into the error of painting a picture of Prince Otto and merely painting a picture of Stevenson! Rather he paints a picture of Prince Otto so that we know the artist is Stevenson. Though he invests Otto with his point of view, Otto has *his* own individual point of view also. It is a characteristic of the genius of Stevenson, in a very limited sense a foreshadowing of a dual personality which was to find such brilliant expression in Dr. Jekyll and Mr. Hyde. Otto is Stevenson, yet Otto is Otto. It is the logical outcome of the genius which is both 'literary' and yet vaguely selfish.

It is perhaps not mere imagination to think that Stevenson must have found the writing of *Prince Otto* far from easy. A political novel, and *Prince Otto* is certainly this, makes very great demands upon its author. He has to avoid a cold and callous disregard of humanity, as he looks for a system of profitable economics; he has to avoid the tendency to lose the political pursuit in the zest of producing a good story. Stevenson does not fall into either of these bottomless pits.

On the one hand *Prince Otto* is a discussion of what people expect of princes and what princes expect of people, on the other there is a vast humanity about the whole book which always gains our sympathies. Now and again we bask in that peculiar charm which is never really too long hid. When Prince Otto lectures on marriage (and the lecture is never tedious), we have a glimpse of something that is the essential Stevenson, the Stevenson far removed from the realm of politics, far from the terror of his own ill-health, far from the dialectical brilliance of his arguments about the ideals of princes. We have Stevenson immersed in his own love of love, his love of the purity of nature, his love of the parallelism between nature and human joy at its most sacred moments.

There is a subtle melancholy in the way in which Otto harps back to the time when he first made love to his Princess. It is almost a parallel to Stevenson looking back from the South Sea Islands, looking back to the countries, the absent friends, he was never to see again. So he writes this exquisite passage:—

'"Do you remember, Seraphina, on our way home, when you saw the roses in the lane, and I got out and plucked them. It was a narrow lane between great trees; the sunset at the end was all gold, and the rooks were flying overhead. There were nine, nine red roses; you gave me a kiss for each, and I told myself that every rose and every kiss should stand for a year of love."'

Again *Prince Otto* is something more that a political novel or a discussion on rule by a Royal House, it is a story of a journey. And it is the journey that all humanity attempts in some way or other to make. It is the journey that a man makes to find his own manhood, a journey that is a harsh and inevitable sifting, a journey that was, for the author of *Prince Otto*, a bitter but splendid revelation.

Prince Otto sets out to find himself, and he finds himself most effectually by hearing what others really think of him, for perhaps Princes and Kings in real life only hear the truth when it is too late. But Prince Otto hears it soon enough to profit by it.

Prince Otto is always his own interpreter. It is he who enunciates the most necessary thing for the good of a country—a good man. It is he who shows with irresistible logic and charm that as a lover he has not changed. It is towards the end of his journey, that Otto learns through a series of adventures, through a series of conversations with all sorts and conditions of men, what is the real lesson that he has to learn. It is the climax to which Stevenson has been so carefully leading us. Once again Otto is his own interpreter.

'"Colonel," said the Prince, "I have now come to that happy moment of my life when I have orders to receive but none to give."'

It is the conclusion of the serious joke that Stevenson seems to intend.

Prince Otto can surely be called one of the masterpieces of Stevenson. It has all the originality of genius. It is a book that combines a serious lesson with a kind of romantic background. Stevenson points an obvious moral. It is a moral that is never more needed to be considered than in this twentieth century. It is the moral that princes can only learn through contact with the people, not only of the people but of themselves. It is the further moral that people can only learn of princes through unknown contact with them, that the manners of courtiers can only be insincere at their best and dangerously false at their worst.

All the best qualities of Stevenson can be found in *Prince Otto*. His admirable commonsense philosophy, his artistic presentment of character, his curious genius for talking through his characters, yet avoiding the creation of puppets. We have glimpses (and they are the more exquisite in that they are somewhat limited in this book), of the fairy-like touch which is so much the essential Stevenson. *Prince Otto* is a discovery, it is a satire, it is a warning.

It was planned when Stevenson thought himself to be dying. Yet nearly fifty years later, not only does it show no sign of death, indeed it would seem as if it had but just been written for us who live so far from the days when Robert Louis Stevenson, through an indomitable will-power, beat his ill-health and his poverty and planned this exquisite romance.

PATRICK BRAYBROOKE

Book one

PRINCE ERRANT

I

In which the Prince departs on an adventure

You shall seek in vain upon the map of Europe for the bygone state of Grünewald. An independent principality, an infinitesimal member of the German Empire, she played, for several centuries, her part in the discord of Europe; and, at last, in the ripeness of time and at the spiriting of several bald diplomatists, vanished like a morning ghost. Less fortunate than Poland, she left not a regret behind her; and the very memory of her boundaries has faded.

It was a patch of hilly country covered with thick wood. Many streams took their beginning in the glens of Grünewald, turning mills for the inhabitants. There was one town, Mittwalden, and many brown, wooden hamlets, climbing roof above roof, along the steep bottom of dells, and communicating by covered bridges over the larger of the torrents. The hum of watermills, the splash of running water, the clean odour of pine sawdust, the sound and smell of the pleasant wind among the innumerable army of the mountain pines, the dropping fire of huntsmen, the dull stroke of the wood-axe, intolerable roads, fresh trout for supper in the clean bare chamber of an inn, and the song of birds and the music of the village-bells—these were the recollections of the Grünewald tourist.

North and east the foothills of Grünewald sank with varying profile into a vast plain. On these sides many small state bordered with the principality, Gerolstein, an extinct grand duchy, among the number. On the south, it marched with the comparatively powerful kingdom of Seaboard Bohemia, celebrated for its flowers and mountain bears, and inhabited by a people of singular simplicity and tenderness of heart. Several inter-marriages had, in the course of centuries, united the crowned families of Grünewald and Maritime Bohemia; and the last Prince of Grünewald, whose history I purpose to relate, drew his descent through Perdita, the only daughter of King Florizel the First of Bohemia. That these inter-marriages had in some degree mitigated the rough, manly stock of the first Grünewalds, was an opinion widely held within the borders of the principality. The charcoal burner, the mountain sawyer, the wielder of the broad axe among the congregated pines of Grünewald, proud of their hard hands, proud of their shrewd ignorance and almost savage lore, looked with an unfeigned contempt on the soft character and manners of the sovereign race.

The precise year of grace in which this tale begins shall be left to the conjecture of the reader. But for the season of the year (which, in such a story, is the more important of the two) it was already so far forward in the spring, that when mountain people heard horns echoing all day about the north-west corner of the principality, they told themselves that Prince Otto and his hunt were up and out for the last time till the return of autumn.

At this point the borders of Grünewald descend somewhat steeply, here and there breaking into crags; and this shaggy and trackless country stands in a bold contrast to the cultivated plain below. It was traversed at that period by two roads alone; one, the imperial highway, bound to Brandenau in Gerolstein, descended the slope obliquely and by the easiest gradients. The other ran like a fillet across the very forehead of the hills, dipping into savage gorges, and wetted by the spray of tiny waterfalls. Once it passed beside a certain tower or castle, built sheer upon the margin of a formidable cliff, and commanding a vast prospect of the skirts of Grünewald and the busy plains of Gerolstein. The Felsenburg (so this tower was called) served now as a prison, now as a hunting-seat; and for all it stood so lonesome to the naked eye, with the aid of a good glass the burghers of Brandenau could count its windows from the lime-tree terrace where they walked at night.

In the wedge of forest hillside enclosed between the roads, the horns continued all day long to scatter tumult; and at length, as the sun began to draw near to the horizon of the plain, a rousing triumph announced the slaughter of the quarry. The first and second huntsman had drawn somewhat aside, and from the summit of a knoll gazed down before them on the drooping shoulders of the hill and across the expanse of plain. They covered their eyes, for the sun was in their faces. The glory of its going down was somewhat pale. Through the confused tracery of many thousands of naked poplars, the smoke of so many houses, and the evening steam ascending from the fields, the sails of a windmill on a gentle eminence moved very conspicuously, like a donkey's ears. And hard by, like an open gash, the imperial high-road ran straight sunward, an artery of travel.

There is one of nature's spiritual ditties, that has not yet been set to words or human music: 'The Invitation to the Road'; an air continually sounding in the ears of gipsies, and to whose inspiration our nomadic fathers journeyed all their days. The hour, the season, and the scene, all were in delicate accordance. The air was full of birds of passage, steering westward and northward over Grünewald, an army of specks to the up looking eye. And below, the great practicable road was bound for the same quarter.

But to the two horsemen on the knoll this spiritual ditty was unheard. They were, indeed, in some concern of mind, scanning every fold of the subjacent forest, and betraying both anger and dismay in their impatient gestures.

'I do not see him, Kuno,' said the first huntsman, 'nowhere —not a trace, not a hair of the mare's tail! No, sir, he's off; broke cover and got away. Why, for twopence I would hunt him with the dogs!'

'Mayhap, he's gone home,' said Kuno, but without conviction.

'Home!' sneered the other. 'I give him twelve days to get home. No, it's begun again; it's as it was three years ago, before he married; a disgrace! Hereditary prince, hereditary fool! There goes the government over the borders on a gray mare. What's that? No, nothing—no, I tell you, on my word, I set more store by a good gelding or an English dog. That for your Otto!'

'He's not my Otto,' growled Kuno.

'Then I don't know whose he is,' was the retort.

'You would put your hand in the fire for him to-morrow,' said Kuno, facing round.

'Me!' cried the huntsman. 'I would see him hanged! I'm a Grünewald patriot—enrolled, and have my medal, too; and I would help a prince! I'm for liberty and Gondremark.'

'Well, it's all one,' said Kuno. 'If anybody said what you said, you would have his blood, and you know it.'

'You have him on the brain,' retorted his companion. 'There he goes!' he cried, the next moment.

And sure enough, about a mile down the mountain, a rider on a white horse was seen to flit rapidly across a heathy open and vanish among the trees on the farther side.

'In ten minutes he'll be over the border into Gerolstein,' said Kuno. 'It's past cure.'

'Well, if he founders that mare, I'll never forgive him,' added the other, gathering his reins.

And as they turned down from the knoll to rejoin their comrades, the sun dipped and disappeared, and the woods fell instantly into the gravity and grayness of the early night.

2

In which the Prince plays Haroun-al-raschid

THE night fell upon the Prince while he was threading green tracks in the lower valleys of the wood; and though the stars came out overhead and displayed the interminable order of the pine-tree pyramids, regular and dark like cypresses, their light was of small service to a traveller in such lonely paths, and from thenceforth he rode at random. The austere face of nature, the uncertain issue of his course, the open sky and the free air, delighted him like wine; and the hoarse chafing of a river on his left sounded in his ears agreeably.

It was past eight at night before his toil was rewarded and he issued at last out of the forest on the firm white high-road. It lay downhill before him, with a sweeping eastward trend, faintly bright between the thickets; and Otto paused and gazed upon it. So it ran, league after league, still joining others, to the farthest ends of Europe, there skirting the sea-surge, here gleaming in the lights of cities; and the innumerable army of tramps and travellers moved upon it in all lands as by a common impulse, and were now in all places drawing near to the inn door and the night's rest. The pictures swarmed and vanished in his brain; a surge of temptation, a beat of all his blood, went over him, to set spur to the mare and to go on into the unknown for ever. And then it passed away; hunger and fatigue, and that habit of middling actions which we call common sense, resumed their empire; and in that changed mood his eyes lighted upon two bright windows on his left hand, between the road and river.

He turned off by a by-road, and in a few minutes he was knocking with his whip on the door of a large farm-house, and a chorus of dogs from the farm-yard were making angry answer. A very tall, old, white-headed man came, shading a candle, at the summons. He had been of great strength in his time, and of a handsome countenance; but now he was fallen away, his teeth were quite gone, and his voice when he spoke was broken and falsetto.

'You will pardon me,' said Otto. 'I am a traveller and have entirely lost my way.'

'Sir,' said the old man, in a very stately, shaky manner, 'you are at the River Farm, and I am Killian Gottesheim, at your disposal. We are here, sir, at about an equal distance from Wittwalden in Grünewald and Brandenau in Gerolstein: six leagues to either, and the road excellent; but there is not a wine bush, not a carter's alehouse, anywhere between. You will have to accept my hospitality for the night; rough hospitality, to which I make you freely welcome; for, sir,' he added with a bow, 'it is God who sends the guest.'

'Amen. And I most heartily thank you,' replied Otto, bowing in his turn.

'Fritz,' said the old man, turning towards the interior, 'lead round this gentleman's horse; and you, sir, condescend to enter.'

Otto entered a chamber occupying the greater part of the ground-floor of the building. It had probably once been divided; for the farther end was raised by a long step above the nearer, and the blazing fire and the white supper-table seemed to stand upon a daïs. All around were dark, brass-mounted cabinets and cupboards; dark shelves carrying ancient country crockery; guns and antlers and broadside ballads on the wall; a tall old clock with roses on the dial; and down in one corner the comfortable promise of a wine barrel. It was homely, elegant, and quaint.

A powerful youth hurried out to attend on the gray mare; and when Mr. Killian Gottesheim had presented him to his daughter Ottilia, Otto followed to the stable as became, not perhaps the Prince, but the good horseman. When he returned, a smoking omelette and some slices of home-cured ham were waiting him; these were followed by a ragout and a cheese; and it was not until his guest had entirely satisfied his hunger, and the whole party drew about the fire over the wine jug, that Killian Gottesheim's elaborate courtesy permitted him to address a question to the Prince.

'You have perhaps ridden far, sir?' he inquired.

'I have, as you say, ridden far,' replied Otto; 'and, as you have seen, I was prepared to do justice to your daughter's cookery.'

'Possibly, sir, from the direction of Brandenau?' continued Killian.

'Precisely: and I should have slept to-night, had I not wandered, in Mittwalden,' answered the Prince, weaving in a patch of truth, according to the habit of all liars.

'Business leads you to Mittwalden?' was the next question.

'Mere curiosity,' said Otto. 'I have never yet visited the principality of Grünewald.'

'A pleasant state, sir,' piped the old man, nodding, 'a very pleasant state, and a fine race, both pines and people. We reckon ourselves part Grünewalders here, lying so near the borders; and the river there is all good Grünewald water, every drop of it. Yes, sir, a fine state. A man of Grünewald now will swing me an axe over his head that many a man of Gerolstein could hardly lift; and the pines, why, deary me, there must be more pines in that little state, sir, than people in this whole big world. 'Tis twenty years now since I crossed the marshes, for we grow home-keepers in old age; but I mind it as if it was yesterday. Up and down, the road keeps right on from here to Mittwalden; and nothing all the way but the good green pine-trees, big and little, and water-power! water-power at every step, sir. We once sold a bit of forest, up there beside the high-road; and the sight of minted money that we got for it has set me ciphering ever since what all the pines in Grünewald would amount to.'

'I suppose you see nothing of the Prince?' inquired Otto.

'No,' said the young man, speaking for the first time, 'nor want to.'

'Why so? is he so much disliked?' asked Otto.

'Not what you might call disliked,' replied the old gentleman, 'but despised, sir.'

'Indeed,' said the Prince, somewhat faintly.

'Yes, sir, despised,' nodded Killian, filling a long pipe, 'and, to my way of thinking, justly despised. Here is a man with great opportunities, and what does he do with them? He hunts, and he dresses very prettily—which is a thing to be ashamed of in a man—and he acts plays; and if he does aught else, the news of it has not come here.'

'Yet these are all innocent,' said Otto. 'What would you have him do—make war?'

'No, sir,' replied the old man. 'But here it is; I have been fifty years upon this River Farm, and wrought in it, day in, day out; I have ploughed and sowed and reaped, and risen early, and waked late; and this is the upshot: that all these years it has supported me and my family; and been the best friend that ever I had, set aside my wife; and now, when my time comes, I leave it a better farm than when I found it. So it is, if a man works hearty in the order of nature, he gets bread and he receives comfort, and whatever he touches breeds. And it humbly appears to me, if that Prince was to labour on his throne, as I have laboured and wrought in my farm, he would find both an increase and a blessing.'

'I believe with you, sir,' Otto said; 'and yet the parallel is inexact. For the farmer's life is natural and simple; but the prince's is both artificial and complicated. It is easy to do right in the one, and exceedingly difficult not to do wrong in the other. If your crop is blighted, you can take off your bonnet and say, "God's will be done"; but if the Prince meets with a reverse, he may have to blame himself for the attempt. And perhaps, if all the kings in Europe were to confine themselves to innocent amusement, the subjects would be better off.'

'Ay,' said the young man Fritz, 'you are in the right of it there. That was a true word spoken. And I see you are like me, a good patriot and an enemy to princes.'

Otto was somewhat abashed at this deduction, and he made haste to change his ground. 'But,' said he, 'you surprise me by what you say of this Prince Otto. I have heard of him, I must own, more favourably painted. I was told he was, in his heart, a good fellow, and the enemy of no one but himself.'

'And so he is, sir,' said the girl, 'a very handsome, pleasant prince; and we know some who would shed their blood for him.'

'O! Kuno!' said Fritz. 'An ignoramus!'

'Ay, Kuno, to be sure,' quavered the old farmer. 'Well, since this gentleman is a stranger to these parts, and curious about the Prince, I do believe that story might divert him. This Kuno, you must know, sir, is one of the hunt servants, and a most ignorant, intemperate man: a right Grünewalder, as we say in Gerolstein. We know him well, in this house; for he has come as far as here after his stray dogs; and I make all welcome, sir, without account of state or nation. And, indeed, between Gerolstein and Grünewald the peace has held so long that the roads stand open like my door; and a man will make no more of the frontier than the very birds themselves.'

'Ay,' said Otto, 'it has been a long peace—a peace of centuries.'

'Centuries, as you say,' returned Killian; 'the more the pity that it should not be for ever. Well, sir, this Kuno was one day in fault, and Otto, who has a quick temper, up with his whip and thrashed him, they do say, soundly. Kuno took it as best he could, but at last he broke out, and dared the Prince to throw his whip away and wrestle like a man; for we are all great at wrestling in these parts, and it's so that we generally settle our disputes. Well, sir, the Prince did so; and, being a weakly creature, found the tables turned, for the man whom he had just been thrashing like a negro slave, lifted him with a back grip and threw him heels overhead.'

'He broke his bridle-arm,' cried Fritz, 'and some say his nose. Serve him right, say I! Man to man, which is the better at that?'

'And then?' asked Otto.

'O, then Kuno carried him home; and they were the best of friends from that day forth. I don't say it's a discreditable story, you observe,' continued Mr. Gottesheim; 'but it's droll, and that's the fact. A man should think before he strikes; for, as my nephew says, man to man was the old valuation.'

'Now, if you were to ask me,' said Otto, 'I should perhaps surprise you. I think it was the Prince that conquered.'

'And, sir, you would be right,' replied Killian seriously. 'In the eyes of God, I do not question but you would be right; but men, sir, look at these things differently and they laugh.'

'They made a song of it,' observed Fritz. 'How does it go? Ta-tum-ta-ra...'

'Well,' interrupted Otto, who had no great anxiety to hear the song, 'the Prince is young; he may yet mend.'

'Not so young, by your leave,' cried Fritz. 'A man of forty.'

'Thirty-six,' corrected Mr. Gottesheim.

'Oh,' cried Ottilia, in obvious disillusion, 'a man of middle age! And they said he was so handsome when he was young!'

'And bald, too,' added Fritz.

Otto passed his hand among his locks. At that moment he was far from happy, and even the tedious evenings at Mittwalden Palace began to smile upon him by comparison.

'O, six-and-thirty!' he protested. 'A man is not yet old at six-and-thirty. I am that age myself.'

'I should have taken you for more, sir,' piped the old farmer. 'But if that be so, you are of an age with Master Ottekin, as people call him; and, I would wager a crown, have done more service in your time. Though it seems young by comparison with men of a great age like me, yet it's some way through life for all that; and the mere fools and fiddlers are beginning to grow weary and to look old. Yes, sir, by six-and-thirty, if a man be a follower of God's laws, he should have made himself a home and a good name to live by; he should have got a wife and a blessing on his marriage; and his works, as the Word says, should begin to follow him.'

'Ah, well, the Prince is married,' cried Fritz, with a coarse burst of laughter.

'That seems to entertain you, sir,' said Otto.

'Ay,' said the young boor. 'Did you not know that? I thought all Europe knew it!' And he added a pantomime of a nature to explain his accusation to the dullest.

'Ah, sir,' said Mr. Gottesheim, 'it is very plain that you are not from hereabouts! But the truth is, that the whole princely family and Court are rips and rascals, not one to mend another. They live, sir, in idleness and—what most commonly follows it—corruption. The Princess has a lover—a Baron, as he calls himself, from East Prussia; and the Prince is so little of a man, sir, that he holds the candle. Nor is that the worst of it, for this foreigner and his paramour are suffered to transact the State affairs, while the Prince takes the salary and leaves all things to go to wrack. There will follow upon this some manifest judgment which, though I am old, I may survive to see.'

'Good man, you are in the wrong about Gondremark,' said Fritz, showing a greatly increased animation; 'but for all the rest, you speak the God's truth like a good patriot. As for the Prince, if he would take and strangle his wife, I would forgive him yet.'

'Nay, Fritz,' said the old man, 'that would be to add iniquity to evil. For you perceive, sir,' he continued, once more addressing himself to the unfortunate Prince, 'this Otto has himself to thank for these disorders. He has his young wife and his principality, and he has sworn to cherish both.'

'Sworn at the altar!' echoed Fritz. 'But put your faith in princes!'

'Well, sir, he leaves them both to an adventurer from East Prussia,' pursued the farmer: 'leaves the girl to be seduced and to go on from bad to worse, till her name's become a tap-room byword, and she not yet twenty; leaves the country to be overtaxed, and bullied with armaments and jockied into war——'

'War!' cried Otto.

'So they say, sir; those that watch their ongoings, say to war,' asseverated Killian. 'Well, sir, that is very sad; it is a sad thing for this poor, wicked girl to go down to hell with people's curses; it's a sad thing for a tight little happy country to be misconducted; but whoever may complain, I humbly conceive, sir, that this Otto cannot. What he has worked for, that he has got; and may God have pity on his soul, for a great and a silly sinner's!'

'He has broken his oath; then he is a perjurer. He takes the money and leaves the work; why, then plainly he's a thief. A cuckold he was before, and a fool by birth. Better me that!' cried Fritz, and snapped his fingers.

'And now, sir, you will see a little,' continued the farmer, 'why we think so poorly of this Prince Otto. There's such a things as a man being pious and honest in the private way; and there's such a thing, sir, as a public virtue; but when a man has neither, the Lord lighten him! Even this Gondremark, that Fritz here thinks so much of——'

'Ay,' interrupted Fritz, 'Gondremark's the man for me. I would we had his like in Gerolstein.'

'He is a bad man,' said the old farmer, shaking his head; 'and there was never good begun by the breach of God's commandments. But so far I will go with you; he is a man that works for what he has.'

'I tell you he's the hope of Grünewald,' cried Fritz. 'He doesn't suit some of your high-and-dry, old, ancient ideas; but he's a downright modern man—a man of the new lights and the progress of the age. He does some things wrong; so they all do; but he has the people's interests next his heart; and you mark me—you, sir, who are a Liberal, and the enemy of all their governments, you please to mark my words—the day will come in Grünewald, when they take out that yellow-headed skulk of a Prince and that dough-faced Messaline of a Princess, march 'em back foremost over the borders, and proclaim the Baron Gondremark first President. I've heard them say it in a speech. I was at a meeting once at Brandenau, and the Mittwalden delegates spoke up for fifteen thousand. Fifteen thousand, all brigaded, and each man with a medal round his neck to rally by. That's all Gondremark.'

'Ay, sir, you see what it leads to; wild talk to-day, and wilder doings to-morrow,' said the old man. 'For there is one thing certain: that this Gondremark has one foot in the Court back-stairs, and the other in the Masons' lodges. He gives himself out, sir, for what nowadays they call a patriot: a man from East Prussia!'

'Gives himself out!' cried Fritz. 'He is! He is to lay by his title as soon as the Republic is declared; I heard it in a speech.'

'Lay by Baron to take up President?' returned Killian. 'King Log, King Stork. But you'll live longer than I, and you will see the fruits of it.'

'Father,' whispered Ottilia, pulling at the speaker's coat, 'surely the gentleman is ill.'

'I beg your pardon,' cried the farmer, rewaking to hospitable thoughts; 'can I offer you anything?'

'I thank you. I am very weary,' answered Otto. 'I have presumed upon my strength. If you would show me to a bed, I should be grateful.'

'Ottilia, a candle!' said the old man. 'Indeed, sir, you look paley. A little cordial water? No? Then follow me, I beseech you, and I will bring you to the stranger's bed. You are not the first by many who has slept well below my roof,' continued the old gentleman, mounting the stairs before his guest; 'for good food, honest wine, a grateful conscience, and a little pleasant chat before a man retires, are worth all the possets and apothecary's drugs. See, sir,' and here he opened a door and ushered Otto into a little whitewashed sleeping room, 'here you are in port. It is small, but it is airy, and the sheets are clean and kept in lavender. The window, too, looks out above the river, and there's no music like a little river's. It plays the same tune (and that's the favourite) over and over again, and yet does not weary of it like men fiddlers. It takes the mind out of doors: and though we should be grateful for good houses, there is, after all, no house like God's out-of-doors. And lastly, sir, it quiets a man down like saying his prayers. So here, sir, I take my kind leave of you until to-morrow; and it is my prayerful wish that you may slumber like a prince.'

And the old man, with the twentieth courteous inclination, left his guest alone.

3

In which the Prince comforts age and beauty and delivers a lecture on discretion in love

THE Prince was early abroad: in the time of the first chorus of birds, of the pure and quiet air, of the slanting sunlight and the mile-long shadows. To one who had passed a miserable night, the freshness of that hour was tonic and reviving; to steal a march upon his slumbering fellows, to be the Adam of the coming day, composed and fortified his spirits; and the Prince, breathing deep and pausing as he went, walked in the wet fields beside his shadow, and was glad.

A trellised path led down into the valley of the brook, and he turned to follow it. The stream was a break-neck boiling Highland river. Hard by the farm, it leaped a little precipice in a thick gray-mare's tail of twisted filaments, and then lay and worked and bubbled in a lynn. Into the middle of this quaking pool a rock protruded, shelving to a cape; and thither Otto scrambled and sat down to ponder.

Soon the sun struck through the screen of branches and thin early leaves that made a hanging bower above the fall; and the golden lights and flitting shadows fell upon and marbled the surface of that seething pot; and rays plunged deep among the turning waters; and a spark, as bright as a diamond, lit upon the swaying eddy. It began to grow warm where Otto lingered, warm and heady; the lights swam, weaving their maze across the shaken pool; on the impending rock, reflections danced like butterflies: and the air was fanned by the waterfall as by a swinging curtain.

Otto, who was weary with tossing and beset with horrid phantoms of remorse and jealousy, instantly fell dead in love with that sun-chequered, echoing corner. Holding his feet, he stared out of a drowsy trance, wondering, admiring, musing, losing his way among uncertain thoughts. There is nothing that so apes the external bearing of free will as that unconscious bustle, obscurely following liquid laws, with which a river contends among obstructions. It seems the very play of man and destiny, and as Otto pored on these recurrent changes, he grew, by equal steps, the sleepier and the more profound. Eddy and Prince were alike jostled in their purpose, alike anchored by intangible influences in one corner of the world. Eddy and Prince were alike useless, starkly useless, in the cosmology of men. Eddy and Prince—Prince and Eddy.

It is probable he had been some while asleep when a voice recalled him from oblivion. 'Sir,' it was saying; and looking round, he saw Mr. Killian's daughter, terrified by her boldness and making bashful signals from the shore. She was a plain, honest lass, healthy and happy and good, and with that sort of beauty that comes of happiness and health. But her confusion lent her for the moment an additional charm.

'Good morning,' said Otto, rising and moving towards her. 'I arose early and was in a dream.'

'O, sir!' she cried, 'I wish to beg of you to spare my father; for I assure your Highness, if he had known who you was, he would have bitten his tongue out sooner. And Fritz, too—how he went on! But I had a notion; and this morning I went straight down into the stable, and there was your Highness's crown upon the stirrup-irons! But O, sir, I made certain you would spare them; for they were as innocent as lambs.'

'My dear,' said Otto, both amused and gratified, 'you do not undertand. It is I who am in the wrong; for I had no business to conceal my name and lead on these gentlemen to speak of me. And it is I who have to beg of you that you will keep my secret and not betray the discourtesy of which I was guilty. As for any fear of me, your friends are safe in Gerolstein: and even in my own territory, you must be well aware I have no power.'

'O, sir,' she said, curtseying, 'I would not say that: the huntsmen would all die for you.'

'Happy Prince!' said Otto. 'But although you are too courteous to avow the knowledge, you have had many opportunities of learning that I am a vain show. Only last night we heard it very clearly stated. You see the shadow flitting on this hard rock? Prince Otto, I am afraid, is but the moving shadow, and the name of the rock is Gondremark. Ah! if your friends had fallen foul of Gondremark! But happily the younger of the two admires him. And as for the old gentleman your father, he is a wise man and an excellent talker, and I would take a long wager he is honest.'

'O, for honest, your Highness, that he is!' exclaimed the girl. 'And Fritz is as honest as he. And as for all they said, it was just talk and nonsense. When countryfolk get gossiping, they go on, I do assure you, for the fun; they don't as much as think of what they say. If you went to the next farm, it's my belief you would hear as much against my father.'

'Nay, nay,' said Otto, 'there you go too fast. For all that was said against Prince Otto——'

'O, it was shameful!' cried the girl.

'Not shameful—true,' returned Otto. 'O, yes—true. I am all they said of me—all that and worse.'

'I never!' cried Ottilia. 'Is that how you do? Well, you would never be a soldier. Now if any one accuses me, I get up and give it them. O, I defend myself. I wouldn't take a fault at another person's hands, no, not if I had it on my forehead. And that's what you must do, if you mean to live it out. But, indeed, I never heard such nonsense. I should think you were ashamed of yourself! You're bald, then, I suppose?'

'O, no,' said Otto, fairly laughing. 'There I acquit myself: not bald!'

'Well, and good,' pursued the girl. 'Come now, you know you are good, and I'll make you say so. . . . Your Highness, I beg your humble pardon. But there's no disrespect intended. And anyhow, you know you are.'

'Why, now, what am I to say?' replied Otto. 'You are a cook, and excellently well you do it; I embrace the chance of thanking you for the ragout. Well now, have you not seen good food so bedevilled by unskilful cookery that no one could be brought to eat the pudding? That is me, my dear. I am full of good ingredients, but the dish is worthless. I am—I give it you in one word—sugar in the salad.'

'Well, I don't care, you're good,' reiterated Ottilia, a little flushed by having failed to understand.

'I will tell you one thing,' replied Otto: 'you are!'

'Ah, well, that's what they all said of you,' moralised the girl; 'such a tongue to come round—such a flattering tongue!'

'O, you forget, I am a man of middle age,' the Prince chuckled.

'Well, to speak to you, I should think you was a boy; and Prince or no Prince, if you came worrying where I was cooking, I would pin a napkin to your tails. . . . And, O Lord, I declare I hope your Highness will forgive me,' the girl added. 'I can't keep it in my mind.'

'No more can I,' cried Otto. 'That is just what they complain of!'

They made a loverly-looking couple; only the heavy pouring

of that horse-tail of water made them raise their voices above lovers' pitch. But to a jealous onlooker from above, their mirth and close proximity might easily give umbrage; and a rough voice out of a tuft of brambles began calling on Ottilia by name. She changed colour at that. 'It is Fritz,' she said. 'I must go.'

'Go, my dear, and I need not bid you go in peace, for I think you have discovered that I am not formidable at close quarters,' said the Prince, and made her a fine gesture of dismissal.

So Ottilia skipped up the bank, and disappeared into the thicket, stopping once for a single blushing bob—blushing, because she had in the interval once more forgotten and remembered the stranger's quality.

Otto returned to his rock promontory; but his humour had in the meantime changed. The sun now shone more fairly on the pool; and over its brown, welling surface the blue of heaven and the golden green of the spring foliage danced in fleeting arabesque. The eddies laughed and brightened with essential colour. And the beauty of the dell began to rankle in the Prince's mind; it was so near to his own borders, yet without. He had never had much of the joy of possessorship in any of the thousand and one beautiful and curious things that were his; and now he was conscious of envy for what was another's. It was, indeed, a smiling, dilettante sort of envy; but yet there it was: the passion of Ahab for the vineyard, done in little; and he was relieved when Mr. Killian appeared upon the scene.

'I hope, sir, that you have slept well under my plain roof,' said the old farmer.

'I am admiring this sweet spot that you are privileged to dwell in,' replied Otto, evading the inquiry.

'It is rustic,' returned Mr. Gottesheim, looking around him with complacency, 'a very rustic corner; and some of the land to the west is most excellent fat land, excellent deep soil. You should see my wheat in the ten-acre field. There is not a farm in Grünewald, no, nor many in Gerolstein, to match the River Farm. Some sixty—I keep thinking when I sow—some sixty, and some seventy, and some an hundredfold; and my own place, six score! But that, sir, is partly the farming.'

'And the stream has fish?' asked Otto.

'A fish-pond,' said the farmer. 'Ay, it is a pleasant bit. It is pleasant even here, if one had time, with the brook drumming in that black pool, and the green things hanging all about the rocks, and, dear heart, to see the very pebbles! all turned to gold and precious stones! But you have come to that time of life, sir, when, if you will excuse me, you must look to have the rheumatism set in. Thirty to forty is, as one may say, their seed-time. And this is a damp cold corner for the early morning and an empty stomach. If I might humbly advise you, sir, I would be moving.'

'With all my heart,' said Otto gravely. 'And so you have lived your life here?' he added, as they turned to go.

'Here I was born,' replied the farmer, 'and here I wish I could say I was to die. But fortune, sir, fortune turns the wheels. They say she is blind, but we will hope she only sees a little farther on. My grandfather and my father and I, we have all tilled these acres, my furrow following theirs. All the three names are on the garden bench, two Killians and one Johann. Yes, sir, good men have prepared themselves for the great change in my old garden. Well do I mind my father, in a woollen night-cap, the good soul, going round and round to see the last of it. "Killian," said he, "do you see the smoke of my tobacco? Why," said he, "that is man's life." It was his last pipe, and I believe he knew it; and it was a strange thing, without doubt, to leave the trees that he had planted, and the son that he had begotten, ay, sir, and even the old pipe with the Turk's head that he had smoked since he was a lad and went a-courting. But here we have no continuing city; and as for the eternal, it's a comfortable thought that we have other merits than our own. And yet you would hardly think how sore it goes against the grain with me, to die in a strange bed.'

'And must you do so? For what reason?' Otto asked.

'The reason? The place is to be sold; three thousand crowns,' replied Mr. Gottesheim. 'Had it been a third of that, I may say without boasting, that, what with my credit and my savings, I could have met the sum. But at three thousand, unless I have singular good fortune and the new proprietor continues me in office, there is nothing left me but to budge.'

Otto's fancy for the place redoubled at the news, and became joined with other feelings. If all he heard were true, Grünewald was growing very hot for a sovereign Prince; it might be well to have a refuge; and if so, what more delightful hermitage could man imagine? Mr. Gottesheim, besides, had touched his sympathies. Every man loves in his soul to play the part of the stage deity. And to step down to the aid of the old farmer, who had so roughly handled him in talk, was the ideal of a Fair Revenge. Otto's thoughts brightened at the prospect, and he began to regard himself with a renewed respect.

'I can find you, I believe, a purchaser,' he said, 'and one who would continue to avail himself of your skill.'

'Can you, sir, indeed?' said the old man. 'Well, I shall be heartily obliged; for I begin to find a man may practise resignation all his days, as he takes physic, and not come to like it in the end.'

'If you will have the papers drawn, you may even burthen the purchase with your interest,' said Otto. 'Let it be assured to you through life.'

'Your friend, sir,' insinuated Killian, 'would not, perhaps, care to make the interest reversible? Fritz is a good lad.'

'Fritz is young,' said the Prince dryly; 'he must earn consideration, not inherit.'

'He has long worked upon the place, sir,' insisted Mr. Gottesheim; 'and at my great age, for I am seventy-eight come harvest, it would be a troublesome thought to the proprietor how to fill my shoes. It would be a care spared to assure yourself of Fritz. And I believe he might be tempted by a permanency.'

'The young man has unsettled views,' returned Otto.

'Possibly the purchaser——' began Killian.

'A little spot of anger burned in Otto's cheek. 'I am the purchaser,' he said.

'It was what I might have guessed,' replied the farmer, bowing with an aged, obsequious dignity. 'You have made an old man very happy; and I may say, indeed, that I have entertained an angel unawares. Sir, the great people of this world—and by that I mean those who are great in station—if they had only hearts like yours, how they would make the fires burn and the poor sing!'

'I would not judge them hardly, sir,' said Otto. 'We all have our frailties.'

'Truly, sir,' said Mr. Gottesheim, with unction. 'And by what name, sir, am I to address my generous landlord?'

The double recollection of an English traveller, whom he had received the week before at court, and of an old English rogue called Transome, whom he had known in youth, came pertinently to the Prince's help. 'Transome,' he answered, 'is my name. I am an English traveller. It is, to-day, Tuesday. On Thursday, before noon, the money shall be ready. Let us meet, if you please, in Mittwalden, at the Morning Star.'

'I am, in all things lawful, your servant to command,' replied the farmer. 'An Englishman! You are a great race of travellers. And has your lordship some experience of land?'

'I have had some interest of the kind before,' returned the Prince; 'not in Gerolstein, indeed. But fortune, as you say, turns the wheel, and I desire to be beforehand with her revolutions.'

'Very right, sir, I am sure,' said Mr. Killian.

They had been strolling with deliberation; but they were

now drawing near to the farm-house, mounting by the trellised pathway to the level of the meadow. A little before them, the sound of voices had been some while audible, and now grew louder and more distinct with every step of their advance. Presently, when they emerged upon the top of the bank, they beheld Fritz and Ottilia some way off; he, very black and bloodshot, emphasising his hoarse speech with the smacking of his fist against his palm; she, standing a little way off in blowzy, voluble distress.

'Dear me!' said Mr. Gottesheim, and made as if he would turn aside.

But Otto went straight towards the lovers, in whose dissension he believed himself to have a share. And, indeed, as soon as he had seen the Prince, Fritz had stood tragic, as if awaiting and defying his approach.

'O, here you are,' he cried, as soon as they were near enough for easy speech. 'You are a man at least, and must reply. What were you after? Why were you two skulking in the bush? God!' he broke out, turning again upon Ottilia, 'to think that I should waste my heart on you!'

'I beg your pardon,' Otto cut in. 'You were addressing me. In virtue of what circumstance am I to render you an account of this young lady's conduct? Are you her father? her brother? her husband?'

'O, sir, you know as well as I,' returned the peasant. 'We keep company, she and I. I love her, and she is by way of loving me; but all shall be above-board, I would have her to know. I have a good pride of my own.'

'Why, I perceive I must explain to you what love is,' said Otto. 'Its measure is kindness. It is very possible that you are proud; but she, too, may have some self-esteem; I do not speak for myself. And perhaps, if your own doings were so curiously examined, you might find it inconvenient to reply.'

'These are all set-offs,' said the young man. 'You know very well that a man is a man, and a woman only a woman. That holds good all over, up and down. I ask you a question, I ask it again, and here I stand.' He drew a mark and toed it.

'When you have studied liberal doctrines somewhat deeper,' said the Prince, 'you will perhaps change your note. You are a man of false weights and measures, my young friend. You have one scale for women, another for men; one for princes, and one for farmer-folk. On the prince who neglects his wife you can be most severe. But what of the lover who insults his mistress? You use the name of love. I should think this lady might very fairly ask to be delivered from love of such a nature.

For if I, a stranger, had been one-tenth part so gross and so discourteous, you would most righteously have broken my head. It would have been in your part, as lover, to protect her from such insolence. Protect her first, then, from yourself.'

'Ay,' quoth Mr. Gottesheim, who had been looking on with his hands behind his tall old back, 'ay, that's Scripture truth.'

Fritz was staggered, not only by the Prince's imperturbable superiority of manner, but by a glimmering consciousness that he himself was in the wrong. The appeal to liberal doctrines had, besides, unmanned him.

'Well,' said he, 'if I was rude, I'll own to it. I meant no ill, and did nothing out of my just rights; but I am above all these old vulgar notions too; and if I spoke sharp, I'll ask her pardon.'

'Freely granted, Fritz,' said Ottilia.

'But all this doesn't answer me,' cried Fritz. 'I ask what you two spoke about. She says she promised not to tell; well, then, I mean to know. Civility is civility, but I'll be no man's gull. I have a right to common justice, if I *do* keep company!'

'If you will ask Mr. Gottesheim,' replied Otto, 'you will find I have not spent my hours in idleness. I have, since I arose this morning, agreed to buy the farm. So far I will go to satisfy a curiosity which I condemn.'

'O, well, if there was business, that's another matter,' returned Fritz. 'Though it beats me why you could not tell. But, of course, if the gentleman is to buy the farm, I suppose there would naturally be an end.'

'To be sure,' said Mr. Gottesheim, with a strong accent of conviction.

But Ottilia was much braver. 'There now!' she cried in triumph. 'What did I tell you? I told you I was fighting your battles. Now you see! Think shame of your suspicious temper! You should go down upon your bended knees both to that gentleman and me.'

4

In which the Prince collects opinions by the way

A LITTLE before noon Otto, by a triumph of manœuvring, effected his escape. He was quit in this way of the ponderous gratitude of Mr. Killian and of the confidential gratitude of poor Ottilia; but of Fritz he was not quit so readily. That young politician, brimming with mysterious glances, offered to lend his convoy as far as to the highroad; and Otto, in fear of some residuary jealousy and for the girl's sake, had not the courage to gainsay him; but he regarded his companion with uneasy glances, and devoutly wished the business at an end. For some time Fritz walked by the mare in silence; and they had already traversed more than half the proposed distance when, with something of a blush, he looked up and opened fire.

'Are you not,' he asked, 'what they call a Socialist?'

'Why, no,' returned Otto, 'not precisely what they call so. Why do you ask?'

'I will tell you why,' said the young man. 'I saw from the first that you were a Red Progressional, and nothing but the fear of old Killian kept you back. And there, sir, you were right: old men are always cowards. But nowadays, you see, there are so many groups: you can never tell how far the likeliest kind of man may be prepared to go; and I was never sure you were one of the strong thinkers, till you hinted about women and free love.'

'Indeed,' cried Otto, 'I never said a word of such a thing.'

'Not you!' cried Fritz. 'Never a word to compromise! You were sowing seed: ground-bait, our president calls it. But it's hard to deceive me, for I know all the agitators and their ways, and all the doctrines; and between you and me,' lowering his voice, 'I am myself affiliated. O yes, I am a Secret Society man, and here is my medal.' And drawing out a green ribbon that he wore about his neck, he held up, for Otto's inspection, a pewter medal bearing the imprint of a Phœnix and the legend *Libertas*. 'And so now you see you may trust me,' added Fritz. 'I am none of your alehouse talkers; I am a convinced revolutionary.' And he looked meltingly upon Otto.

'I see,' replied the Prince; 'that is very gratifying. Well, sir, the great thing for the good of one's country is, first of all, to be a good man. All springs from there. For my part, although you are right in thinking that I have to do with politics, I am unfit by intellect and temper for a leading rôle. I was intended, I fear, for a subaltern. Yet we have all something to command, Mr. Fritz, if it be only our own temper; and a man about to marry must look closely to himself. The husband's, like the prince's, is a very artificial standing; and it is hard to be kind in either. Do you follow that?'

'O yes, I follow that,' replied the young man, sadly chop-fallen over the nature of the information he had elicited; and then brightening up: 'Is it,' he ventured, 'is it for an arsenal that you have bought the farm?'

'We'll see about that,' the Prince answered, laughing. 'You must not be too zealous. And in the meantime, if I were you, I would say nothing on the subject.'

'O, trust me, sir, for that,' cried Fritz, as he pocketed a crown. 'And you've let nothing out; for I suspected—I might say I knew it—from the first. And mind you, when a guide is required,' he added, 'I know all the forest paths.'

Otto rode away, chuckling. This talk with Fritz had vastly entertained him; nor was he altogether discontented with his bearing at the farm; men, he was able to tell himself, had behaved worse under smaller provocation. And, to harmonise all, the road and the April air were both delightful to his soul.

Up and down, and to and fro, ever mounting through the wooded foothills, the broad white highroad wound onward into Grünewald. On either hand the pines stood coolly rooted—green moss prospering, springs welling forth between their knuckled spurs; and though some were broad and stalwart, and others spiry and slender, yet all stood firm in the same attitude and with the same expression like a silent army presenting arms.

The road lay all the way apart from towns and villages, which it left on either hand. Here and there, indeed, in the bottom of green glens, the Prince could spy a few congregated roofs, or perhaps above him, on a shoulder, the solitary cabin of a woodman. But the highway was an international undertaking, and with its face set for distant cities, scorned the little life of Grünewald. Hence it was exceeding solitary. Near the frontier Otto met a detachment of his own troops marching in the hot dust; and he was recognised and somewhat feebly cheered as he rode by. But from that time forth and for a long while he was alone with the great woods.

Gradually the spell of pleasure relaxed; his own thoughts returned, like stinging insects, in a cloud; and the talk of the night before, like a shower of buffets, fell upon his memory. He looked east and west for any comforter; and presently he was aware of a cross-road coming steeply down-hill, and a horseman cautiously descending. A human voice or presence, like a spring in the desert, was now welcome in itself, and Otto drew bridle to await the coming of this stranger. He proved to be a very red-faced, thick-lipped countryman, with a pair of fat saddle-bags and a stone bottle at his waist; who, as soon as the Prince hailed him, jovially if somewhat thickly answered. At the same time he gave a beery yaw in the saddle. It was clear his bottle was no longer full.

'Do you ride towards Mittwalden?' asked the Prince.

'As far as the cross-road to Tannenbrunn,' the man replied. 'Will you bear company?'

'With pleasure. I have even waited for you on the chance,' answered Otto.

By this time they were close alongside; and the man, with the countryfolk instinct, turned his cloudy vision first of all on his companion's mount. 'The devil!' he cried. 'You ride a bonny mare, friend!' And then, his curiosity being satisfied about the essential, he turned his attention to that merely secondary matter, his companion's face. He started. 'The Prince!' he cried, saluting, with another yaw that came near dismounting him. 'I beg your pardon, your Highness, not to have reco'nised you at once.'

The Prince was vexed out of his self-possession. 'Since you know me,' he said, 'it is unnecessary we should ride together. I will precede you, if you please.' And he was about to set spur to the gray mare, when the half-drunken fellow, reaching over, laid his hand upon the rein.

'Hark you,' he said, 'prince or no prince, that is not how one man should conduct himself with another. What! You'll ride with me incog, and set me talking! But if I know you, you'll preshede me, if you please! Spy!' And the fellow, crimson with drink and injured vanity, almost spat the word into the Prince's face.

A horrid confusion came over Otto. He perceived that he had acted rudely, grossly presuming on his station. And perhaps a little shiver of physical alarm mingled with his remorse, for the fellow was very powerful and not more than half in the possession of his senses. 'Take your hand from my rein,' he said, with a sufficient assumption of command; and when the man, rather to his wonder, had obeyed: 'You should understand, sir,' he added, 'that while I might be glad to ride with you as one person of sagacity with another, and so receive your true opinions, it would amuse me very little to hear the empty compliments you would address to me as Prince.'

'You think I would lie, do you?' cried the man with the bottle, purpling deeper.

'I know you would,' returned Otto, entering entirely into his self-possession. 'You would not even show me the medal you wear about your neck.' For he had caught a glimpse of a green ribbon at the fellow's throat.

The change was instantaneous: the red face became mottled with yellow: a thick-fingered, tottering hand made a clutch at a tell-tale ribbon. 'Medal!' the man cried, wonderfully sobered. 'I have no medal.'

'Pardon me,' said the Prince. 'I will even tell you what that medal bears: a Phœnix burning, with the word *Libertas*.' The medallist remaining speechless. 'You are a pretty fellow,' continued Otto, smiling, 'to complain of incivility from the man whom you conspire to murder.'

'Murder!' protested the man. 'Nay, never that; nothing criminal for me!'

'You are strangely misinformed,' said Otto. 'Conspiracy itself is criminal, and ensures the pain of death. Nay, sir, death it is; I will guarantee my accuracy. Not that you need be so deplorably affected, for I am no officer. But those who mingle with politics should look at both sides of the medal.'

'Your Highness——' began the knight of the bottle.

'Nonsense! you are a Republican,' cried Otto; 'what have you to do with highnesses? But let us continue to ride forward. Since you so much desire it, I cannot find it in my heart to deprive you of my company. And for that matter, I have a question to address to you. Why, being so great a body of men—for you are a great body—fifteen thousand, I have heard, but that will be understated; am I right?'

The man gurgled in his throat.

'Why, then, being so considerable a party,' resumed Otto, 'do you not come before me boldly with your wants?—what do I say? with your commands? Have I the name of being passionately devoted to my throne? I can scarce suppose it. Come, then; show me your majority, and I will instantly resign. Tell this to your friends; assure them from me of my docility; assure them that, however they conceive of my deficiencies, they cannot suppose me more unfit to be a ruler than I do myself. I am one of the worst princes in Europe; will they improve on that?'

'Far be it from me——' the man began.

'See, now, if you will not defend my government!' cried Otto. 'If I were you, I would leave conspiracies. You are as little fit to be a conspirator as I to be a king.'

'One thing I will say out,' said the man. 'It is not so much you that we complain of, it's your lady.'

'Not a word, sir,' said the Prince; and then, after a moment's pause, and in tones of some anger and contempt: 'I once more advise you to have done with politics,' he added; 'and when next I see you, let me see you sober. A morning drunkard is the last man to sit in judgment even upon the worst of princes.'

'I have had a drop, but I had not been drinking,' the man replied, triumphing in a sound distinction. 'And if I had, what then? Nobody hangs by me. But my mill is standing idle, and I blame it on your wife. Am I alone in that? Go round and ask Where are the mills? Where are the young men that should be working? Where is the currency? All paralysed. No, sir, it is not equal; for I suffer for your faults—I pay for them, by George out of a poor man's pocket. And what have you to do with mine? Drunk or sober, I can see my country going to hell, and I can see whose fault it is. And so now, I've said my say, and you may drag me to a stinking dungeon; what care I? I've spoken the truth, and so I'll hold hard, and not intrude upon your Highness's society.'

And the miller reined up and, clumsily enough, saluted.

'You will observe, I have not asked your name,' said Otto. 'I wish you a good ride,' and he rode on hard. But let him ride as he pleased, this interview with the miller was a chokepear, which he could not swallow. He had begun by receiving a reproof in manners, and ended by sustaining a defeat in logic, both from a man whom he despised. All his old thoughts returned with fresher venom. And by three in the afternoon, coming to the cross-roads for Beckstein, Otto decided to turn aside and dine there leisurely. Nothing at least could be worse than to go on as he was going.

In the inn at Beckstein he remarked, immediately upon his entrance, an intelligent young gentleman dining, with a book in front of him. He had his own place laid close by the reader, and with a proper apology, broke ground by asking what he read.

'I am perusing,' answered the young gentleman, 'the last work of the Herr Doctor Hohenstockwitz, cousin and librarian of your Prince here in Grünewald—a man of great erudition and some lambencies of wit.'

'I am acquainted,' said Otto, 'with the Herr Doctor, though not yet with his work.'

'Two privileges that I must envy you,' replied the young man politely: 'an honour in hand, a pleasure in the bush.'

'The Herr Doctor is a man much respected, I believe, for his attainments?' asked the Prince.

'He is, sir, a remarkable instance of the force of intellect,' replied the reader. 'Who, of our young men know anything of his cousin, all reigning Prince although he be? Who but has heard of Doctor Gotthold? But intellectual merit, alone of all distinctions, has its base in nature.'

'I have the gratification of addressing a student—perhaps an author?' Otto suggested.

The young man somewhat flushed. 'I have some claim to both distinctions, sir, as you suppose,' said he; 'there is my card. I am the licentiate Roederer, author of several works on the theory and practice of politics.'

'You immensely interest me,' said the Prince; 'the more so as I gather that here in Grünewald we are on the brink of revolution. Pray, since these have been your special studies, would you augur hopefully of such a movement?'

'I perceive,' said the young author, with a certain vinegary twitch, 'that you are unacquainted with my opuscula. I am a convinced authoritarian. I share none of those illusory, Utopian fancies with which empirics blind themselves and exasperate the ignorant. The day of these ideas is, believe me, past, or at least passing.'

'When I look about me——' began Otto.

'When you look about you,' interrupted the licentiate, 'you behold the ignorant. But in the laboratory of opinion, beside the studious lamp, we begin already to discard these figments. We begin to return to nature's order, to what I might call, if I were to borrow from the language of therapeutics, the expectant treatment of abuses. You will not misunderstand me,' he continued, 'a country in the condition in which we find Grünewald, a prince such as your Prince Otto, we must explicitly condemn; they are behind the age. But I would look for a remedy not to brute convulsions, but to the natural supervenience of a more able sovereign. I should amuse you, perhaps,' added the licentiate, with a smile, 'I think I should amuse you if I were to explain my notion of a prince. We who have studied in the closet, no longer, in this age, propose ourselves for active service. The paths, we have perceived, are incompatible. I would not have a student on the throne, though I would have one near by for an adviser. I would set forward as a prince a man of a good medium understanding, lively rather than deep; a man of courtly manner, possessed of the double art to ingratiate and to command; receptive, accommodating, seductive. I have been observing you since your first entrance. Well, sir, were I a subject of Grünewald I should pray heaven to set upon the seat of government just such another as yourself.'

'The devil you would!' exclaimed the Prince.

The licentiate Roederer laughed most heartily. 'I thought I should astonish you,' he said. 'These are not the ideas of the masses.'

'They are not, I can assure you,' Otto said.

'Or rather,' distinguished the licentiate, 'not to-day. The time will come, however, when these ideas shall prevail.'

'You will permit me, sir, to doubt it,' said Otto.

'Modesty is always admirable,' chuckled the theorist. 'But yet I assure you, a man like you, with such a man as, say, Doctor Gotthold at your elbow, would be, for all practical issues, my ideal ruler.'

At this rate the hours sped pleasantly for Otto. But the licentiate unfortunately slept that night at Beckstein, where he was, being dainty in the saddle and given to half stages. And to find a convoy to Mittwalden, and thus mitigate the company of his own thoughts, the Prince had to make favour with a certain party of wood-merchants from various states of the empire, who had been drinking together somewhat noisily at the far end of the apartment.

The night had already fallen when they took the saddle. The merchants were very loud and mirthful; each had a face like a nor'west moon; and they played pranks with each other's horses, and mingled songs and choruses, and alternately remembered and forgot the companion of their ride. Otto thus combined society and solitude, hearkening now to their chattering and empty talk, now to the voices of the encircling forest. The starlit dark, the faint wood airs, the clank of the horse-shoes making broken music, accorded together and attuned his mind. And he was still in a most equal temper when the party reached the top of that long hill that overlooks Mittwalden.

Down in the bottom of a bowl of forest, the lights of the little formal town glittered in a pattern, street crossing street; away by itself on the right, the palace was glowing like a factory.

Although he knew not Otto, one of the wood-merchants was a native of the state. 'There,' said he, pointing to the palace with his whip, 'there is Jezebel's inn.'

'What, do you call it that?' cried another, laughing.

'Ay, that's what they call it,' returned the Grünewalder; and he broke into a song, which the rest, as people well acquainted with the words and air, instantly took up in chorus. Her Serene Highness Amalia Seraphina, Princess of Grünewald, was the heroine, Gondremark the hero of this ballad. Shame hissed in Otto's ears. He reined up short and sat stunned in the saddle; and the singers continued to descend the hill without him.

The song went to a rough, swashing, popular air; and long after the words because inaudible the swing of the music, rising and falling, echoed insult to the Prince's brain. He fled the sounds. Hard by him on his right a road struck towards the palace, and he followed it through the thick shadows and branching alleys of the park. It was a busy place on a fine summer's afternoon, when the court and burghers met and saluted; but at that hour of the night in the early spring it was deserted to the roosting birds. Hares rustled among the covert; here and there a statue stood glimmering, with its eternal gesture; here and there the echo of an imitation temple clattered ghostly to the trampling of the mare. Ten minutes brought him to the upper end of his own home garden, where the small stables opened, over a bridge, upon the park. The yard clock was striking the hour of ten; so was the big bell in the palace bell-tower; and, farther off, the belfries of the town. About the stable all else was silent but the stamping of stalled horses and the rattle of halters. Otto dismounted; and as he did so a memory came back to him; a whisper of dishonest grooms and stolen corn, once heard, long forgotten, and now recurring in the nick of opportunity. He crossed the bridge, and, going up to a window, knocked six or seven heavy blows in a particular cadence, and, as he did so, smiled. Presently a wicket was opened in the gate, and a man's head appeared in the dim starlight.

'Nothing to-night,' said a voice.

'Bring a lantern,' said the Prince.

'Dear heart a' mercy!' cried the groom. 'Who's that?'

'It is I, the Prince,' replied Otto. 'Bring a lantern, take in the mare, and let me through into the garden.'

The man remained silent for a while, his head still projecting through the wicket.

'His Highness!' he said at last. 'And why did your Highness knock so strange?'

'It is a superstition in Mittwalden,' answered Otto, 'that it cheapens corn.'

With a sound like a sob the groom fled. He was very white when he returned, even by the light of the lantern; and his hand trembled as he undid the fastenings and took the mare.

'Your Highness,' he began at last, 'for God's sake . . .' And there he paused, oppressed with guilt.

'For God's sake, what?' asked Otto cheerfully. 'For God's sake let us have cheaper corn, say I. Good-night!' And he strode off into the garden, leaving the groom petrified once more.

The garden descended by a succession of stone terraces to the level of the fish-pond. On the far side the ground rose again, and was crowned by the confused roofs and gables of the palace. The modern pillared front, the ball-room, the great library, the princely apartments, the busy and illuminated quarters of that great house, all faced the town. The garden side was much older; and here it was almost dark; only a few windows quietly lighted at various elevations. The great square tower rose, thinning by stages like a telescope; and on the top of all the flag hung motionless.

The garden, as it now lay in the dusk and glimmer of the starshine, breathed of April violets. Under night's cavern arch the shrubs obscurely bustled. Through the plotted terraces and down the marble stairs the Prince rapidly descended, fleeing before uncomfortable thoughts. But alas! from these there is no city of refuge. And now, when he was about midway of the descent, distant strains of music began to fall upon his ear from the ball-room, where the court was dancing. They reached him faint and broken, but they touched the keys of memory; and through and above them Otto heard the ranting melody of the wood-merchant's song. Mere blackness seized upon his mind. Here he was, coming home; the wife was dancing, the husband had been playing a trick upon a lackey; and meanwhile, all about them, they were a byword to their subjects. Such a prince, such a husband, such a man, as this Otto had become! And he sped the faster onward.

Some way below he came unexpectedly upon a sentry; yet a little farther, and he was challenged by a second; and as he crossed the bridge over the fish-pond, an officer making the rounds stopped him once more. The parade of watch was more than usual; but curiosity was dead in Otto's mind, and he only chafed at the interruption. The porter of the back postern admitted him, and started to behold him so disordered. Thence, hasting by private stairs and passages, he came at length unseen to his own chamber, tore off his clothes, and threw himself upon his bed in the dark. The music of the ball-room still continued to a very lively measure; and still, behind that, he heard in spirit the chorus of the merchants clanking down the hill.

Book Two

OF LOVE AND POLITICS

5

What happened in the library

At a quarter before six on the following morning Doctor Gotthold was already at his desk in the library; and with a small cup of black coffee at his elbow, and an eye occasionally wandering to the busts and the long array of many-coloured books, was quietly reviewing the labours of the day before. He was a man of about forty, flaxen-haired, with refined features a little worn, and bright eyes somewhat faded. Early to bed and early to rise, his life was devoted to two things: erudition and Rhine wine. An ancient friendship existed latent between him and Otto; they rarely met, but when they did it was to take up at once the thread of their suspended intimacy. Gotthold, the virgin priest of knowledge, had envied his cousin, for half a day, when he was married; he had never envied him his throne.

Reading was not a popular diversion at the court of Grünewald; and that great, pleasant, sunshiny gallery of books and statues was, in practice, Gotthold's private cabinet. On this particular Wednesday morning, however, he had not been long about his manuscript when a door opened and the Prince stepped into the apartment. The doctor watched him as he drew near, receiving from each of the embayed windows in succession, a flush of morning sun; and Otto looked so gay, and walked so airily, he was so well dressed and brushed and frizzled, so point-device, and of such a sovereign elegance, that the heart of his cousin the recluse was rather moved against him.

'Good-morning, Gotthold,' said Otto, dropping in a chair.

'Good-morning, Otto,' returned the librarian. 'You are an early bird. Is this an accident, or do you begin reforming?'

'It is about time, I fancy,' answered the Prince.

'I cannot imagine,' said the Doctor. 'I am too sceptical to be an ethical adviser; and as for good resolutions, I believed in them when I was young. They are the colours of hope's rainbow.'

'If you come to think of it,' said Otto, 'I am not a popular sovereign.' And with a look he changed his statement to a question.

'Popular? Well, there I would distinguish,' answered Gotthold, leaning back and joining the tips of his fingers. 'There are various kinds of popularity; the bookish, which is perfectly impersonal, as unreal as the nightmare; the politician's, a mixed variety; and yours, which is the most personal of all. Women take to you; footmen adore you; it is as natural to like you as to pat a dog; and were you a saw-miller you would be the most popular citizen in Grünewald. As a prince—well, you are in the wrong trade. It is perhaps philosophical to recognise it as you do.'

'Perhaps philosophical?' repeated Otto.

'Yes, perhaps. I would not be dogmatic,' answered Gotthold.

'Perhaps philosophical, and certainly not virtuous,' Otto resumed.

'Not of a Roman virtue,' chuckled the recluse.

Otto drew his chair nearer to the table, leaned upon it with his elbow, and looked his cousin squarely in the face. 'In short,' he asked, 'not manly?'

'Well,' Gotthold hesitated, 'not manly, if you will.' And then, with a laugh, 'I did not know that you gave yourself out to be manly,' he added. 'It was one of the points that I inclined to like about you; inclined, I believe, to admire. The names of virtues exercise a charm on most of us; we must lay claim to all of them, however incompatible; we must all be both daring and prudent; we must all vaunt our pride and go to the stake for our humility. Not so you. Without compromise you were yourself: a pretty sight. I have always said it: none so void of all pretence as Otto.'

'Pretence and effort both!' cried Otto. 'A dead dog in a canal is more alive. And the question, Gotthold, the question that I have to face is this: Can I not, with effort and self-denial, can I not become a tolerable sovereign?'

'Never,' replied Gotthold. 'Dismiss the notion. And besides, dear child, you would not try.'

'Nay, Gotthold, I am not to be put by,' said Otto. 'If I am constitutionally unfit to be a sovereign, what am I doing with this money, with this palace, with these guards? And I—a thief—am to execute the law on others?'

'I admit the difficulty,' said Gotthold.

'Well, can I not try?' continued Otto. 'Am I not bound to try? And with the advice and help of such a man as you——'

'Me!' cried the librarian. 'Now, God forbid!'

Otto, though he was in no very smiling humour, could not forbear to smile. 'Yet I was told last night,' he laughed, 'that with a man like me to impersonate, and a man like you to touch the springs, a very possible government could be composed.'

'Now, I wonder in what diseased imagination,' Gotthold said, 'that preposterous monster saw the light of day?'

'It was one of your own trade—a writer: one Roederer,' said Otto.

'Roederer! an ignorant puppy!' cried the librarian.

'You are ungrateful,' said Otto. 'He is one of your professed admirers.'

'Is he?' cried Gotthold, obviously impressed. 'Come, that is a good account of the young man. I must read his stuff again. It is the rather to his credit, as our views are opposite. The east and west are not more opposite. Can I have converted him? But no; the incident belongs to Fairyland.'

'You are not then,' asked the Prince 'an authoritarian?'

'I? God bless me, no!' said Gotthold. 'I am a red, dear child.'

'That brings me then to my next point, and by a natural transition. If I am so clearly unfitted for my post,' the Prince asked; 'if my friends admit it, if my subjects clamour for my downfall, if revolution is preparing at this hour, must I not go forth to meet the inevitable? should I not save these horrors and be done with these absurdities? in a word, should I not abdicate? O, believe me, I feel the ridicule, the vast abuse of language,' he added, wincing, 'but even a principulus like me cannot resign; he must make a great gesture, and come buskined forth, and abdicate.'

'Ay,' said Gotthold, 'or else stay where he is. What gnat has bitten you to-day? Do you not know that you are touching, with lay hands, the very holiest inwards of philosophy, where madness dwells? Ay, Otto, madness; for in the serene temples of the wise, the inmost shrine, which we carefully keep locked, is full of spiders' webs. All men, all, are fundamentally useless; nature tolerates, she does not need, she does not use them: sterile flowers! All—down to the fellow swinking in a byre, whom fools point out for the exception—all are useless; all weave ropes of sand; or like a child that has breathed on a window, write and obliterate, write and obliterate idle words! Talk of it no more. That way, I tell you, madness lies.' The speaker rose from his chair and then sat down again. He laughed a little laugh, and then, changing his tone, resumed: 'Yes, dear child, we are not here to do battle with giants; we are here to be happy like the flowers, if we can be. It is because you could, that I have always secretly admired you. Cling to that trade; believe me, it is the right one. Be happy, be idle, be airy. To the devil with all casuistry! and leave the state to Gondremark, as heretofore. He does it well enough, they say; and his vanity enjoys the situation.'

'Gotthold,' cried Otto, 'what is this to me? Useless is not the question; I cannot rest at uselessness; I must be useful or I must be noxious—one or other. I grant you the whole thing, prince and principality alike, is pure absurdity, a stroke of satire; and that a banker or the man who keeps an inn has graver duties. But now, when I have washed my hands of it three years, and left all—labour, responsibility, and honour and enjoyment too, if there be any—to Gondremark and to—Seraphina——' He hesitated at the name, and Gotthold glanced aside. 'Well,' the Prince continued, 'what has come of it? Taxes, army, cannon—why, it's like a box of lead soldiers! And the people sick at the folly of it, and fired with the injustice! And war, too—I hear of war—war in this teapot! What a complication of absurdity and disgrace! And when the inevitable end arrives—the revolution—who will be to blame in the sight of God, who will be gibbeted in public opinion? I! Prince Puppet!'

'I thought you had despised public opinion,' said Gotthold.

'I did,' said Otto sombrely, 'but now I do not. I am growing old. And then, Gotthold, there is Seraphina. She is loathed in this country that I brought her to and suffered her to spoil. Yes, I gave it her as a plaything, and she has broken it: a fine Prince, an admirable Princess! Even her life—I ask you, Gotthold, is her life safe?'

'It is safe enough to-day,' replied the librarian: 'but since you ask me seriously, I would not answer for to-morrow. She is ill-advised.'

'And by whom? By this Gondremark, to whom you counsel me to leave my country,' cried the Prince. 'Rare advice! The course that I have been following all these years, to come at last to this. O, ill-advised! if that were all! See now, there is no sense in beating about the bush between two men: you know what scandal says of her?'

Gotthold, with pursed lips, silently nodded.

'Well, come, you are not very cheering as to my conduct as the Prince; have I even done my duty as a husband?' Otto asked.

'Nay, nay,' said Gotthold, earnestly and eagerly, 'this is another chapter. I am an old celibate, an old monk. I cannot advise you in your marriage.'

'Nor do I require advice,' said Otto, rising. 'All of this must cease.' And he began to walk to and fro with his hands behind his back.

'Well, Otto, may God guide you!' said Gotthold, after a considerable silence. 'I cannot.'

'From what does all this spring?' said the Prince, stopping in his walk. 'What am I to call it? Diffidence? The fear of ridicule? Inverted vanity? What matter names, if it has brought me to this? I could never bear to be bustling about nothing; I was ashamed of this toy kingdom from the first; I could not tolerate that people should fancy I believed in a thing so patently absurd! I would do nothing that cannot be done smiling. I have a sense of humour, forsooth! I must know better than my Maker. And it was the same thing in my marriage,' he added more hoarsely. 'I did not believe this girl could care for me; I must not intrude; I must preserve the foppery of my indifference. What an impotent picture!'

'Ay, we have the same blood,' moralised Gotthold. 'You are drawing, with fine strokes, the character of the born sceptic.'

'Sceptic?—coward!' cried Otto. 'Coward is the word. A springless, putty-hearted, cowering coward!'

And as the Prince rapped out the words in tones of unusual vigour, a little, stout, old gentleman, opening a door behind Gotthold, received them fairly in the face. With his parrot's beak for a nose, his pursed mouth, his little goggling eyes, he was the picture of formality; and in ordinary circumstances, strutting behind the drum of his corporation, he impressed the beholder with a certain air of frozen dignity and wisdom. But at the smallest contrariety, his trembling hands and disconnected gestures betrayed the weakness at the root. And now, when he was thus surprisingly received in that library of Mittwalden Palace, which was the customary haunt of silence, his hands went up into the air as if he had been shot, and he cried aloud with the scream of an old woman.

'O!' he gasped, recovering, 'your Highness! I beg ten thousand pardons. But your Highness at such an hour in the library!—a circumstance so unusual as your Highness's presence was a thing I could not be expected to foresee.'

'There is no harm done, Herr Cancellarius,' said Otto.

'I came upon the errand of a moment: some papers I left over-night with the Herr Doctor,' said the Chancellor of Grünewald. 'Herr Doctor, if you will kindly give me them, I will intrude no longer.'

Gotthold unlocked a drawer and handed a bundle of manuscript to the old gentleman, who prepared, with fitting salutations, to take his departure.

'Herr Greisengesang, since we have met,' said Otto, 'let us talk.'

'I am honoured by his Highness's commands,' replied the Chancellor.

'All has been quiet since I left?' asked the Prince, resuming his seat.

'The usual business, your Highness,' answered Greisengesang;

'punctual trifles: huge, indeed, if neglected, but trifles when discharged. Your Highness is most zealously obeyed.'

'Obeyed, Herr Cancellarius?' returned the Prince. 'And when have I obliged you with an order? Replaced, let us rather say. But to touch upon these trifles; instance me a few.'

'The routine of government, from which your Highness has so wisely dissociated his leisure——' began Greisengesang.

'We will leave my leisure, sir,' said Otto. 'Approach the facts.'

'The routine of business was proceeded with,' replied the official, now visibly twittering.

'It is very strange, Herr Cancellarius, that you should so persistently avoid my questions,' said the Prince. 'You tempt me to suppose a purpose in your dullness. I have asked you whether all was quiet; do me the pleasure to reply.'

'Perfectly—O, perfectly quiet,' jerked the ancient puppet, with every signal of untruth.

'I make a note of these words,' said the Prince gravely. 'You assure me, your sovereign, that since the date of my departure nothing has occurred of which you owe me an account.'

'I take your Highness, I take the Herr Doctor to witness,' cried Greisengesang, 'that I have had no such expression.'

'Halt!' said the Prince; and then, after a pause: 'Herr Greisengesang, you are an old man, and you served my father before you served me,' he added. 'It consists neither with your dignity nor mine that you should babble excuses and stumble possibly upon untruths. Collect your thoughts; and then categorically inform me of all you have been charged to hide.'

Gotthold, stooping very low over his desk, appeared to have resumed his labours; but his shoulders heaved with subterranean merriment. The Prince waited, drawing his handkerchief quietly through his fingers.

'Your Highness, in this informal manner,' said the old gentleman at last, 'and being unavoidably deprived of documents, it would be difficult, it would be impossible, to do justice to the somewhat grave occurrences which have transpired.'

'I will not criticise your attitude,' replied the Prince. 'I desire that between you and me, all should be done gently; for I have not forgotten, my old friend, that you were kind to me from the first, and for a period of years a faithful servant. I will thus dismiss the matters on which you waive immediate inquiry. But you have certain papers actually in your hand. Come, Herr Greisengesang, there is at least one point for which you have authority. Enlighten me on that.'

'On that?' cried the old gentleman. 'O, that is a trifle; a

matter, your Highness, of police; a detail of a purely administrative order. These are simply a selection of the papers seized upon the English traveller.'

'Seized?' echoed Otto. 'In what sense? Explain yourself.'

'Sir John Crabtree,' interposed Gotthold, looking up, 'was arrested yesterday evening.'

'Is this so, Herr Cancellarius?' demanded Otto sternly.

'It was judged right, your Highness,' protested Greisengesang. 'The decree was in due form, invested with your Highness's authority by procuration. I am but an agent; I had no status to prevent the measure.'

'This man, my guest, has been arrested,' said the Prince. 'On what grounds, sir? With what colour of pretence?'

The Chancellor stammered.

'Your Highness will perhaps find the reason in these documents,' said Gotthold, pointing with the tail of his pen.

Otto thanked his cousin with a look. 'Give them to me,' he said, addressing the Chancellor.

But that gentleman visibly hesitated to obey. 'Baron von Gondremark,' he said, 'has made the affair his own. I am in this case a mere messenger; and, as such, I am not clothed with any capacity to communicate the documents I carry. Herr Doctor, I am convinced you will not fail to bear me out.'

'I have heard a great deal of nonsense,' said Gotthold, 'and most of it from you; but this beats all.'

'Come, sir,' said Otto, rising, 'the papers. I command.'

Herr Greisengesang instantly gave way.

'With your Highness's permission,' he said, 'and laying at his feet my most submiss apologies, I will now hasten to attend his further orders in the Chancery.'

'Herr Cancellarius, do you see this chair?' said Otto. 'There is where you shall attend my further orders. O, now, no more!' he cried, with a gesture, as the old man opened his lips. 'You have sufficiently marked your zeal to your employer; and I begin to weary of a moderation you abuse.'

The Chancellor moved to the appointed chair and took his seat in silence.

'And now,' said Otto, opening the roll, 'what is all this? it looks like the manuscript of a book.'

'It is,' said Gotthold, 'the manuscript of a book of travels.'

'You have read it, Doctor Hohenstockwitz?' asked the Prince.

'Nay, but I saw the title-page,' replied Gotthold. 'But the roll was given to me open, and I heard no word of any secrecy.'

Otto dealt the Chancellor an angry glance.

'I see,' he went on. 'The papers of an author seized at this date of the world's history, in a state so petty and so ignorant as Grünewald, here is indeed an ignominious folly. Sir,' to the Chancellor, 'I marvel to find you in so scurvy an employment. On your conduct to your Prince I will not dwell: but to descend to be a spy! For what else can it be called? To seize the papers of this gentleman, the private papers of a stranger, the toil of a life, perhaps—to open, and to read them. And what have we to do with books? The Herr Doctor might perhaps be asked for his advice; but we have no *index expurgatorius* in Grünewald. Had we but that, we should be the most absolute parody and farce upon this tawdry earth.'

Yet, even while Otto spoke, he had continued to unfold the roll; and now, when it lay fully open, his eye rested on the title-page elaborately written in red ink. It ran thus:—

MEMOIRS
OF A VISIT TO THE VARIOUS
COURTS OF EUROPE,
BY
SIR JOHN CRABTREE, BARONET.

Below was a list of chapters, each bearing the name of one of the European Courts; and among these the nineteenth and the last upon the list was dedicated to Grünewald.

'Ah! The Court of Grünewald!' said Otto, 'that should be droll reading.' And his curiosity itched for it.

'A methodical dog, this English Baronet,' said Gotthold. 'Each chapter written and finished on the spot. I shall look for his work when it appears.'

'It would be odd, now, just to glance at it,' said Otto, wavering.

Gotthold's brow darkened, and he looked out of window.

But though the Prince understood the reproof, his weakness prevailed. 'I will,' he said, with an uneasy laugh, 'I will, I think, just glance at it.'

So saying, he resumed his seat and spread the traveller's manuscript upon the table.

6

'On the Court of Grünewald' being a portion of the traveller's manuscript

It may well be asked (*it was thus the English traveller began his nineteenth chapter*) why I should have chosen Grünewald out of so many other states equally petty, formal, dull, and corrupt. Accident, indeed, decided, and not I; but I have seen no reason to regret my visit. The spectacle of this small society macerating in its own abuses was not perhaps instructive, but I have found it exceedingly diverting.

The reigning Prince, Otto Johann Friedrich, a young man of imperfect education, questionable valour, and no scintilla of capacity, has fallen into entire public contempt. It was with difficulty that I obtained an interview, for he is frequently absent from a court where his presence is unheeded, and where his only rôle is to be a cloak for the amours of his wife. At last, however, on the third occasion when I visited the palace, I found the sovereign in the exercise of his inglorious function, with the wife on one hand, and the lover on the other. He is not ill-looking; he has hair of a ruddy gold, which naturally curls, and his eyes are dark, a combination which I always regard as the mark of some congenital deficiency, physical or moral; his features are irregular, but pleasing; the nose perhaps a little short, and the mouth a little womanish; his address is excellent, and he can express himself with point. But to pierce below these externals is to come on a vacuity of any sterling quality, a deliquescence of the moral nature, a frivolity and inconsequence of purpose that mark the nearly perfect fruit of a decadent age. He has a worthless smattering of many subjects, but a grasp of none. 'I soon weary of a pursuit,' he said to me, laughing; it would almost appear as if he took a pride in his incapacity and lack of moral courage. The results of his dilettanteism are to be seen in every field; he is a bad fencer, a second-rate horseman, dancer, shot; he sings—I have heard him—and he sings like a child; he writes intolerable verses in more than doubtful French; he acts like the common amateur; and in short there is no end to the number of the things that he does, and does badly. His one manly taste is for the chase. In sum, he is but a plexus of weaknesses; the singing chambermaid of the stage, tricked out in man's apparel, and mounted on a circus horse. I have seen this poor phantom of a prince riding out alone or with a few huntsmen, disregarded by all, and I have been even grieved for the bearer of so futile and melancholy an existence. The last Merovingians may have looked not otherwise.

The Princess Amalia Seraphina, a daughter of the Grand-Ducal house of Toggenburg-Tannhäuser, would be equally inconsiderable if she were not a cutting instrument in the hands of an ambitious man. She is much younger than the Prince, a girl of two-and-twenty, sick with vanity, superficially clever, and fundamentally a fool. She has a red-brown rolling eye, too large for her face, and with sparks of both levity and ferocity; her forehead is high and narrow, her figure thin and a little stooping. Her manners, her conversation, which she interlards with French, her very tastes and ambitions, are alike assumed; and the assumption is ungracefully apparent: Hoyden playing Cleopatra. I should judge her to be incapable of truth. In private life a girl of this description embroils the peace of families, walks attended by a troop of scowling swains, and passes, once at least, through the divorce court; it is a common and, except to the cynic, an uninteresting type. On the throne, however, and in the hands of a man like Gondremark, she may become the authoress of serious public evils.

Gondremark, the true ruler of this unfortunate country, is a more complex study. His position in Grünewald, to which he is a foreigner, is eminently false; and that he should maintain it as he does, a very miracle of impudence and dexterity. His speech, his face, his policy, are all double: heads and tails. Which of the two extremes may be his actual design he were a bold man who should offer to decide. Yet I will hazard the guess that he follows both experimentally, and awaits, at the hand of destiny, one of those directing hints of which she is so lavish to the wise.

On the one hand, as *Maire du Palais* to the incompetent Otto, and using the love-sick Princess for a tool and mouthpiece, he pursues a policy of arbitrary power and territorial aggrandisement. He has called out the whole capable male population of the state to military service; he has bought cannon; he has tempted away promising officers from foreign armies; and he now begins, in his international relations, to assume the swaggering port and the vague, threatful language of a bully. The idea of extending Grünewald may appear absurd, but the little state is advantageously placed, its neighbours are all defenceless; and if at any moment the jealousies of the greater courts should neutralise each other, an active policy might double the principality both in population and extent. Certainly at least the scheme is entertained in the court of Wittwalden; nor do I myself regard it as entirely desperate. The margravate of Brandenburg has grown from as small beginnings to a formidable power; and though it is late in the day to try adventurous policies, and the age of war seems ended, Fortune, we must not forget, still blindly turns her wheel for men and nations. Concurrently with, and tributary to, these warlike preparations, crushing taxes have been levied, journals have been suppressed, and the country, which three years ago was prosperous and happy, now stagnates in a forced inaction, gold has become a curiosity, and the mills stand idle on the mountain streams.

On the other hand, in his second capacity of popular tribune, Gondremark is the incarnation of the free lodges, and sits at the centre of an organised conspiracy against the state. To any such movement my sympathies were early acquired, and I would not willingly let fall a word that might embarrass or retard the revolution. But to show that I speak of knowledge, and not as the reporter of mere gossip, I may mention that I have myself been present at a meeting where the details of a republican Constitution were minutely debated and arranged; and I may add that Gondremark was throughout referred to by the speakers as their captain in action and the arbiter of their disputes. He has taught his dupes (for so I must regard them) that his power of resistance to the Princess is limited, and at each fresh stretch of authority persuades them, with specious reasons, to postpone the hour of insurrection. Thus (to give some instance of his astute diplomacy) he salved over the decree enforcing military service, under the plea that to be well drilled and exercised in arms was even a necessary preparation for revolt. And the other day, when it began to be rumoured abroad that a war was being forced on a reluctant neighbour, the Grand Duke of Gerolstein, and I made sure it would be the signal for an instant rising, I was struck dumb with wonder to find that even this had been prepared and was to be accepted. I went from one to another in the Liberal camp, and all were in the same story, all had been drilled and schooled and fitted out with vacuous argument. 'The lads had better see some real fighting,' they said; 'and besides, it will be as well to capture Gerolstein: we can then extend to our neighbours the blessing of liberty on the same day that we snatch it for ourselves; and the republic will be all the stronger to resist, if the kings of Europe should band themselves together to reduce it.' I know not which of the two I should admire the more: the simplicity of the multitude or the audacity of the adventurer. But such are the subtleties, such the quibbling reasons, with which he blinds and leads this people. How long a course so tortuous can be pursued with safety I am incapable of guessing; not long, one would suppose; and yet this singular man has been treading the mazes for five years, and his favour at court and his popularity among the lodges still endure unbroken.

I have the privilege of slightly knowing him. Heavily and somewhat clumsily built, of a vast, disjointed, rambling frame, he can still pull himself together, and figure, not without admiration, in the saloon or the ball-room. His hue and temperament are plentifully bilious; he has a saturnine eye; his cheek is of a dark blue where he has been shaven. Essentially he is to be numbered among the man-haters, a convinced contemner of his fellows. Yet he is himself of a commonplace ambition and greedy of applause. In talk, he is remarkable for a thirst of information, loving rather to hear than to communicate; for sound and studious views; and, judging by the extreme short-sightedness of common politicians, for a remarkable prevision of events. All this, however, without grace, pleasantry, or charm, heavily set forth, with a dull countenance. In our numerous conversations, although he has always heard me with deference, I have been conscious throughout of a sort of ponderous finessing hard to tolerate. He produces none of the effect of a gentleman; devoid not merely of pleasantry, but of all attention or communicative warmth of bearing. No gentleman, besides, would so parade his amours with the Princess; still less repay the Prince for his long-suffering with a studied insolence of demeanour and the fabrication of insulting nicknames, such as Prince Featherhead, which run from ear to ear and create a laugh throughout the country. Gondremark has thus some of the clumsier characters of the self-made man, combined with an inordinate, almost a besotted, pride of intellect and birth. Heavy, bilious, selfish, inornate, he sits upon this court and country like an incubus.

But it is probable that he preserves softer gifts for necessary purposes. Indeed, it is certain, although he vouchsafed none of it to me, that this cold and stolid politician possesses to a great degree the art of ingratiation, and can be all things to all men. Hence there has probably sprung up the idle legend that in private life he is a gross romping voluptuary. Nothing, at least, can well be more surprising than the terms of his connection with the Princess. Older than her husband, certainly uglier, and according to the feeble ideas common among women, in every particular less pleasing, he has not only seized the complete command of all her thought and action, but has imposed on her in public a humiliating part. I do not here refer to the complete sacrifice of every rag of her reputation; for to many women these extremities are in themselves attractive. But there is about the court a certain lady of a dishevelled reputation, a Countess von

Rosen, wife or widow of a cloudy count, no longer in her second youth, and already bereft of some of her attractions, who unequivocally occupies the station of the Baron's mistress. I had thought, at first, that she was but a hired accomplice, a mere blind or buffer for the more important sinner. A few hours' acquaintance with Madame von Rosen for ever dispelled the illusion. She is one rather to make than to prevent a scandal, and she values none of those bribes—money, honours, or employment—with which the situation might be gilded. Indeed, as a person frankly bad, she pleased me, in the court of Grünewald, like a piece of nature.

The power of this man over the Princess is, therefore, without bounds. She has sacrificed to the adoration with which he has inspired her not only her marriage vow and every shred of public decency, but that vice of jealousy which is so much dearer to the female sex than either intrinsic honour or outward consideration. Nay, more: a young, although not a very attractive woman, and a princess both by birth and fact, she submits to the triumphant rivalry of one who might be her mother as to years, and who is so manifestly her inferior in station. This is one of the mysteries of the human heart. But the rage of illicit love, when it is once indulged, appears to grow by feeding; and to a person of the character and temperament of this unfortunate young lady, almost any depth of degradation is within the reach of possibility.

7

The Prince and the English traveller

So far Otto read, with waxing indignation; and here his fury overflowed. He tossed the roll upon the table and stood up. 'This man,' he said, 'is a devil. A filthy imagination, an ear greedy of evil, a ponderous malignity of thought and language: I grow like him by the reading! Chancellor, where is this fellow lodged?'

'He was committed to the Flag Tower,' replied Greisengesang, 'in the Gamiani apartment.'

'Lead me to him,' said the Prince; and then, a thought striking him, 'Was it for that,' he asked, 'that I found so many sentries in the garden?'

'Your Highness, I am unaware,' answered Greisengesang, true to his policy. 'The disposition of the guards is a matter distinct from my functions.'

Otto turned upon the old man fiercely, but ere he had time to speak, Gotthold touched him on the arm. He swallowed his wrath with a great effort. 'It is well,' he said, taking the roll. 'Follow me to the Flag Tower.'

The Chancellor gathered himself together, and the two set forward. It was a long and complicated voyage; for the library was in the wing of the new buildings, and the tower which carried the flag was in the old schloss upon the garden. By a great variety of stairs and corridors, they came out at last upon a patch of gravelled court; the garden peeped through a high grating with a flash of green; tall, old gabled buildings mounted on every side; the Flag Tower climbed, stage after stage, into the blue; and high over all, among the building daws, the yellow flag wavered in the wind. A sentinel at the foot of the tower stairs presented arms; another paced the first landing; and a third was stationed before the door of the extemporised prison.

'We guard this mud-bag like a jewel,' Otto sneered.

The Gamiani apartment was so called from an Italian doctor who had imposed on the credulity of a former prince. The rooms were large, airy, pleasant, and looked upon the gardens; but the walls were of great thickness (for the tower was old), and the windows were heavily barred. The Prince, followed by the Chancellor, still trotting to keep up with him, brushed swiftly through the little library and the long saloon, and burst like a thunderbolt into the bedroom at the farther end. Sir John was finishing his toilet; a man of fifty, hard, uncompromising, able, with the eye and teeth of physical courage. He was unmoved by the irruption, and bowed with a sort of sneering ease.

'To what am I to attribute the honour of this visit?' he asked.

'You have eaten my bread,' replied Otto, 'you have taken my hand, you have been received under my roof. When did I fail you in courtesy? What have you asked that was not granted as to an honoured guest? And here, sir,' tapping fiercely on the manuscript, 'here is your return.'

'Your Highness has read my papers?' said the Baronet. 'I am honoured indeed. But the sketch is most imperfect. I shall now have much to add. I can say that the Prince, whom I have accused of idleness, is zealous in the department of police, taking upon himself those duties that are most distasteful. I shall be able to relate the burlesque incident of my arrest, and the singular interview with which you honour me at present. For the rest, I have already communicated with my Ambassador at Vienna; and unless you propose to murder me, I shall be at liberty, whether you please or not, within the week. For I hardly fancy the future empire of Grünewald is yet ripe to go to war with England. I conceive I am a little more than quits. I owe you no explanation; yours has been the wrong. You, if you have studied my writing with intelligence, owe me a large debt of gratitude. And to conclude, as I have not yet finished my toilet, I imagine the courtesy of a turnkey to a prisoner would induce you to withdraw.'

There was some paper on the table, and Otto, sitting down, wrote a passport in the name of Sir John Crabtree.

'Affix the seal, Herr Cancellarius,' he said, in his most princely manner, as he rose.

Greisengesang produced a red portfolio, and affixed the seal in the unpoetic guise of an adhesive stamp; nor did his perturbed and clumsy movements at all lessen the comedy of the performance. Sir John looked on with a malign enjoyment; and Otto chafed, regretting, when too late, the unnecessary loyalty of his command and gesture. But at length the Chancellor had finished his piece of prestidigitation, and, without waiting for an order, had countersigned the passport. Thus regularised, he returned it to Otto with a bow.

'You will now,' said the Prince, 'order one of my own carriages to be prepared; see it, with your own eyes, charged with Sir John's effects, and have it waiting within the hour behind the Pheasant House. Sir John departs this morning for Vienna.'

The Chancellor took his elaborate departure.

'Here, sir, is your passport,' said Otto, turning to the Baronet. 'I regret it from my heart that you have met inhospitable usage.'

'Well, there will be no English war,' returned Sir John.

'Nay, sir,' said Otto, 'you surely owe me your civility. Matters are now changed, and we stand again upon the footing of two gentlemen. It was not I who ordered your arrest; I returned late last night from hunting; and as you cannot blame me for your imprisonment, you may even thank me for your freedom.'

'And yet you read my papers,' said the traveller shrewdly.

'There, sir, I was wrong,' returned Otto; 'and for that I ask your pardon. You can scarce refuse it, for your own dignity, to one who is a plexus of weaknesses. Nor was the fault entirely mine. Had the papers been innocent, it would have been at most an indiscretion. Your own guilt is the sting of my offence.'

Sir John regarded Otto with an approving twinkle; then he bowed, but still in silence.

'Well, sir, as you are now at your entire disposal, I have a favour to beg of your indulgence,' continued the Prince. 'I have to request that you will walk with me alone into the garden so soon as your convenience permits.'

'From the moment that I am a free man,' Sir John replied, this time with perfect courtesy, 'I am wholly at your Highness's command; and if you will excuse a rather summary toilet, I will even follow you, as I am.'

'I thank you, sir,' said Otto.

So without more delay, the Prince leading, the pair proceeded down through the echoing stairway of the tower, and out through the grating, into the ample air and sunshine of the morning, and among the terraces and flower-beds of the garden. They crossed the fish-pond, where the carp were leaping as thick as bees; they mounted, one after another, the various flights of stairs, snowed upon, as they went, with April blossoms, and marching in time to the great orchestra of birds. Nor did Otto pause till they had reached the highest terrace of the garden. Here was a gate into the park, and hard by, under a tuft of laurel, a marble garden seat. Hence they looked down on the green tops of many elm-trees, where the rooks were busy; and, beyond that, upon the palace roof, and the yellow banner flying in the blue. 'I pray you to be seated, sir,' said Otto.

Sir John complied without a word; and for some seconds Otto walked to and fro before him, plunged in angry thought. The birds were all singing for a wager.

'Sir,' said the Prince at length, turning towards the Englishman, 'you are to me, except by the conventions of society, a perfect stranger. Of your character and wishes I am ignorant. I have never wittingly disobliged you. There is a difference in station, which I desire to waive. I would, if you still think me entitled to so much consideration—I would be regarded simply as a gentleman. Now, sir, I did wrong to glance at these papers, which I here return to you; but if curiosity be undignified, as I am free to own, falsehood is both cowardly and cruel. I opened your roll; and what did I find—what did I find about my wife; Lies!' he broke out. 'They are lies! There are not, so help me God! four words of truth in your intolerable libel! You are a man; you are old, and might be the girl's father; you are a gentleman; you are a scholar, and have learned refinement; and you rake together all this vulgar scandal, and propose to print it in a public book! Such is your chivalry! But, thank God, sir, she has still a husband. You say, sir, in that paper in your hand, that I am a bad fencer; I have to request from you a lesson in the art. The park is close behind; yonder is the Pheasant House, where you will find your carriage; should I fall, you know, sir—you have written it in your paper—how little my movements are regarded; I am in the custom of disappearing; it will be one more disappearance; and long before it has awakened a remark, you may be safe across the border.'

'You will observe,' said Sir John, 'that what you ask is impossible.'

'And if I struck you?' cried the Prince, with a sudden menacing flash.

'It would be a cowardly blow,' returned the Baronet, unmoved, 'for it would make no change. I cannot draw upon a reigning sovereign.'

'And it is this man, to whom you dare not offer satisfaction, that you choose to insult!' cried Otto.

'Pardon me,' said the traveller, 'you are unjust. It is because you are a reigning sovereign that I cannot fight with you; and it is for the same reason that I have a right to criticise your action and your wife. You are in everything a public creature; you belong to the public, body and bone. You have with you the law, the muskets of the army, and the eyes of spies. We, on our side, have but one weapon—truth.'

'Truth!' echoed the Prince, with a gesture.

There was another silence.

'Your Highness,' said Sir John at last, 'you must not expect grapes from a thistle. I am old and a cynic. Nobody cares a rush for me; and on the whole, after the present interview, I scarce know anybody that I like better than yourself. You see, I have changed my mind, and have the uncommon virtue to avow the change. I tear up this stuff before you, here in your own garden; I ask your pardon, I ask the pardon of the Princess; and I give you my word of honour as a gentleman and an old man, that when my book of travel shall appear it shall not contain so much as the name of Grünewald. And yet it was a racy chapter! But had your Highness only read about the other courts! I am a carrion crow; but it is not my fault, after all, that the world is such a nauseous kennel.'

'Sir,' said Otto, 'is the eye not jaundiced?'

'Nay,' cried the traveller, 'very likely. I am one who goes sniffing; I am no poet. I believe in a better future for the world; or, at all accounts, I do most potently disbelieve in the present. Rotten eggs is the burthen of my song. But indeed, your Highness, when I meet with any merit, I do not think that I am slow to recognise it. This is a day that I shall still recall with gratitude, for I have found a sovereign with some manly virtues; and for once—old courtier and old radical as I am—it is from the heart and quite sincerely that I can request the honour of kissing your Highness's hand?'

'Nay, sir,' said Otto, 'to my heart!'

And the Englishman, taken at unawares, was clasped for a moment in the Prince's arms.

'And now, sir,' added Otto, 'there is the Pheasant House; close behind it you will find my carriage, which I pray you to accept. God speed you to Vienna!'

'In the impetuosity of youth,' replied Sir John, 'your Highness has overlooked one circumstance. I am still fasting.'

'Well, sir,' said Otto, smiling, 'you are your own master; you may go or stay. But I warn you, your friend may prove less powerful than your enemies. The Prince, indeed, is thoroughly on your side; he has all the will to help; but to whom do I speak?—you know better than I do, he is not alone in Grünewald.'

'There is a deal in position,' returned the traveller, gravely nodding. 'Gondremark loves to temporise; his policy is below ground, and he fears all open courses; and now that I have seen you act with so much spirit, I will cheerfully risk myself on your protection. Who knows? You may be yet the better man.'

'Do you indeed believe so?' cried the Prince. 'You put life into my heart!'

'I will give up sketching portraits,' said the Baronet. 'I am a blind owl; I had misread you strangely. And yet remember this; a spring is one thing, and to run all day another. For I still mistrust your constitution; the short nose, the hair and eyes of several complexions; no, they are diagnostic; and I must end, I see, as I began.'

'I am still a singing chambermaid?' said Otto.

'Nay, your Highness, I pray you to forget what I had written,' said Sir John; 'I am not like Pilate; and the chapter is no more. Bury it, if you love me.'

8

While the Prince is in the anteroom...

GREATLY comforted by the exploits of the morning, the Prince turned towards the Princess's anteroom, bent on a more difficult enterprise. The curtains rose before him, the usher called his name, and he entered the room with an exaggeration of his usual mincing and airy dignity. There were about a score of persons waiting, principally ladies; it was one of the few societies in Grünewald where Otto knew himself to be popular; and while a maid of honour made her exit by a side door to announce his arrival to the Princess, he moved round the apartment, collecting homage and bestowing compliments with friendly grace. Had this been the sum of his duties, he had been an admirable monarch. Lady after lady was impartially honoured by his attention.

'Madam,' he said to one, 'how does this happen? I find you daily more adorable.'

'And your Highness daily browner,' replied the lady. 'We began equal; O, there I will be bold: we have both beautiful complexions. But while I study mine, your Highness tans himself.'

'A perfect negro, madam; and what so fitly—being beauty's slave?' said Otto.—'Madame Grafinski, when is our next play? I have just heard that I am a bad actor.'

'*O ciel!*' cried Madame Grafinski. 'Who could venture? What a bear!'

'An excellent man, I can assure you,' returned Otto.

'O, never! O, is it possible!' fluted the lady. 'Your Highness plays like an angel.'

'You must be right, madam; who could speak falsely and yet look so charming?' said the Prince. 'But this gentleman, it seems, would have preferred me playing like an actor.'

A sort of hum, a falsetto, feminine cooing, greeted the tiny sally: and Otto expanded like a peacock. This warm atmosphere of women and flattery and idle chatter pleased him to the marrow.

'Madame von Eisenthal, your coiffure is delicious,' he remarked.

'Every one was saying so,' said one.

'If I have pleased Prince Charming?' And Madame von Eisenthal swept him a deep curtsey with a killing glance of adoration.

'It is new?' he asked. 'Vienna fashion.'

'Mint new,' replied the lady, 'for your Highness's return. I felt young this morning; it was a premonition. But why, Prince, do you ever leave us?'

'For the pleasure of the return,' said Otto. 'I am like a dog; I must bury my bone, and then come back to gloat upon it.'

'O, a bone! Fie, what a comparison! You have brought back the manners of the wood,' returned the lady.

'Madam, it is what the dog has dearest,' said the Prince. 'But I observe Madame von Rosen.'

And Otto, leaving the group to which he had been piping, stepped towards the embrasure of a window where a lady stood.

The Countess von Rosen had hitherto been silent, and a thought depressed, but on the approach of Otto she began to brighten.

She was tall, slim as a nymph, and of a very airy carriage; and her face, which was already beautiful in repose, lightened and changed, flashed into smiles, and glowed with lovely colour at the touch of animation. She was a good vocalist; and, even in speech, her voice commanded a great range of changes, the low notes rich with tenor quality, the upper ringing, on the brink of laughter, into music. A gem of many facets and variable hues of fire; a woman who withheld the better portion of her beauty, and then, in a caressing second, flashed it like a weapon full on the beholder; now merely a tall figure and a sallow handsome face, with the evidences of a reckless temper; anon opening like a flower to life and colour, mirth and tenderness:—Madame von Rosen had always a dagger in reserve for the dispatch of ill-assured admirers. She met Otto with the dart of tender gaiety.

'You have come to me at last, Prince Cruel,' she said. 'Butterfly! Well, and am I not to kiss your hand?' she added.

'Madam, it is I who must kiss yours.' And Otto bowed and kissed it.

'You deny me every indulgence,' she said, smiling.

'And now what news in Court?' inquired the Prince. 'I come to you for my gazette.'

'Ditch-water!' she replied. 'The world is all asleep, grown gray in slumber; I do not remember any waking movement since quite an eternity; and the last thing in the nature of a sensation was the last time my governess was allowed to box my ears. But yet I do myself and your unfortunate enchanted palace some injustice. Here is the last—O positively!' And she told him the story from behind her fan, with many glances, many cunning strokes of the narrator's art. The others had drawn away, for it was understood that Madame von Rosen was in favour with the Prince. None the less, however, did the Countess lower her voice at times to within a semitone of whispering; and the pair leaned together over the narrative.

'Do you know,' said Otto, laughing, 'you are the only entertaining woman on this earth!'

'O, you have found out so much,' she cried.

'Yes, madam, I grow wiser with advancing years,' he returned.

'Years,' she repeated. 'Do you name the traitors? I do not believe in years; the calendar is a delusion.'

'You must be right, madam,' replied the Prince. 'For six years that we have been good friends, I have observed you to grow younger.'

'Flatterer!' cried she, and then with a change, 'but why should I say so,' she added, 'when I protest I think the same? A week ago I had a council with my father director, the glass;

and the glass replied, " Not yet "! I confess my face in this way once a month. O! a very solemn moment. Do you know what I shall do when the mirror answers, " Now "? '

'I cannot guess,' said he.

'No more can I,' returned the Countess. 'There is such a choice! Suicide, gambling, a nunnery, a volume of memoirs, or politics—the last, I am afraid.'

'It is a dull trade,' said Otto.

'Nay,' she replied, 'it is a trade I rather like. It is, after all, first cousin to gossip, which no one can deny to be amusing. For instance, if I were to tell you that the Princess and the Baron rode out together daily to inspect the cannon, it is either a piece of politics or scandal, as I turn my phrase. I am the alchemist that makes the transmutation. They have been everywhere together since you left,' she continued, brightening as she saw Otto darken; 'that is a poor snippet of malicious gossip —and they were everywhere cheered—and with that addition all becomes political intelligence.'

'Let us change the subject,' said Otto.

'I was about to propose it,' she replied, 'or rather to pursue the politics. Do you know? this war is popular—popular to the length of cheering Princess Seraphina.'

'All things, madam, are possible,' said the Prince; 'and this among others, that we may be going into war, but I give you my word of honour, I do not know with whom.'

'And you put up with it?' she cried. 'I have no pretensions to morality; and I confess I have always abominated the lamb, and nourished a romantic feeling for the wolf. O, be done with lambiness! Let us see there is a prince, for I am weary of the distaff.'

'Madam,' said Otto, 'I thought you were of that faction.'

'I should be of yours, *mon Prince*, if you had one,' she retorted. 'Is it true that you have no ambition? There was a man once in England whom they call the kingmaker. Do you know,' she added, 'I fancy I could make a prince?'

'Some day, madam,' said Otto, 'I may ask you to help make a farmer.'

'Is that a riddle?' asked the Countess.

'It is,' replied the Prince, 'and a very good one too.'

'Tit for tat. I will ask you another,' she returned. 'Where is Gondremark?'

'The Prime Minister? In the prime-ministry, no doubt,' said Otto.

'Precisely,' said the Countess; and she pointed with her fan to the door of the Princess's apartments. 'You and I, *mon Prince*, are in the anteroom. You think me unkind,' she added. 'Try me and you will see. Set me a task, put me a question; there is no enormity I am not capable of doing to oblige you, and no secret that I am not ready to betray.'

'Nay, madam, but I respect my friend too much,' he answered, kissing her hand. 'I would rather remain ignorant of all. We fraternise like foemen soldiers at the outposts, but let each be true to his own army.'

'Ah,' she cried, 'if all men were generous like you, it would be worth while to be a woman!' Yet, judging by her looks, his generosity, if anything, had disappointed her; she seemed to seek a remedy, and, having found it, brightened once more. 'And now,' she said, 'may I dismiss my sovereign? This is rebellion and a *cas pendable*; but what am I to do? My bear is jealous!'

'Madam, enough!' cried Otto. 'Ahasuerus reaches you the sceptre; more, he will obey you in all points. I should have been a dog to come to whistling.'

And so the Prince departed, and fluttered round Grafinski and von Eisenthal. But the Countess knew the use of her offensive weapons, and had left a pleasant arrow in the Prince's heart. That Gondremark was jealous—here was an agreeable revenge! And Madame von Rosen, as the occasion of the jealousy, appeared to him in a new light.

9

...Gondremark is in my Lady's chamber

THE Countess von Rosen spoke the truth. The great Prime Minister of Grünewald was already closeted with Seraphina. The toilet was over; and the Princess, tastefully arrayed, sat face to face with a tall mirror. Sir John's description was unkindly true, true in terms and yet a libel, a misogynistic masterpiece. Her forehead was perhaps too high, but it became her; her figure somewhat stooped, but every detail was formed and finished like a gem; her hand, her foot, her ear, the set of her comely head, were all dainty and accordant; if she was not beautiful, she was vivid, changeful, coloured, and pretty with a thousand various prettinesses; and her eyes, if they indeed rolled too consciously, yet rolled to purpose. They were her most attractive feature, yet they continually bore eloquent false witness to her thoughts; for while she herself, in the depths of her immature, unsoftened heart, was given altogether to manlike ambition and the desire of power, the eyes were by turns bold, inviting, fiery, melting, and artful, like the eyes of a rapacious siren. And artful, in a sense, she was. Chafing that she was not a man, and could not shine by action, she had conceived a woman's part, of answerable domination; she sought to subjugate for by-ends, to rain influence and be fancy free; and, while she loved not man, loved to see man obey her. It is a common girl's ambition. Such was perhaps that lady of the glove, who sent her lover to the lions. But the snare is laid alike for male and female, and the world most artfully contrived.

Near her, in a low chair, Gondremark had arranged his limbs into a cat-like attitude, high-shouldered, stooping, and submiss. The formidable blue jowl of the man, and the dull bilious eye, set perhaps a higher value on his evident desire to please. His face was marked by capacity, temper, and a kind of bold, piratical dishonesty which it would be calumnious to call deceit. His manners, as he smiled upon the Princess, were over-fine, yet hardly elegant.

'Possibly,' said the Baron, 'I should now proceed to take my leave. I must not keep my sovereign in the anteroom. Let us come at once to a decision.'

'It cannot, cannot be put off?' she asked.

'It is impossible,' answered Gondremark. 'Your Highness sees it for herself. In the earlier stages, we might imitate the serpent; but for the ultimatum, there is no choice but to be bold like lions. Had the Prince chosen to remain away, it had been better; but we have gone too far forward to delay.'

'What can have brought him?' she cried. 'To-day of all days?'

'The marplot, madam, has the instinct of his nature,' returned Gondremark. 'But you exaggerate the peril. Think, madam, how far we have prospered, and against what odds! Shall a Featherhead?—but no!' And he blew upon his fingers lightly with a laugh.

'Featherhead,' she replied, 'is still the Prince of Grünewald.'

'On your suffrance only, and so long as you shall please to be indulgent,' said the Baron. 'There are rights of nature; power to the powerful is the law. If he shall think to cross your destiny—well, you have heard of the brazen and the earthen pot.'

'Do you call me pot? You are ungallant, Baron,' laughed the Princess.

'Before we are done with your glory, I shall have called you by many different titles,' he replied.

The girl flushed with pleasure. 'But Frédéric is still the

Prince, *monsieur le flatteur*,' she said. 'You do not propose a revolution?—you of all men?'

'Dear madam, when it is already made!' he cried. 'The Prince reigns indeed in the almanac; but my Princess reigns and rules.' And he looked at her with a fond admiration that made the heart of Seraphina swell. Looking on her huge slave, she drank the intoxicating joys of power. Meanwhile he continued with that sort of massive archness that so ill became him: 'She has but one fault; there is but one danger in the great career that I foresee for her. May I name it? may I be so irreverent? It is in herself—her heart is soft.'

'Her courage is faint, Baron,' said the Princess. 'Suppose we have judged ill, suppose we were defeated?'

'Defeated, madam?' returned the Baron, with a touch of ill-humour. 'Is the dog defeated by the hare? Our troops are all cantoned along the frontier; in five hours the vanguard of five thousand bayonets shall be hammering on the gates of Brandenau; and in all Gerolstein there are not fifteen hundred men who can manœuvre. It is as simple as a sum. There can be no resistance.'

'It is no great exploit,' she said. 'Is that what you call glory? It is like beating a child.'

'The courage, madam, is diplomatic,' he replied. 'We take a grave step; we fix the eyes of Europe, for the first time, on Grünewald; and in the negotiations of the next three months, mark me, we stand or fall. It is there, madam, that I shall have to depend upon your counsels,' he added, almost gloomily. 'If I had not seen you at work, if I did not know the fertility of your mind, I own I should tremble for the consequence. But it is in this field that men must recognise their inability. All the great negotiators when they have not been women, have had women at their elbows. Madame de Pompadour was ill served; she had not found her Gondremark; but what a mighty politician! Catherine de' Medici, too, what justice of sight, what readiness of means, what elasticity against defeat! But alas! madam, her Featherheads were her own children; and she had that one touch of vulgarity, that one trait of the good-wife, that she suffered family ties and affections to confine her liberty.'

These singular views of history, strictly *ad usum Seraphinæ*, did not weave their usual soothing spell over the Princess. It was plain that she had taken a momentary distaste to her own resolutions; for she continued to oppose her counsellor, looking upon him out of half-closed eyes and with the shadow of a sneer upon her lips. 'What boys men are!' she said; 'what lovers of big words! Courage, indeed! If you had to scour pans,

Herr von Gondremark, you would call it, I suppose, Domestic Courage?'

'I would, madam,' said the Baron stoutly, 'if I scoured them well. I would put a good name upon a virtue; you will not overdo it: they are not so enchanting in themselves.'

'Well, but let me see,' she said. 'I wish to understand your courage. Why we asked leave, like children! Our grannie in Berlin, our uncle in Vienna, the whole family, have patted us on the head and sent us forward. Courage? I wonder when I hear you!'

'My Princess is unlike herself,' returned the Baron. 'She has forgotten where the peril lies. True, we have received encouragement on every hand; but my Princess knows too well on what untenable conditions; and she knows besides how, in the publicity of the diet, these whispered conferences are forgotten and disowned. The danger is very real'—he raged inwardly at having to blow the very coal he had been quenching—'none the less real in that it is not precisely military, but for that reason the easier to be faced. Had we to count upon your troops, although I share your Highness's expectations of the conduct of Alvenau, we cannot forget that he has not been proved in chief command. But where negotiation is concerned, the conduct lies with us; and with your help, I laugh at danger.'

'It may be so,' said Seraphina, sighing. 'It is elsewhere that I see danger. The people, these abominable people—suppose they should instantly rebel? What a figure we should make in the eyes of Europe to have undertaken an invasion while my own throne was tottering to its fall!'

'Nay, madam,' said Gondremark, smiling, 'here you are beneath yourself. What is it that feeds their discontent? What but the taxes? Once we have seized Gerolstein, the taxes are remitted, the sons return covered with renown, the houses are adorned with pillage, each tastes his little share of military glory, and behold us once again a happy family! "Ay," they will say, in each other's long ears, "the Princess knew what she was about; she was in the right of it; she has a head upon her shoulders; and here we are, you see, better off than before." But why should I say all this? It is what my Princess pointed out to me herself; it was by these reasons that she converted me to this adventure.'

'I think, Herr von Gondremark,' said Seraphina, somewhat tartly, 'you often attribute your own sagacity to your Princess.'

For a second Gondremark staggered under the shrewdness of the attack; the next, he had perfectly recovered. 'Do I?' he said. 'It is very possible. I have observed a similar tendency in your Highness.'

It was so openly spoken, and appeared so just, that Seraphina breathed again. Her vanity had been alarmed, and the greatness of the relief improved her spirits. 'Well,' she said, 'all this is little to the purpose. We are keeping Frédéric without, and I am still ignorant of our line of battle. Come, co-admiral, let us consult. . . . How am I to receive him now? And what are we to do if he should appear at the council?'

'Now,' he answered. 'I shall leave him to my Princess for just now! I have seen her at work. Send him off to his theatricals! But in all gentleness,' he added. 'Would it, for instance, would it displease my sovereign to affect a headache?'

'Never!' said she. 'The woman who can manage, like the man who can fight, must never shrink from an encounter. The knight must not disgrace his weapons.'

'Then let me pray my *belle dame sans merci*,' he returned, 'to affect the only virtue that she lacks. Be pitiful to the poor young man; affect an interest in his hunting; be weary of politics; find in his society, as it were, a grateful repose from dry considerations. Does my Princess authorise the line of battle?'

'Well, that is a trifle,' answered Seraphina. 'The council—there is the point.'

'The council?' cried Gondremark. 'Permit me, madam.' And he rose and proceeded to flutter about the room, counterfeiting Otto both in voice and gesture not unhappily. '"What is there to-day, Herr von Gondremark? Ah, Herr Cancellarius, a new wig! You cannot deceive me; I know every wig in Grünewald; I have the sovereign's eye. What are these papers about? O, I see. O, certainly. Surely, surely. I wager none of you remarked that wig. By all means. I know nothing about that. Dear me, are there as many as all that? Well, you can sign them; you have the procuration. You see, Herr Cancellarius, I know your wig." And so,' concluded Gondremark, resuming his own voice, 'our sovereign, by the particular grace of God, enlightens and supports his privy councillors.'

But when the Baron turned to Seraphina for approval, he found her frozen. 'You are pleased to be witty, Herr von Gondremark,' she said, 'and have perhaps forgotten where you are. But these rehearsals are apt to be misleading. Your master, the Prince of Grünewald, is sometimes more exacting.'

Gondremark cursed her in his soul. Of all injured vanities, that of the reproved buffoon is the most savage; and when grave issues are involved, these petty stabs become unbearable. But Gondremark was a man of iron; he showed nothing; he did not even, like the common trickster, retreat because he had presumed, but held to his point bravely. 'Madam,' he said, 'if, as you say, he prove exacting, we must take the bull by the horns.'

'We shall see,' she said, and she arranged her skirt like one about to rise. Temper, scorn, disgust, all the more acrid feelings, became her like jewels; and she now looked her best.

'Pray God they quarrel,' thought Gondremark. 'The damned minx may fail me yet, unless they quarrel. It is time to let him in. Zz—fight, dogs!' Consequent on these reflections, he bent a stiff knee and chivalrously kissed the Princess's hand. 'My Princess,' he said, 'must now dismiss her servant. I have much to arrange against the hour of council.'

'Go,' she said, and rose.

And as Gondremark tripped out of a private door, she touched a bell, and gave the order to admit the Prince.

10

The Prince delivers a lecture on marriage, with practical illustrations of divorce

With what a world of excellent intentions Otto entered his wife's cabinet! how fatherly, how tender! how morally affecting were the words he had prepared! Nor was Seraphina unamiably inclined. Her usual fear of Otto as a marplot in her great designs was now swallowed up in a passing distrust of the designs themselves. For Gondremark, besides, she had conceived an angry horror. In her heart she did not like the Baron. Behind his impudent servility, behind the devotion which, with indelicate delicacy, he still forced on her attention, she divined the grossness of his nature. So a man may be proud of having tamed a bear, and yet sicken at his captive's odour. And above all, she had certain jealous intimations that the man was false and the deception double. True, she falsely trifled with his love; but he, perhaps, was only trifling with her vanity. The insolence of his late mimicry, and the odium of her own position as she sat and watched it, lay besides like a load upon her conscience. She met Otto almost with a sense of guilt, and yet she welcomed him as a deliverer from ugly things.

But the wheels of an interview are at the mercy of a thousand ruts; and even at Otto's entrance, the first jolt occurred. Gondremark, he saw, was gone; but there was the chair drawn close for consultation; and it pained him not only that this man had been received, but that he should depart with such an air of secrecy. Struggling with this twinge, it was somewhat sharply that he dismissed the attendant who had brought him in.

'You make yourself at home, *chez moi*,' she said, a little ruffled both by his tone of command and by the glance he had thrown upon the chair.

'Madam,' replied Otto, 'I am here so seldom that I have almost the rights of a stranger.'

'You choose your own associates, Frédéric,' she said.

'I am here to speak of it,' he returned. 'It is now four years since we were married; and these four years, Seraphina, have not perhaps been happy either for you or for me. I am well aware I was unsuitable to be your husband. I was not young, I had no ambition, I was a trifler; and you despised me, I dare not say unjustly. But to do justice on both sides, you must bear in mind how I have acted. When I found it amused you to play the part of Princess on this little stage, did I not immediately resign to you my box of toys, this Grünewald? And when I found I was distasteful as a husband, could any husband have been less intrusive? You will tell me that I have no feelings, no preference, and thus no credit; that I go before the wind; that all this was in my character. And indeed, one thing is true, that it is easy, too easy, to leave things undone. But Seraphina, I begin to learn it is not always wise. If I were too old and too uncongenial for your husband, I should still have remembered that I was the Prince of that country to which you came, a visitor and a child. In that relation also there were duties, and these duties I have not performed.'

To claim the advantage of superior age is to give sure offence. 'Duty!' laughed Seraphina, 'and on your lips, Frédéric! You make me laugh. What fancy is this? Go, flirt with the maids, and be a prince in Dresden china, as you look. Enjoy yourself, *mon enfant*, and leave duty and the state to us.'

The plural grated on the Prince. 'I have enjoyed myself too much,' he said, 'since enjoyment is the word. And yet there were much to say upon the other side. You must suppose me desperately fond of hunting. But indeed there were days when I found a great deal of interest in what it was courtesy to call my government. And I have always had some claim to taste; I could tell live happiness from dull routine; and between hunting, and the throne of Austria, and your society, my choice had never wavered, had the choice been mine. You were a girl, a bud, when you were given me——'

'Heavens!' she cried, 'is this to be a love-scene?'

'I am never ridiculous,' he said; 'it is my only merit; and you may be certain this shall be a scene of marriage *à la mode*.

But when I remember the beginning, it is bare courtesy to speak in sorrow. Be just, madam: you would think me strangely uncivil to recall these days without the decency of a regret. Be yet a little juster, and own, if only in complaisance, that you yourself regret that past.'

'I have nothing to regret,' said the Princess. 'You surprise me. I thought you were so happy.'

'Happy and happy, there are so many hundred ways,' said Otto. 'A man may be happy in revolt; he may be happy in sleep; wine, change, and travel make him happy; virtue, they say, will do the like—I have not tried; and they say also that in old, quiet, and habitual marriages there is yet another happiness. Happy, yes; I am happy if you like; but I will tell you frankly, I was happier when I brought you home.'

'Well,' said the Princess, not without constraint, 'it seems you changed your mind.'

'Not I,' returned Otto, 'I never changed. Do you remember, Seraphina, on our way home, when you saw the roses in the lane, and I got out and plucked them? It was a narrow lane between great trees; the sunset at the end was all gold, and the rooks were flying overhead. There were nine, nine red roses; you gave me a kiss for each, and I told myself that every rose and every kiss should stand for a year of love. Well, in eighteen months there was an end. But do you fancy, Seraphina, that my heart has altered?'

'I am sure I cannot tell,' she said, like an automaton.

'It has not,' the Prince continued. 'There is nothing ridiculous, even from a husband, in a love that owns itself unhappy and that asks no more. I built on sand; pardon me, I do not breathe a reproach—I built, I suppose, upon my own infirmities; but I put my heart in the building, and it still lies among the ruins.'

'How very poetical!' she said, with a little choking laugh, unknown relentings, unfamiliar softnesses, moving within her. 'What would you be at?' she added, hardening her voice.

'I would be at this,' he answered; 'and hard it is to say. I would be at this:—Seraphina, I am your husband after all, and a poor fool that loves you. Understand,' he cried almost fiercely, 'I am no suppliant husband; what your love refuses I would scorn to receive from your pity. I do not ask, I would not take it. And for jealousy, what ground have I? A dog-in-the-manger jealousy is a thing the dogs may laught at. But at least, in the world's eye, I am still your husband; and I ask you if you treat me fairly? I keep to myself, I leave you free, I have given you in everything your will. What do you in return? I find, Seraphina, that you have been too thoughtless. But between persons such as we are, in our conspicuous station, particular care and a particular courtesy are owing. Scandal is perhaps not easy to avoid; but it is hard to bear.'

'Scandal!' she cried, with a deep breath. 'Scandal! It is for this you have been driving!'

'I have tried to tell you how I feel,' he replied. 'I have told you that I love you—love you in vain—a bitter thing for a husband; I have laid myself open that I might speak without offence. And now that I have begun, I will go on and finish.'

'I demand it,' she said. 'What is this about?'

Otto flushed crimson. 'I have to say what I would fain not,' he answered. 'I counsel you to see less of Gondremark.'

'Of Gondremark? And why?' she asked.

'Your intimacy is the ground of scandal, madam,' said Otto, firmly enough—'of a scandal that is agony to me, and would be crushing to your parents if they knew it.'

'You are the first to bring me word of it,' said she. 'I thank you.'

'You have perhaps cause,' he replied. 'Perhaps I am the only one among your friends——'

'O, leave my friends alone,' she interrupted. 'My friends are of a different stamp. You have come to me here and made a parade of sentiment. When have I last seen you? I have governed your kingdom for you in the meanwhile, and there I got no help. At last, when I am weary with a man's work, and you are weary of your playthings, you return to make me a scene of conjugal reproaches—the grocer and his wife! The positions are too much reversed; and you should understand, at least, that I cannot at the same time do your work of government and behave myself like a little girl. Scandal is the atmosphere in which we live, we princes; it is what a prince should know. You play an odious part. Do you believe this rumour?'

'Madam, should I be here?' said Otto.

'It is what I want to know!' she cried, the tempest of her scorn increasing. 'Suppose you did—I say, suppose you did believe it?'

'I should make it my business to suppose the contrary,' he answered.

'I thought so. O, you are made of baseness!' said he.

'Madam,' he cried, roused at last, 'enough of this. You wilfully misunderstand my attitude; you outwear my patience. In the name of your parents, in my own name, I summon you to be more circumspect.'

'Is this a request, *monsieur mon mari*?' she demanded.

'Madam, if I chose, I might command,' said Otto.

'You might, sir, as the law stands, make me prisoner,' returned Seraphina. 'Short of that you will gain nothing.'

'You will continue as before?' he asked.

'Precisely as before,' said she. 'As soon as this comedy is over, I shall request the Freiherr von Gondremark to visit me. Do you understand?' she added, rising. 'For my part, I have done.'

'I will then ask the favour of your hand, madam,' said Otto, palpitating in every pulse with anger. 'I have to request that you will visit in my society another part of my poor house. And reassure yourself—it will not take long—and it is the last obligation that you shall have the chance to lay me under.'

'The last?' she cried. 'Most joyfully!'

She offered her hand, and he took it; on each side with an elaborate affectation, each inwardly incandescent. He led her out by the private door, following where Gondremark had passed; they threaded a corridor or two, little frequented, looking on a court, until they came at last into the Prince's suite. The first room was an armoury, hung all about with the weapons of various countries, and looking forth on the front terrace.

'Have you brought me here to slay me?' she inquired.

'I have brought you, madam, only to pass on,' replied Otto.

Next they came to a library, where an old chamberlain sat half asleep. He rose and bowed before the princely couple, asking for orders.

'You will attend us here,' said Otto.

The next stage was a gallery of pictures, where Seraphina's portrait hung conspicuous, dressed for the chase, red roses in her hair, as Otto, in the first months of marriage, had directed. He pointed to it without a word; she raised her eyebrows in silence; and they passed still forward into a matted corridor where four doors opened. One led to Otto's bedroom; one was the private door to Seraphina's. And here, for the first time, Otto left her hand, and, stepping forward, shot the bolt.

'It is long, madam,' said he, 'since it was bolted on the other side.'

'One was effectual,' returned the Princess. 'Is this all?'

'Shall I reconduct you?' he asked, bowing.

'I should prefer,' she asked, in ringing tones, 'the conduct of the Freiherr von Gondremark.'

Otto summoned the chamberlain. 'If the Freiherr von Gondremark is in the palace,' he said, 'bid him attend the Princess here.' And when the official had departed, 'Can I do more to serve you, madam?' the Prince asked.

'Thank you, no. I have been much amused,' she answered.

'I have now,' continued Otto, 'given you your liberty complete. This has been for you a miserable marriage.'

'Miserable!' said she.

'It has been made light to you; it shall be lighter still,' continued the Prince. 'But one thing, madam, you must still continue to bear—my father's name, which is now yours. I leave it in your hands. Let me see you, since you will have no advice of mine, apply the more attention of your own to bear it worthily.'

'Herr von Gondremark is long in coming,' she remarked.

'O Seraphina, Seraphina!' he cried. And that was the end of their interview.

She tripped to a window and looked out; and a little after the chamberlain announced the Freiherr von Gondremark, who entered with something of a wild eye and changed complexion, confounded, as he was, at this unusual summons. The Princess faced round from the window with a pearly smile; nothing but her heightened colour spoke of discomposure. Otto was pale, but he was otherwise master of himself.

'Herr von Gondremark,' said he, 'oblige me so far: reconduct the Princess to her own apartment.'

The Baron, still all at sea, offered his hand, which was smilingly accepted, and the pair sailed forth through the picture-gallery.

As soon as they were gone, and Otto knew the length and breadth of his miscarriage, and how he had done the contrary of all that he intended, he stood stupefied. A fiasco so complete and sweeping was laughable, even to himself; and he laughed aloud in his wrath. Upon this mood there followed the sharpest violence of remorse; and to that again, as he recalled his provocation, anger succeeded afresh. So he was tossed in spirit; now bewailing his inconsequence and lack of temper, now flaming up in white-hot indignation and a noble pity for himself.

He paced his apartment like a leopard. There was danger in Otto, for a flash. Like a pistol, he could kill at one moment, and the next he might be kicked aside. But just then, as he walked the long floors in his alternate humours, tearing his handkerchief between his hands, he was strung to his top note, every nerve attent. The pistol, you might say, was charged. And when jealousy from time to time fetched him a lash across the tenderest of his feeling, and sent a string of her fire-pictures glancing before his mind's eye, the contraction of his face was even dangerous. He disregarded jealousy's inventions, yet they stung. In this height of anger, he still preserved his faith in

Seraphina's innocence; but the thought of her possible misconduct was the bitterest ingredient in his pot of sorrow.

There came a knock at the door, and the chamberlain brought him a note. He took it and ground it in his hand, continuing his march, continuing his bewildered thoughts; and some minutes had gone by before the circumstance came clearly to his mind. Then he paused and opened it. It was a pencil scratch from Gotthold, thus conceived:—

'The council is privately summoned at once.

'G. v. H.'

If the council was thus called before the hour, and that privately, it was plain they feared his interference. Feared: here was a sweet thought. Gotthold, too—Gotthold, who had always used and regarded him as a mere peasant lad, had now been at the pains to warn him; Gotthold looked for something at his hands. Well, none should be disappointed; the Prince, too long beshadowed by the uxorious lover, should now return and shine. He summoned his valet, repaired the disorder of his appearance with elaborate care; and then, curled and scented and adorned, Prince Charming in every line, but with a twitching nostril, he set forth unattended for the council.

II

The Prince dissolves the Council

It was as Gotthold wrote. The liberation of Sir John, Greisengesang's uneasy narrative, last of all, the scene between Seraphina and the Prince, had decided the conspirators to take a step of bold timidity. There had been a period of bustle, liveried messengers speeding here and there with notes; and at half-past ten in the morning, about an hour before its usual hour, the council of Grünewald sat around the board.

It was not a large body. At the instance of Gondremark, it had undergone a strict purgation, and was now composed exclusively of tools. Three secretaries sat at a side-table. Seraphina took the head; on her right was the Baron, on her left Greisengesang; below these Grafinski the treasurer, Count Eisenthal, a couple of non-combatants, and, to the surprise of all, Gotthold. He had been named a privy councillor by Otto, merely that he might profit by the salary; and as he was never known to attend a meeting, it had occurred to nobody to cancel his appointment. His present appearance was the more ominous, coming when it did. Gondremark scowled upon him; and the non-combatant on his right, intercepting this black look, edged away from one who was so clearly out of favour.

'The hour presses, you Highness,' said the Baron; 'may we proceed to business?'

'At once,' replied Seraphina.

'Your Highness will pardon me,' said Gotthold; 'but you are still, perhaps, unacquainted with the fact that Prince Otto has returned.'

'The Prince will not attend the council,' replied Seraphina, with a momentary blush. 'The despatches, Herr Cancellarius? There is one for Gerolstein?'

A secretary brought a paper.

'Here, madam,' said Greisengesang. 'Shall I read it?'

'We are all familiar with its terms,' replied Gondremark. 'Your Highness approves?'

'Unhesitatingly,' said Seraphina.

'It may then be held as read,' concluded the Baron. 'Will your Highness sign?'

The Princess did so; Gondremark, Eisenthal, and one of the non-combatants followed suit; and the paper was then passed across the table to the librarian. He proceeded leisurely to read.

'We have no time to spare, Herr Doctor,' cried the Baron brutally. 'If you do not choose to sign on the authority of your sovereign, pass it on. Or you may leave the table,' he added, his temper ripping out.

'I decline your invitation, Herr von Gondremark; and my sovereign, as I continue to observe with regret, is still absent from the board,' replied the Doctor calmly; and he resumed the perusal of the paper, the rest chafing and exchanging glances. 'Madam and gentlemen,' he said at last, 'what I hold in my hand is simply a declaration of war.'

'Simply,' said Seraphina, flashing defiance.

'The sovereign of this country is under the same roof with us,' continued Gotthold, 'and I insist he shall be summoned. It is needless to adduce my reasons; you are all ashamed at heart of this projected treachery.'

The council waved like a sea. There were various outcries.

'You insult the Princess,' thundered Gondremark.

'I maintain my protest,' replied Gotthold.

At the height of this confusion the door was thrown open; an usher announced, 'Gentlemen, the Prince!' and Otto, with his most excellent bearing, entered the apartment. It was like oil upon the troubled waters; every one settled instantly into his place, and Greisengesang, to give himself a countenance, became absorbed in the arrangement of his papers; but in their eagerness to dissemble, one and all neglected to rise.

'Gentlemen,' said the Prince, pausing.

They all got to their feet in a moment; and this reproof still further demoralised the weaker brethren.

The Prince moved slowly towards the lower end of the table; then he paused again, and, fixing his eye on Greisengesang, 'How comes it, Herr Cancellarius,' he asked, 'that I have received no notice of the change of hour?'

'Your Highness,' replied the Chancellor, 'her Highness the Princess...' and there paused.

'I understood,' said Seraphina, taking him up, 'that you did not purpose to be present.'

Their eyes met for a second, and Seraphina's fell; but her anger only burned the brighter for that private shame.

'And now, gentlemen,' said Otto, taking his chair, 'I pray you to be seated. I have been absent: there are doubtless some arrears; but ere we proceed to business, Herr Grafinski, you will direct four thousand crowns to be sent to me at once. Make a note, if you please,' he added, as the treasurer still stared in wonder.

'Four thousand crowns?' asked Seraphina. 'Pray, for what?'

'Madam,' returned Otto, smiling, 'for my own purposes.'

Gondremark spurred up Grafinski underneath the table.

'If your Highness will indicate the destination...' began the puppet.

'You are not here, sir, to interrogate your Prince,' said Otto.

Grafinski looked for help to his commander; and Gondremark came to his aid, in suave and measured tones.

'Your Highness may reasonably be surprised,' he said; 'and Herr Grafinski, although I am convinced he is clear of the intention of offending, would have perhaps done better to begin with an explanation. The resources of the state are at the present moment entirely swallowed up, or, as we hope to prove, wisely invested. In a month from now, I do not question we shall be able to meet any command your Highness may lay upon us; but at this hour I fear that, even in so small a matter, he must prepare himself for disappointment. Our zeal is no less, although our power may be inadequate.'

'How much, Herr Grafinski, have we in the treasury?' asked Otto.

'Your Highness,' protested the treasurer, 'we have immediate need of every crown.'

'I think, sir, you evade me,' flashed the Prince; and then

turning to the side-table, 'Mr. Secretary,' he added, 'bring me, if you please, the treasury docket.'

Herr Grafinski became deadly pale; the Chancellor, expecting his own turn, was probably engaged in prayer; Gondremark was watching like a ponderous cat. Gotthold, on his part, looked on with wonder at his cousin; he was certainly showing spirit, but what, in such a time of gravity, was all this talk of money? and why should he waste his strength upon a personal issue?

'I find,' said Otto, with his finger on the docket, 'that we have 20,000 crowns in case.'

'That is exact, your Highness,' replied the Baron. But our liabilities, all of which are happily not liquid, amount to a far larger sum; and at the present point of time it would be morally impossible to divert a single florin. Essentially, the case is empty. We have, already presented, a large note for material of war.'

'Material of war?' exclaimed Otto, with an excellent assumption of surprise. 'But if my memory serves me right, we settled these accounts in January.'

'There have been further orders,' the Baron explained. 'A new park of artillery has been completed; five hundred stand of arms, seven hundred baggage mules—the details are in a special memorandum.—Mr. Secretary Holtz, the memorandum, if you please.'

'One would think, gentlemen, that we were going to war,' said Otto.

'We are,' said Seraphina.

'War!' cried the Prince, 'and, gentlemen, with whom? The peace of Grünewald has endured for centuries. What aggression, what insult, have we suffered?'

'Here, your Highness,' said Gotthold, 'is the ultimatum. It was in the very article of signature when your Highness so opportunely entered.'

Otto laid the paper before him; as he read, his fingers played tattoo upon the table. 'Was it proposed,' he inquired, 'to send this paper forth without a knowledge of my pleasure?'

One of the non-combatants, eager to trim, volunteered an answer. 'The Herr Doctor von Hohenstockwitz had just entered his dissent,' he added.

'Give me the rest of this correspondence,' said the Prince. It was handed to him, and he read it patiently from end to end, while the councillors sat foolishly enough looking before them on the table. The secretaries, in the background, were exchanging glances of delight; a row at the council was for them a rare and welcome feature.

'Gentlemen,' said Otto, when he had finished, 'I have read with pain. This claim upon Obermünsterol is palpably unjust; it has not a tincture, not a show, of justice. There is not in all this ground enough for after-dinner talk, and you propose to force it as a *casus belli.*'

'Certainly, your Highness,' returned Gondremark, too wise to defend the indefensible, 'the claim on Obermünsterol is simply a pretext.'

'It is well,' said the Prince. 'Herr Cancellarius, take your pen. "The council,"' he began to dictate—'I withhold all notice of my intervention,' he said, in parenthesis, and addressing himself more directly to his wife; 'and I say nothing of the strange suppression by which this business has been smuggled past my knowledge. I am content to be in time—"The council,"' he resumed, '"on a further examination of the facts, and enlightened by the note in the last despatch from Gerolstein, have the pleasure to announce that they are entirely at one, both as to fact and sentiment, with the Grand-Ducal Court of Gerolstein." You have it? Upon these lines, sir, you will draw up the despatch.'

'If your Highness will allow me,' said the Baron, 'your Highness is so imperfectly acquainted with the internal history of this correspondence, that any interference will be merely hurtful. Such a paper as your Highness proposes would be to stultify the whole previous policy of Grünewald.'

'The policy of Grünewald!' cried the Prince. 'One would suppose you had no sense of humour! Would you fish in a coffee cup?'

'With deference, your Highness,' returned the Baron, 'even in a coffee cup there may be poison. The purpose of this war is not simply territorial enlargement; still less is it a war of glory; for, as your Highness indicates, the state of Grünewald is too small to be ambitious. But the body politic is seriously diseased; republicanism, socialism, many disintegrating ideas are abroad; circle within circle, a really formidable organisation has grown up about your Highness's throne.'

'I have heard of it, Herr von Gondremark,' put in the Prince; 'but I have reason to be aware that yours is the more authoritative information.'

'I am honoured by this expression of my Prince's confidence,' returned Gondremark, unabashed. 'It is, therefore, with a single eye to these disorders that our present external policy has been shaped. Something was required to divert public attention, to employ the idle, to popularise your Highness's rule, and, if it were possible, to enable him to reduce the taxes at a blow and to a notable amount. The proposed expedition—for it cannot without hyperbole be called a war—seemed to the council to combine the various characters required; a marked improvement in the public sentiment has followed even upon our preparations; and I cannot doubt that when success shall follow, the effect will surpass even our boldest hopes.'

'You are very adroit, Herr von Gondremark,' said Otto. 'You fill me with admiration. I had not heretofore done justice to your qualities.'

Seraphina looked up with joy, supposing Otto conquered; but Gondremark still waited, armed at every point; he knew how very stubborn is the revolt of a weak character.

'And the territorial army scheme, to which I was persuaded to consent—was it secretly directed to the same end?' the Prince asked.

'I still believe the effect to have been good,' replied the Baron; 'discipline and mounting guard are excellent sedatives. But I will avow to your Highness, I was unaware at the date of that decree, of the magnitude of the revolutionary movement; nor did any of us, I think, imagine that such a territorial army was a part of the republican proposals.'

'It was?' asked Otto. 'Strange! Upon what fancied grounds?'

'The grounds were indeed fanciful,' returned the Baron. 'It was conceived among the leaders that a territorial army, drawn from and returning to the people, would, in the event of any popular uprising, prove lukewarm or unfaithful to the throne.'

'I see,' said the Prince. 'I begin to understand.'

'His Highness begins to understand?' repeated Gondremark, with the sweetest politeness. 'May I beg of him to complete the phrase?'

'The history of the revolution,' replied Otto dryly. 'And now,' he added, 'what do you conclude?'

'I conclude, your Highness, with a simple reflection,' said the Baron, accepting the stab without a quiver, 'the war is popular; were the rumour contradicted to-morrow, a considerable disappointment would be felt in many classes; and in the present tension of spirits, the most lukewarm sentiment may be enough to precipitate events. There lies the danger. The revolution hangs imminent; we sit, at this council board, below the sword of Damocles.'

'We must then lay our heads together,' said the Prince, 'and devise some honourable means of safety.'

Up to this moment, since the first note of opposition fell from the librarian, Seraphina had uttered about twenty words. With a somewhat heightened colour, her eyes generally lowered, her foot sometimes nervously tapping on the floor, she had kept her own counsel and commanded her anger like a hero. But at this stage of the engagement she lost control of her impatience.

'Means!' she cried. 'They have been found and prepared before you knew the need for them. Sign the despatch, and let us be done with this delay.'

'Madam, I said "honourable,"' returned Otto, bowing. 'This war is, in my eyes, and by Herr von Gondremark's account, an inadmissible expedient. If we have misgoverned here in Grünewald, are the people of Gerolstein to bleed and pay for our misdoings? Never, madam; not while I live. But I attach so much importance to all that I have heard to-day for the first time—and why only to-day, I do not even stop to ask—that I am eager to find some plan that I can follow with credit to myself.'

'And should you fail?' she asked.

'Should I fail, I will then meet the blow halfway,' replied the Prince. 'On the first open discontent, I shall convoke the States, and, when it pleases them to bid me, abdicate.'

Seraphina laughed angrily. 'This is the man for whom we have been labouring!' she cried. 'We tell him of change; he will devise the means, he says; and his device is abdication? Sir, have you no shame to come here at the eleventh hour among those who have borne the heat and burthen of the day? Do you not wonder at yourself? I, sir, was here in my place, striving to uphold your dignity alone. I took counsel with the wisest I could find, while you were eating and hunting. I have laid my plans with foresight; they were ripe for action; and then'—she choked—'then you return—for a forenoon—to ruin all! To-morrow, you will be once more about your pleasures; you will give us leave once more to think and work for you; and again you will come back, and again you will thwart what you had not the industry, or knowledge to conceive. O! it is intolerable. Be modest, sir. Do not presume upon the rank you cannot worthily uphold. I would not issue my commands with so much gusto—it is from no merit in yourself they are obeyed. What are you? What have you to do in this grave council? Go,' she cried, 'go among your equals? The very people in the streets mock at you for a prince.'

At this surprising outburst the whole council sat aghast.

'Madam,' said the Baron, alarmed out of his caution, 'command yourself.'

'Address yourself to me, sir!' cried the Prince. 'I will not bear these whisperings!'

Seraphina burst into tears.

'Sir,' cried the Baron, rising, 'this lady——'

'Herr von Gondremark,' said the Prince, 'one more observation, and I place you under arrest.'

'Your Highness is the master,' replied Gondremark, bowing.

'Bear it in mind more constantly,' said Otto. 'Herr Cancellarius, bring all the papers to my cabinet. Gentlemen, the council is dissolved.'

And he bowed and left the apartment, followed by Greisengesang and the secretaries, just at the moment when the Princess's ladies, summoned in all haste, entered by another door to help her forth.

12

The Party of war takes action

HALF an hour after, Gondremark was once more closeted with Seraphina.

'Where is he now?' she asked, on his arrival.

'Madam, he is with the Chancellor,' replied the Baron. 'Wonder of wonders, he is at work!'

'Ah,' she said, 'he was born to torture me! O what a fall, what a humiliation! Such a scheme to wreck upon so small a trifle! But now all is lost.'

'Madam,' said Gondremark, 'nothing is lost. Something, on the other hand, is found. You have found your senses; you see him as he is—see him as you see everything where your too-good heart is not in question—with the judicial, with the statesman's eye. So long as he had a right to interfere, the empire that may be was still distant. I have not entered on this course without the plain foresight of its dangers; and even for this I was prepared. But, madam, I knew two things: I knew that you were born to command, that I was born to serve; I knew that, by a rare conjuncture, the hand had found the tool; and from the first I was confident, as I am confident to-day, that no hereditary trifler has the power to shatter that alliance.'

'I, born to command!' she said. 'Do you forget my tears?'

'Madam, they were the tears of Alexander,' cried the Baron. 'They touched, they thrilled me; I forgot myself a moment—even I! But do you suppose that I had not remarked, that I had not admired, your previous bearing? your great self-command? Ay, that was princely!' He paused. 'It was a thing to see. I drank confidence! I tried to imitate your calm. And I was well inspired; in my heart, I think that I was well inspired; that any man, within the reach of argument, had been convinced! But it was not to be; nor, madam, do I regret the failure. Let us be open; let me disclose my heart. I have loved two things, not unworthily: Grünewald and my sovereign!' Here he kissed her hand. 'Either I must resign my ministry, leave the land of my adoption and the queen whom I had chosen to obey—or——' He paused again.

'Alas, Herr von Gondremark, there is no "or,"' said Seraphina.

'Nay, madam, give me time,' he replied. 'When first I saw you, you were still young; not every man would have remarked your powers; but I had not been twice honoured by your conversation ere I had found my mistress. I have, madam, I believe, some genius; and I have much ambition. But the genius is of the serving kind; and to offer a career to my ambition, I had to find one born to rule. This is the base and essence of our union; each had need of the other; each recognised, master and servant, lever and fulcrum, the complement of his endowment. Marriages, they say, are made in heaven: how much more these pure, laborious, intellectual fellowships, born to found empires! Nor is this all. We found each other ripe, filled with great ideas that took shape and clarified with every word. We grew together—ay, madam, in mind we grew together like twin children. All of my life until we met was petty and groping; was it not—I will flatter myself openly—it *was* the same with you! Not till then had you those eagle surveys, that wide and hopeful sweep of intuition! Thus we had formed ourselves and we were ready.'

'It is true,' she cried. 'I feel it. Yours is the genius; your generosity confounds your insight; all I could offer you was the position, was this throne, to be a fulcrum. But I offered it without reserve; I entered at least warmly into all your thoughts; you were sure of me—sure of my support—certain of justice. Tell me, tell me again, that I have helped you.'

'Nay, madam,' he said, 'you made me. In everything you were my inspiration. And as we prepared our policy, weighing every step, how often have I had to admire your perspicacity, your man-like diligence and fortitude! You know that these are not the words of flattery; your conscience echoes them; have you spared a day? have you indulged yourself in any pleasure? Young and beautiful, you have lived a life of high intellectual effort, or irksome intellectual patience with details. Well, you have your reward: with the fall of Brandenau, the throne of your Empire is founded.'

'What thought have you in your mind?' she asked. 'Is not all ruined?'

'Nay, my Princess, the same thought is in both our minds,' he said.

'Herr von Gondremark,' she replied, 'by all that I hold sacred, I have none; I do not think at all; I am crushed.'

'You are looking at the passionate side of a rich nature, misunderstood and recently insulted,' said the Baron. 'Look into your intellect, and tell me.'

'I find nothing, nothing but tumult,' she replied.

'You find one word branded, madam,' returned the Baron: '"Abdication"!'

'O!' she cried. 'The coward! He leaves me to bear all, and in the hour of trial he stabs me from behind. There is nothing in him, not respect, not love, not courage—his wife, his dignity, his throne, the honour of his father, he forgets them all!'

'Yes,' pursued the Baron, 'the word Abdication. I perceive a glimmering there.'

'I read your fancy,' she returned. 'It is mere madness, midsummer madness. Baron, I am more unpopular than he. You know it. They can excuse, they can love, his weakness; but me, they hate.'

'Such is the gratitude of peoples,' said the Baron. 'But we trifle. Here, madam, are my plain thoughts. The man who in the hour of danger speaks of abdication is, for me, a venomous animal. I speak with the bluntness of gravity, madam; this is no hour for mincing. The coward, in a station of authority, is more dangerous than fire. We dwell on a volcano; if this man can have his way, Grünewald before a week will have been deluged with innocent blood. You know the truth of what I say; we have looked unblenching into this ever-possible catastrophe. To him it is nothing: he will abdicate! Abdicate, just God! and this unhappy country committed to his charge, and the lives of men and the honour of women ...' His voice appeared to fail him; in an instant he had conquered his emotion and resumed: 'But you, madam, conceive more worthily of your responsibilities. I am with you in the thought; and in the face of the horrors that I see impending, I say, and your heart repeats it—we have gone too far to pause. Honour, duty, ay, and the care of our own lives, demand we should proceed.'

She was looking at him, her brow thoughtfully knitted. 'I feel it,' she said. 'But how? He has the power.'

'The power, madam? The power is in the army,' he replied; and then hastily, ere she could intervene, 'we have to save ourselves,' he went on; 'I have to save my Princess, she has to save her minister; we have both of us to save this infatuated youth from his own madness. He in the outbreak would be the earliest victim; I see him,' he cried, 'torn in pieces; and Grünewald, unhappy Grünewald! Nay, madam, you who have the power must use it; it lies hard upon your conscience.'

'Show me how!' she cried. 'Suppose I were to place him under some constraint, the revolution would break upon us instantly.'

The Baron feigned defeat. 'It is true,' he said. 'You see more clearly than I do. Yet there should, there must be, some way.' And he waited for his chance.

'No,' she said; 'I told you from the first there is no remedy. Our hopes are lost: lost by one miserable trifler, ignorant, fretful, fitful—who will have disappeared to-morrow, who knows? to his boorish pleasures!'

Any peg would do for Gondremark. 'The thing!' he cried, striking his brow. 'Fool, not to have thought of it! Madam, without perhaps knowing it, you have solved our problem.'

'What do you mean? Speak!' she said.

He appeared to collect himself; and then, with a smile, 'The Prince,' he said, 'must go once more a-hunting.'

'Ay, if he would!' cried she, 'and stay there!'

'And stay there,' echoed the Baron. It was so significantly said, that her face changed; and the schemer, fearful of the sinister ambiguity of his expressions, hastened to explain. 'This time he shall go hunting in a carriage, with a good escort of our foreign lancers. His destination shall be the Felsenburg; it is healthy, the rock is high, the windows are small and barred; it might have been built on purpose. We shall entrust the captaincy to the Scotsman Gordon; he at least will have no scruple. Who will miss the sovereign? He is gone hunting; he came home on Tuesday, on Thursday he returned; all is usual in that. Meanwhile the war proceeds; our Prince will soon weary of his solitude; and about the time of our triumph, or, if he prove very obstinate, a little later, he shall be released upon a proper understanding, and I see him once more directing his theatricals.'

Seraphina sat gloomy, plunged in thought. 'Yes,' she said suddenly, 'and the despatch? He is now writing it.'

'It cannot pass the council before Friday,' replied Gondremark; 'and as for any private note, the messengers are all at my disposal. They are picked men, madam. I am a person of precaution.'

'It would appear so,' she said, with a flash of her occasional repugnance to the man; and then after a pause, 'Herr von Gondremark,' she added, 'I recoil from this extremity.'

'I share your Highness's repugnance,' answered he. 'But what would you have? We are defenceless, else.'

'I see it, but this is sudden. It is a public crime,' she said, nodding at him with a sort of horror.

'Look but a little deeper,' he returned, 'and whose is the crime?'

'His!' she cried. 'His, before God! And I hold him liable. But still——'

'It is not as if he would be harmed,' submitted Gondremark.

'I know it,' she replied, but it was still unheartily.

And then, as brave men are entitled, by prescriptive right as old as the world's history, to the alliance and the active help of fortune, the punctual goddess stepped down from the machine. One of the Princess's ladies begged to enter; a man, it appeared, had brought a line for the Freiherr von Gondremark. It proved to be a pencil billet, which the crafty Greisengesang had found the means to scribble and despatch under the very guns of Otto; and the daring of the act bore testimony to the terror of the actor. For Greisengesang had but one influential motive: fear. 'At the first council, procuration to be withdrawn.—CORN. GREIS.'

So, after three years of exercise, the right of signature was to be stript from Seraphina. It was more than an insult; it was a public disgrace; and she did not pause to consider how she had earned it, but morally bounded under the attack as bounds the wounded tiger.

'Enough,' she said; 'I will sign the order. When shall he leave?'

'It will take me twelve hours to collect my men, and it had best be done at night. To-morrow midnight, if you please?' answered the Baron.

'Excellent,' she said. 'My door is always open to you, Baron. As soon as the order is prepared, bring it me to sign.'

'Madam,' he said, 'alone of all of us you do not risk your head in this adventure. For that reason, and to prevent all hesitation, I venture to propose the order should be in your hand throughout.'

'You are right,' she replied.

He laid a form before her, and she wrote the order in a clear hand, and re-read it. Suddenly a cruel smile came on her face. 'I had forgotten his puppet,' said she. 'They will keep each other company.' And she interlined and initialed the condemnation of Doctor Gotthold.'

'Your Highness has more memory than your servant,' said

the Baron; and then he, in his turn, carefully perused the fateful paper. 'Good!' said he.

'You will appear in the drawing-room, Baron?' she asked.

'I thought it better,' said he, 'to avoid the possibility of a public affront. Anything that shook my credit might hamper us in the immediate future.'

'You are right,' she said; and she held out her hand as to an old friend and equal.

13

The price of the river farm; in which vainglory goes before a fall

THE pistol had been practically fired. Under ordinary circumstances the scene at the council table would have entirely exhausted Otto's store both of energy and anger; he would have begun to examine and condemn his conduct, have remembered all that was true, forgotten all that was unjust in Seraphina's onslaught; and by half an hour after would have fallen into that state of mind in which a Catholic flees to the confessional and a sot takes refuge with the bottle. Two matters of detail preserved his spirits. For, first, he had still an infinity of business to transact; and to transact business, for a man of Otto's neglectful and procrastinating habits, is the best anodyne for conscience. All afternoon he was hard at it with the Chancellor, reading, dictating, signing, and despatching papers; and this kept him in a glow of self-approval. But, secondly, his vanity was still alarmed; he had failed to get the money; tomorrow before noon he would have to disappoint old Killian; and in the eyes of that family which counted him so little, and to which he had sought to play the part of the heroic comforter, he must sink lower than at first. To a man of Otto's temper, this was death. He could not accept the situation. And even as he worked, and worked wisely and well, over the hated details of his principality, he was secretly maturing a plan by which to turn the situation. It was a scheme as pleasing to the man as it was dishonourable in the prince; in which his frivolous nature found and took vengeance for the gravity and burthen of the afternoon. He chuckled as he thought of it: and Greisengesang heard him with wonder, and attributed his lively spirits to the skirmish of the morning.

Led by this idea, the antique courtier ventured to compliment his sovereign on his bearing. It reminded him, he said, of Otto's father.

'What?' asked the Prince, whose thoughts were miles away.

'Your Highness's authority at the board,' explained the flatterer.

'O, that! O yes,' returned Otto; but for all his carelessness, his vanity was delicately tickled, and his mind returned and dwelt approvingly over the details of his victory. 'I quelled them all,' he thought.

When the more pressing matters had been dismissed, it was already late, and Otto kept the Chancellor to dinner, and was entertained with a leash of ancient histories and modern compliments. The Chancellor's career had been based, from the first off-put, on entire subserviency; he had crawled into honours and employments; and his mind was prostitute. The instinct of the creature served him well with Otto. First, he let fall a sneering word or two upon the female intellect; thence he proceeded to a closer engagement; and before the third course he was artfully dissecting Seraphina's character to her approving husband. Of course no names were used; and of course the identity of that abstract or ideal man, with whom she was currently contrasted, remained an open secret. But this stiff old gentleman had a wonderful instinct for evil, thus to wind his way into man's citadel; thus ho harp by the hour on the virtues of his hearer and not once alarm his self-respect. Otto was all roseate, in and out, with flattery and Tokay and an approving conscience. He saw himself in the most attractive colours. If even Greisengesang, he thought, could thus espy the loose stitches in Seraphina's character, and thus disloyally impart them to the opposite camp, he, the discarded husband—the dispossessed Prince—could scarce have erred to the side of severity.

In this excellent frame he bade adieu to the old gentleman, whose voice had proved so musical, and set forth for the drawing-room. Already on the stair, he was seized with some compunction; but when he entered the great gallery and beheld his wife, the Chancellor's abstract flatteries fell from him like rain, and he re-awoke to the poetic facts of life. She stood a good way off below a shining lustre, her back turned. The bend of her waist overcame him with physical weakness. This was the girl-wife who had lain in his arms and whom he had sworn to cherish; there was she, who was better than success.

It was Seraphina who restored him from the blow. She swam forward and smiled upon her husband with a sweetness that was insultingly artificial. 'Frédéric,' she lisped, 'you are late.'

It was a scene of high comedy, such as is proper to unhappy marriages; and her *aplomb* disgusted him.

There was no etiquette at these small drawing-rooms. People came and went at pleasure. The window embrasures became the roost of happy couples; at the great chimney the talkers mostly congregated, each full-charged with scandal; and down at the farther end the gamblers gambled. It was towards this point that Otto moved, not ostentatiously, but with a gentle insistence, and scattering attentions as he went. Once abreast of the card-table, he placed himself opposite to Madame von Rosen, and, as soon as he had caught her eye, withdrew to the embrasure of a window. There she had speedily joined him.

'You did well to call me,' she said, a little wildly. 'These cards will be my ruin.'

'Leave them,' said Otto.

'I!' she cried, and laughed; 'they are my destiny. My only chance was to die of a consumption; now I must die in a garret.'

'You are bitter to-night,' said Otto.

'I have been losing,' she replied. 'You do not know what greed is.'

'I have come, then, in an evil hour,' said he.

'Ah, you wish a favour!' she cried, brightening beautifully.

'Madam,' said he, 'I am about to found my party, and I come to you for a recruit.'

'Done,' said the Countess. 'I am a man again.'

'I may be wrong,' continued Otto, 'but I believe upon my heart you wish me no ill.'

'I wish you so well,' she said, 'that I dare not tell it you.'

'Then if I ask my favour?' quoth the Prince.

'Ask it, *mon Prince*,' she answered. 'Whatever it is, it is granted.'

'I wish you,' he returned, 'this very night to make the farmer of our talk.'

'Heaven knows your meaning!' she exclaimed. 'I know not, neither care; there are no bounds to my desire to please you. Call him made.'

'I will put it in another way,' returned Otto. 'Did you ever steal?'

'Often!' cried the Countess. 'I have broken all the ten commandments; and if there were more to-morrow, I should not sleep till I had broken these.'

'This is a case of burglary: to say the truth, I thought it would amuse you,' said the Prince.

'I have no practical experience,' she replied, 'but O! the good-will! I have broken a workbox in my time, and several hearts, my own included. Never a house! But it cannot be difficult; sins are so unromantically easy! What are we to break?'

'Madam, we are to break the treasury,' said Otto; and he sketched to her briefly, wittily, with here and there a touch of pathos, the story of his visit to the farm, of his promise to buy it, and of the refusal with which his demand for money had been met that morning at the council; concluding with a few practical words as to the treasury windows, and the helps and hindrances of the proposed exploit.

'They refused you the money,' she said, when he had done. 'And you accepted the refusal? Well!'

'They gave their reasons,' replied Otto, colouring. 'They were not such as I could combat; and I am driven to dilapidate the funds of my own country by a theft. It is not dignified; but it is fun.'

'Fun,' she said; 'yes.' And then she remained silently plunged in thought for an appreciable time. 'How much do you require?' she asked at length.

'Three thousand crowns will do,' he answered, 'for I have still some money of my own.'

'Excellent,' she said, regaining her levity. 'I am your true accomplice. And where are we to meet?'

'You know the Flying Mercury,' he answered, 'in the Park? Three pathways intersect; there they have made a seat and raised the statue. The spot is handy and the deity congenial.'

'Child,' she said, and tapped him with her fan. 'But do you know, my Prince, you are an egoist—your handy trysting-place is miles from me. You must give me ample time; I cannot, I think, possibly be there before two. But as the bell beats two, your helper shall arrive: welcome, I trust. Stay—do you bring any one?' she added. 'O, it is not for a chaperon—I am not a prude!'

'I shall bring a groom of mine,' said Otto. 'I caught him stealing corn.'

'His name?' she asked.

'I profess I know not. I am not yet intimate with my corn-stealer,' returned the Prince. 'It was in a professional capacity——'

'Like me! Flatterer!' she cried. 'But oblige me in one thing. Let me find you waiting at the seat—yes, you shall await me; for on this expedition it shall be no longer Prince and Countess, it shall be the lady and the squire—and your friend the thief shall be no nearer than the fountain. Do you promise?'

'Madam, in everything you are to command; you shall be captain, I am but supercargo,' answered Otto.

'Well, Heaven bring all safe to port!' she said. 'It is not Friday!'

Something in her manner had puzzled Otto, had possibly touched him with suspicion.

'Is it not strange,' he remarked, 'that I should choose my accomplice from the other camp?'

'Fool!' she said. 'But it is your only wisdom that you know your friends.' And suddenly in the vantage of the deep window, she caught up his hand and kissed it with a sort of passion. 'Now go,' she added, 'go at once.'

He went, somewhat staggered, doubting in his heart that he was over-bold. For in that moment she had flashed upon him like a jewel; and even through the strong panoply of a previous love he had been conscious of a shock. Next moment he had dismissed the fear.

Both Otto and the Countess retired early from the drawing-room; and the Prince, after an elaborate feint, dismissed his valet, and went forth by the private passage and the back postern in quest of the groom.

Once more the stable was in darkness, once more Otto employed the talismanic knock, and once more the groom appeared and sickened with terror.

'Good-evening, friend,' said Otto pleasantly. 'I want you to bring a corn sack—empty this time—and to accompany me. We shall be gone all night.'

'Your Highness,' groaned the man, 'I have the charge of the small stables. I am here alone.'

'Come,' said the Prince, 'you are no such martinet in duty.' And then seeing that the man was shaking from head to foot, Otto laid a hand upon his shoulder. 'If I meant you harm,' he said, 'should I be here?'

The fellow became instantly reassured. He got the sack; and Otto led him round by several paths and avenues, conversing pleasantly by the way, and left him at last planted by a certain fountain where a goggle-eyed Triton spouted intermittently into a rippling laver. Thence he proceeded alone to where, in a round clearing, a copy of Gian Bologna's Mercury stood tiptoe in the twilight of the stars. The night was warm and windless. A shaving of new moon had lately arisen; but it was still too small and too low down in heaven to contend with the immense host of lesser luminaries; and the rough face of the earth was drenched with starlight. Down one of the alleys, which widened as it receded, he could see a part of the lamplit terrace where a sentry silently paced, and beyond that a corner of the town with interlacing street-lights. But all around him the young trees stood mystically blurred in the dim shine; and in the stock-still quietness the upleaping god appeared alive.

In this dimness and silence of the night, Otto's conscience became suddenly and staringly luminous, like the dial of a city clock. He averted the eyes of his mind, but the finger, rapidly travelling, pointed to a series of misdeeds that took his breath away. What was he doing in that place? The money had been wrongly squandered, but that was largely by his own neglect. And he now proposed to embarrass the finances of this country which he had been too idle to govern. And he now proposed to squander the money once again, and this time for a private, if a generous end. And the man whom he had reproved for stealing corn he was now to set stealing treasure. And then there was Madame von Rosen, upon whom he looked down with some of that ill-favoured contempt of the chaste male for the imperfect woman. Because he thought of her as one degraded below scruples, he had picked her out to be still more degraded, and to risk her whole irregular establishment in life by complicity in this dishonourable act. It was uglier than a seduction.

Otto had to walk very briskly and whistle very busily; and when at last he heard steps in the narrowest and darkest of the alleys, it was with a gush of relief that he sprang to meet the Countess. To wrestle alone with one's good angel is so hard! and so precious, at the proper time, is a companion certain to be less virtuous than oneself!

It was a young man who came towards him—a young man of small stature and a peculiar gait, wearing a wide flapping hat, and carrying, with great weariness, a heavy bag. Otto recoiled; but the young man held up his hand by way of signal, and coming up with a panting run, as if with the last of his endurance, laid the bag upon the ground, threw himself upon the bench, and disclosed the features of Madame von Rosen.

'You, Countess!' cried the Prince.

'No, no,' she panted, 'the Count von Rosen—my young brother. A capital fellow. Let him get his breath.'

'Ah, madam . . .' said he.

'Call me Count,' she returned, 'respect my incognito.'

'Count be it, then,' he replied. 'And let me implore that gallant gentleman to set forth at once on our enterprise.'

'Sit down beside me here,' she returned, patting the farther corner of the bench. 'I will follow you in a moment. O, I am so tired—feel how my heart leaps! Where is your thief?'

'At his post,' replied Otto. 'Shall I introduce him? He seems an excellent companion.'

'No,' she said, 'do not hurry me yet. I must speak to you.

Not but I adore your thief; I adore any one who has the spirit to do wrong. I never cared for virtue till I fell in love with my Prince.' She laughed musically. 'And even so, it is not for your virtues,' she added.

Otto was embarrassed. 'And now,' he asked, 'if you are anyway rested?'

'Presently, presently. Let me breathe,' she said, panting a little harder than before.

'And what has so wearied you?' he asked. 'This bag? And why, in the name of eccentricity, a bag? For an empty one, you might have relied on my own foresight; and this one is very far from being empty. My dear Count, with what trash have you come laden? But the shortest method is to see for myself.' And he put down his hand.

She stopped him at once. 'Otto,' she said, 'no—not that way. I will tell, I will make a clean breast. It is done already. I have robbed the treasury single-handed. There are three thousand two hundred crowns. O, I trust it is enough!'

Her embarrassment was so obvious that the Prince was struck into a muse, gazing in her face, with his hand still outstretched, and she still holding him by the wrist. 'You!' he said at last. 'How?' And then drawing himself up, 'O madam,' he cried, 'I understand. You must indeed think meanly of the Prince.'

'Well, then, it was a lie!' she cried. 'The money is mine, honestly my own—now yours. This was an unworthy act that you proposed. But I love your honour, and I swore to myself that I should save it in your teeth. I beg of you to let me save it'—with a sudden lovely change of tone. 'Otto, I beseech you let me save it. Take this dross from your poor friend who loves you!'

'Madam, madam,' babbled Otto, in the extreme of misery, 'I cannot—I must go.'

And he half rose; but she was on the ground before him in an instant, clasping his knees. 'No,' she gasped, 'you shall not go. Do you despise me so entirely? It is dross; I hate it; I should squander it at play and be no richer; it is an investment, it is to save me from ruin. Otto,' she cried, as he again feebly tried to put her from him, 'if you leave me alone in this disgrace, I will die here!' He groaned aloud. 'O,' she said, 'think what I suffer! If you suffer from a piece of delicacy, think what I suffer in my shame! To have my trash refused! You would rather steal, you think of me so basely! You would rather tread my heart in pieces! O, unkind! O my Prince! O Otto! O pity me!' She was still clasping him; then she found his hand and covered it with kisses, and at this his head began to turn. 'O,' she cried again, 'I see it! O what a horror! It is because I am old, because I am no longer beautiful.' And she burst into a storm of sobs.

This was the *coup de grâce*. Otto had now to comfort and compose her as he could, and before many words, the money was accepted. Between the woman and the weak man such was the inevitable end. Madame von Rosen instantly composed her sobs. She thanked him with a fluttering voice, and resumed her place upon the bench, at the far end from Otto. 'Now you see,' she said, 'why I bade you keep the thief at distance, and why I came alone. How I trembled for my treasure!'

'Madam,' said Otto, with a tearful whimper in his voice, 'spare me! You are too good, too noble!'

'I wonder to hear you,' she returned. 'You have avoided a great folly. You will be able to meet your good old peasant. You have found an excellent investment for a friend's money. You have preferred essential kindness to an empty scruple; now you are ashamed of it! You have made your friend happy; and now you mourn as the dove! Come, cheer up. I know it is depressing to have done exactly right; but you need not make a practice of it. Forgive yourself this virtue; come now, look me in the face and smile!'

He did look at her. When a man has been embraced by a woman, he sees her in a glamour; and at such a time, in the baffling glimmer of the stars, she will look wildly well. The hair is touched with light; the eyes are constellations; the face sketched in shadows—a sketch, you might say, by passion. Otto became consoled for his defeat; he began to take an interest. 'No,' he said, 'I am no ingrate.'

'You promised me fun,' she returned, with a laugh. 'I have given you as good. We have had a stormy *scena*.'

He laughed in his turn, and the sound of the laughter, in either case, was hardly reassuring.

'Come, what are you going to give me in exchange,' she continued, 'for my excellent declamation?'

'What you will,' he said.

'Whatever I will? Upon your honour? Suppose I asked the crown?' She was flashing upon him, beautiful in triumph.

'Upon my honour,' he replied.

'Shall I ask the crown?' she continued. 'Nay; what should I do with it? Grünewald is but a petty state; my ambition swells above it. I shall ask—I find I want nothing,' she concluded. 'I will give you something instead. I will give you leave to kiss me—once.'

Otto drew near, and she put up her face; they were both smiling, both on the brink of laughter, all was so innocent and playful; and the Prince, when their lips encountered, was dumbfoundered by the sudden convulsion of his being. Both drew instantly apart, and for an appreciable time sat tongue-tied. Otto was indistinctly conscious of a peril in the silence, but could find no words to utter. Suddenly the Countess seemed to awake. 'As for your wife——' she began in a clear and steady voice.

The word recalled Otto, with a shudder, from his trance. 'I will hear nothing against my wife,' he cried wildly; and then, recovering himself and in a kindlier tone, 'I will tell you my one secret,' he added. 'I love my wife.'

'You should have let me finish,' she returned, smiling. 'Do you suppose I did not mention her on purpose? You know you had lost your head. Well, so had I. Come now, do not be abashed by words,' she added somewhat sharply. 'It is the one thing I despise. If you are not a fool, you will see that I am building fortresses about your virtue. And at any rate, I choose that you shall understand that I am not dying of love for you. It is a very smiling business; no tragedy for me! And now here is what I have to say about your wife; she is not and she never has been Gondremark's mistress. Be sure he would have boasted if she had. Good-night!'

And in a moment she was gone down the alley, and Otto was alone with the bag of money and the flying god.

14

Gotthold's revised opinion; and the fall completed

THE Countess left poor Otto with a caress and buffet simultaneously administered. The welcome word about his wife and the virtuous ending of his interview should doubtless have delighted him. But for all that, as he shouldered the bag of money and set forward to rejoin his groom, he was conscious of many aching sensibilities. To have gone wrong and to have been set right makes but a double trial for man's vanity. The discovery of his own weakness and possible unfaith had staggered him to the heart; and to hear, in the same hour, of his wife's fidelity from one who loved her not, increased the bitterness of the surprise.

He was about half-way between the fountain and the Flying Mercury before his thoughts began to clear; and he was surprised to find them resentful. He paused in a kind of temper, and struck with his hand a little shrub. Thence there arose instantly a cloud of awakened sparrows, which as instantly dispersed and disappeared into the thicket. He looked at them stupidly, and when they were gone continued staring at the stars. 'I am angry. By what right? By none!' he thought; but he was still angry. He cursed Madame von Rosen and instantly repented. Heavy was the money on his shoulders.

When he reached the fountain, he did, out of ill-humour and parade, an unpardonable act. He gave the money bodily to the dishonest groom. 'Keep this for me,' he said, 'until I call for it to-morrow. It is a great sum, and by that you will judge that I have not condemned you.' And he strode away ruffling, as if he had done something generous. It was a desperate stroke to re-enter at the point of the bayonet into his self-esteem; and, like all such, it was fruitless in the end. He got to bed with the devil, it appeared: kicked and tumbled till the gray of the morning; and then fell inopportunely into a leaden slumber, and awoke to find it ten. To miss the appointment with old Killian after all, had been too tragic a miscarriage: and he hurried with all his might, found the groom (for a wonder) faithful to his trust, and arrived only a few minutes before noon in the guest-chamber of the Morning Star. Killian was there in his Sunday's best and looking very gaunt and rigid; a lawyer from Brandenau stood sentinel over his outspread papers; and the groom and the landlord of the inn were called to serve as witnesses. The obvious deference of that great man, the innkeeper, plainly affected the old farmer with surprise; but it was not until Otto had taken the pen and signed that the truth flashed upon him fully. Then, indeed, he was beside himself.

'His Highness!' he cried, 'His Highness!' and repeated the exclamation till his mind had grappled fairly with the facts. Then he turned to the witnesses. 'Gentlemen,' he said, 'you dwell in a country highly favoured by God; for of all generous gentlemen, I will say it on my conscience, this one is the king. I am an old man, and I have seen good and bad, and the year of the great famine; but a more excellent gentleman, no, never.'

'We know that,' cried the landlord, 'we know that well in Grünewald. If we saw more of his Highness we should be the better pleased.'

'It is the kindest Prince,' began the groom, and suddenly closed his mouth upon a sob, so that every one turned to gaze upon his emotion—Otto not last; Otto struck with remorse, to see the man so grateful.

Then it was the lawyer's turn to pay a compliment. 'I do not know what Providence may hold in store,' he said, 'but this day should be a bright one in the annals of your reign. The shouts of armies could not be more eloquent than the emotion on these honest faces.' And the Brandenau lawyer bowed, skipped, stepped back, and took snuff, with the air of a man who has found and seized an opportunity.

'Well, young gentleman,' said Killian, 'if you will pardon me the plainness of calling you a gentleman, many a good day's work you have done, I doubt not, but never a better, or one that will be better blessed; and whatever, sir, may be your happiness and triumph in that high sphere to which you have been called, it will be none the worse, sir, for an old man's blessing!'

The scene had almost assumed the proportions of an ovation; and when the Prince escaped he had but one thought: to go wherever he was most sure of praise. His conduct at the board of council occurred to him as a fair chapter; and this evoked the memory of Gotthold. To Gotthold he would go.

Gotthold was in the library as usual, and laid down his pen, a little angrily, on Otto's entrance. 'Well,' he said, 'here you are.'

'Well,' returned Otto, 'we made a revolution, I believe.'

'It is what I fear,' returned the Doctor.

'How?' said Otto. 'Fear? Fear is the burnt child. I have learned my strength and the weakness of others, and I now mean to govern.'

Gotthold said nothing, but he looked down and smoothed his chin.

'You disapprove?' cried Otto. 'You are a weather-cock.'

'On the contrary,' replied the Doctor. 'My observation has confirmed my fears. It will not do, Otto, not do.'

'What will not do?' demanded the Prince, with a sickening stab of pain.

'None of it,' answered Gotthold. 'You are unfitted for a life of action; you lack the stamina, the habit, the restraint, the patience. Your wife is greatly better, vastly better; and though she is in bad hands, displays a very different aptitude. She is a woman of affairs; you are—dear boy, you are yourself. I bid you back to your amusements; like a smiling dominie, I give you holidays for life. Yes,' he continued, 'there is a day appointed for all when they shall turn again upon their own philosophy. I had grown to disbelieve impartially in all; and if in the atlas of the sciences there were two charts I disbelieved in more than all the rest, they were politics and morals. I had a sneaking kindness for your vices; as they were negative, they flattered my philosophy; and I called them almost virtues. Well, Otto, I was wrong; I have forsworn my sceptical philosophy; and I perceive your faults to be unpardonable. You are unfit to be a

Prince, unfit to be a husband. And I give you my word, I would rather see a man capably doing evil than blundering about good.'

Otto was still silent, in extreme dudgeon.

Presently the Doctor resumed: 'I will take the smaller matter first: your conduct to your wife. You went, I hear, and had an explanation. That may have been right or wrong; I know not; at least, you had stirred her temper. At the council she insults you; well, you insult her back—a man to a woman, a husband to his wife, in public! Next upon the back of this, you propose—the story runs like wildfire—to recall the power of signature. Can she ever forgive that? a woman—a young woman—ambitious, conscious of talents beyond yours? Never, Otto. And to sum all, at such a crisis in your married life, you get into a window corner with that ogling dame von Rosen. I do not dream that there was any harm; but I do say it was an idle disrespect to your wife. Why, man, the woman is not decent.

'Gotthold,' said Otto, 'I will hear no evil of the Countess.'

'You will certainly hear no good of her,' returned Gotthold; 'and if you wish your wife to be the pink of nicety, you should clear your court of demi-reputations.'

'The commonplace injustice of a byword,' Otto cried. 'The partiality of sex. She is a demirep; what then is Gondremark? Were she a man——'

'It would be all one,' retorted Gotthold roughly. 'When I see a man, come to years of wisdom, who speaks in double-meanings and is the braggart of his vices, I spit on the other side. "You, my friend," say I, "are not even a gentleman." Well, she's not even a lady.'

'She is the best friend I have, and I choose that she shall be respected,' Otto said.

'If she is your friend, so much the worse,' replied the Doctor. 'It will not stop there.'

'Ah!' cried Otto, 'there is the charity of virtue! All evil in the spotted fruit. But I can tell you, sir, that you do Madame von Rosen prodigal injustice.'

'You can tell me!' said the Doctor shrewdly. 'Have you tried? have you been riding the marches?'

The blood came into Otto's face.

'Ah!' cried Gotthold, 'look at your wife and blush! There's a wife for a man to marry and then lose! She's a carnation, Otto. The soul is in her eyes.'

'You have changed your note for Seraphina, I perceive,' said Otto.

'Changed it!' cried the Doctor, with a flush. 'Why, when

was it different? But I own I admired her at the council. When she sat there silent, tapping with her foot, I admired her as I might a hurricane. Were I one of those who venture upon matrimony, there had been the prize to tempt me! She invites, as Mexico invited Cortez; the enterprise is hard, the natives are unfriendly—I believe them cruel too—but the metropolis is paved with gold and the breeze blows out of paradise. Yes, I could desire to be that conqueror. But to philander with von Rosen! never! Senses? I discard them; what are they?—pruritus! Curiosity? Reach me my Anatomy!'

'To whom do you address yourself?' cried Otto. 'Surely you, of all men, know that I love my wife!'

'O, love!' cried Gotthold; 'love is a great word; it is in all the dictionaries. If you had loved—she would have paid you back. What does she ask? A little ardour!'

'It is hard to love for two,' replied the Prince.

'Hard? Why, there's the touchstone! O, I know my poets!' cried the Doctor. 'We are but dust and fire, too arid to endure life's scorching; and love, like the shadow of a great rock, should lend shelter and refreshment, not to the lover only, but to his mistress and to the children that reward them; and their very friends should seek repose in the fringes of that peace. Love is not love that cannot build a home. And you call it love to grudge and quarrel and pick faults? You call it love to thwart her to her face, and bandy insults? Love!'

'Gotthold, you are unjust. I was then fighting for my country,' said the Prince.

'Ay, and there's the worst of all,' returned the Doctor. 'You could not even see that you were wrong; that being where they were, retreat was ruin.'

'Why, you supported me!' cried Otto.

'I did. I was a fool like you,' replied Gotthold. 'But now my eyes are open. If you go on as you have started, disgrace this fellow Gondremark, and publish the scandal of your divided house, there will befall a most abominable thing in Grünewald. A revolution, friend—a revolution.'

'You speak strangely for a red,' said Otto.

'A red republican, but not a revolutionary,' returned the Doctor. 'An ugly thing is a Grünewalder drunk! One man alone can save the country from this pass, and that is the double-dealer Gondremark, with whom I conjure you to make peace. It will not be you; it never can be you:—you, who can do nothing, as your wife said, but trade upon your station—you, who spent the hours in begging money! And in God's name, what for? Why money? What mystery of idiocy was this?'

'It was to no ill end. It was to buy a farm,' quoth Otto sulkily.

'To buy a farm!' cried Gotthold. 'Buy a farm!'

'Well, what then?' returned Otto. 'I have bought it, if you come to that.'

Gotthold fairly bounded on his seat. 'And how that?' he cried.

'How?' repeated Otto, startled.

'Ay, verily, how!' returned the Doctor. 'How came you by the money?'

The Prince's countenance darkened. 'That is my affair,' said he.

'You see you are ashamed,' retorted Gotthold. 'And so you bought a farm in the hour of your country's need—doubtless to be ready for the abdication; and I put it that you stole the funds. There are not three ways of getting money: there are but two: to earn and steal. And now, when you have combined Charles the Fifth and Long-fingered Tom, you come to me to fortify your vanity! But I will clear my mind upon this matter: until I know the right and wrong of the transaction, I put my hand behind my back. A man may be the pitifullest prince; he must be a spotless gentleman.'

The Prince had gotten to his feet, as pale as paper. 'Gotthold,' he said, 'you drive me beyond bounds. Beware, sir, beware!'

'Do you threaten me, friend Otto?' asked the Doctor grimly. 'That would be a strange conclusion.'

'When have you ever known me use my power in any private animosity?' cried Otto. 'To any private man your words were an unpardonable insult, but at me you shoot in full security, and I must turn aside to compliment you on your plainness. I must do more than pardon, I must admire, because you have faced this—this formidable monarch, like a Nathan before David. You have uprooted an old kindness, sir, with an unsparing hand. You leave me very bare. My last bond is broken; and though I take Heaven to witness that I sought to do the right, I have this reward: to find myself alone. You say I am no gentleman; yet the sneers have been upon your side; and though I can very well perceive where you have lodged your sympathies, I will forbear the taunt.'

'Otto, are you insane?' cried Gotthold, leaping up. 'Because I ask you how you came by certain moneys, and because you refuse——'

'Herr von Hohenstockwitz, I have ceased to invite your aid in my affairs,' said Otto. 'I have heard all that I desire, and you have sufficiently trampled on my vanity. It may be that I cannot govern, it may be that I cannot love—you tell me so with every mark of honesty; but God has granted me one virtue, and I can still forgive. I forgive you; even in this hour of passion, I can perceive my faults and your excuses; and if I desire that in future I may be spared your conversation, it is not, sir, from resentment—not resentment—but, by Heaven, because no man on earth could endure to be so rated. You have the satisfaction to see your sovereign weep; and that person whom you have so often taunted with his happiness reduced to the last pitch of solitude and misery. No—I will hear nothing; I claim the last word, sir, as your Prince; and that last word shall be forgiveness.'

And with that Otto was gone from the apartment, and Doctor Gotthold was left alone with the most conflicting sentiments of sorrow, remorse, and merriment; walking to and fro before his table, and asking himself, with hands uplifted, which of the pair of them was most to blame for this unhappy rupture. Presently, he took from a cupboard a bottle of Rhine wine and a goblet of the deep Bohemian ruby. The first glass a little warmed and comforted his bosom; with the second he began to look down upon these troubles from a sunny mountain; yet a while, and filled with this false comfort and contemplating life throughout a golden medium, he owned to himself, with a flush, a smile, and a half-pleasurable sigh, that he had been somewhat over plain in dealing with his cousin. 'He said the truth, too,' added the penitent librarian, 'for in my monkish fashion I adore the Princess.' And then, with a still deepening flush and a certain stealth, although he sat all alone in that great gallery, he toasted Seraphina to the dregs.

15

Providence von Rosen: Act I.: She beguiles the Baron

At a sufficiently late hour, or to be more exact, at three in the afternoon, Madame von Rosen issued on the world. She swept downstairs and out across the garden, a black mantilla thrown over her head, and the long train of her black velvet dress ruthlessly sweeping in the dirt.

At the other end of that long garden and, back to back with the villa of the Countess, stood the large mansion where the Prime Minister transacted his affairs and pleasures. This distance, which was enough for decency by the easy canons of Mittwalden, the Countess swiftly traversed, opened a little door with a key, mounted a flight of stairs, and entered unceremoniously into

Gondremark's study. It was a large and very high apartment; books all about the walls, papers on the table, papers on the floor; here and there a picture, somewhat scant of drapery; a great fire glowing and flaming in the blue tiled hearth; and the daylight streaming through a cupola above. In the midst of this sat the great Baron Gondremark in his shirt-sleeves, his business for that day fairly at an end, and the hour arrived for relaxation. His expression, his very nature, seemed to have undergone a fundamental change. Gondremark at home appeared the very antipode of Gondremark on duty. He had an air of massive jollity that well became him; grossness and geniality sat upon his features; and along with his manners, he had laid aside his sly and sinister espression. He lolled there, sunning his bulk before the fire, a noble animal.

'Hey!' he cried. 'At last!'

The Countess stepped into the room in silence, threw herself on a chair, and crossed her legs. In her lace and velvet, with a good display of smooth black stocking and of snowy petticoat, and with the refined profile of her face and slender plumpness of her body, she showed in singular contrast to the big, black, intellectual satyr by the fire.

'How often do you send for me?' she cried. 'It is compromising.'

Gondremark laughed. 'Speaking of that,' said he, 'what in the devil's name were you about? You were not home till morning.'

'I was giving alms,' she said.

The Baron again laughed loud and long, for in his shirt-sleeves he was a very mirthful creature. 'It is fortunate I am not jealous,' he remarked. 'But you know my way: pleasure and liberty go hand in hand. I believe what I believe; it is not much, but I believe it.—But now to business. Have you not read my letter?'

'No,' she said; 'my head ached.'

'Ah, well! then I have news indeed!' cried Gondremark. 'I was mad to see you all last night and all this morning: for yesterday afternoon I brought my long business to a head; the ship has come home; one more dead lift, and I shall cease to fetch and carry for the Princess Ratafia. Yes, 'tis done. I have the order all in Ratafia's hand; I carry it on my heart. At the hour of twelve to-night, Prince Featherhead is to be taken in his bed and, like the bambino, whipped into a chariot; and by next morning he will command a most romantic prospect from the donjon of the Felsenburg. Farewell, Featherhead! The war goes on, the girl is in my hand; I have long been indispensable, but now I shall be sole. I have long,' he added exultingly, 'long carried this intrigue upon my shoulders, like Samson with the gates of Gaza; now I discharge that burthen.'

She had sprung to her feet a little paler. 'Is this true?' she cried.

'I tell you a fact,' he asseverated. 'The trick is played.'

'I will never believe it,' she said. 'An order? In her own hand? I will never believe it, Heinrich.'

'I swear to you,' said he.

'O, what do you care for oaths—or I either? What would you swear by? Wine, women, and song? It is not binding,' she said. She had come quite close up to him and laid her hand upon his arm. 'As for the order—no, Heinrich, never! I will never believe it. I will die ere I believe it. You have some secret purpose—what, I cannot guess—but not one word of it is true.'

'Shall I show it you?' he asked.

'You cannot,' she answered. 'There is no such thing.'

'Incorrigible Sadducee!' he cried. 'Well, I will convert you; you shall see the order.' He moved to a chair where he had thrown his coat, and then drawing forth and holding out a paper, 'Read,' said he.

She took it greedily, and her eye flashed as she perused it.

'Hey!' cried the Baron, 'there falls a dynasty, and it was I that felled it; and I and you inherit!' He seemed to swell in stature; and next moment, with a laugh, he put his hand forward. 'Give me the dagger,' said he.

But she whisked the paper suddenly behind her back and faced him, lowering. 'No, no,' she said. 'You and I have first a point to settle. Do you suppose me blind? She could never have given that paper but to one man, and that man her lover. Here you stand—her lover, her accomplice, her master—O, I well believe it, for I know your power. But what am I?' she cried; 'I, whom you deceive?'

'Jealousy!' cried Gondremark. 'Anna, I would never have believed it! But I declare to you by all that's credible that I am not her lover. I might be, I suppose; but I never yet durst risk the declaration. The chit is so unreal; a mincing doll; she will and she will not; there is no counting on her, by God! And hitherto I have had my own way without, and keep the lover in reserve. And I say, Anna,' he added with severity, 'you must break yourself of this new fit, my girl; there must be no combustion. I keep the creature under the belief that I adore her; and if she caught a breath of you and me, she is such a fool, prude, and dog in the manger, that she is capable of spoiling all.'

'All very fine,' returned the lady. 'With whom do you pass your days? and which am I to believe, your words or your actions?'

'Anna, the devil take you, are you blind?' cried Gondremark. 'You know me. Am I likely to care for such a preciosa? 'Tis hard that we should have been together for so long, and you should still take me for a troubadour. But if there is one thing that I despise and deprecate, it is all such figures in Berlin wool. Give me a human woman—like yourself. You are my mate; you were made for me; you amuse me like the play. And what have I to gain that I should pretend to you? If I do not love you, what use are you to me? Why, none. It is as clear as noon-day.'

'Do you love me, Heinrich?' she asked, languishing. 'Do you truly?'

'I tell you,' he cried, 'I love you next after myself. I should be all abroad if I had lost you.'

'Well, then,' said she, folding up the paper and putting it calmly in her pocket, 'I will believe you, and I join the plot. Count upon me. At midnight, did you say? It is Gordon, I see, that you have charged with it. Excellent; he will stick at nothing.'

Gondremark watched her suspiciously. 'Why do you take the paper?' he demanded. 'Give it here.'

'No,' she returned; 'I mean to keep it. It is I who must prepare the stroke; you cannot manage it without me; and to do my best I must possess the paper. Where shall I find Gordon? In his rooms?' She spoke with a rather feverish self-possession.

'Anna,' he said sternly, the black, bilious countenance of his palace rôle taking the place of the more open favour of his hours at home, 'I ask you for that paper. Once, twice, and thrice.'

'Heinrich,' she returned, looking him in the face, 'take care. I will put up with no dictation.'

Both looked dangerous; and the silence lasted for a measurable interval of time. Then she made haste to have the first word; and with a laugh that rang clear and honest, 'Do not be a child,' she said. 'I wonder at you. If your assurances are true, you can have no reason to mistrust me, nor I to play you false. The difficulty is to get the Prince out of the palace without scandal. His valets are devoted; his chamberlain a slave; and yet one cry might ruin all.'

'They must be overpowered,' he said, following her to the new ground, 'and disappear along with him.'

'And your whole scheme along with them!' she cried. 'He

does not take his servants when he goes a-hunting: a child could read the truth. No, no; the plan is idiotic; it must be Ratafia's. But hear me. You know the Prince worships me?'

'I know,' he said. 'Poor Featherhead, I cross his destiny!'

'Well, now,' she continued, 'what if I bring him alone out of the palace, to some quiet corner of the Park—the Flying Mercury, for instance? Gordon can be posted in the thicket; the carriage wait behind the temple; not a cry, not a scuffle, not a footfall; simply, the Prince vanishes!—What do you say? Am I an able ally? Are my *beaux yeux* of service? Ah, Heinrich, do not lose your Anna!—she has power!'

He struck with his open hand upon the chimney. 'Witch!' he said, 'there is not your match for devilry in Europe. Service! the thing runs on wheels.'

'Kiss me, then, and let me go. I must not miss my Featherhead,' she said.

'Stay, stay,' said the Baron; 'not so fast. I wish, upon my soul, that I could trust you; but you are, out and in, so whimsical a devil that I dare not. Hang it, Anna, no; it's not possible!'

'You doubt me, Heinrich?' she cried.

'Doubt is not the word,' said he. 'I know you. Once you were clear of me with that paper in your pocket, who knows what you would do with it?—not you, at least—nor I. You see,' he added, shaking his head paternally upon the Countess, 'you are as vicious as a monkey.'

'I swear to you,' she cried, 'by my salvation. . . .'

'I have no curiosity to hear you swearing,' said the baron.

'You think that I have no religion? You suppose me destitute of honour. Well,' she said, 'see here: I will not argue, but I tell you once for all: leave me this order, and the Prince shall be arrested—take it from me, and, as certain as I speak, I will upset the coach. Trust me, or fear me: take your choice.' And she offered him the paper.

The Baron in a great contention of mind, stood irresolute, weighing the two dangers. Once his hand advanced, then dropped. 'Well,' he said, 'since trust is what you call it. . . .'

'No more,' she interrupted, 'Do not spoil your attitude. And now since you have behaved like a good sort of fellow in the dark, I will condescend to tell you why. I go to the palace to arrange with Gordon; but how is Gordon to obey me? And how can I foresee the hours? It may be midnight; ay, and it may be nightfall; all's a chance; and to act, I must be free and hold the strings of the adventure. And now,' she cried, 'your Vivien goes. Dub me your knight!' And she held out her arms and smiled upon him radiant.

'Well,' he said, when he had kissed her, 'every man must have his folly; I thank God mine is no worse. Off with you! I have given a child a squib.'

16

Providence von Rosen: Act II.: She informs the Prince

It was the first impulse of Madame von Rosen to return to her own villa and revise her toilette. Whatever else should come of this adventure, it was her firm design to pay a visit to the Princess. And before that woman, so little beloved, the Countess would appear at no disadvantage. It was the work of minutes. Von Rosen had the captain's eye in the matters of the toilette; she was none of those who hang in Fabian helplessness among their finery and, after hours, come forth upon the world as dowdies. A glance, a loosened curl, a studied and admired disorder in the hair, a bit of lace, a touch of colour, a yellow rose in the bosom; and the instant picture was complete.

'That will do,' she said. 'Bid my carriage follow me to the palace. In half an hour it should be there in waiting.'

The night was beginning to fall and the shops to shine with lamps along the tree-shadowed thoroughfares of Otto's capital, when the Countess started on her high emprise. She was jocund at heart; pleasure and interest had winged her beauty, and she knew it. She paused before the glowing jeweller's; she remarked and praised a costume in the milliner's window; and when she reached the lime-tree walk, with its high, umbrageous arches and stir of passers-by in the dim alleys, she took her place upon a bench and began to dally with the pleasures of the hour. It was cold, but she did not feel it, being warm within; her thoughts, in that dark corner, shone like the gold and rubies at the jeweller's; her ears, which heard the brushing of so many footfalls, transposed it into music.

What was she to do? She held the paper by which all depended. Otto and Gondremark and Ratafia, and the state itself, hung light in her balances, as light as dust; her little finger laid in either scale would set all flying: and she hugged herself upon her huge preponderance, and then laughed aloud to think how giddily it might be used. The vertigo of omnipotence, the disease of Cæsars, shook her reason. 'O the mad world!' she thought, and laughed aloud in exultation.

A child, finger in mouth, had paused a little way from where she sat, and stared with cloudy interest upon this laughing lady.

She called it nearer; but the child hung back. Instantly, with that curious passion which you may see any woman in the world display, on the most odd occasions, for a similar end, the Countess bent herself with singleness of mind to overcome this diffidence; and presently, sure enough, the child was seated on her knee, thumbing and glowering at her watch.

'If you had a clay bear and a china monkey,' asked von Rosen, 'which would you prefer to break?'

'But I have neither,' said the child.

'Well,' she said, 'here is a bright florin, with which you may purchase both the one and the other; and I shall give it you at once, if you will answer my question. The clay bear or the china monkey—come?'

But the unbreeched soothsayer only stared upon the florin with big eyes; the oracle could not be persuaded to reply; and the Countess kissed him lightly, gave him the florin, set him down upon the path, and resumed her way with swinging and elastic gait.

'Which shall I break?' she wondered; and she passed her hand with delight among the careful disarrangement of her locks. 'Which?' and she consulted heaven with her bright eyes. 'Do I love both or neither? A little—passionately—not at all? Both or neither—both, I believe; but at least I will make hay of Ratafia.'

By the time she had passed the iron gates, mounted the drive, and set her foot upon the broad flagged terrace, the night had come completely; the palace front was thick with lighted windows; and along the balustrade, the lamp on every twentieth baluster shone clear. A few withered tracks of sunset, amber and glow-worm green, still lingered in the western sky; and she paused once again to watch them fading.

'And to think,' she said, 'that here am I—destiny embodied, a norn, a fate, a providence—and have no guess upon which side I shall declare myself! What other woman in my place would not be prejudiced, and think herself committed? But, thank Heaven! I was born just!' Otto's windows were bright among the rest, and she looked on them with rising tenderness. 'How does it feel to be deserted?' she thought. 'Poor dear fool! The girl deserves that he should see this order.'

Without more delay, she passed into the palace and asked for an audience of Prince Otto. The Prince, she was told, was in his own apartment, and desired to be private. She sent her name. A man presently returned with word that the Prince tendered his apologies, but could see no one. Then I will write,' she said, and scribbled a few lines alleging urgency of life and death. 'Help me, my Prince,' she added; 'none but you can help me.' This time the messenger returned more speedily, and begged the Countess to follow him: the Prince was graciously pleased to receive the Frau Gräfin von Rosen.

Otto sat by the fire in his large armoury, weapons faintly glittering all about him in the changeful light. His face was disfigured by the marks of weeping; he looked sour and sad; nor did he rise to greet his visitor, but bowed, and bade the man begone. That kind of general tenderness which served the Countess for both heart and conscience, sharply smote her at this spectacle of grief and weakness; she began immediately to enter into the spirit of her part; and as soon as they were alone, taking one step forward and with a magnificent gesture—'Up!' she cried.

'Madame von Rosen,' replied Otto dully, 'you have used strong words. You speak of life and death. Pray, madam, who is threatened? Who is there,' he added bitterly, 'so destitute that even Otto of Grünewald can assist him?'

'First learn,' said she, 'the names of the conspirators: the Princess and the Baron Gondremark. Can you not guess the rest?' And then, as he maintained his silence—'You!' she cried, pointing at him with her finger. ''Tis you they threaten! Your rascal and mine have laid their heads together and condemned you. But they reckoned without you and me. We make a *partie carrée*, Prince, in love and politics. They lead an ace, but we shall trump it. Come, partner, shall I draw my card?'

'Madam,' he said, 'explain yourself. Indeed I fail to comprehend.'

'See, then,' said she; and handed him the order.

He took it, looked upon it with a start; and then, still without speech, he put his hand before his face. She waited for a word in vain.

'What!' she cried, 'do you take the thing down-heartedly? As well seek wine in a milkpail as love in that girl's heart! Be done with this, and be a man. After the league of the lions, let us have a conspiracy of mice, and pull this piece of machinery to ground. You were brisk enough last night when nothing was at stake and all was frolic. Well, here is better sport; here is life indeed.'

He got to his feet with some alacrity, and his face, which was a little flushed, bore the marks of resolution.

'Madame von Rosen,' said he, 'I am neither unconscious nor ungrateful; this is the true continuation of your friendship; but I see that I must disappoint your expectations. You seem to expect from me some effort of resistance; but why should I resist? I have not much to gain; and now that I have read this paper, and the last of a fool's paradise is shattered, it would be hyperbolical to speak of loss in the same breath with Otto of Grünewald. I have no party, no policy; no pride, nor anything to be proud of. For what benefit or principle under Heaven do you expect me to contend? Or would you have me bite and scratch like a trapped weasel? No, madam; signify to those who sent you my readiness to go. I would at least avoid a scandal.'

'You go?—of your own will, you go?' she cried.

'I cannot say so much, perhaps,' he answered; 'but I go with good alacrity. I have desired a change some time; behold one offered me! Shall I refuse? Thank God, I am not so destitute of humour as to make a tragedy of such a farce.' He flicked the order on the table. 'You may signify my readiness,' he added grandly.

'Ah,' she said, 'you are more angry than you own.'

'I, madam? angry?' he cried. 'You rave! I have no cause for anger. In every way I have been taught my weakness, my instability, and my unfitness for the world. I am a plexus of weaknesses, an impotent Prince, a doubtful gentleman; and you yourself, indulgent as you are, have twice reproved my levity. And shall I be angry? I may feel the unkindness, but I have sufficient honesty of mind to see the reasons of this *coup d'état*.'

'From whom have you got this?' she cried in wonder. 'You think you have not behaved well? My Prince, were you not young and handsome, I should detest you for your virtues. You push them to the verge of commonplace. And this ingratitude——'

'Understand me, Madame von Rosen,' returned the Prince, flushing a little darker, 'there can be here no talk of gratitude, none of pride. You are here, by what circumstance I know not, but doubtless led by your kindness, mixed up in what regards my family alone. You have no knowledge what my wife, your sovereign, may have suffered; it is not for you—no, nor for me—to judge. I own myself in fault; and were it otherwise, a man were a very empty boaster who should talk of love and start before a small humiliation. It is in all the copybooks that one should die to please his lady-love; and shall a man not go to prison?'

'Love? And what has love to do with being sent to gaol?' exclaimed the Countess, appealing to the walls and roof. 'Heaven knows I think as much of love as any one; my life would prove it; but I admit no love, at least for a man, that is not equally returned. The rest is moonshine.'

'I think of love more absolutely, madam, though I am certain no more tenderly, than a lady to whom I am indebted for such kindnesses,' returned the Prince. 'But this is unavailing. We are not here to hold a court of troubadours.'

'Still,' she replied, 'there is one thing you forget. If she conspires with Gondremark against your liberty, she may conspire with him against your honour also.'

'My honour?' he repeated. 'For a woman, you surprise me. If I have failed to gain her love or play my part of husband, what right is left me? or what honour can remain in such a scene of defeat? No honour that I recognise. I am become a stranger. If my wife no longer loves me, I will go to prison, since she wills it; if she love another, where should I be more in place? or whose fault is it but mine? You speak, Madame von Rosen, like too many women, with a man's tongue. Had I myself fallen into temptation (as, Heaven knows, I might) I should have trembled, but still hoped and asked for her forgiveness; and yet mine had been a treason in the teeth of love. But let me tell you, madam,' he pursued, with rising irritation, 'where a husband by futility, facility, and ill-timed humours has outwearied his wife's patience, I will suffer neither man nor woman to misjudge her. She is free; the man has been found wanting.'

'Because she loves you not?' the Countess cried. 'You know she is incapable of such a feeling.'

'Rather, it was I who was born incapable of inspiring it,' said Otto.

Madame von Rosen broke into sudden laughter. 'Fool,' she cried, 'I am in love with you myself.'

'Ah, madam, you are most compassionate,' the Prince retorted, smiling. 'But this is waste debate. I know my purpose. Perhaps, to equal you in frankness, I know and embrace my advantage. I am not without the spirit of adventure. I am in a false position—so recognised by public acclamation: do you grudge me, then, my issue?'

'If your mind is made up, why should I dissuade you?' said the Countess. 'I own, with a bare face, I am the gainer. Go, you take my heart with you, or more of it than I desire; I shall not sleep at night for thinking of your misery. But do not be afraid; I would not spoil you, you are such a fool and hero.'

'Alas! madam,' cried the Prince, 'and your unlucky money! I did amiss to take it, but you are a wonderful persuader. And I thank God, I can still offer you the fair equivalent.' He took some papers from the chimney. 'Here, madam, are the title-deeds,' he said; 'where I am going, they can certainly be of no use to me, and I have now no other hope of making up to you your kindness. You made the loan without formality, obeying your kind heart. The parts are somewhat changed; the sun of this Prince of Grünewald is upon the point of setting; and I know you better than to doubt you will once more waive ceremony, and accept the best that he can give you. If I may look for any pleasure in the coming time, it will be to remember that the peasant is secure, and my most generous friend no loser.'

'Do you not understand my odious position?' cried the Countess. 'Dear Prince, it is upon your fall that I begin my fortune.'

'It was the more like you to tempt me to resistance,' returned Otto. 'But this cannot alter our relations; and I must, for the last time, lay my commands upon you in the character of Prince.' And with his loftiest dignity, he forced the deeds on her acceptance.

'I hate the very touch of them,' she cried.

There followed upon this a little silence. 'At what time,' resumed Otto, '(if indeed you know) am I to be arrested?'

'Your Highness, when you please!' exclaimed the Countess. 'Or, if you choose to tear that paper, never!'

'I would rather it were done quickly,' said the Prince. 'I shall take but time to leave a letter for the Princess.'

'Well,' said the Countess, 'I have advised you to resist; at the same time, if you intend to be dumb before your shearers, I must say that I ought to set about arranging your arrest. I offered'—she hesitated—'I offered to manage it, intending, my dear friend—intending, upon my soul, to be of use to you. Well, if you will not profit by my goodwill, then be of use to me; and as soon as ever you feel ready, go to the Flying Mercury where we met last night. It will be none the worse for you; and to make it quite plain, it will be better for the rest of us.'

'Dear madam, certainly,' said Otto. 'If I am prepared for the chief evil, I shall not quarrel with details. Go, then, with my best gratitude; and when I have written a few lines of leave-taking, I shall immediately hasten to keep tryst. To-night I shall not meet so dangerous a cavalier,' he added, with a smiling gallantry.

As soon as Madame von Rosen was gone, he made a great call upon his self-command. He was face to face with a miserable passage where, if it were possible, he desired to carry himself with dignity. As to the main fact, he never swerved or faltered; he had come so heart-sick and so cruelly humiliated from his talk with Gotthold, that he embraced the notion of imprisonment with something bordering on relief. Here was, at least, a step which he thought blameless; here was a way out of his troubles. He sat down to write to Seraphina; and his anger blazed. The tale of his forbearances mounted, in his eyes, to something monstrous; still more monstrous, the coldness, egoism, and cruelty that had required and thus requited them. The pen which he had taken shook in his hand. He was amazed to find his resignation fled, but it was gone beyond his recall. In a few white-hot words, he bade adieu, dubbing desperation by the name of love, and calling his wrath forgiveness; then he cast but one look of leave-taking on the place that had been his for so long and was now to be his no longer; and hurried forth—love's prisoner—or pride's.

He took that private passage which he had trodden so often in less momentous hours. The porter let him out; and the bountiful, cold air of the night and the pure glory of the stars received him on the threshold. He looked round him, breathing deep of earth's plain fragrance; he looked up into the great array of heaven, and was quieted. His little turgid life dwindled to its true proportions; and he saw himself (that great flame-hearted martyr!) stand like a speck under the cool cupola of the night. Thus he felt his careless injuries already soothed; the live air of out-of-doors, the quiet of the world, as if by their silent music, sobering and dwarfing his emotions.

'Well, I forgive her,' he said. 'If it be of any use to her, I forgive.'

And with brisk steps he crossed the garden, issued upon the Park, and came to the Flying Mercury. A dark figure moved forward from the shadow of the pedestal.

'I have to ask your pardon, sir,' a voice observed, 'but if I am right in taking you for the Prince, I was given to understand that you would be prepared to meet me.'

'Herr Gordon, I believe?' said Otto.

'Herr Oberst Gordon,' replied that officer. 'This is rather a ticklish business for a man to be embarked in; and to find that all is to go pleasantly is a great relief to me. The carriage is at hand; shall I have the honour of following your Highness?'

'Colonel,' said the Prince, 'I have now come to that happy moment of my life when I have orders to receive but none to give.'

'A most philosophical remark,' returned the Colonel. 'Begad, a very pertinent remark! it might be Plutarch. I am not a drop's blood to your Highness, or indeed to any one in this principality; or else I should dislike my orders. But as it is, and since there is nothing unnatural or unbecoming on my side, and your Highness takes it in good part, I begin to believe we may have a capital time together, sir—a capital time. For a gaoler is only a fellow-captive.'

'May I inquire, Herr Gordon,' asked Otto, 'what led you to accept this dangerous and I would fain hope thankless office?'

'Very natural, I am sure,' replied the officer of fortune. 'My pay, is, in the meanwhile, doubled.'

'Well, sir, I will not presume to criticise,' returned the Prince. 'And I perceive the carriage.'

Sure enough, at the intersection of two alleys of the Park, a coach and four, conspicuous by its lanterns, stood in waiting. And a little way off about a score of lancers were drawn up under the shadow of the trees.

17

Providence von Rosen: Act III: She enlightens Seraphina

When Madame von Rosen left the Prince, she hurried straight to Colonel Gordon; and not content with directing the arrangements, she had herself accompanied the soldier of fortune to the Flying Mercury. The Colonel gave her his arm, and the talk between this pair of conspirators ran high and lively. The Countess, indeed, was in a whirl of pleasure and excitement; her tongue stumbled upon laughter, her eyes shone, the colour that was usually wanting now perfected her face. It would have taken little more to bring Gordon to her feet—or so, at least, she believed, disdaining the idea.

Hidden among some lilac bushes, she enjoyed the great decorum of the arrest, and heard the dialogue of the two men die away along the path. Soon after, the rolling of a carriage and the beat of hoofs arose in the still air of the night, and passed speedily farther and fainter into silence. The Prince was gone.

Madame von Rosen consulted her watch. She had still, she thought, time enough for the tit-bit of her evening; and hurrying to the palace, winged by the fear of Gondremark's arrival, she sent her name and a pressing request for a reception to the Princess Seraphina. As the Countess von Rosen unqualified, she was sure to be refused; but as an emissary of the Baron's, for so she chose to style herself, she gained immediate entry.

The Princess sat alone at table, making a feint of dining. Her cheeks were mottled, her eyes heavy; she had neither slept nor eaten; even her dress had been neglected. In short, she was out of health, out of looks, out of heart, and hag-ridden by her conscience. The Countess drew a swift comparison, and shone brighter in beauty.

'You come, madam, *de la part de Monsieur le Baron*,' drawled the Princess. 'Be seated! What have you to say?'

'To say?' repeated Madame von Rosen. 'O, much to say! Much to say that I would rather not, and much to leave unsaid that I would rather say. For I am like St. Paul, your Highness, and always wish to do the things I should not. Well! to be categorical—that is the word?—I took the Prince your order. He could not credit his senses. "Ah," he cried, "dear Madame von Rosen, it is not possible—it cannot be—I must hear it from your lips. My wife is a poor girl misled, she is only silly, she is not cruel." "*Mon Prince*," said I, "a girl—and therefore cruel; youth kills flies."—He had such pain to understand it!'

'Madame von Rosen,' said the Princess, in most steadfast tones, but with a rose of anger in her face, 'who sent you here, and for what purpose? Tell your errand.'

'O, madam, I believe you understand me very well,' returned von Rosen. 'I have not your philosophy. I wear my heart upon my sleeve, excuse the indecency! It is a very little one,' she laughed, 'and I so often change the sleeve!'

'Am I to understand the Prince has been arrested?' asked the Princess, rising.

'While you sat there dining!' cried the Countess, still nonchalantly seated.

'You have discharged your errand,' was the reply; 'I will not detain you.'

'O no, madam,' said the Countess, 'with your permission, I have not yet done. I have borne much this evening in your service. I have suffered. I was made to suffer in your service.' She unfolded her fan as she spoke. Quick as her pulses beat, the fan waved languidly. She betrayed her emotion only by the brightness of her eyes and face, and by the almost insolent triumph with which she looked down upon the Princess. There were old scores of rivalry between them in more than one field; so at least von Rosen felt; and now she was to have her hour of victory in them all.

'You are no servant, Madame von Rosen, of mine,' said Seraphina.

'No, madam, indeed,' returned the Countess; 'but we both serve the same person, as you know—or if you do not, then I have the pleasure of informing you. Your conduct is so light—so light,' she repeated, the fan wavering higher like a butterfly, 'that perhaps you do not truly understand.' The Countess rolled her fan together, laid it in her lap, and rose to a less languorous position. 'Indeed,' she continued, 'I should be sorry to see any young woman in your situation. You began with every advantage—birth, a suitable marriage—quite pretty too—and see what you have come to! My poor girl, to think of it!

But there is nothing that does so much harm,' observed the Countess finely, 'as giddiness of mind.' And she once more unfurled the fan, and approvingly fanned herself.

'I will no longer permit you to forget yourself,' cried Seraphina. 'I think you are mad.'

'Not mad,' returned von Rosen. 'Sane enough to know you dare not break with me to-night, and to profit by the knowledge. I left my poor, pretty Prince Charming crying his eyes out for a wooden doll. My heart is soft; I love my pretty Prince; you will never understand it, but I long to give my Prince his doll, dry his poor eyes, and send him off happy. O, you immature fool!' the Countess cried, rising to her feet, and pointing at the Princess the closed fan that now began to tremble in her hand. 'O wooden doll!' she cried, 'have you a heart, or blood, or any nature? This is a man, child—a man who loves you. O, it will not happen twice! it is not common; beautiful and clever women look in vain for it. And you, you pitiful schoolgirl, tread this jewel under foot! you stupid with your vanity! Before you try to govern kingdoms, you should first be able to behave yourself at home; home is the woman's kingdom.' She paused and laughed a little, strangely to hear and look upon. 'I will tell you one of the things,' she said, 'that were to stay unspoken. Von Rosen is a better woman than you, my Princess, though you will never have the pain of understanding it; and when I took the Prince your order, and looked upon his face, my soul was melted—O, I am frank—here, within my arms, I offered him repose!' She advanced a step superbly as she spoke, with outstretched arms; and Seraphina shrank. 'Do not be alarmed!' the countess cried; 'I am not offering that hermitage to you; in all the world there is but one who wants to, and him you have dismissed! "If it will give her pleasure I should wear the martyr's crown," he cried, "I will embrace the thorns." I tell you—I am quite frank—I put the order in his power and begged him to resist. You, who have betrayed your husband, may betray me to Gondremark; my Prince would betray no one. Understand it plainly,' she cried, ''tis of his pure forbearance that you sit there; he had the power—I gave it him—to change the parts; and he refused, and went to prison in your place.'

The Princess spoke with some distress. 'Your violence shocks me and pains me,' she began, 'but I cannot be angry with what at least does honour to the mistaken kindness of your heart; it was right for me to know this. I will condescended to tell you. It was with deep regret that I was driven to this step. I admire in many ways the Prince—I admit his amiability. It was our great misfortune, it was perhaps somewhat of my fault, that we were so unsuited to each other; but I have a regard, a sincere regard, for all his qualities. As a private person I should think as you do. It is difficult, I know, to make allowances for state considerations. I have only with deep reluctance obeyed the call of a superior duty; and so soon as I dare do it for the safety of the state, I promise you the Prince shall be released. Many in my situation would have resented your freedoms. I am not '—and she looked for a moment rather piteously upon the Countess—' I am not altogether so inhuman as you think.'

'And you can put these troubles of the state,' the Countess cried, 'to weigh with a man's love?'

'Madame von Rosen, these troubles are affairs of life and death to many; to the Prince, and perhaps even to yourself, among the number,' replied the Princess, with dignity. 'I have learned, madam, although still so young, in a hard school, that my own feelings must everywhere come last.'

'O callow innocence!' exclaimed the other. 'Is it possible you do not know, or do not suspect, the intrigue in which you move? I find it in my heart to pity you! We are both women after all—poor girl, poor girl!—and who is born a woman is born a fool. And though I hate all women—come, for the common folly, I forgive you. Your Highness '—she dropped a deep stage curtsey and resumed her fan—' I am going to insult you, to betray one who is called my lover, and if it pleases you to use the power I now put unreservedly into your hands, to ruin my dear self. O what a French comedy! You betray, I betray, they betray. It is now my cue. The letter, yes. Behold the letter, madam, its seal unbroken as I found it by my bed this morning; for I was out of humour, and I get many, too many, of these favours. For your own sake, for the sake of my Prince Charming, for the sake of this great principality that sits so heavy on your conscience, open it and read!'

'Am I to understand,' inquired the Princess, 'that this letter in any way regards me?'

'You see I have not opened it,' replied von Rosen; 'but 'tis mine, and I beg you to experiment.'

'I cannot look at it till you have,' returned Seraphina, very seriously. 'There may be matter there not meant for me to see; it is a private letter.'

The Countess tore it open, glanced it through, and tossed it back; and the Princess, taking up the sheet, recognised the hand of Gondremark, and read with a sickening shock the following lines:—

'Dearest Anna, come at once. Ratafia has done the deed, her husband is to be packed to prison. This puts the minx entirely in my power; *le tour est joué*; she will now go steady in harness, or I will know the reason why. Come. 'HEINRICH.'

'Command yourself, madam,' said the Countess, watching with some alarm the white face of Seraphina. 'It is in vain for you to fight with Gondremark; he has more strings than mere court favour, and could bring you down to-morrow with a word. I would not have betrayed him otherwise; but Heinrich is a man, and plays with all of you like marionettes. And now at least you see for what you sacrificed my Prince. Madam, will you take some wine? I have been cruel.'

'Not cruel, madam—salutary,' said Seraphina, with a phantom smile. 'No, I thank you, I require no attentions. The first surprise affected me: will you give me time a little? I must think.'

She took her head between her hands, and contemplated for a while the hurricane confusion of her thoughts.

'This information reaches me,' she said, 'when I have need of it. I would not do as you have done, but yet I thank you. I have been much deceived in Baron Gondremark.'

'O, madam, leave Gondremark, and think upon the Prince!' cried von Rosen.

'You speak once more as a private person,' said the Princess; 'nor do I blame you. But my own thoughts are more distracted. However, as I believe you are truly a friend to my—to the—as I believe,' she said, 'you are a friend to Otto, I shall put the order for his release into your hands this moment. Give me the ink-dish. There! And she wrote hastily, steadying her arm upon the table, for she trembled like a reed. 'Remember, madam,' she resumed, handing her the order, 'this must not be used nor spoken of at present; till I have seen the Baron, any hurried step—I lose myself in thinking. The suddenness has shaken me.'

'I promise you I will not use it,' said the Countess, 'till you give me leave, although I wish the Prince could be informed of it, to comfort his poor heart. And O, I had forgotten, he has left a letter. Suffer me, madam, I will bring it you. This is the door, I think?' And she sought to open it.

'The bolt is pushed,' said Seraphina, flushing.

'O! O!' cried the Countess.

A silence fell between them.

'I will get it for myself,' said Seraphina; 'and in the meanwhile I beg you to leave me. I thank you, I am sure, but I shall be obliged if you will leave me.'

The Countess deeply curtseyed, and withdrew.

18

Relates the cause and outbreak of the revolution

Brave as she was, and brave by intellect, the Princess, when first she was alone, clung to the table for support. The four corners of her universe had fallen. She had never liked nor trusted Gondremark completely; she had still held it possible to find him false to friendship; but from that to finding him devoid of all those public virtues for which she had honoured him, a mere commonplace intriguer, using her for his own ends, the step was wide and the descent giddy Light and darkness succeeded each other in her brain; now she believed, and now she could not. She turned, blindly groping for the note. But von Rosen, who had not forgotten to take the warrant from the Prince, had remembered to recover her note from the Princess: von Rosen was an old campaigner, whose most violent emotion aroused rather than clouded the vigour of her reason.

The thought recalled to Seraphina the remembrance of the other letter—Otto's. She rose and went speedily, her brain still wheeling, and burst into the Prince's armoury. The old chamberlain was there in waiting; and the sight of another face, prying (or so she felt) on her distress, struck Seraphina into childish anger.

'Go!' she cried; and then, when the old man was already half-way to the door, 'Stay!' she added. 'As soon as Baron Gondremark arrives, let him attend me here.'

'It shall be so directed,' said the chamberlain.

'There was a letter . . . ' she began, and paused.

'Her Highness,' said the chamberlain, 'will find a letter on the table. I had received no orders, or Her Highness had been spared this trouble.'

'No, no, no,' she cried. 'I thank you. I desire to be alone.'

And then, when he was gone, she leaped upon the letter. Her mind was still obscured; like the moon upon a night of clouds and wind, her reason shone and was darkened, and she read the words by flashes.

'Seraphina,' the Prince wrote, 'I will write no syllable of reproach. I have seen your order, and I go. What else is left me? I have wasted my love, and have no more. To say that I forgive you is not needful; at least, we are now separate for ever; by your own act, you free me from my willing bondage:

I go free to prison. This is the last that you will hear of me in love or anger. I have gone out of your life; you may breathe easy; you have now rid yourself of the husband who allowed you to desert him, of the Prince who gave you his rights, and of the married lover who made it his pride to defend you in your absence. How you have requited him, your own heart more loudly tells you than my words. There is a day coming when your vain dreams will roll away like clouds, and you will find yourself alone. Then you will remember.

'OTTO.'

She read with a great horror on her mind; that day, of which he wrote, was come. She was alone; she had been false, she had been cruel; remorse rolled in upon her; and then with a more piercing note, vanity bounded on the stage of consciousness. She a dupe! she helpless! she to have betrayed herself in seeking to betray her husband! she to have lived these years upon flattery, grossly swallowing the bolus, like a clown with sharpers! she—Seraphina! Her swift mind drank the consequences; she foresaw the coming fall, her public shame; she saw the odium, disgrace, and folly of her story flaunt through Europe. She recalled the scandal she had so royally braved; and alas! she had now no courage to confront it with. To be thought the mistress of that man: perhaps for that. . . . She closed her eyes on agonising vistas. Swift as thought she had snatched a bright dagger from the weapons that shone along the wall. Ay, she would escape. From that world-wide theatre of nodding heads and buzzing whisperers, in which she now beheld herself unpitiably martyred, one door stood open. At any cost, through any stress of suffering, that greasy laughter should be stifled. She closed her eyes, breathed a wordless prayer, and pressed the weapon to her bosom.

At the astonishing sharpness of the prick, she gave a cry and awoke to a sense of undeserved escape. A little ruby spot of blood was the reward of that great act of desperation; but the pain had braced her like a tonic, and her whole design of suicide had passed away.

At the same instant regular feet drew near along the gallery, and she knew the tread of the big Baron, so often gladly welcome, and even now rallying her spirits like a call to battle. She concealed the dagger in the folds of her skirt; and drawing her stature up, she stood firm-footed, radiant with anger, waiting for the foe.

The Baron was announced and entered. To him, Seraphina was a hated task: like the schoolboy with his Virgil, he had neither will nor leisure to remark her beauties; but when he now beheld her standing illuminated by her passion, new feelings flashed upon him, a frank admiration, a brief sparkle of desire. He noted both with joy; they were means. 'If I have to play the lover,' thought he, for that was his constant preoccupation, 'I believe I can put soul into it.' Meanwhile, with his usual ponderous grace, he bent before the lady.

'I propose,' she said in a strange voice, not known to her till then, 'that we release the Prince and do not prosecute the war.'

'Ah, madam,' he replied, ''tis as I knew it would be! Your heart, I knew, would wound you when we came to this distasteful but most necessary step. Ah, madam, believe me, I am not unworthy to be your ally; I know you have qualities to which I am a stranger, and count them the best weapons in the armoury of our alliance:—the girl in the queen—pity, love, tenderness, laughter; the smile that can reward. I can only command; I am the frowner. But you! And you have the fortitude to command these comely weaknesses, to tread them down at the call of reason. How often have I not admired it even to yourself! Ay, even to yourself,' he added tenderly, dwelling, it seemed, in memory on hours of more private admiration. 'But now, madam——'

'But now, Herr von Gondremark, the time for these declarations has gone by,' she cried. 'Are you true to me? are you false? Look in your heart and answer: it is your heart I want to know.'

'It has come,' thought Gondremark. 'You, madam!' he cried, starting back—with fear, you would have said, and yet a timid joy. 'You! yourself, you bid me look into my heart?'

'Do you suppose I fear?' she cried, and looked at him with such a heightened colour, such bright eyes, and a smile of so abstruse a meaning, that the baron discarded his last doubt.

'Ah, madam!' he cried, plumping on his knees. 'Seraphina! Do you permit me? have you divined my secret? It is true—I put my life with joy into your power—I love you, love with ardour, as an equal, as a mistress, as a brother-in-arms, as an adored, desired, sweet-hearted woman. O Bride!' he cried, waxing dithyrambic, 'bride of my reason and my senses, have pity, have pity on my love!'

She heard him with wonder, rage, and then contempt. His words offended her to sickness; his appearance, as he grovelled bulkily upon the floor, moved her to such laughter as we laugh in nightmares.

'O shame!' she cried. 'Absurd and odious! What would the Countess say?'

That great Baron Gondremark, the excellent politician, remained for some little time upon his knees in a frame of mind which perhaps we are allowed to pity. His vanity, within his iron bosom, bled and raved. If he could have blotted all, if he could have withdrawn part, if he had not called her bride—with a roaring in his ears, he thus regretfully reviewed his declaration. He got to his feet tottering; and then, in that first moment when a dumb agony finds a vent in words, and the tongue betrays the inmost and worst of a man, he permitted himself a retort which, for six weeks to follow, he was to repent at leisure.

'Ah,' said he, 'the Countess? Now I perceive the reason of your Highness's disorder.'

The lackey-like insolence of the words was driven home by a more insolent manner. There fell upon Seraphina one of those storm-clouds which had already blackened upon her reason; she heard herself cry out; and when the cloud dispersed, flung the blood-stained dagger on the floor, and saw Gondremark reeling back with open mouth and clapping his hand upon the wound. The next moment, with oaths that she had never heard, he leaped at her in savage passion; clutched her as she recoiled; and in the very act, stumbled and drooped. She had scarce time to fear his murderous onslaught ere he fell before her feet.

He rose upon one elbow; she still staring upon him, white with horror.

'Anna!' he cried, 'Anna! Help!'

And then his utterance failed him, and he fell back, to all appearance dead.

Seraphina ran to and fro in the room; she wrung her hands and cried aloud; within she was all one uproar of terror, and conscious of no articulate wish but to awake.

There came a knocking at the door; and she sprang to it and held it, panting like a beast, and with the strength of madness in her arms, till she had pushed the bolt. At this success a certain calm fell upon her reason. She went back and looked upon her victim, the knocking growing louder. O yes, he was dead. She had killed him. He had called upon von Rosen with his latest breath; ah! who would call on Seraphina? She had killed him. She, whose irresolute hand could scarce prick blood from her own bosom, had found strength to cast down that great colossus at a blow.

All this while the knocking was growing more uproarious and more unlike the staid career of life in such a palace. Scandal was at the door, with what a fatal following she dreaded to conceive; and at the same time among the voices that now began to summon her by name, she recognised the Chancellor's. He or another, somebody must be the first.

'Is Herr von Greisengesang without?' she called.

'Your Highness—yes!' the old gentleman answered. 'We have heard cries, a fall. Is anything amiss?'

'Nothing,' replied Seraphina. 'I desire to speak with you. Send off the rest.' She panted between each phrase; but her mind was clear. She let the looped curtain down upon both sides before she drew the bolt; and, thus secure from any sudden eyeshot from without, admitted the obsequious Chancellor, and again made fast the door.

Greisengesang clumsily revolved among the wings of the curtain, so that she was clear of it as soon as he.

'My God!' he cried. 'The Baron!'

'I have killed him,' she said. 'O, killed him!'

'Dear me,' said the old gentleman, 'this is most unprecedented. Lovers' quarrels,' he added ruefully, 'redintegratio——' and then paused. 'But, my dear madam,' he broke out again, 'in the name of all that is practical, what are we to do? This is exceedingly grave; morally, madam, it is appalling. I take the liberty, your Highness, for one moment, of addressing you as a daughter, a loved although respected daughter; and I must say that I cannot conceal from you that this is morally most questionable. And, O dear me, we have a dead body!'

She had watched him closely; hope fell to contempt; she drew away her skirts from his weakness, and, in the act, her own strength returned to her.

'See if he be dead,' she said; not one word of explanation or defence; she had scorned to justify herself before so poor a creature; 'See if he be dead,' was all.

With the greatest compunction, the Chancellor drew near; and as he did so the wounded Baron rolled his eyes.

'He lives,' cried the old courtier, turning effusively to Seraphina. 'Madam, he still lives.'

'Help him, then,' returned the Princess, standing fixed. 'Bind up his wound.'

'Madam, I have no means,' protested the Chancellor.

'Can you not take your handkerchief, your neckcloth, anything?' she cried; and at the same moment, from her light muslin gown she rent off a flounce and tossed it on the floor. 'Take that,' she said, and for the first time directly faced Greisengesang.

But the Chancellor held up his hands and turned away his head in agony. The grasp of the falling Baron had torn down the dainty fabric of the bodice; and—'O Highness!' cried Greisengesang, appalled, 'the terrible disorder of your toilette!'

'Take up that flounce,' she said; 'the man may die.'

Greisengesang turned in a flutter to the Baron, and attempted some innocent and bungling measures. 'He still breathes,' he kept saying. 'All is not yet over; he is not yet gone.'

'And now,' said she, 'if that is all you can do, begone and get some porters; he must instantly go home.'

'Madam,' cried the Chancellor, 'if this most melancholy sight were seen in town—O dear, the State would fall!' he piped.

'There is a litter in the Palace,' she replied. 'It is your part to see him safe. I lay commands upon you. On your life it stands.'

'I see it, dear Highness,' he jerked. 'Clearly I see it. But how? what men? The Prince's servants—yes. They had a personal affection. They will be true, if any.'

'O, not them!' she cried. 'Take Sabra, my own man.'

'Sabra! The grand-mason?' returned the Chancellor, aghast. 'If he but saw this, he would sound the tocsin—we should all be butchered.'

She measured the depth of her abasement steadily. 'Take whom you must,' she said, 'and bring the litter here.'

Once she was alone she ran to the Baron, and with a sickening heart sought to allay the flux of blood. The touch of the skin of that great charlatan revolted her to the toes; the wound, in her ignorant eyes, looked deathly; yet she contended with her shuddering, and, with more skill at least than the Chancellor's, stanched the welling injury. An eye unprejudiced with hate would have admired the Baron in his swoon; he looked so great and shapely; it was so powerful a machine that lay arrested; and his features, cleared for the moment both of temper and dissimulation, were seen to be so purely modelled. But it was not thus with Seraphina. Her victim, as he lay outspread, twitching a little, his big chest unbared, fixed her with his ugliness; and her mind flitted for a glimpse to Otto.

Rumours began to sound about the Palace of feet running and of voices raised; the echoes of the great arched staircase were voluble of some confusion; and then the gallery jarred with a quick and heavy tramp. It was the Chancellor, followed by four of Otto's valets and a litter. The servants, when they were admitted, stared at the dishevelled Princess and the wounded man; speech was denied them, but their thoughts were riddled with profanity. Gondremark was bundled in; the curtains of the litter were lowered; the bearers carried it forth, and the Chancellor followed behind with a white face.

Seraphina ran to the window. Pressing her face upon the pane, she could see the terrace, where the lights contended; thence, the avenue of lamps that joined the Palace and town; and overhead the hollow night and the larger stars. Presently the small procession issued from the Palace, crossed the parade, and began to thread the glittering alley: the swinging couch with its four porters, the much-pondering Chancellor behind. She watched them dwindle with strange thoughts: her eyes fixed upon the scene, her mind still glancing right and left on the overthrow of her life and hopes. There was no one left in whom she might confide; none whose hand was friendly, or on whom she dared to reckon for the barest loyalty. With the fall of Gondremark, her party, her brief popularity, had fallen. So she sat crouched upon the window-seat, her brow to the cool pane; her dress in tatters, barely shielding her; her mind revolving bitter thoughts.

Meanwhile, consequences were fast mounting; and in the deceptive quiet of the night, downfall and red revolt were brewing. The litter had passed forth between the iron gates and entered on the streets of the town. By what flying panic, by what thrill of air communicated, who shall say? but the passing bustle in the Palace had already reached and re-echoed in the region of the burghers. Rumour, with her loud whispers, hissed about the town; men left their homes without knowing why; knots formed along the boulevard; under the rare lamps and the great limes the crowd grew blacker.

And now through the midst of that expectant company, the unusual sight of a closed litter was observed approaching, and trotting hard behind it that great dignitary Cancellarius Greisengesang. Silence looked on as it went by; and as soon as it was passed, the whispering seethed over like a boiling pot. The knots were sundered; and gradually, one following another, the whole mob began to form into a procession and escort the curtained litter. Soon spokesmen, a little bolder than their mates, began to ply the Chancellor with questions. Never had he more need of that great art of falsehood, by whose exercise he had so richly lived. And yet now he stumbled, the master passion, fear, betraying him. He was pressed; he became incoherent; and then from the jolting litter came a groan. In the instant hubbub and the gathering of the crowd as to a natural signal, the clear-eyed, quavering Chancellor heard the catch of the clock before it strikes the hour of doom; and for ten seconds he forgot himself. This shall atone for many sins. He plucked a bearer by the sleeve. 'Bid the Princess flee. All is lost,' he whispered. And the next moment he was babbling for his life among the multitude.

Five minutes later the wild-eyed servant burst into the armoury. 'All is lost!' he cried. 'The Chancellor bids you flee.' And at the same time, looking through the window, Seraphina saw the black rush of the populace begin to invade the lamplit avenue.

'Thank you, Georg,' she said. 'I thank you. Go.' And as the man still lingered, 'I bid you go,' she added. 'Save yourself.'

Down by the private passage, and just some two hours later, Amalia Seraphina, the last Princess, followed Otto Johann Friedrich, the last Prince of Grünewald.

Book Three

FORTUNATE MISFORTUNE

19

Princess Cinderella

THE porter, drawn by the growing turmoil, had vanished from the postern, and the door stood open on the darkness of the night. As Seraphina fled up the terraces, the cries and loud footing of the mob drew nearer the doomed palace; the rush was like the rush of cavalry; the sound of shattering lamps tingled above the rest; and, over-towering all, she heard her own name bandied among the shouters. A bugle sounded at the door of the guard-room; one gun was fired; and then, with the yell of hundreds, Mittwalden Palace was carried at a rush.

Sped by these dire sounds and voices, the Princess scaled the long garden, skimming like a bird the starlit stairways; crossed the Park, which was in that place narrow; and plunged upon the farther side into the rude shelter of the forest. So, at a bound, she left the discretion and the cheerful lamps of Palace evenings; ceased utterly to be a sovereign lady; and, falling from the whole height of civilisation, ran forth into the woods, a ragged Cinderella.

She went direct before her through an open tract of the forest, full of brush and birches, and where the starlight guided her; and, beyond that again, must thread the columned blackness of a pine grove joining overhead the thatch of its long branches. At that hour the place was breathless; a horror of night like a presence occupied that dungeon of the wood; and she went groping, knocking against the boles—her ear, betweenwhiles, strained to aching and yet unrewarded.

But the slope of the ground was upward, and encouraged her; and presently she issued on a rocky hill that stood forth above the sea of forest. All around were other hilltops, big and little; sable vales of forest between; overhead the open heaven and the brilliancy of countless stars; and along the western sky the dim forms of mountains. The glory of the great night laid hold upon her; her eyes shone with stars; she dipped her sight into the coolness and brightness of the sky, as she might have dipped her wrist into a spring; and her heart, at that ethereal shock, began to move more soberly. The sun that sails overhead, ploughing into gold the fields of daylight azure and uttering the signal to man's myriads, has no word apart for man the individual;

and the moon, like a violin, only praises and laments our private destiny. The stars alone, cheerful whisperers, confer quietly with each of us like friends; they give ear to our sorrows smilingly, like wise old men, rich in tolerance; and by their double scale, so small to the eye, so vast to the imagination, they keep before the mind the double character of man's nature and fate.

There sat the Princess, beautifully looking upon beauty, in council with these glad advisers. Bright like pictures, clear like a voice in the porches of her ear, memory re-enacted the tumult of the evening: the Countess and the dancing fan, the big Baron on his knees, the blood on the polished floor, the knocking, the swing of the litter down the avenue of lamps, the messenger, the cries of the charging mob; and yet all were far away and phantasmal, and she was still healingly conscious of the peace and glory of the night. She looked towards Mittwalden; and above the hill-top, which already hid it from her view, a throbbing redness hinted of fire. Better so: better so, that she should fall with tragic greatness, lit by a blazing palace! She felt not a trace of pity for Gondremark or of concern for Grünewald: that period of her life was closed for ever, a wrench of wounded vanity alone surviving. She had but one clear idea: to flee; —and another, obscure and half-rejected, although still obeyed: to flee in the direction of the Felsenburg. She had a duty to perform, she must free Otto—so her mind said, very coldly; but her heart embraced the notion of that duty even with ardour, and her hands began to yearn for the grasp of kindness.

She rose, with a start of recollection, and plunged down the slope into the covert. The woods received and closed upon her. Once more, she wandered and hasted in a blot, uncheered, unpiloted. Here and there, indeed, through rents in the wood-roof, a glimmer attracted her; here and there a tree stood out among its neighbours by some force of outline; here and there a brushing among the leaves, a notable blackness, a dim shine, relieved, only to exaggerate, the solid oppression of the night and silence. And betweenwhiles, the unfeatured darkness would redouble and the whole ear of night appear to be gloating on her steps. Now she would stand still, and the silence would grow and grow, till it weighed upon her breathing; and then she would address herself again to run, stumbling, falling, and still hurrying the more. And presently the whole wood rocked and began to run along with her. The noise of her own mad passage through the silence spread and echoed, and filled the night with terror. Panic hunted her: Panic from the trees reached forth with clutching branches; the darkness was lit up and peopled with strange forms and faces. She strangled and fled before her fears. And yet in the last fortress, reason, blown upon by these gusts of terror, still shone with a troubled light. She knew, yet could not act upon her knowledge; she knew that she must stop, and yet she still ran.

She was already near madness, when she broke suddenly into a narrow clearing. At the same time the din grew louder, and she became conscious of vague forms and fields of whiteness. And with that the earth gave way; she fell and found her feet again with an incredible shock to her senses, and her mind was swallowed up.

When she came again to herself, she was standing to the mid-leg in an icy eddy of a brook, and leaning with one hand on the rock from which it poured. The spray had wet her hair. She saw the white cascade, the stars wavering in the shaken pool, foam flitting, and high overhead the tall pines on either hand serenely drinking starshine; and in the sudden quiet of her spirit she heard with joy the firm plunge of the cataract in the pool. She scrambled forth dripping. In the face of her proved weakness, to adventure again upon the horror of blackness in the groves were a suicide of life or reason. But here, in the alley of the brook, with the kind stars above her, and the moon presently swimming into sight, she could await the coming of day without alarm.

This lane of pine-trees ran very rapidly down-hill and wound among the woods; but it was a wider thoroughfare than the brook needed, and here and there were little dimpling lawns and coves of the forest, where the starshine slumbered. Such a lawn she paced, taking patience bravely; and now she looked up the hill and saw the brook coming down to her in a series of cascades; and now approached the margin, where it welled among the rushes silently; and now gazed at the great company of heaven with an enduring wonder. The early evening had fallen chill, but the night was now temperate; out of the recesses of the wood there came mild airs as from a deep and peaceful breathing; and the dew was heavy on the grass and the tight-shut daisies. This was the girl's first night under the naked heaven; and now that her fears were overpast, she was touched to the soul by its serene amenity and peace. Kindly the host of heaven blinked down upon that wandering Princess; and the honest brook had no words but to encourage her.

At last she began to be aware of a wonderful revolution, compared to which the fire of Mittwalden Palace was but the crack and flash of a percussion-cap. The countenance with which the pines regarded her began insensibly to change; the grass too, short as it was, and the whole winding staircase of the brook's course, began to wear a solemn freshness of appearance. And this slow transfiguration reached her heart, and played upon it, and transpierced it with a serious thrill. She looked about; the whole face of nature looked back, brimful of meaning, finger on lip, leaking its glad secret. She looked up. Heaven was almost emptied of stars. Such as still lingered shone with a changed and waning brightness, and began to faint in their stations. And the colour of the sky itself was the most wonderful; for the rich blue of the night had now melted and softened and brightened; and there had succeeded in its place a hue that has no name, and that is never seen but as the herald of morning. 'O!' she cried, joy catching at her voice, 'O! it is the dawn!'

In a breath she passed over the brook, and looped up her skirts and fairly ran in the dim alleys. As she ran, her ears were aware of many pipings, more beautiful than music; in the small dish-shaped houses in the fork of giant arms, where they had lain all night, lover by lover, warmly pressed, the bright-eyed, big-hearted singers began to awaken for the day. Her heart melted and flowed forth to them in kindness. And they, from their small and high perches in the clerestories of the wood cathedral, peered down sidelong at the ragged Princess as she flitted below them on the carpet of the moss and tassel.

Soon she had struggled to a certain hill-top, and saw far below her the silent inflooding of the day. Out of the East it welled and whitened; the darkness trembled into light; and the stars were extinguished like the street-lamps of a human city. The whiteness brightened into silver, the silver warmed into gold, the gold kindled into pure and living fire; and the face of the East was barred with elemental scarlet. The day drew its first long breath, steady and chill; and for leagues around the woods sighed and shivered. And then, at one bound, the sun had floated up; and her startled eyes received day's first arrow, and quailed under the buffet. On every side, the shadows leaped from their ambush and fell prone. The day was come, plain and garish; and up the steep and solitary eastern heaven, the sun, victorious over his competitors, continued slowly and royally to mount.

Seraphina drooped for a little, leaning on a pine, the shrill joy of the woodlands mocking her. The shelter of the night, the thrilling and joyous changes of the dawn, were over; and now, in the hot eye of the day, she turned uneasily and looked sighingly about her. Some way off among the lower woods, a pillar of smoke was mounting and melting in the gold and blue. There, surely enough were human folk, the hearth-surrounders. Man's fingers had laid the twigs; it was man's breath that had quickened and encouraged the baby flames; and now, as the fire caught, it would be playing ruddily on the face of its creator. At the thought, she felt a-cold and little and lost in that great out-of-doors. The electric shock of the young sunbeams and the unhuman beauty of the woods began to irk and daunt her. The covert of the house, the decent privacy of rooms, the swept and regulated fire, all that denotes or beautifies the home life of man, began to draw her as with cords. The pillar of smoke was now risen into some stream of moving air; it began to lean out sideways in a pennon; and thereupon, as though the change had been a summons, Seraphina plunged once more into the labyrinth of the wood.

She left day upon the high ground. In the lower groves there still lingered the blue early twilight and the seizing freshness of the dew. But here and there, above this field of shadow, the head of a great outspread pine was already glorious with day; and here and there, through the breaches of the hills, the sunbeams made a great and luminous entry. Here Seraphina hastened along forest paths. She had lost sight of the pilot smoke, which blew another way, and conducted herself in that great wilderness by the direction of the sun. But presently fresh signs bespoke the neighbourhood of man; felled trunks, white slivers from the axe, bundles of green boughs, and stacks of firewood. These guided her forward; until she came forth at last upon the clearing whence the smoke arose. A hut stood in the clear shadow, hard by a brook which made a series of inconsiderable falls; and on the threshold the Princess saw a sunburnt and hard-featured woodman, standing with his hands behind his back and gazing skyward.

She went to him directly: a beautiful, bright-eyed, and haggard vision; splendidly arrayed and pitifully tattered; the diamond ear-drops still glittering in her ears; and with the movement of her coming, one small breast showing and hiding among the ragged covert of the laces. At that ambiguous hour, and coming as she did from the great silence of the forest, the man drew back from the Princess as from something elfin.

'I am cold,' she said, 'and weary. Let me rest beside your fire.'

The woodman was visibly commoved, but answered nothing.

'I will pay,' she said, and then repented of the words, catching perhaps a spark of terror from his frightened eyes. But, as usual, her courage rekindled brighter for the check. She put him from the door and entered; and he followed her in superstitious wonder.

Within, the hut was rough and dark; but on the stone that served as hearth, twigs and a few dry branches burned with the brisk sounds and all the variable beauty of fire. The very sight of it composed her; she crouched hard by on the earth floor and shivered in the glow, and looked upon the eating blaze with admiration. The woodman was still staring at his guest: at the wreck of the rich dress, the bare arms, the bedraggled laces and the gems. He found no word to utter.

'Give me food,' said she—'here, by the fire.'

He set down a pitcher of coarse wine, bread, a piece of cheese, and a handful of raw onions. The bread was hard and sour, the cheese like leather; even the onion, which ranks with the truffle and the nectarine in the chief place of honour of earth's fruits, is not perhaps a dish for princesses when raw. But she ate, if not with appetite, with courage; and when she had eaten, did not disdain the pitcher. In all her life before, she had not tasted of gross food nor drunk after another; but a brave woman far more readily accepts a change of circumstances than the bravest man. All that while, the woodman continued to observe her furtively, many low thoughts of fear and greed contending in his eyes. She read them clearly and she knew she must begone.

Presently she arose and offered him a florin.

'Will that repay you?' she asked.

But here the man found his tongue. 'I must have more than that,' said he.

'It is all I have to give you,' she returned, and passed him by serenely.

Yet her heart trembled, for she saw his hand stretched forth as if to arrest her, and his unsteady eyes wandering to his axe. A beaten path led westward from the clearing, and she swiftly followed it. She did not glance behind her. But as soon as the least turning of the path had concealed her from the woodman's eyes, she slipped among the trees and ran till she deemed herself in safety.

By this time the strong sunshine pierced in a thousand places the pine-thatch of the forest, fired the red boles, irradiated the cool aisles of shadow, and burned in jewels on the grass. The gum of these trees was dearer to the senses than the gums of Araby; each pine, in the lusty morning sunlight, burned its own wood-incense; and now and then a breeze would rise and toss these rooted censers, and send shade and sun-gem flitting, swift as swallows, thick as bees; and wake a brushing bustle of sounds that murmured and went by.

On she passed, and up and down, in sun and shadow; now aloft on the bare ridge among the rocks and birches, with the lizards and the snakes; and anon in the deep grove among sunless pillars. Now she followed wandering wood-paths, in the maze of valleys; and again, from a hill-top, beheld the distant mountains and the great birds circling under the sky. She would see afar off a nestling hamlet, and go round to avoid it. Below, she traced the course of the foam of mountain torrents. Nearer hand, she saw where the tender springs welled up in silence, or oozed in green moss; or in the more favoured hollows a whole family of infant rivers would combine, and tinkle in the stones, and lie in pools to be a bathing-place for sparrows, or fall from the sheer rock in rods of crystal. Upon all these things, as she still sped along in the bright air, she looked with a rapture of surprise and a joyful fainting of the heart; they seemed so novel, they touched so strangely home, they were so hued and scented, they were so beset and canopied by the dome of the blue air of heaven.

At length, when she was well weary, she came upon a wide and shallow pool. Stones stood in it, like islands; bulrushes fringed the coast; the floor was paved with the pine needles; and the pines themselves, whose roots made promontories, looked down silently on their green images. She crept to the margin and beheld herself with wonder, a hollow and bright-eyed phantom, in the ruins of her palace robes. The breeze now shook her image; now it would be marred with flies; and at that she smiled; and from the fading circles, her counterpart smiled back to her and looked kind. She sat long in the warm sun, and pitied her bare arms that were all bruised and marred with falling, and marvelled to see that she was dirty and could not grow to believe that she had gone so long in such a strange disorder.

Then, with a sigh, she addressed herself to make a toilette by that forest mirror, washed herself pure from all the stains of her adventure, took off her jewels and wrapped them in her handkerchief, re-arranged the tatters of her dress, and took down the folds of her hair. She shook it round her face, and the pool repeated her thus veiled. Her hair had smelt like violets, she remembered Otto saying; and so now she tried to smell it, and then shook her head, and laughed a little, sadly, to herself.

The laugh was returned upon her in a childish echo. She looked up; and lo! two children looking on—a small girl and a yet smaller boy, standing like playthings, by the pool, below a spreading pine. Seraphina was not fond of children, and now she was startled to the heart.

'Who are you?' she cried hoarsely.

The mites huddled together and drew back; and Seraphina's heart reproached her that she should have frightened things so quaint and little, and yet alive with sense. She thought upon the birds and looked again at her two visitors; so little larger and so far more innocent. On their clear faces, as in a pool, she saw the reflection of their fears. With gracious purpose she arose.

'Come,' she said, 'do not be afraid of me,' and took a step towards them.

But alas! at the first moment, the two poor babes in the wood turned and ran helter-skelter from the Princess.

The most desolate pang was struck into the girl's heart. Here she was, twenty-two—soon twenty-three—and not a creature loved her; none but Otto; and would even he forgive? If she began weeping in these woods alone, it would mean death or madness. Hastily she trod the thoughts out like a burning paper; hastily rolled up her locks, and with terror dogging her, and her whole bosom sick with grief, resumed her journey.

Past ten in the forenoon, she struck a high-road, marching in that place uphill between two stately groves, a river of sunlight; and here, dead weary, careless of consequences, and taking some courage from the human and civilised neighbourhood of the road, she stretched herself on the green margin in the shadow of a tree. Sleep closed on her, at first with a horror of fainting, but when she ceased to struggle, kindly embracing her. So she was taken home for a little, from all her toils and sorrows, to her Father's arms. And there in the meanwhile her body lay exposed by the highwayside, in tattered finery; and on either hand from the woods the birds came flying by and calling upon others, and debated in their own tongue this strange appearance.

The sun pursued his journey; the shadow flitted from her feet, shrank higher and higher, and was upon the point of leaving her altogether, when the rumble of a coach was signalled to and fro by the birds. The road in that part was very steep; the rumble drew near with great deliberation; and ten minutes passed before a gentleman appeared, walking with a sober, elderly gait upon the grassy margin of the highway, and looking pleasantly around him as he walked. From time to time he paused, took out his notebook and made an entry with a pencil; and any spy who had been near enough would have heard him mumbling words as though he were a poet testing verses. The voice of the wheels was still faint, and it was plain the traveller had far outstripped his carriage.

He had drawn very near to where the Princess lay asleep, before his eye alighted on her; but when it did he started, pocketed his notebook, and approached. There was a milestone close to where she lay; and he sat down on that and coolly studied her. She lay upon one side, all curled and sunken, her brow on one bare arm, the other stretched out, limp and dimpled. Her young body, like a thing thrown down, had scarce a mark of life. Her breathing stirred her not. The deadliest fatigue was thus confessed in every language of the sleeping flesh. The traveller smiled grimly. As though he had looked upon a statue, he made a grudging inventory of her charms: the figure in that touching freedom of forgetfulness surprised him; the flush of slumber became her like a flower.

'Upon my word,' he thought, 'I did not think the girl could be so pretty. And to think,' he added, 'that I am under obligation not to use one word of this!'

He put forth his stick and touched her; and at that she awoke, sat up with a cry, and looked upon him wildly.

'I trust your Highness has slept well,' he said, nodding.

But she only uttered sounds.

'Compose yourself,' said he, giving her certainly a brave example in his own demeanour. 'My chaise is close at hand; and I shall have, I trust, the singular entertainment of abducting a sovereign Princess.'

'Sir John!' she said, at last.

'At your Highness's disposal,' he replied.

She sprang to her feet. 'O!' she cried, 'have you come from Mittwalden?'

'This morning,' he returned, 'I left it; and if there is any one less likely to return to it than yourself, behold him!'

'The Baron—— ' she began, and paused.

'Madam,' he answered, 'it was well meant, and you are quite a Judith; but after the hours that have elapsed, you will probably be relieved to hear that he is fairly well. I took his news this morning ere I left. Doing fairly well, they said, but suffering acutely. Hey?—acutely. They could hear his groans in the next room.'

'And the Prince,' she asked, 'is anything known of him?'

'It is reported,' replied Sir John, with the same pleasurable deliberation, 'that upon that point your Highness is the best authority.'

'Sir John,' she said eagerly, 'you were generous enough to speak about your carriage. Will you, I beseech you, will you take me to the Felsenburg? I have business there of an extreme importance.'

'I can refuse you nothing,' replied the old gentleman, gravely and seriously enough. 'Whatever, madam, it is in my power to do for you, that shall be done with pleasure. As soon as my chaise shall overtake us, it is yours to carry you where you will. But,' added he, reverting to his former manner, 'I observe you ask me nothing of the Palace.'

'I do not care,' she said. 'I thought I saw it burning.'

'Prodigious!' said the Baronet. 'You thought? And can the loss of forty toilettes leave you cold? Well, madam, I admire your fortitude. And the state, too? As I left, the government was sitting,—the new government of which at least two members must be known to you by name: Sabra, who had, I believe, the benefit of being formed in your employment—a footman,—am I right?—and our old friend the Chancellor, in something of a subaltern position. But in these convulsions the last shall be first, and the first last.'

'Sir John,' she said, with an air of perfect honesty, 'I am sure you mean most kindly, but these matters have no interest for me.'

The Baronet was so utterly discountenanced that he hailed the appearance of his chaise with welcome, and, by way of saying something, proposed that they should walk back to meet it. So it was done; and he helped her in with courtesy, mounted to her side, and from various receptacles (for the chaise was most completely fitted out) produced fruits and truffled liver, beautiful white bread, and a bottle of delicate wine. With these he served her like a father, coaxing and praising her to fresh exertions; and during all that time, as though silenced by the laws of hospitality, he was not guilty of the shadow of a sneer. Indeed his kindness seemed so genuine that Seraphina was moved to gratitude.

'Sir John,' she said, 'you hate me in your heart; why are you so kind to me?'

'Ah, my good lady,' said he, with no disclaimer of the accusation, 'I have the honour to be much your husband's friend, and somewhat his admirer.'

'You!' she cried. 'They told me you wrote cruelly of both of us.'

'Such was the strange path by which we grew acquainted,' said Sir John. 'I had written, madam, with particular cruelty (since that shall be the phrase) of your fair self. Your husband set me at liberty, gave me a passport, ordered a carriage, and then, with the most boyish spirit, challenged me to fight. Knowing the nature of his married life, I thought the dash and loyalty he showed delightful. "Do not be afraid," says he; "if I am killed, there is nobody to miss me." It appears you subsequently thought of that yourself. But I digress. I explained to him it was impossible that I could fight! "Not if I strike you?" says he. Very droll; I wish I could have put it in my book. However, I was conquered, took the young gentleman to my high favour, and tore up my bits of scandal on the spot. That is one of the little favours, madam, that you owe your husband.'

Seraphina sat for some while in silence. She could bear to be misjudged without a pang by those whom she contemned; she had none of Otto's eagerness to be approved, but went her own way straight and head in air. To Sir John, however, after what he had said, and as her husband's friend, she was prepared to stoop.

'What do you think of me?' she asked abruptly.

'I have told you already,' said Sir John: 'I think you want another glass of my good wine.'

'Come,' she said, 'this is unlike you. You are not wont to be afraid. You say that you admire my husband: in his name, be honest.'

'I admire your courage,' said the Baronet. 'Beyond that, as you have guessed, and indeed said, our natures are not sympathetic.'

'You spoke of scandal,' pursued Seraphina. 'Was the scandal great?'

'It was considerable,' said Sir John.

'And you believed it?' she demanded.

'O, madam,' said Sir John, 'the question!'

'Thank you for that answer!' cried Seraphina. 'And now here, I will tell you, upon my honour, upon my soul, in spite of all the scandal in this world, I am as true a wife as ever stood.'

'We should probably not agree upon a definition,' observed Sir John.

'O!' she cried, 'I have abominably used him—I know that; it is not that I mean. But if you admire my husband, I insist that you shall understand me: I can look him in the face without a blush.'

'It may be, madam,' said Sir John; 'nor have I presumed to think the contrary.'

'You will not believe me?' she cried. 'You think I am a guilty wife? You think he was my lover?'

'Madam,' returned the Baronet, 'when I tore up my papers, I promised your good husband to concern myself no more with your affairs; and I assure you for the last time that I have no desire to judge you.'

'But you will not acquit me! Ah!' she cried, '*he* will—he knows me better!'

Sir John smiled.

'You smile at my distress?' asked Seraphina.

'At your woman's coolness,' said Sir John. 'A man would scarce have had the courage of that cry, which was, for all that, very natural, and I make no doubt quite true. But remark, madam—since you do me the honour to consult me gravely—I have no pity for what you call your distresses. You have been completely selfish, and now reap the consequence. Had you once thought of your husband, instead of singly thinking of yourself, you would not now have been alone, a fugitive, with blood upon your hands, and hearing from a morose old Englishman truth more bitter than scandal.'

'I thank you,' she said, quivering. 'This is very true. Will you stop the carriage?'

'No, child,' said Sir John, 'not until I see you mistress of yourself.'

There was a long pause during which the carriage rolled by rock and woodland.

'And now,' she resumed, with perfect steadiness, 'will you consider me composed? I request you, as a gentleman, to let me out.'

'I think you do unwisely,' he replied. 'Continue, if you please, to use my carriage.'

'Sir John,' she said, 'if death were sitting on that pile of stones, I would alight! I do not blame, I thank you; I now know how I appear to others; but sooner than draw breath beside a man who can so think of me, I would——O!' she cried, and was silent.

Sir John pulled the string, alighted, and offered her his hand; but she refused the help.

The road had now issued from the valleys in which it had been winding, and come to that part of its course where it runs, like a cornice, along the brow of the steep northward face of Grünewald. The place where they had alighted was at a salient angle; a bold rock and some wind-tortured pine-trees overhung it from above; far below the blue plains lay forth and melted into heaven; and before them the road, by a succession of bold zig-zags, was seen mounting to where a tower upon a tall cliff closed the view.

'There,' said the Baronet, pointing to the tower, 'you see the Felsenburg, your goal. I wish you a good journey, and regret I cannot be of more assistance.'

He mounted to his place and gave a signal, and the carriage rolled away.

Seraphina stood by the wayside, gazing before her with blind eyes. Sir John she had dismissed already from her mind: she hated him, that was enough; for whatever Seraphina hated or contemned fell instantly to Lilliputian smallness, and was thenceforward steadily ignored in thought. And now she had matter for concern indeed. Her interview with Otto, which she had never yet forgiven him, began to appear before her in a very different light. He had come to her, still thrilling under recent insult, and not yet breathed from fighting her own cause; and how that knowledge changed the value of his words! Yes, he must have loved her! this was a brave feeling—it was no mere weakness of the will. And she, was she incapable of love? It would appear so; and she swallowed her tears, and yearned to see Otto, to explain all, to ask pity upon her knees for her transgressions, and, if all else were now beyond the reach of reparation, to restore at least the liberty of which she had deprived him.

Swiftly she sped along the highway, and, as the road wound out and in about the bluffs and gullies of the mountain, saw and lost by glimpses the tall tower that stood before and above her, purpled by the mountain air.

20

Treats of a Christian virtue

WHEN Otto mounted to his rolling prison he found another occupant in a corner of the front seat; but as this person hung his head and the brightness of the carriage lamps shone outward, the Prince could only see it was a man. The Colonel followed his prisoner and clapped-to the door; and at that the four horses broke immediately into a swinging trot.

'Gentlemen,' said the Colonel, after some little while had passed, 'if we are to travel in silence, we might as well be at home. I appear, of course, in an invidious character; but I am a man of taste, fond of books and solidly informing talk, and unfortunately condemned for life to the guardroom. Gentlemen, this is my chance: don't spoil it for me. I have here the pick of the whole court, barring lovely woman; I have a great author in the person of the Doctor—— '

'Gotthold!' cried Otto.

'It appears,' said the Doctor bitterly, 'that we must go together. Your Highness had not calculated upon that.'

'What do you infer?' cried Otto; 'that I had you arrested?'

'The inference is simple,' said the Doctor.

'Colonel Gordon,' said the Prince, 'oblige me so far, and set me right with Herr von Hohenstockwitz.'

'Gentlemen,' said the Colonel, 'you are both arrested on the same warrant in the name of the Princess Seraphina, acting regent, countersigned by Prime Minister Freiherr von Gondremark, and dated the day before yesterday, the twelfth. I reveal to you the secrets of the prison-house,' he added.

'Otto,' said Gotthold, 'I ask you to pardon my suspicions.'

'Gotthold,' said the Prince, 'I am not certain I can grant you that.'

'Your Highness is, I am sure, far too magnanimous to hesitate,' said the Colonel. 'But allow me: we speak at home in my religion of the means of grace: and I now propose to offer them.' So saying, the Colonel lighted a bright lamp which he attached to one side of the carriage, and from below the front seat produced a goodly basket adorned with the long necks of bottles. '*Tu spem reducis*—how does it go, Doctor?' he asked gaily. 'I am, in a sense, your host; and I am sure you are both far too considerate of my embarrassing position to refuse to do me honour. Gentlemen, I drink to the Prince!'

'Colonel,' said Otto, 'we have a jovial entertainer. I drink to Colonel Gordon.'

Thereupon all three took their wine very pleasantly; and even as they did so, the carriage with a lurch turned into the high-road and began to make better speed.

All was bright within; the wine had coloured Gotthold's cheek; dim forms of forest trees, dwindling and spiring, scarves of the starry sky, now wide and now narrow, raced past the windows; through one that was left open the air of the woods came in with a nocturnal raciness; and the roll of wheels and the tune of the trotting horses sounded merrily on the ear. Toast followed toast; glass after glass was bowed across and emptied by the trio; and presently there began to fall upon them a luxurious spell, under the influence of which little but the sound of quiet and confidential laughter interrupted the long intervals of meditative silence.

'Otto,' said Gotthold, after one of these seasons of quiet, 'I do not ask you to forgive me. Were the parts reversed, I could not forgive you.'

'Well,' said Otto, 'it is a phrase we use. I do forgive you, but your words and your suspicions rankle; and not yours alone. It is idle, Colonel Gordon, in view of the order you are carrying out, to conceal from you the dissensions of my family; they have gone so far that they are now public property. Well, gentlemen, can I forgive my wife? I can, of course, and do; but in what sense? I would certainly not stoop to any revenge; as certainly I could not think of her but as one changed beyond my recognition.'

'Allow me,' returned the Colonel. 'You will permit me to hope that I am addressing Christians? We are all conscious, I trust, that we are miserable sinners.'

'I disown the consciousness,' said Gotthold. 'Warmed with this good fluid, I deny your thesis.'

'How, sir? You never did anything wrong? and I heard you asking pardon but this moment, not of your God, sir, but of a common fellow-worm!' the Colonel cried.

'I own you have me; you are expert in argument, Herr Oberst,' said the Doctor.

'Begad, sir, I am proud to hear you say so,' said the Colonel. 'I was well grounded indeed at Aberdeen. And as for this matter of forgiveness, it comes, sir, of loose views and (what is if anything more dangerous) a regular life. A sound creed and a bad morality, that's the root of wisdom. You two gentlemen are too good to be forgiving.'

'The paradox is somewhat forced,' said Gotthold.

'Pardon me, Colonel,' said the Prince; 'I readily acquit you of any design of offence, but your words bite like satire. Is this a time, do you think, when I can wish to hear myself called good, now that I am paying the penalty (and am willing like yourself to think it just) of my prolonged misconduct?'

'O, pardon me!' cried the Colonel. 'You have never been expelled from the divinity hall; you have never been broke. I was: broke for a neglect of military duty. To tell you the open truth, your Highness, I was the worse of drink; it's a thing I never do now,' he added, taking out his glass. 'But a man, you see, who has really tasted the defects of his own character, as I have, and has come to regard himself as a kind of blind teetotum knocking about life, begins to learn a very different view about forgiveness. I will talk of not forgiving others, sir, when I have made out to forgive myself, and not before; and the date is like to be a long one. My father, the Reverend Alexander Gordon, was a good man, and damned hard upon others. I am what they call a bad one, and that is just the difference. The man who cannot forgive any mortal thing is a green hand in life.'

'And yet I have heard of you, Colonel, as a duellist,' said Gotthold.

'A different thing, sir,' replied the soldier. 'Professional etiquette. And I trust without unchristian feeling.'

Presently after the Colonel fell into a deep sleep; and his companions looked upon each other, smiling.

'And odd fish,' said Gotthold.

'And a strange guardian,' said the Prince. 'Yet what he said was true.'

'Rightly looked upon,' mused Gotthold, 'it is ourselves that we cannot forgive, when we refuse forgiveness to our friend. Some strand of our own misdoing is involved in every quarrel.'

'Are there not offences that disgrace the pardoner?' asked Otto. 'Are there not bounds of self-respect?'

'Otto,' said Gotthold, 'does any man respect himself? To this poor waif of a soldier of fortune we may seem respectable gentlemen; but to ourselves, what are we unless a pasteboard portico and a deliquium of deadly weaknesses within?'

'I? yes,' said Otto; 'but you, Gotthold—you, with your interminable industry, your keen mind, your books—serving mankind, scorning pleasures and temptations! You do not know how I envy you.'

'Otto,' said the Doctor, 'in one word, and a bitter one to say: I am a secret tippler. Yes, I drink too much. The habit has robbed these very books, to which you praise my devotion, of the merits that they should have had. It has spoiled my temper. When I spoke to you the other day, how much of my warmth was in the cause of virtue? how much was the fever of last night's wine? Ay, as my poor fellow-sot there said, and as I vaingloriously denied, we are all miserable sinners, put here for a moment, knowing the good, choosing the evil, standing naked and ashamed in the eye of God.'

'Is it so?' said Otto. 'Why, then, what are we? Are the very best——'

'There is no best in man,' said Gotthold. 'I am not better, it is likely I am not worse, than you or that poor sleeper. I was a sham, and now you know me: that is all.'

'And yet it has not changed my love,' returned Otto softly. 'Our misdeeds do not change us. Gotthold, fill your glass. Let us drink to what is good in this bad business; let us drink to our old affection; and, when we have done so, forgive your too just grounds of offence, and drink with me to my wife, whom I have so misused, who has so misused me, and whom I have left, I fear, I greatly fear, in danger. What matters it how bad we are, if others can still love us, and we can still love others?'

'Ay!' replied the Doctor. 'It is very well said. It is the true answer to the pessimist, and the standing miracle of mankind. So you still love me? and so you can forgive your wife? Why, then, we may bid conscience "Down, dog," like an ill-trained puppy yapping at shadows.'

The pair fell into silence, the Doctor tapping on his empty glass.

The carriage swung forth out of the valleys on that open balcony of high-road that runs along the front of Grünewald, looking down on Gerolstein. Far below, a white waterfall was shining to the stars from the falling skirts of forest, and beyond that, the night stood naked above the plain. On the other hand, the lamplight skimmed the face of the precipices, and the dwarf pine-trees twinkled with all their needles, and were gone again into the wake. The granite roadway thundered under wheels and hoofs; and at times, by reason of its continual winding, Otto could see the escort on the other side of a ravine, riding well together in the night. Presently the Felsenburg came plainly in view, some way above them, on a bold projection of the mountain, and planting its bulk against the starry sky.

'See, Gotthold,' said the Prince, 'our destination.'

Gotthold awoke as from a trance.

'I was thinking,' said he, 'if there is any danger, why did you not resist? I was told you came of your free will; but should you not be there to help her?'

The colour faded from the Prince's cheeks.

21

Providence von Rosen: Act the Last: In which she gallops off

WHEN the busy Countess came forth from her interview with Seraphina, it is not too much to say that she was beginning to be terribly afraid. She paused in the corridor and reckoned up her doings with an eye to Gondremark. The fan was in requisition in an instant; but her disquiet was beyond the reach of fanning. 'The girl has lost her head,' she thought; and then dismally, 'I have gone too far.' She instantly decided on secession. Now the *Mons Sacer* of the Frau von Rosen was a certain rustic villa in the forest, called by herself, in a smart attack of poesy, Tannen Zauber, and by everybody else plain Kleinbrunn.

Thither, upon the thought, she furiously drove, passing Gondremark at the entrance to the Palace avenue, but feigning not to observe him; and as Kleinbrunn was seven good miles away, and in the bottom of a narrow dell, she passed the night without any rumour of the outbreak reaching her; and the glow of the conflagration was concealed by intervening hills. Frau von Rosen did not sleep well; she was seriously uneasy as to the results of her delightful evening, and saw herself condemned to quite a lengthy sojourn in her deserts and a long defensive correspondence, ere she could venture to return to Gondremark. On the other hand, she examined, by way of pastime, the deeds she had received from Otto; and even here saw cause for disappointment. In these troublous days she had no taste for landed property, and she was convinced, besides, that Otto had paid dearer than the farm was worth. Lastly, the order for the Prince's release fairly burned her meddling fingers.

All things considered, the next day beheld an elegant and beautiful lady, in a riding-habit and a flapping hat, draw bridle at the gate of the Felsenburg, not perhaps with any clear idea of her purpose, but with her usual experimental views on life. Governor Gordon, summoned to the gate, welcomed the omnipotent Countess with his most gallant bearing, though it was wonderful how old he looked in the morning.

'Ah, Governor,' she said, 'we have surprises for you, sir,' and nodded at him meaningly.

'Eh, madam, leave me my prisoners,' he said; 'and if you will but join the band, begad, I'll be happy for life.'

'You would spoil me, would you not?' she asked.

'I would try, I would try,' returned the Governor, and he offered her his arm.

She took it, picked up her skirt, and drew him close to her. 'I have come to see the Prince,' she said. 'Now, infidel! on business. A message from that stupid Gondremark, who keeps me running like a courier. Do I look like one, Herr Gordon?' And she planted her eyes in him.

'You look like an angel, ma'am,' returned the Governor, with a great air of finished gallantry.

The Countess laughed. 'An angel on horseback!' she said. 'Quick work.'

'You came, you saw, you conquered,' flourished Gordon, in high good humour with his own wit and grace. 'We toasted you, madam, in the carriage, in an excellent good glass of wine; toasted you fathom deep; the finest woman, with, begad, the finest eyes in Grünewald. I never saw the like of them but once, in my own country, when I was a young fool at College: Thomasina Haig her name was. I give you my word of honour she was as like you as two peas.'

'And so you were merry in the carriage?' asked the Countess, gracefully dissembling a yawn.

'We were; we had a very pleasant conversation; but we took perhaps a glass more than that fine fellow of a Prince has been accustomed to,' said the Governor; 'and I observe this morning that he seems a little off his mettle. We'll get him mellow again ere bedtime. This is his door.'

'Well,' she whispered, 'let me get my breath. No, no; wait. Have the door ready to open.' And the Countess, standing like one inspired, shook out her fine voice in 'Lascia ch'io pianga'; and when she had reached the proper point, and lyrically uttered forth her sighings after liberty, the door, at a sign, was flung wide open, and she swam into the Prince's sight, bright-eyed, and with her colour somewhat freshened by the exercise of singing. It was a great dramatic entrance, and to the somewhat doleful prisoner within the sight was sunshine.

'Ah, madam,' he cried, running to her—'you here!'

She looked meaningly at Gordon; and as soon as the door was closed she fell on Otto's neck. 'To see you here!' she moaned and clung to him.

But the Prince stood somewhat stiffly in that enviable situation, and the Countess instantly recovered from her outburst.

'Poor child,' she said, 'poor child! Sit down beside me here, and tell me all about it. My heart really bleeds to see you. How does time go?'

'Madam,' replied the Prince, sitting down beside her, his gallantry recovered, 'the time will now go all too quickly till you leave. But I must ask you for the news. I have most bitterly condemned myself for my inertia of last night. You wisely counselled me; it was my duty to resist. You wisely and nobly counselled me; I have since thought of it with wonder. You have a noble heart.'

'Otto,' she said, 'spare me. Was it even right, I wonder? I have duties, too, you poor child; and when I see you they all melt—all my good resolutions fly away.'

'And mine still come too late,' he replied, sighing. 'O, what would I not give to have resisted? What would I not give for freedom?'

'Well, what would you give?' she asked; and the red fan was spread; only her eyes, as if from over battlements, brightly surveyed him.

'I? What do you mean? Madam, you have some news for me,' he cried.

'O, O!' said madam dubiously.

He was at her feet. 'Do not trifle with my hopes,' he pleaded.

'Tell me, dearest Madame von Rosen, tell me! You cannot be cruel: it is not in your nature. Give? I can give nothing; I have nothing; I can only plead in mercy.'

'Do not,' she said; 'it is not fair. Otto, you know my weakness. Spare me. Be generous.'

'O, madam,' he said, 'it is for you to be generous, to have pity.' He took her hand and pressed it; he plied her with caresses and appeals. The Countess had a most enjoyable sham siege, and then relented. She sprang to her feet, she tore her dress open, and, all warm from her bosom, threw the order on the floor.

'There!' she cried. 'I forced it from her. Use it, and I am ruined!' And she turned away as if to veil the force of her emotions.

Otto sprang upon the paper, read it, and cried out aloud. 'O, God bless her!' he said, 'God bless her.' And he kissed the writing.

Von Rosen was a singularly good-natured woman but her part was now beyond her. 'Ingrate!' she cried; 'I wrung it from her, I betrayed my trust to get it, and 'tis she you thank.'

'Can you blame me?' said the Prince. 'I love her.'

'I see that,' she said. 'And I?'

'You, Madame von Rosen? You are my dearest, my kindest and most generous of friends,' he said, approaching her. 'You would be a perfect friend, if you were not so lovely. You have a great sense of humour, you cannot be unconscious of your charm, and you amuse yourself at times by playing on my weakness; and at times I can take pleasure in the comedy. But not to-day: to-day you will be the true, the serious, the manly friend, and you will suffer me to forget that you are lovely and that I am weak. Come, dear Countess, let me to-day repose in you entirely.'

He held out his hand, smiling, and she took it frankly. 'I vow you have bewitched me,' she said; and then with a laugh, 'I break my staff,' she added; 'and I must pay you my best compliment. You made a difficult speech. You are as adroit, dear Prince, as I am—charming.' And as she said the word with a great curtsey, she justified it.

'You hardly keep the bargain, madam, when you make yourself so beautiful,' said the Prince, bowing.

'It was my last arrow,' she returned. 'I am disarmed. Blank cartridge, *O mon Prince!* And now I tell you, if you choose to leave this prison, you can, and I am ruined. Choose!'

'Madame von Rosen,' replied Otto, 'I choose, and I will go. My duty points me, duty still neglected by this Featherhead. But do not fear to be a loser. I propose instead that you should take me with you, a bear in chains, to Baron Gondremark. I am become perfectly unscrupulous: to save my wife I will do all, all he can ask or fancy. He shall be filled; were he huge as leviathan and greedy as the grave, I will content him. And you, the fairy of our pantomime, shall have the credit.'

'Done!' she cried. 'Admirable! Prince Charming no longer—Prince Sorcerer, Prince Solon! Let us go this moment. Stay,' she cried, pausing. 'I beg, dear Prince, to give you back these deeds. 'Twas you who liked the farm—I have not seen it; and it was you who wished to benefit the peasants. And, besides,' she added, with a comical change of tone, 'I should prefer the ready money.'

Both laughed. 'Here I am, once more a farmer,' said Otto, accepting the papers, 'but overwhelmed in debt.'

The Countess touched a bell, and the Governor appeared.

'Governor,' she said, 'I am going to elope with his Highness. The result of our talk has been a thorough understanding, and the *coup d'état* is over. Here is the order.'

Colonel Gordon adjusted silver spectacles upon his nose. 'Yes,' he said, 'the Princess: very right. But the warrant, madam, was countersigned.'

'By Heinrich!' said von Rosen. 'Well, and here am I to represent him.'

'Well, your Highness,' resumed the soldier of fortune, 'I must congratulate you upon my loss. You have been cut out by beauty, and I am left lamenting. The Doctor still remains to me: *probus, doctus, lepidus, jucundus:* a man of books.'

'Ay, there is nothing about poor Gotthold,' said the Prince.

'The Governor's consolation? Would you leave him bare?' asked von Rosen.

'And your Highness,' resumed Gordon, 'may I trust that in the course of this temporary obscuration, you have found me discharge my part with suitable respect and, I may add, tact? I adopted purposely a cheerfulness of manner; mirth, it appeared to me, and a good glass of wine, were the fit alleviations.'

'Colonel,' said Otto, holding out his hand, 'your society was of itself enough. I do not merely thank you for pleasant spirits; I have to thank you, besides, for some philosophy, of which I stood in need. I trust I do not see you for the last time; and in the meanwhile, as a memento of our strange acquaintance, let me offer you these verses on which I was but now engaged. I am so little of a poet, and was so ill inspired by prison bars, that they have some claim to be at least a curiosity.'

The Colonel's countenance lighted as he took the paper; the silver spectacles were hurriedly replaced. 'Ha!' he said, 'Alexandrines, the tragic metre. I shall cherish this, your Highness, like a relic; no more suitable offering, although I say it, could be made. "*Dieux de l'immense plaine et des vastes forêts.*" Very good,' he said, 'very good indeed! "*Et du geôlier lui-même apprendre des leçons.*" Most handsome, begad!'

'Come, Governor,' cried the Countess, 'you can read his poetry when we are gone. Open your grudging portals.'

'I ask your pardon,' said the Colonel. 'To a man of my character and tastes, these verses, this handsome reference—most moving, I assure you. Can I offer you an escort?'

'No, no,' replied the Countess. 'We go incogniti, as we arrived. We ride together; the Prince will take my servant's horse. Hurry and privacy, Herr Oberst, that is all we seek.' And she began impatiently to lead the way.

But Otto had still to bid farewell to Dr. Gotthold; and the Governor following, with his spectacles in one hand and the paper in the other, had still to communicate his treasured verses, piece by piece, as he succeeded in deciphering the manuscript, to all he came across; and still his enthusiasm mounted. 'I declare,' he cried at last, with the air of one who has at length divined a mistery, 'they remind me of Robbie Burns!'

But there is an end to all things; and at length Otto was walking by the side of Madame von Rosen, along that mountain wall, her servant following with both the horses, and all about them sunlight, and breeze, and flying bird, and the vast regions of the air, and the capacious prospect: wildwood and climbing pinnacle, and the sound and voice of mountain torrents, at their hand: and far below them, green melting into sapphire on the plains.

They walked at first in silence; for Otto's mind was full of the delight of liberty and nature, and still, betweenwhiles, he was preparing his interview with Gondremark. But when the first rough promontory of the rock was turned, and the Felsenburg concealed behind its bulk, the lady paused.

'Here,' she said, 'I will dismount poor Karl, and you and I must ply our spurs. I love a wild ride with a good companion.'

As she spoke, a carriage came into sight round the corner next below them in the order of the road. It came heavily creaking, and a little ahead of it a traveller was soberly walking, notebook in hand.

'It is Sir John,' cried Otto, and he hailed him.

The Baronet pocketed his notebook, stared through an eyeglass, and then waved his stick; and he on his side, and the Countess and the Prince on theirs, advanced with somewhat quicker steps. They met at the re-entrant angle, where a thin stream sprayed across a boulder and was scattered in rain among the brush; and the Baronet saluted the Prince with much punctilio. To the Countess, on the other hand, he bowed with a kind of sneering wonder.

'Is it possible, madam, that you have not heard the news?' he asked.

'What news?' she cried.

'News of the first order,' returned Sir John: 'a revolution in the State, a Republic declared, the Palace burned to the ground, the Princess in flight, Gondremark wounded——'

'Heinrich wounded?' she screamed.

'Wounded and suffering acutely,' said Sir John. 'His groans——'

There fell from the lady's lips an oath so potent that, in smoother hours, it would have made her hearers jump. She ran to her horse, scrambled to the saddle, and, yet half seated, dashed down the road at full gallop. The groom, after a pause of wonder, followed her. The rush of her impetuous passage almost scared the carriage horses over the verge of the steep hill; and still she clattered further, and the crags echoed to her flight, and still the groom flogged vainly in pursuit of her. At the fourth corner, a woman trailing slowly up leaped back with a cry and escaped death by a hand's-breadth. But the Countess wasted neither glance nor thought upon the incident. Out and in, about the bluffs of the mountain wall, she fled, loose-reined, and still the groom toiled in her pursuit.

'A most impulsive lady!' said Sir John. 'Who would have thought she cared for him?' And before the words were uttered, he was struggling in the Prince's grasp.

'My wife! the Princess? What of her?'

'She is down the road,' he gasped. 'I left her twenty minutes back.'

And next moment, the choked author stood alone and the Prince on foot was racing down the hill behind the Countess.

22

Babes in the wood

While the feet of the Prince continued to run swiftly, his heart, which had at first by far outstripped his running, soon began to linger and hang back. Not that he ceased to pity the misfortune or to yearn for the sight of Seraphina; but the memory of her obdurate coldness awoke within him, and woke in turn his own habitual diffidence of self. Had Sir John been given time to tell him all, had he even known that she was speeding to the Felsenburg, he would have gone to her with ardour. As it was, he began to see himself once more intruding, profiting, perhaps, by her misfortune, and now that she was fallen, proffering unloved caresses to the wife who had spurned him in prosperity. The sore spots upon his vanity began to burn; once more, his anger assumed the carriage of a hostile generosity; he would utterly forgive indeed; he would help, save, and comfort his unloving wife; but all with distant self-denial, imposing silence on his heart, respecting Seraphina's disaffection as he would the innocence of a child. So, when at length he turned a corner and beheld the Princess, it was his first thought to reassure her of the purity of his respect, and he at once ceased running and stood still. She, upon her part, began to run to him with a little cry; then, seeing him pause, she paused also, smitten with remorse; and at length, with the most guilty timidity, walked nearly up to where he stood.

'Otto,' she said, 'I have ruined all!'

'Seraphina!' he cried with a sob, but did not move, partly withheld by his resolutions, partly struck stupid at the sight of her weariness and disorder. Had she stood silent, they had soon been locked in an embrace. But she too had prepared herself against the interview, and must spoil the golden hour with protestations.

'All!' she went on, 'I have ruined all! But, Otto, in kindness you must hear me—not justify, but own, my faults. I have been taught so cruelly; I have had such time for thought, and see the world so changed. I have been blind, stone-blind; I have let all true good go by me, and lived on shadows. But when this dream fell, and I had betrayed you, and thought I had killed—— ' She paused. 'I thought I had killed Gondremark,' she said with a deep flush, 'and I found myself alone, as you said.'

The mention of the name of Gondremark pricked the Prince's generosity like a spur. 'Well,' he cried, 'and whose fault was it but mine? It was my duty to be beside you, loved or not. But I was a skulker in the grain, and found it easier to desert than to oppose you. I could never learn that better part of love, to fight love's battles. But yet the love was there. And now when this toy kingdom of ours has fallen, first of all by my demerits, and next by your inexperience, and we are here alone together, as poor as Job and merely a man and a woman—let me conjure you to forgive the weakness and to repose in the love. Do not mistake me!' he cried, seeing her about to speak, and imposing silence with uplifted hand. 'My love is changed; it is purged of any conjugal pretension; it does not ask, does not hope, does not wish for a return in kind. You may forget for ever that part in which you found me so distasteful, and accept without embarrassment the affection of a brother.'

'You are too generous, Otto,' she said. 'I know that I have forfeited your love. I cannot take this sacrifice. You had far better leave me. O, go away, and leave me to my fate!'

'O no!' said Otto; 'we must first of all escape out of this hornet's nest, to which I led you. My honour is engaged. I said but now we were as poor as Job; and behold! not many miles from here I have a house of my own to which I will conduct you. Otto the Prince being down, we must try what luck remains to Otto the Hunter. Come, Seraphina; show that you forgive me, and let us set about this business of escape in the best spirits possible. You used to say, my dear, that, except as a husband and a prince, I was a pleasant fellow. I am neither now, and you may like my company without remorse. Come, then; it were idle to be captured. Can you still walk? Forth, then,' said he, and he began to lead the way.

A little below where they stood, a good-sized brook passed below the road, which overleapt it in a single arch. On one bank of that loquacious water a footpath descended a green dell. Here it was rocky and stony, and lay on the steep scarps of the ravine; here it was choked with brambles; and there, in fairy haughs, it lay for a few paces evenly on the green turf. Like a sponge, the hillside oozed with well-water. The burn kept growing both in force and volume; at every leap it fell with heavier plunges and span more widely in the pool. Great had been the labours of that stream, and great and agreeable the changes it had wrought. It had cut through dykes of stubborn rock, and now, like a blowing dolphin, spouted through the orifice; along all its humble coasts, it had undermined and rafted-down the goodlier timber of the forest; and on these rough clearings it now set and tended primrose gardens, and planted woods of willow, and made a favourite of the silver birch. Through all these friendly features the path, its human acolyte, conducted our two wanderers downward,—Otto before, still pausing at the more difficult passages to lend assistance; the Princess following. From time to time, when he turned to help her, her face would lighten upon his—her eyes, half desperately, woo him. He saw, but dared not understand. 'She does not love me,' he told himself, with magnanimity. 'This is remorse or gratitude;

I were no gentleman, no, nor yet a man, if I presumed upon these pitiful concessions.'

Some way down the glen, the stream, already grown to a good bulk of water, was rudely damned across, and about a third of it abducted in a wooden trough. Gaily the pure water, air's first cousin, fleeted along the rude aqueduct, whose sides and floor it had made green with grasses. The path, bearing it close company, threaded a wilderness of brier and wild-rose. And presently, a little in front, the brown top of a mill and the tall mill-wheel, spraying diamonds, arose in the narrows of the glen; at the same time the snoring music of the saws broke the silence.

The miller, hearing steps, came forth to his door, and both he and Otto started.

'Good-morning, miller,' said the Prince. 'You were right, it seems, and I was wrong. I give you the news, and bid you to Mittwalden. My throne has fallen—great was the fall of it!—and your good friends of the Phœnix bear the rule.'

The red-faced miller looked supreme astonishment. 'And your Highness?' he gasped.

'My Highness is running away,' replied Otto, 'straight for the frontier.'

'Leaving Grünewald?' cried the man. 'Your father's son? It's not to be permitted!'

'Do you arrest us, friend?' asked Otto, smiling.

'Arrest you? I?' exclaimed the man. 'For what does your Highness take me? Why, sir, I make sure there is not a man in Grünewald would lay hands upon you.'

'O, many, many,' said the Prince; 'but from you, who were bold with me in my greatness, I should even look for aid in my distress.'

The miller became the colour of beetroot. 'You may say so indeed,' said he. 'And meanwhile, will you and your lady step into my house?'

'We have not time for that,' replied the Prince; 'but if you would oblige us with a cup of wine without here, you will give a pleasure and a service, both in one.'

The miller once more coloured to the nape. He hastened to bring forth wine in a pitcher and three bright crystal tumblers. 'Your Highness must not suppose,' he said, as he filled them, 'that I am an habitual drinker. The time when I had the misfortune to encounter you, I was a trifle overtaken, I allow; but a more sober man than I am in my ordinary, I do not know where you are to look for; and even this glass that I drink to you (and to the lady) is quite an unusual recreation.'

The wine was drunk with due rustic courtesies; and then, refusing further hospitality, Otto and Seraphina once more proceeded to descend the glen, which now began to open and to be invaded by the taller trees.

'I owed that man a reparation,' said the Prince; 'for when we met I was in the wrong and put a sore affront upon him. I judge by myself, perhaps; but I begin to think that no one is the better for a humiliation.'

'But some have to be taught so,' she replied.

'Well, well,' he said, with a painful embarrassment. 'Well, well. But let us think of safety. My miller is all very good, but I do not pin my faith to him. To follow down this stream will bring us, but after innumerable windings, to my house. Here, up this glade, there lies a cross-cut—the world's end for solitude—the very deer scarce visit it. Are you too tired, or could you pass that way?'

'Choose the path, Otto. I will follow you,' she said.

'No,' he replied, with a singular imbecility of manner and appearance, 'but I meant the path was rough. It lies, all the way, by glade and dingle, and the dingles are both deep and thorny.'

'Lead on,' she said. 'Are you not Otto the Hunter?'

They had now burst across a veil of underwood, and were come into a lawn among the forest, very green and innocent, and solemnly surrounded by trees. Otto paused on the margin, looking about him with delight; then his glance returned to Seraphina, as she stood framed in that silvan pleasantness and looking at her husband with undecipherable eyes. A weakness both of the body and mind fell on him like the beginnings of sleep; the cords of his activity were relaxed, his eyes clung to her. 'Let us rest,' he said; and he made her sit down, and himself sat down beside her on the slope of an inconsiderable mound.

She sat with her eyes downcast, her slim hand dabbling in grass, like a maid waiting for love's summons. The sound of the wind in the forest swelled and sank, and drew near them with a running rush, and died away and away in the distance into fainting whispers. Nearer hand, a bird out of the deep covert uttered broken and anxious notes. All this seemed but a halting prelude to speech. To Otto it seemed as if the whole frame of nature were waiting for his words; and yet his pride kept him silent. The longer he watched that slender and pale hand plucking at the grasses, the harder and rougher grew the fight between pride and its kindly adversary.

'Seraphina,' he said at last, 'it is right you should know one thing: I never . . .' He was about to say 'doubted you,' but was that true? And, if true, was it generous to speak of it? Silence succeeded.

'I pray you, tell it me,' she said; 'tell it me, in pity.'

'I mean only this,' he resumed, 'that I understand all, and do not blame you. I understand how the brave woman must look down on the weak man. I think you were wrong in some things; but I have tried to understand it, and I do. I do not need to forget or to forgive, Seraphina, for I have understood.'

'I know what I have done,' she said. 'I am not so weak that I can be deceived with kind speeches. I know what I have been—I see myself. I am not worth your anger, how much less to be forgiven! In all this downfall and misery, I see only me and you: you, as you have been always; me, as I was—me, above all! O yes, I see myself: and what can I think?'

'Ah, then, let us reverse the parts!' said Otto. 'It is ourselves we cannot forgive, when we deny forgiveness to another—so a friend told me last night. On these terms, Seraphina, you see how generously I have forgiven myself. But am not *I* to be forgiven? Come, then, forgive yourself—and me.'

She did not answer in words, but reached out her hand to him quickly. He took it; and as the smooth fingers settled and nestled in his, love ran to and fro between them in tender and transforming currents.

'Seraphina,' he cried, 'O, forget the past! Let me serve and help you; let me be your servant; it is enough for me to serve you and to be near you, let me be near you, dear—do not send me away.' He hurried his pleading like the speech of a frightened child. 'It is not love,' he went on; 'I do not ask for love; my love is enough. . . .'

'Otto!' she said, as if in pain.

He looked up into her face. It was wrung with the very ecstasy of tenderness and anguish; on her features, and most of all in her changed eyes, there shone the very light of love.

'Seraphina?' he cried aloud, and with a sudden, tuneless voice, 'Seraphina?'

'Look round you at this glade,' she cried, 'and where the leaves are coming on young trees, and the flowers begin to blossom. This is where we meet, meet for the first time; it is so much better to forget and to be born again. O what a pit there is for sins—God's mercy, man's oblivion!'

'Seraphina,' he said, 'let it be so, indeed; let all that was be merely the abuse of dreaming; let me begin again, a stranger. I have dreamed, in a long dream, that I adored a girl unkind and beautiful; in all things my superior, but still cold, like ice.

And again I dreamed, and thought she changed and melted, glowed and turned to me. And I—who had no merit but a love, slavish and unerect—lay close, and durst not move for fear of waking.'

'Lie close,' she said, with a deep thrill of speech.

So they spake in the spring woods; and meanwhile, in Mittwalden Rath-haus, the Republic was declared.

BIBLIOGRAPHICAL POSTSCRIPT

To complete the Story

The reader well informed in modern history, will not require details as to the fate of the Republic. The best account is to be found in the memoirs of Herr Greisengesang (7 Bände: Leipzig), by our passing acquaintance the licentiate Roederer. Herr Roederer, with too much of an author's licence, makes a great figure of his hero—poses him, indeed, to be the centre-piece and cloud-compeller of the whole. But, with due allowance for this bias, the book is able and complete.

The reader is of course acquainted with the vigorous and bracing pages of Sir John (2 vols.: London: Longman, Hurst, Rees, Orme and Brown). Sir John, who plays but a tooth-comb in the orchestra of this historical romance, blows in his own book the big bassoon. His character is there drawn at large; and the sympathy of Landor has countersigned the admiration of the public. One point, however, calls for explanation; the chapter on Grünewald was torn by the hand of the author in the palace gardens; how comes it, then, to figure at full length among my more modest pages, the Lion of the caravan? That eminent literatus was a man of method; 'Juvenal by double entry,' he was once profanely called; and when he tore the sheets in question, it was rather, as he has since explained, in the search for some dramatic evidence of his sincerity, than with the thought of practical deletion. At that time, indeed, he was possessed of two blotted scrolls and a fair copy in double. But the chapter, as the reader knows, was honestly omitted from the famous *Memoirs on the various Courts of Europe*. It has been mine to give it to the public.

Bibliography still helps us with a further glimpse of our characters. I have here before me a small volume (printed for private circulation: no printer's name; n.d.), *Poésies par Frédéric et Amélie*. Mine is a presentation copy, obtained for me by Mr. Bain in the Haymarket; and the name of the first owner is written on the fly-leaf in the hand of Prince Otto himself. The modest epigraph—' Le rime n'est pas riche '—may be attributed, with a good show of likelihood, to the same collaborator. It is strikingly appropriate, and I have found the volume very dreary. Those pieces in which I seem to trace the hand of the Princess are particularly dull and conscientious. But the booklet had a fair success with that public for which it was designed; and I have come across some evidences of a second venture of the same sort, now unprocurable. Here, at least, we may take leave of Otto and Seraphina—what do I say? of Frédéric and Amélie—ageing together peaceably at the court of the wife's father, jingling French rhymes and correcting joint proofs.

Still following the book-lists, I perceive that Mr. Swinburne has dedicated a rousing lyric and some vigorous sonnets to the memory of Gondremark; that name appears twice at least in Victor Hugo's trumpet-blasts of patriot enumeration; and I came latterly, when I supposed my task already ended, on a trace of the fallen politician and his Countess. It is in the *Diary of J. Hogg Cotterill, Esq.*, (that very interesting work). Mr. Cotterill being at Naples, is introduced (May 27th) to 'a Baron and Baroness Gondremark—he a man who once made a noise—she still beautiful—both witty. She complimented me much upon my French—should never have known me to be English—had known my uncle, Sir John, in Germany—recognised in me, as a family trait, some of his *grand air* and studious courtesy—asked me to call.' And again (May 30th), 'visited the Baronne de Gondremark—much gratified—a most *refined*, *intelligent* Roman, quite of the old school, now, *hélas!* extinct—had read my *Remarks on Sicily*—it reminds her of my uncle, but with more of grace—I feared she thought there was less energy—assured no—a softer style of presentation, more of the *literary grace*, but the same firm grasp of circumstance and force of thought—in short, just Buttonhole's opinion. Much encouraged. I have a real esteem for this patrician lady.' The acquaintance lasted some time; and when Mr. Cotterill left in the suite of Lord Protocol, and, as he is careful to inform us, in Admiral Yardarm's flag-ship, one of his chief causes of regret is to leave 'that most *spirituelle* and sympathetic lady, who already regards me as a younger brother.'

BIBLIOGRAPHY

NOVELS AND SHORT STORIES:

1882 - The Story of a Lie.
New Arabian Nights (2 vols.).
1883 - Treasure Island.
1885 - Prince Otto.
More New Arabian Nights.
1886 - The Strange Case of Dr. Jekyll and Mr. Hyde.
Kidnapped.
1887 - The Merry Men, and Other Tales.
1888 - The Black Arrow.
1889 - The Misadventures of John Nicholson.
The Master of Ballantrae.
The Wrong Box.
1892 - The Wrecker.
1893 - Island Night's Entertainments.
Catriona.
1894 - The Ebb-Tide.
1895 - The Body-Snatcher.
1896 - Weir of Hermiston.
1897 - St. Ives (Finished by Sir A. T. Quiller-Couch).

POSTHUMOUSLY PUBLISHED:

1916 - The Waif Woman.
1921 - When the Devil Was Well.
1923 - Ticonderoga.

POEMS AND PLAYS:

1880 - Deacon Brodie
1884 - Beau Austin
Admiral Guinea
1885 - Macaire
(Written in conjunction with W. E. Henley and privately printed.)
1885 - A Child's Garden of Verses.
1887 - Underwoods.
Ticonderoga (privately printed).
1890 - Ballads.
1896 - Songs of Travel and Other Verses.
1898 - Three Short Poems.
1899 - R. L. S. Teuila.

POSTHUMOUSLY PUBLISHED:

1913 - Complete Edition of Poems and Ballads (New York Edition).
1914 - The Hanging Judge.
1916 - An Ode of Horace (privately printed).
Poems Hitherto Unpublished (Boston Bibliophile Soc.).
1918 - New Poems and Variant Readings (Boston Bibliophile Soc.).

NUMEROUS ESSAYS AND OTHER MISCELLANEOUS WRITINGS INCLUDING:

1878 - An Inland Voyage.
1879 - Travels with a Donkey in the Cevennes.
1892 - A Footnote to History.
1893 - War in Samoa (privately printed).

Also the *Vailima Letters* and other published collections of his correspondences.

COLLECTED EDITIONS OF HIS WORKS:

Edinburgh Edition 1894-98 (28 vols.)
Vailima Edition 1922-23 (26 vols.)
Tusitala Edition 1923-24 (35 vols.)

FOLLOWING CONTAIN INFORMATION ON HIS LIFE AND WORKS:

Partial Portraits (1888) and *Notes on Novelists* (1914) by Henry James.
Robert Louis Stevenson by Sir W. Raleigh (1895)
Robert Louis Stevenson by L. C. Cornford (1899)
Life of Robert Louis Stevenson by Graham Balfour (1901)
With Stevenson in Samoa by H. J. Moore (1911)
Memories of Vailima by I. Strong and Lloyd Osbourne (1911)
On the Trail of Stevenson by H. Clayton
R. L. S. A Critical Study by F. Swinnerton (1914)
Life of Robert Louis Stevenson by R. O. Masson (1923)
An Intimate Portrait of Robert Louis Stevenson by Lloyd Osbourne (New York, 1924)
* *Robert Louis Stevenson* by J. A. Stewart (1924)
The True Stevenson by G. S. Hellman (Boston, 1925)
Robert Louis Stevenson by G. K. Chesterton (1927)
Robert Louis Stevenson by Janet Smith (1937)
Presbyterian Pirate by Doris N. Dalglish (1937)
Home from the Sea by Richard A. Berman (1939)

Selected Writings of Robert Louis Stevenson Ed. by Saxe Commins (1947)

Novels and Stories by Robert Louis Stevenson by V. S. Pritchett (1947)

Robert Louis Stevenson by Lettice Cooper (1947)

Our Mountain Hermitage (*Silverado and Robert Louis Stevenson*) by Anne Roller Issler (1950)

Stevenson and Edinburgh (A Centenary Study) by Moray MacLaren (1951)

The Strange Case of Robert Louis Stevenson by Malcolm Elwin (1951)

Collected Poems (Editor) Janet Adam Smith (1951)

Robert Louis Stevenson: Collected Poems (Editor) Janet Adam Smith (1951)

Voyage to Windward: The Life of Robert Louis Stevenson by G. C. Furness (1951)

Tusitala of the South Seas: The Story of Robert Louis Stevenson's Life in the South Pacific by Joseph W. Ellison (1953)

R.L.S.: Stevenson's Letters to Charles Baxter Edited by DeLancey Ferguson and Marshall Waingrow (1956)

Our Samoan Adventure by Fanny and Robert Louis Stevenson (1956)

Portrait of a Rebel by Richard Aldington (1957)